Praise for

HEATHER
GRAHAM

"A suspenseful, sexy thriller...Graham builds
jagged suspense that will keep readers
guessing up to the final pages."
— *Publishers Weekly*

"An incredible storyteller!"
— *Los Angeles Daily News*

"Award-winning [Heather Graham] combines
mystery with sizzling romance."
— *Publishers Weekly*

"Refreshing, unique...Graham does it
better than anyone."
— *Publishers Weekly*

HEATHER GRAHAM

Dead on the dance floor

MIRA® BOOKS

MIRA is a registered trademark of Harlequin Enterprises Limited, used under licence.

First published in Great Britain in 2004.
MIRA Books, Eton House, 18-24 Paradise Road,
Richmond, Surrey, TW9 1SR

© Heather Graham Pozzessere 2004

ISBN 0 7783 0057 9

58-0704

Printed and bound in Spain
by Litografía Rosés S.A., Barcelona

For Ana and John,
with congratulations on their
tremendous successes and best of luck, always,
in the future!

For Shirley Johnson,
with the deepest thanks for all your
instruction, your smile—and the laughter!

For Vickie Regan,
eternally gorgeous, and of course, our
true reigning diva, Honey Bunch.

And for Victor,
who always does me so much
better than me! But teaches so much and, with
his work, gives to so many.

CHAPTER 1

There was always something to see on South Beach.

Always.

Glittering, balmy, radiant by virtue of the sun by day and neon by night. The rich and beautiful came and played, and everyone else came and watched. The beach sparkled, offering the most spectacular eye candy, gossip, scandal, traffic jams and more. Nearly bare bodies that were beautiful. Nearly bare bodies that were not so beautiful.

Models, rockers, skaters, bikers, would-be-surfers-were-there-only-some-surf, the MTV crowd, the very old, the very young.

But tonight there was even more.

One of the largest and most prestigious ballroom dance competitions in the world was taking place at one of the best-known hotels ever to grace the strip of sand called Miami Beach.

And with it came Lara Trudeau.

She spun, she twirled, she floated on air, a blur of crystal color and grace.

She was, quite simply, beauty in motion.

Lara demonstrated a grace and perfection of movement that few could even begin to emulate. She had it all, a flair to pin down the unique character of every dance, a face that came alive to the music, a smile that never failed. Judges were known to have said that it was difficult to look down and judge her footwork, much less notice the other couples on the floor, because her smile and her face were so engaging they almost forgot their duties. They had been known to admit that they hadn't marked other couples as accurately as they might have; Lara was simply so beautiful and spectacular and point-blank good that it was hard to draw their eyes away from her.

Tonight was no exception.

Indeed, tonight Lara was more incredible than ever, more seductive, alluring, and glorious. To watch her was to feel that the senses were teased, stroked, awakened, caressed, excited and eased.

She was alone on the floor, or rather, alone with her partner, Jim Burke. During the cabaret routines, each of the couples in the finals took the floor alone, so there she was, her body a lithe example of feminine perfection in her formfitting ball gown of a thousand colors. Jim, as talented as he was, had become nothing more than an accessory.

Those who loved her watched in awe, while those who despised her watched with envy.

Shannon Mackay, current manager of Moonlight Sonata, the independent studio where Lara had long ago begun her career and continued to coach, watched with mixed feelings of wry amusement, not at all sure herself whether she loved Lara or despised her. But there was no denying her talent. Even among the spectacular performances by the best and most accomplished artists in the world community of professional dance, Lara stood out.

"She is simply incredible," Shannon said aloud.

At her side, Ben Trudeau, Lara's ex, snorted. "Oh, yeah. Just incredible."

Jane Ulrich, who had made it to the semifinals but been edged out at the end, as usual, by Lara, turned to Ben with a brilliant smile.

"Oh, Ben. You can't still be bitter. She's so good, it's as if she's not really of this earth."

Shannon smiled at Jane's compliment. Jane was stunning that night herself; her figure lean and trim, and her waltz gown, a deep crimson, set off her dark coloring in a blaze of glittering fire.

"I'd rather dance with you," Jane's partner, Sam Railey, said softly, giving her a squeeze. "You, my love, actually dance *with* someone. Lara uses her partner like a prop."

"But she *is* brilliant, just brilliant," Gordon Henson, owner of the studio, said. He was the one who had first taught Lara, and his pride was justified.

"Let's face it—she's a mean, ambitious bitch who'd walk over a friend's dead body to get where she wanted to go," said Justin Garcia, one of the studio's upcoming salsa specialists.

Next to him, Rhianna Markham, another contender, laughed delightedly. "C'mon, Justin, say what you really feel."

Shannon nudged Rhianna and said softly, "Careful. We're surrounded by our students." And they were, since the hotel was just north of the South Beach area where the studio was located. As a teaching institution, it was the envy of many a competitor, for not only was it located in the limelight of a varied and heavily populated area, it was situated right on top of a club that had turned into a true hot spot over the past few years, since it had been bought by charismatic young Latin American entrepreneur Gabriel Lopez—

who had come this evening, as well, in support of his friends. Due to the proximity of the event, even a number of the studio's more casual students had come, entranced to see the very best of the best, competitors from all over the world.

"She's just gorgeous," Rhianna said loudly enough to be overheard, making a conspiratorial face at Shannon and lowering her head. Shannon had to grin.

But then Gordon whispered to her softly, "*You* should have been out there. You could have been more gorgeous."

She shook her head. "I like teaching, not competing."

"Chicken?"

She grinned. "I know when I'm outclassed."

"Never outclassed," he said, and squeezed her hand.

On the dance floor, Lara executed another perfect lift, spiraling down her partner's body in perfect unity with the music.

There was a tap on Shannon's shoulder. At first, she paid no attention to it. The crowd was massive, including students, teachers, amateurs, professionals, press and those who just liked to watch. A jostle meant nothing as everyone vied for space from which to watch the spectacle.

The tap came again. Frowning, Shannon half turned. The sides of the stage were dark, cast in shadow by the spotlights on the floor. She couldn't see the person summoning her, but it might have been the waiter behind her, a man dressed in tails. Strange, tonight the wait staff, some of the judges and many of the contenders were dressed almost alike.

"Yes?" she murmured, puzzled.

"You're next," he said.

"Next?" she queried. But the man, whose face she hadn't really seen, was already gone. He must have been mistaken. She wasn't competing.

"Ooh!" Jane said. "She's unbelievable!"

Shannon looked quickly back to the floor, forgetting the man who had been trying to reach her in a case of mistaken identity. She wasn't particularly concerned. Whoever was up next would know. They would already be waiting on the sidelines.

Waiting in a nerve-wracking situation. Following Lara would never be easy.

"Excellent," Ben admitted. "Every step perfectly executed."

From the crowd, a collective "Ahh!" arose.

And then, suddenly, Lara Trudeau went poetically still. Her hands, so elegant with their long, tapered fingers and polished nails, flew dramatically to her left breast. There was a moment of stillness, with the music still playing a Viennese waltz as sweet and lilting as the cool air.

Then, still graceful, she dropped.

Her fall was as elegant as any dance movement, a melting into the ground, a dip that was slow, supple....

Until her head fell to the dance floor in perfect complement to the length of her body and she did not move again.

"That wasn't in her routine," Gordon whispered to Shannon.

"No," Shannon murmured back, frowning. "Do you think it's something she added at the last minute for dramatic effect?"

"If so, she's milking it too far," Gordon replied, frowning as he stared at the floor.

At first, there was a hushed, expectant silence from the crowd. Then, as Jim Burke remained standing at her side, the room began to fill with the thunder of applause.

It ebbed awkwardly to a hollow clap here and there, then faded altogether, as those who knew dance and knew Lara began to frown, realizing that they hadn't witnessed a dramatic finale but that something was wrong.

A collective "What…?" rose from the crowd.

Shannon started to move forward, frowning, wondering if Lara hadn't decided to make use of a new ploy.

Gordon caught her arm.

"Something's wrong," he said. "I think she needs medical help."

That must have been apparent, because the first person to rush forward was Dr. Richard Long, a handsome young surgeon, as well as a student at Moonlight Sonata. He fell to his knees at Lara's side, felt deftly for a pulse. He raised his head, looking around stunned for a split second, then yelled out hoarsely, "Call an ambulance!" He quickly looked down again and began performing CPR.

The room was still for a second, as if the hundreds of people in it had become collectively paralyzed with shock. Then dozens of cell phones were suddenly whipped out from pockets and purses.

Whispers and murmurs rose from all around the dance floor, then went still.

Richard valiantly continued his efforts.

"My God, what on earth happened to her?" Gordon said, the tension in his eyes showing his inner debate on whether to rush up himself or not.

"Drugs?" Ben suggested.

"Lara? Never," Jane said vehemently.

"No," Shannon murmured, shaking her head.

"Yeah, right, no, never," Ben said with a sniff. "Let's see, drugs on South Beach? In Miami, Florida, gateway to South America? Right, never."

"Never for Lara Trudeau," Shannon snapped.

"There are different drugs," Justin said.

"Maybe," Gordon agreed ruefully. "She's been known to swallow a few Xanax when she's nervous."

"Or maybe alcohol?" Justin said worriedly.

"When she's dancing?" Rhianna protested, shaking her head.

"She truly considers her body a temple," Sam informed them with complete assurance. "But sometimes the temple needs a few offerings, she says," he added. "She must have taken something. I mean, look at her."

"I hope she's going to be all right. She's got to be all right!" Shannon said, sharing Gordon's concern regarding whether or not she should step forward.

Gordon set his hand on Shannon's shoulders. "No," he said softly.

She stared at him, puzzled.

"It's too late," he told her.

"What?" Shannon said, disbelieving.

Yet even as she asked the question, Richard Long rose. "Clear the floor, please. I'm afraid it's too late," he said quietly.

"Too late?" came a shout.

"She's...gone," Richard said awkwardly, as if sorry that his words gave the final ring of reality to the unbelievable.

"Dead?" Someone in the crowd said.

Richard sighed, dismayed that he couldn't get his words to sink through the collective head of those surrounding him. "I'm afraid...yes."

The sound of sirens filled the night.

Seconds later the crowd parted and medical techs swept into the room. They added emergency equipment and a desperately administered injection to the CPR efforts.

But in the end, no matter how hard they tried, it was over. Those watching kept their distance but could not turn away.

Shannon stared at the uniformed men, frozen in disbelief, along with the others. And as she watched, unbidden, a strange whisper filtered back into her mind.

You're next.

Insane. Silly. Someone had mistaken her for the next dancer to compete, that was all. Everything was a mess, Lara had fallen, but would be all right in the end. The CPR would work. She would suddenly inhale and stand up, and soon they would all be talking about her again, saying that she would do anything to create the biggest impression of the evening. She meant to be remembered, to be immortal.

But no one lived forever.

As the crowd left the floor at last, still stunned, there were murmurs everywhere.

Lara Trudeau. Gone. Impossible. And yet, she had died as she had lived. Glorious, beautiful, graceful, and now… dead.

Dead on the dance floor.

CHAPTER 2

"Hey, Quinn, someone to see you."

Quinn O'Casey was startled to see Amber Larkin standing at the top of the ladder as he crawled his way up. He was in full dive gear, having spent the past forty-five minutes scraping barnacles from the hull of the *Twisted Time,* his boat.

To the best of his knowledge, Amber had been in Key Largo, at work at the office, where she should have been. He was on vacation. She wasn't.

He arched a brow, indicating that she should step back so he could come aboard. She did so, ignoring the look that also questioned her arrival when he should have been left the hell alone. So much for chasing a man down.

She backed up, giving him room, and when he stepped on deck, tossing down his flippers, pulling off his dive mask, he saw the reason she had come. His brother was standing behind her.

"Hey, Doug," he said, frowning at them both.

"You might have mentioned you were coming up. I

wouldn't have had to drive down to Key Largo just to make Amber drive back up to Miami with me."

Maybe he should have mentioned his vacation time to his brother, but why drag him down? Doug had gone through the police academy less than a year ago. An enthusiastic and ambitious patrolman, he was a younger brother to be proud of, having survived his teen years and young adulthood without the growing pains that had plagued Quinn's younger years—and a few of his older ones, for that matter. But hell, that was why he was back in South Florida, despite the gut-wrenching work he'd found instead of the easy slide he'd expected at the beginning.

Quinn shook his head. He was glad to be back home in South Florida. It could be one hell of a great place to live.

It could also showcase the most blatant forms of man's inhumanity to his fellow man.

And thus, the vacation. It wasn't as if he felt shattered or anything like that. Hell, he knew he couldn't control the evils of the world, or even those of a single man. But who the hell had ever expected what had happened to Nell Durken? He should be glad that the scum who had killed her was under arrest and would either be put away for life or meet a date with death. Still, whatever Art Durken's sentence, Nell was gone. And maybe he did blame himself a little, wonder if he shouldn't have told her to get away from the man immediately. But she had just come in to hire Quinn for routine surveillance, so who the hell knew until it was too late just what kind of a hornets' nest they'd stirred up. Eventually he *had* suggested that she part from her husband, and he had assumed she meant to do so, armed with the information regarding the man that Quinn had been able to give her.

But she hadn't left fast enough. Art hadn't been abusive, not physically, though he had been sexually demanding of

Nell while spending his own time in a number of places out-side his own home—and with a number of women who had not been his wife.

Who the hell could have known the guy would suddenly become homicidal?

He should have—he should have suspected Nell could be in danger.

Today he felt something like the boat—his time on that particular case had caused a growth of barnacles over his skin. Some time off might help scrape off the festering scabs of surprise and bitterness.

Vacation. From work, from family, from friends.

Maybe especially family. Doug didn't deserve any of his foul mood or foul temper.

And also, he hadn't actually been up to spending time with Doug. His brother could be a royal pain in the ass, a nonstop barrage of questions and inquiries. Like an intern in an emergency room, ready to diagnose a malady in any tic of the body, Doug was ready to find evil in every off-the-wall movement in the people around him.

A tough way to be in Miami-Dade County, where more than half the inhabitants could be considered a bit off-the-wall.

Quinn didn't know whether to groan or be concerned. Doug wouldn't have hunted him down to ask hypothetical questions. A tinge of unease hit him suddenly.

"Mom?" Quinn said worriedly.

"Heart ticking like an industrial clock," Doug assured him quickly. "However, she did mention that you hadn't been by lately, and she enjoys it when you come around to dinner once a week. You might want to give her a call."

"I left her a message that I was fine, just kind of busy."

"Yeah, but she's a smart woman, you know. She reads the newspapers."

"Is that why you're here?" Quinn demanded, arching a brow.

"I have a case for you," Doug said, moving around his brother to grab the dive tank Quinn had just unbuckled.

"Guess what, baby bro? I don't need you to find cases for me. The agency does that very well—too well. Besides, I'm on vacation."

"Yeah, Amber told me. That's why I thought it would be a great time for you to take on something private I've been thinking about."

Quinn went ahead and groaned. "Dammit, Doug. You mean you want me to do a bunch of prying around for free." He glared at Amber.

"Hey, he's your brother," she said defensively. "And you know what? Now that we've found you, I think I'll let you two talk. I'm going over to Nick's for a hamburger." Tossing her long blond hair over her shoulder, she started off the boat, casting back a single glance so she could try to read Quinn's scowl and figure out just how annoyed he was with her.

Doug wore a rueful grin on his face. "Hey, I'll rinse your equipment for you," he said, as if offering some kind of an apology.

"Good. Go ahead. I'll be in the cabin."

Quinn took the two steps down to the *Twisted Time*'s head, stripped and stepped beneath a spray of fresh water for a moment, then wrapped a towel around his waist and dug a clean pair of cutoffs out of the wicker laundry basket on the bed of the main cabin. Barefoot and still damp, he returned to the main cabin area, pulled a Miller from the fridge in the galley and sat on the sofa just beyond it, waiting, fingers drumming, scowl still in place.

Doug came down the steps, nimble and quick, a grimace on his face as he, too, went to the fridge, helped himself to a beer and sat on the port-side sofa, facing Quinn.

"You want me to do something for free, right?" Quinn said, scowling.

"Well…sort of. Actually, it's going to cost you."

"What?"

"I need you to take dance lessons."

Quinn stared at his younger brother, stunned speechless for several seconds. "You're out of your mind," he told Doug.

"No, no, I'm not, and you'll understand in a few minutes."

"No, I won't."

"Yes, you will. It's about a death."

"Do you know how many people die everyday, Doug? Hey, you're the cop. If this was suspicious death, it was— or will be—investigated. And even if it was deemed natural or accidental, you must know someone in the department who can look into it."

Quinn shook his head. Looking at Doug was almost like seeing himself a number of years ago. There was an eight-year age gap between them. They looked something alike, identical in height at six-two, but Doug still had the lean, lanky strength of a young man in his early twenties, while Quinn himself had broadened out. Quinn's hair was dark, while Doug's was a wheaten color, but they both had their father's deep blue, wide-set eyes and hard-angled face. Sometimes they moved alike, using their hands when they spoke, as if words weren't quite enough, and folding them prayer fashion or tapping them against their chins when they were in deep thought. For a moment Quinn reflected on his irritation at being interrupted here, but Doug had always been a damned good brother, looking up to him, being there for him, never losing faith, even when Quinn had gone through his own rough times.

"I can't get anyone in the department interested in this,"

Doug admitted. "There's been too much going on in the county lately. They're hunting a serial rapist who's getting more violent with each victim, a guard was killed at a recent robbery…trust me, homicide is occupied. Too busy to get involved when it looks like an accidental death. There's no one who's free right now."

"No one?"

Doug made a face. "All right, there were a few suspicious factors, so there is a guy assigned to follow up. But he's an asshole, Quinn, really."

"Who?"

Sometimes guys just didn't like each other, so rumors went around about their capabilities. The metro department had endured its share of troubles through the years with a few bad cops, but for the most part, the officers were good men, underpaid and overworked.

Then again, sometimes they *were* just assholes.

"Pete Dixon."

Quinn frowned. "Old Pete's not that bad."

"Hell no. Give him a smoking gun in a guy's hand, and he can catch the perp every time."

"That from a rookie," Quinn muttered.

"Look, Dixon's not a ball of fire. And he's just following up on what the M.E. has ruled as an accidental death. He isn't going to go around looking under any carpets. He's not interested. He'll just do some desk work by rote. He doesn't care."

"And therefore I should? To the point of taking dance lessons? Like I said, bro, I think you've lost your mind," Quinn said flatly.

Doug smiled, reaching into the back pocket of his jeans. He pulled out his wallet and, from it, a carefully folded newspaper clipping. That was just like Doug. He was one of the most orderly human beings Quinn had ever come across. The clipping hadn't been ripped out but cut, then folded meticulously. He shook his head at the thought, knowing that his own organizational skills were lacking in comparison.

"What is it?" Quinn asked, taking the paper.

"Read."

Quinn unfolded it and looked at the headline. "'Diva Lara Trudeau Dead on the Dance Floor at Thirty-eight.'" He cocked his head toward his brother.

"Keep reading."

Quinn scanned the article. He'd never heard of Lara Trudeau, but that didn't mean anything. He wouldn't have recognized the name of any dancer, ballroom or otherwise. He could free-dive to nearly four hundred feet, bench-press nearly four hundred pounds and rock climb with the best of them. But in a salsa club, hell, he was best as a bar support.

Puzzled, he scanned the article. Lara Trudeau, thirty-eight, winner of countless dance championships, had died as she had lived—on the dance floor. A combination of tranquilizers and alcohol had caused a cardiac arrest. Those closest to the dancer were distraught, and apparently stunned that, despite her accomplishments, she had felt the need for artificial calm.

Quinn looked back at his brother and shook his head. "I don't get it. An aging beauty got nervous and took too many pills. Tragic. But hardly diabolical."

"You're not reading between the lines," Doug said with dismay.

Quinn suppressed a grin. "And I take it no one in the homicide division 'read between the lines,' either?"

Doug smacked the article. "Quinn, a woman like Lara Trudeau wouldn't take pills. She was a perfectionist. And a winner. She would have taken the championship. She had no reason to be nervous."

"Doug, are you even reading the lines yourself? We're talking about something that no one can outrun—age. Here's this Lara Trudeau—*thirty-eight*. With a horde of twenty-somethings following in her wake. Hell, yes, she was nervous."

"What, you think people keel over at thirty-eight?" Doug said.

"When you're a quarterback, you're damn near retirement," Quinn said.

"She wasn't a quarterback."

Quinn let out an impatient sigh. "It's the same thing. Sports, dancing. People slow down with age."

"Some get better with age. *She* was still winning. And hell, in ballroom dance, people compete at all ages."

"And that's really great. More power to them. I just don't understand why you chased me down about this. According to the paper *and* everything you're telling me, the death was accidental. It's all here. She dropped dead in public on a ballroom floor, so naturally there was an autopsy, and the findings indicated nothing suspicious."

"Right. They found the physical cause of death. Cardiac arrest brought on by a mixture of alcohol and pills. How she happened to ingest that much isn't in the M.E.'s report."

Quinn groaned and pulled over the day's newspaper, flipping quickly to the local section. "'Mother and Two Children Found Shot to Death in North Miami Apartment,'" he read, glaring at his brother over the headlines. "'Body Found in Car Trunk at Mall,'" he continued. "Want me to go on? Violence is part of life in the big city, bro. You've been through the academy. There's a lot out there that's real bad. You know it, and I know it. Things that need to be questioned, and I'm sure the homicide guys are on them. But a drugged-out dancer drops dead, and you want to make something more out of it. You'll make detective soon enough. Give yourself time."

"Quinn, this is important to me."

"Why?"

"Because I'm afraid that someone else is going to die."

Quinn frowned, staring at his younger brother, wondering if he wasn't being overly dramatic. Doug looked dead calm and serious, though.

Quinn threw up his hands. "Is this based on anything, Doug? Was someone else threatened? If so, you're a cop. You know the guys in homicide, including Dixon. And he's not that bad. He knows the law, and on a paper chase, he's great."

"You know them better."

"*Knew* them better," Quinn corrected. "I was away a long time, before I started working with Dane down in the Keys. Anyway, we're getting away from my point. Doug, take a look at the facts. There was an autopsy, and the medical examiner was convinced that her death was accidental. The cops must see it that way, too, if all they're doing is a bit of follow-up investigation. So...? Did you hear someone threaten her before she died? Do you have any reason whatsoever to suspect murder? And if so, do you have any idea who might have wanted to kill her?"

Doug shrugged, contemplating his answer. "Several people, actually."

"And what makes you say that?"

"She could be the world's biggest bitch."

"And you know this for a fact?"

"Yes."

"How?"

Again Doug hesitated, then cocked his head to the side as he surveyed his brother. "I was sleeping with her."

Quinn groaned, set his beer on the table and pressed his temples between his palms. "You were sleeping with a woman more than ten years your senior?"

"There's something wrong with that?"

"I didn't say that."

"You sure as hell did."

"All right, it just seems a little strange to me, that's all."

"She was quite a woman."

"If you say so, Doug, I'm sure she was." He hesitated. "Were you emotionally involved, or was it more of a sexual thing?"

"I can't say that I thought I wanted to spend the rest of my life with her or anything like that. And I know damn well she didn't feel that way about me. But whether she could be a bitch or not, and whether or not we were meant for the ages, hell, yes, I cared about her."

"And are you asking me to look into this because your feelings are ruling your mind?" Quinn asked seriously.

Doug shook his head. "We weren't a 'thing,' by any means. And I wasn't the only one involved with her. She could play games. Or maybe, in her mind, she wasn't playing games. She kind of considered herself a free spirit." He shrugged, not looking at Quinn. "Kind of as if she was a gift to the world and the men in it, and she bestowed herself when she felt it was warranted, or when she was struck by whim, I guess. At any rate, I wasn't the only one she was sleeping with," Doug said flatly.

"Great. You know who else she was seeing?"

"I know who she might have been seeing—anyone around the studio."

"And how many people knew about your relationship?"

"I don't know," Doug admitted.

"This is pretty damn vague."

"It wouldn't need to be—if you would just agree to look into what happened."

Quinn surveyed his younger brother thoughtfully. He was caught up in this thing emotionally. And maybe that was why he didn't want it to have happened the way it appeared.

"Maybe you should make it a point to stay *away* from the homicide guys, Doug. If the police suspected someone of murder, you might be first in line."

"But I didn't kill her. I'm a cop. And even if I wasn't, I'd never murder anyone, Quinn. You know that."

"You had a relationship with the woman. If you convince people that she was killed, you could wind up under investigation yourself, you understand that?"

"Of course. But I'm innocent."

Quinn looked at the newspaper again. "She died because of an overdose of the prescription drug Xanax. The alcohol might have enhanced the drug, bringing on cardiac arrest."

"Yes," Doug said. "And the cop on the case is certain that in her pigheaded quest for eternal fame—my adjective, not his—she got nervous."

"Doug, I'm sorry to say it, but I've seen people do a lot of stupid things. It may be tragic, but it looks as if she got nervous, took the pills, then drank."

Doug groaned, shaking his head. "No."

"You don't think that's even possible?"

"No."

"The prescription was in her name. Her doctor was contacted. According to him, she'd been taking a few pills before performances for the past several years. It's in the article."

"That's right," Doug agreed calmly.

"Doug, unless you've got more to go on...I can't even understand what you think I can do for you."

"I've got more to go on. A hunch. A feeling. A certainty, actually," his brother said firmly. Quinn knew Doug. He was capable of being as steadfast as an oak. That was what had gotten him through school and into the academy, where he had graduated with honors. The kid was going to make a fine detective one day.

"There are times to hold and times to fold, you know," Quinn said quietly.

Doug suddenly looked as if he was about to lose it. "*I'll* pay you."

"We charge way too much," Quinn told him brusquely.

"Give me two weeks," Doug said. "Quinn, dammit, I need your help! Just come into the studio and see if you don't think people are behaving strangely, that people besides me believe she was murdered."

"They've told you this?"

"Not in so many words. In fact, those who knew her well all admit she took pills now and then. She had a drink here and there, too. And yeah, she was getting up there for a woman determined on maintaining her championships in both the smooth and rhythm categories, and in cabaret."

"Doug, you might as well be speaking a foreign language," Quinn said irritably.

"Rhythm is the faster dances, rumba, cha-cha, swing, hustle, merengue, West Coast swing, polka. Smooth is the fox-trot, waltz, tango. And cabaret is for partners and combines different things."

"All right, all right, never mind. I get the picture."

"So?"

"Doug…"

"Dammit, Quinn, there were plenty of people who hated her. Plenty of suspects. But if I push any further, someone will start investigating me. Will they ever be able to prove I caused her death? No, because I didn't. Can my career be ruined? Can people look at me with suspicion for the rest of my life? You bet, and you know it. Quinn, I'm not asking a lot. Just go and take a few dance lessons. It won't kill you."

It won't kill you. An odd sensation trickled down Quinn's spine. He wondered if he wouldn't come to remember those words.

"Doug, no one will believe I've come in for dance lessons. I can't dance to save my life."

"Why do you think guys take lessons?" Doug demanded.

"To pick up women at the salsa clubs on the beach," he said flatly.

"See? A side benefit. What are you going to do—hole up like a hermit for the rest of your life?"

"I haven't holed up like a hermit at all." Did he actually sound defensive?

His brother just stared at him. Quinn sat back and said, "Wait a minute—is this how you got into the whole thing to begin with? *Dance* lessons." He couldn't have been more surprised if he'd heard that Doug had taken up knitting. Doug had nearly gone the route of a pro athlete. He remained an exceptional golfer and once a week coached a Little League team.

"Yeah, I was taking lessons," Doug said.

"I see." He paused thoughtfully. "No, I don't see at all. Why did you decide to take dance lessons?"

Doug grinned sheepishly. "Randy Torres is getting married. I agreed to be his best man. He and his fiancée, Sheila, started taking lessons for the wedding. I figured, what the hell? I'd go with him a few times and be a good best man. There aren't nearly as many guys taking lessons as females. The place seemed to be a gold mine of really great looking women. The studio is on South Beach, right above one of the hottest salsa clubs out there. Nice place to go after classes and make use of what you've learned. So I started taking lessons."

"And wound up…dating an older diva?"

"That's the way it went. She wasn't actually a teacher there—she got paid big bucks to come in and coach now and then. So she wasn't really in on the teacher rules."

"What are the teacher rules?"

"Teachers aren't supposed to fraternize with students. A loose rule there, because everyone goes down to the salsa club now and then. Let me tell you, Moonlight Sonata has the best location in history for a dance studio. Sometimes couples come in, and they can dance with each other. But for singles…well, they're still nervous at first. So if you can go to a club and have a few drinks and have a teacher there to dance with you, make you look good—well, it's a nice setup. And hey, South Beach, you know. It's one of those places where rockers and movie stars stop in sometimes."

"So there are a lot of players hanging around. And, I imagine, drugs up the wazoo. What's the name of the club?"

"Suede."

Quinn arched a brow. "I know the name, and I never hang out on South Beach. I hate South Beach," he added. And he meant it. The place was plastic, at best. People never doing anything—just coming out to be seen. Trying to make the society pages by being in the right club when Madonna came by. Proving their worth by getting a doorman to let them into one of the new hot spots when the line was down the street.

The only good thing in his opinion was Lincoln Road, where some good foreign and independent films occasionally made it to the theater, a few of the restaurants were authentic and reasonable, and every canine maniac in the city felt free to walk a dog.

"Come on, the beach isn't really that bad. Okay, it's not as laid-back as your precious Keys, but still… And as for Suede, there was an investigation not long ago. A runaway-turned-prostitute was found about a block away, just lying on the sidewalk. Heroin overdose. So Narcotics did a sweep, but Suede came out clean. Hell, maybe the girl did get her drugs from someone at the bar. You know as well as I do that dealers don't have to look like bums. And there's money on the beach. Big money people pop in at Suede. But as for the management and the club itself, everything came out squeaky clean. In fact, they're known for enforcing the twenty-one-and-over law on drinking, and there was a big thing in the paper a few months ago when one of the bartenders threw out a rock star, said he wasn't serving him any more alcohol. It's a good club, and like I said, students and teachers see one another and dance, maybe have a drink or two—it gives the school a real edge, because people can use what they learn. But outside of that, teachers and students really aren't supposed to hang around together."

"Why?"

Doug sighed as if his brother had gotten old and dense. "Favoritism. Dance classes are expensive. Someone could get pissed if their teacher was seeing someone outside the studio and maybe giving that student extra attention. Still, it's a rule that gets broken. You need to come down there, Quinn. Could it really hurt you to take a few lessons, ask a few questions, make a few inquiries—get into it in a way I can't?" Doug asked.

Quinn winced. "Doug, one day, I'd like to take up sky-diving. I'd like to up my scuba certification to a higher level. I'd like to speak Spanish better, and I kind of always wanted to go on safari in Africa. Never in my life have I wanted to take dance lessons."

"You might be surprised," Doug said. "Quinn, please."

Quinn looked down at his hands. He'd thought he would clean up the boat and head out to the Bahamas. Spend two weeks with nothing but fish, sea, sun and sand. Listening to calypso music and maybe some reggae. Listening to it. Not dancing to it.

But this seemed to matter to Doug. Really matter. And maybe something *had* been going on. Doug wouldn't be here if he didn't have a real feeling about it. Better he find it out before the police, because Doug would be a natural suspect.

He looked up at Doug, ready to agree that it wouldn't kill him just to check the place out and ask a few questions. Then he hesitated. "I need a break," he said honestly. "I'm not even sure you want me handling a case that means so much to you."

Doug shook his head angrily. "Quinn, you know better than to blame yourself for anything that's happened—lately. You do your best with what you've learned and what you know. And sometimes knowledge and laws work, and sometimes they don't. I still have faith in you—even if you've lost it in yourself."

"I haven't lost faith in myself," Quinn said. Shit. Beyond a doubt, he was sounding defensive.

"No?" Doug asked. "Good. Because I've got some news for you that I think will change your mind about this case— among other things."

Quinn looked at him questioningly.

"Your girl took lessons at the Moonlight Sonata studios. Right up until last November."

Quinn frowned. "My girl? My girl who?"

"Nell Durken. I managed to sneak a look in the file cabinet at Moonlight Sonata, and Nell Durken's name is there, right in the record books."

Quinn hadn't known a damn thing about Nell Durken's dance lessons. But then again, he hadn't known all that much about her, really. She had just hired him to find out what her husband spent his time doing.

So he had found out.

And the bastard had killed her.

"Actually," Doug continued, "Nell was one of their advanced students. Then, last November, she just quit going. Never mentioned it to you, I guess. Curious, though. The records indicate that she was gung ho—and then just gone. Makes you wonder, huh?"

"Fine," Quinn said flatly. "I'll do some checking. I'll take a few fucking dance lessons."

CH**A**PTER 3

"H_{ey}, how's it going?"

Ella Rodriguez tapped on Shannon's half-open door, then walked the few feet to the desk and perched on the corner of it. Shannon sat back in her desk chair, contemplating a reply to her receptionist.

"I don't know. How do you think it's going? Personally, I think we should have shut down for the week," Shannon said.

"We shut down for three days," Ella reminded her. "That's about what most corporations are willing to give for members of the immediate family when someone has passed away."

"Her pictures are all over the walls," Shannon reminded Ella.

"Right. And teachers and really serious students are going to miss her—one way or another—for a long time. But you have some students who aren't all that serious, who never want to see a competition floor, and who are getting married in a matter of weeks, left feet and all. They need the studio open, Shannon." Ella had short, almost platinum hair, cut stylishly. She had a gamine's face, with incredible dark eyes and one of the world's best smiles. She considered herself the least talented employee in the studio, but whether she was right about that or not, her warmth and easy charm surely accounted for many of their students.

Except that now Ella made a face that was hardly warm or charming. "Shannon, I'm well aware you're not supposed to speak ill of the dead. But truth be told, I didn't like Lara. And I'm not the only one. There are even people who think that her dropping dead on the dance floor was a piece of poetic justice."

"Ella!"

"I know that sounds terrible, and I'm really sorry. I certainly didn't want anything to happen to her," Ella said. She stared at Shannon. "Come on, you've got admit it—she couldn't possibly have been your favorite person."

"Whether she was or wasn't, she was a dynamic force in our industry, and she started here. So this was her home, so to speak," Shannon said.

"We're all sorry, we know she was a professional wonder, and I don't think there's a soul out there who didn't respect her talent." Ella met Shannon's eyes. "Hey, I even said all that when the detective talked to me."

"You told him that you hadn't liked Lara?" Shannon asked.

"I was dead honest. Sorry, no pun intended. Oh, come on, he was just questioning us because he had to. You know—when someone dies that way, they have to do an autopsy, and they had to question a bunch of people, too, but hell, everyone saw what happened." Ella arched a brow. "Did you tell them you had adored her?"

"I was dead honest, as well—no pun intended," Shannon said dryly. "Well, for all of the four and a half minutes he questioned me."

Ella shook her head. "What did you expect? There's no

trick here. Her dance is on tape—her death is on tape." Ella shivered. "Creepy. Except Lara probably would have loved it. Even her demise was as dramatic as possible, captured on film for all eternity. She got carried away, and she died. A foolish waste. There's nothing anyone can do now. But you closed the studio in her honor. Now we're open again. And you've got a new student arriving in fifteen minutes."

"*I* have a new student?"

"Yeah, you."

Shannon frowned and said, "Wait, wait, wait, I'm not taking on any of the new students. Me being the studio manager and all? I have too much paperwork and too many administration duties, plus planning for the Gator Gala. Remember what we decided at the last meeting?"

"Of course I remember. But as I'm sure you've noticed, Jane isn't in yet. She has a dental appointment—which she announced at the same meeting. Rhianna couldn't change her weekly two-o'clock, because we don't open until then and her guy works nights. And this new guy is coming in because Doug bought him a guest pass. Actually, it's Doug's brother. Personally, I can't wait to see him."

"I keep telling you that you should go ahead and get your certification to teach," Shannon said. Ella had the natural ability to become an excellent teacher. But she had come to the studio two years ago looking for a clerical position and still shied away from anything else.

As for herself, at this particular time, Shannon just didn't want to teach, which was odd, because watching the growth of a student was something she truly enjoyed.

Everything, however, had seemed off-kilter since Lara had dropped dead. Naturally it had shaken the entire dance world. Sudden death was always traumatic.

But it was true as well that Lara Trudeau hadn't been her favorite person.

Championships—no matter how many—didn't guarantee a decent living, not in the States. Lara had coached to supplement her income. Gordon Henson had been her first ballroom instructor. He had maintained his pride in his prize student, and, to her credit, Lara had come to the Moonlight Sonata studio whenever he asked her, within reason. But after he had begun to groom Shannon to take over management of the studio, he had left the hiring of coaches to her.

And because Lara was excellent and a real draw for the students, Shannon had continued to bring her in. But unlike a number of the other coaches they hired, Lara was not averse to making fun of the students—or the teachers—after a coaching session.

Shannon also had other, more personal, reasons for disliking Lara. Even so, it still bothered her deeply that Lara had died. It might have been the simple fact that no one so young should perish. Or perhaps it was impossible to see anyone who was so much a part of one's life—liked or disliked—go so abruptly from it without feeling a sense of mourning and loss. Part of it was a sense of confusion, or of disbelief, that remained. Whatever the reasons, Shannon simply felt off, and it was difficult enough to maintain a working mentality to deal with the needs of the upcoming Gator Gala, much less consider teaching a beginner with a smile and the enthusiasm necessary to bring them into the family fold of the studio.

"She hasn't even been dead a week yet," Shannon said. "She hasn't even been buried yet." Because Lara's death had to be investigated, she had been taken to the county morgue until her body could be released by the medical examiner. But once his findings had been complete, Ben, Lara's ex, along with Gordon, had gotten together to make the arrangements. Lara had come to Miami for college almost twenty years ago, and sometime during the next few years, her parents had passed away. She'd never had children, and if she had any close relatives, they hadn't appeared in all the years. Because she was a celebrity, even after her death had officially been declared accidental, the two men had opted for a Saturday morning funeral.

"Shannon, she breezed through here to dance now and then, and yes, we knew her. She wasn't like a sister. We need to get past this," Ella insisted. "Honestly, if anyone really knew her, it was Gordon, and *he's* moving on."

Yes, their boss was definitely moving on, Shannon thought. He had spent yesterday in his office, giving great concern to swatches of fabric he had acquired, trying to determine which he liked best for the new drapes he was putting in his living room.

"I don't know about you," Ella said, shaking her head. "You were all upset when Nell Durken died, and she hadn't been in here in a year."

"Nell Durken didn't just die. Her husband killed her. He probably realized he was about to lose his meal ticket," Shannon said bitterly. Nell Durken had been one of the most amazing students to come through the door. Bubbly, beautiful and always full of life, she had been a ray of sunshine. She'd been friendly with all the students, wry about the fact that she couldn't drag her husband in, but determined to learn on her own. Hearing that the man had killed her had been horribly distressing.

"Jeez," Shannon breathed suddenly.

"What?" Ella said.

"It's just strange…isn't it?"

"What's strange?" Ella asked, shaking her head.

"Nell Durken died because her husband forced an overdose of sleeping pills down her throat."

"Yes? The guy was a bastard—we all thought that," Ella said. "No one realized he was a lethal bastard, but…anyway, the cops got him. He was having an affair, but Nell was the one with the trust fund. He probably thought he'd get away with forcing all those pills down her throat. It would look like an accident, and he'd get to keep the money," Ella said. "But they've got him. He could even get the death penalty— his motive was evident and his fingerprints were all over the bottle of pills."

"Have you been watching too many cop shows?" came a query from the open door. A look of amusement on his face, Gordon was staring in at the two women.

"No, Gordon," Ella said. "I'm just pointing out what happened to Nell Durken. And hoping the bastard will fry."

"Fry?" Gordon said.

"Okay, so now it's usually lethal injection. He was so mean to her, long before he killed her," Ella said, shaking her head.

Gordon frowned. "What brought up Nell Durken?"

"Talking about Lara," Ella said.

Gordon didn't seem to see the correlation. "We've lost Lara. That's that. She was kind of like Icarus, I guess, trying to fly too high. As to Nell…hell, we all knew she needed to leave that bastard. It's too bad she didn't. I wish she'd kept dancing."

"She stopped coming in when he planned that Caribbean vacation for her, remember?" Shannon said thoughtfully. "They were going on a second honeymoon. He was going to make everything up to her."

"And we all figured they got on great and things were lovey-dovey again, because she called in afterward saying that she wasn't going to schedule any more lessons for a while because they were going to be traveling. And, of course," Ella added pointedly, since Gordon was staring at her, his mouth open as if he were about to speak, "like a good receptionist, I followed up with calls, but I always got her answering machine, and then, I guess, after about six months, she kind of slipped off the 'things to do' list."

"It's horrible, though, isn't it?" Shannon murmured. "I hope we're not bad luck. I mean, an ex-student is murdered by her husband, and then…then Lara drops dead."

"You think we're jinxed?"

Shannon looked past Gordon's shoulder. Sam Railey was right behind Gordon, staring in.

"Jinxed?" Gordon protested. "Don't even suggest such a thing. Nell was long gone from here when she was murdered. And Lara…Lara is simply a tragedy." He held up three fingers. "The Broward studio lost two students and an instructor last year."

Shannon hid a smile, her brow quirking upward. "Gordon, the students were Mr. and Mrs. Hallsly, ninety and ninety three, respectively. It wasn't such a shock that they died with a few months of one another. And," she added softly, since she had been very fond of Dick Graft, the instructor who had died, "Dick had an aneurism."

"I'm pointing out the fact that people die and *we're* not jinxed," Gordon said.

"Man, I hope not," Sam said. "Because that would be two for us. And you know, things happen in threes."

"Sam!" Gordon said.

"Oh, man, sorry. Hey, don't worry, I'd never say anything like that in front of the students."

"I should hope not," Gordon admonished.

Gordon might have given the management over to Shannon, but if he were to decide that an instructor was detrimental to the studio, that teacher would be out in seconds flat.

"Hey," another voice chimed in. Justin Garcia, five-eight tops, slim, with an ability to move with perfect rhythm, was on his toes, trying to look over the shoulders of the others gathered at Shannon's door. "Psst." He stared at Ella, still perched on the desk. "New student out front. I'd try to start the lesson myself, but he's one big guy, and I think he'd cream me if I gave it a try."

"Doug's brother," Ella said, jumping up.

Doug was definitely one of their favorite new students. He'd come in to learn salsa for a friend's wedding and started out as stiff as a board, but within a week, he'd fallen in love with Cuban motion and wanted to learn everything.

He was a cop and he would laugh about the fact that his fellow officers teased him.

He was definitely appreciated by the studio's many female students—not to mention his teacher, Jane Ulrich. Jane loved the dramatic. With Doug, she could leap, spin and almost literally fly. She was an excellent dancer, and he had the strength to allow her to do any lift she wanted to do. He was tall, blond, blue eyed and ready to go, everything one could want in a student.

Ella pushed past the men, hurrying toward the front of the studio, where she could greet their new student and get him started on paperwork.

Shannon, rising, was startled when Ella burst her way back in almost instantly, her eyes wide. "Damn, is Jane going to be sorry she had that dental appointment. Get up! You gotta see this guy." Ella flew out again.

"Makes mincemeat out of me," Justin told Shannon with a shrug.

Curious, Shannon followed the group on out. By then, Ella was greeting the man politely, and the others were standing around, waiting to meet him.

They didn't usually circle around to greet their new clients.

Doug's brother. Yes, the resemblance was there. They were of a similar height. But where Doug had nice shoulders and a lithe build, this guy looked like he'd walked out of a barbarian movie. His hair was dark, his eyes a penetrating blue. Nice face, hard, but even lines. In a cartoon, he might have been labeled Joe, the truck driver.

Just before she could step forward, Sam placed his hands on her shoulders, pulling her back against him. He whispered teasingly to her, "Too bad it's against policy to fraternize with our students, huh?"

"Sam," she chastised with a soft, weary sigh. It was policy, yes, though Gordon had always preferred not to know what he didn't have to. She had maintained the same *Don't tell me what I don't need to know* attitude.

As she stepped away from him, she heard Justin whisper, "Policy? Like hell. For some of us, maybe, but not for others."

Even as she extended a hand to the Atlas standing before her, Shannon wondered just what his words meant.

Who, exactly, had been fraternizing with whom?

And why the hell did this simple question suddenly make her feel so uneasy?

She forced a smile. "So you're Doug's brother. We're delighted to have you. Doug is something of a special guy around here, you know." She hesitated slightly. "Did he drag you in by the ears?"

The man smiled. Dimple in his left cheek. "Something like that," he said. "He has a knack for coming up with just the right come-on." His handshake was firm. "I'm Quinn. Quinn O'Casey. I'm afraid that you're going to find me to be the brother with two left feet. You've got one hell of a challenge before you."

Her smile stayed in place, though the uneasy sense swept through her again.

One hell of a challenge.

She had a feeling that he was right. On more than one level.

What the hell was he really doing here? she wondered.

"Ella, could I get a chart for Mr. O'Casey, please?" she said aloud. "Come into our conference room, and we'll see what we can do for you."

The conference room wasn't really much of a room, just a little eight-by-eight enclosure. There was a round table in the middle that seated five at most, surrounded by a few shelves and a few displays. Some of the teachers' trophies were there, along with a few she had acquired herself, and several indicating that they had won in the division of best independent studio for the past two years.

Ella handed Shannon a chart, and the others, rather than discreetly going about their business, stared. Shannon arched a brow, which sent them scurrying off. Then she closed the door and indicated a chair to Quinn O'Casey.

"Have a seat."

"You learn to dance at a table?" he queried lightly as he sat.

"I learn a little bit about what sort of dancing you're interested in," she replied. Obviously, they were interested in selling dance lessons, and the conference room was sometimes referred to—jokingly—as the shark-attack haven; however, she'd never felt as if she were actually going into a hostile environment herself. She prided herself on offering the best and never forcing anyone into anything. Students didn't return if they didn't feel that they were getting the most for their money. And the students who came into it for the long haul were the ones who went into competition and kept them all afloat.

"So, Mr. O'Casey, just which dances do you want to learn?"

"Which dances?"

The dark-haired hunk across from Shannon lifted his brows, as if she had asked a dangerous question and was ready to suck him right in.

"We teach a lot of dances here, including country and western and polka. People usually have some kind of a plan in mind when they come in."

"Right, well, sorry, no real plan. Doug talked me into this. Um, which dances. Well, I…I can't dance at all," he said. "So…uh, Doug said something about smooth, so that's what I want, I guess," he said.

"So you'd like a concentration on waltz, fox-trot and tango."

"Tango?"

"Yes, tango."

"That's what you call a smooth dance?"

"There are quick movements, yes, and sharpness of motion is an important characteristic, but it's considered a smooth dance. Do you want to skip the tango?"

He shrugged. "No, I haven't a thing in the world against tango." They might have been discussing a person. He flashed a dry smile, and she was startled by his electric appeal. He wasn't just built. He had strong, attractive facial features, and that dimple. His eyes appealed, too, the color very deep, his stare direct. Despite herself, she felt a little flush of heat surge through her. Simple chemistry. He was something. She was professional and mature and quite able to keep any reaction under control—but she wasn't dead.

He leaned forward suddenly. "I think I'd love to tango," he said, as if he'd given it serious thought.

And probably every woman out there would love to tango with you, too, buddy, she thought.

She had to smile suddenly. "Are you sure you really want to take dance lessons?" she asked him.

"Yes. No." He shrugged. "Doug really wanted me to get into it."

Shannon suddenly felt hesitant about him. She didn't know why—he was so physically impressive that any teacher should be glad to have him, as a challenge, at the least.

A challenge. That was it exactly. Just as he appealed to her, he created a sense of wariness in her, as well. She didn't understand it.

She sat back, smiling, tapping her pencil idly against the table as she looked at him. She spoke casually. "Your brother is a police officer. Are you in the same line of work, Mr. O'Casey?"

"Quinn. Please, call me Quinn. And no, I'm not a cop. Although I was a cop once."

He didn't offer any further details.

"So, what *do* you do?"

"I'm with a charter service down in the Keys."

"Fishing? Diving?"

He smiled slowly. "Yes, both. Why? Are only certain men involved in certain lines of work supposed to take dance lessons?"

She shook her head, annoyed to know that her cheeks were reddening. She stared down at the paper. "No, of course not, and I'm sorry. We just try to tailor a program toward what an individual really wants."

"Well, I guess I just want to be able to dance socially. And I'm not kidding when I say that I can't dance."

Those words were earnest. The dimple in his cheek flashed.

She smiled. "Doug came in with the movement ability of a deeply rooted tree...Quinn." His name rolled strangely on her tongue. "He's made incredible progress."

"Well, he just kind of fell in love with it, huh?"

Her smile deepened, and she nodded. "You don't think you're going to fall in love with it, do you?"

He shrugged, lifting his hands. Large hands, long fingered. Clean and neat, though. Of course. Fishing and diving. He was in the water constantly. Face deeply bronzed, making the blue of his eyes a sharp contrast. "What about you?"

"Pardon?" she said, startled that they had suddenly changed course.

"When did you fall in love with it?"

"When I could walk," she admitted.

"Ah, so you're one of those big competitors," he said.

She shook her head. "No. I'm an instructor."

He arched a brow, and she felt another moment's slight unease as she realized he was assessing her appearance.

"I bet you would make a great competitor."

She shrugged. "I really like what I do."

"I guess competition can be dangerous."

His words sounded casual enough. She felt herself stiffen. "Dangerous? Dancing?"

He shrugged again. "Doug told me someone had a heart attack and died at the last big competition."

She shook her head. "What happened was tragic. But it was an isolated incident. I've certainly never seen anything like it before. We're all shattered, of course…but, no, competition isn't usually dangerous." She was tempted to say more but pulled back, telling herself not to be an absolute idiot. She certainly wasn't going to spill out her own discomfort before a man she'd just met, even if he was Doug's brother. Doug was a student, a promising one, but even he was far from a confident one. "I would assume, Mr. O'Casey, that boating and diving are far more dangerous than dancing."

"I wasn't worried," he said. "Just…well, sorry about the loss, of course. And curious."

Obviously, people would be upset. And yes, curious. In the world of dance, Lara had reigned as a queen. Though most people might not have known her name—any more than Shannon might have known that of the leading Nascar racer—such a death still made the newspapers and even a number of news broadcasts. Several stations had been there filming when she had died.

Sure, people were going to be curious.

Gordon had given a speech to her; she had given one to the teachers, and she'd also written up a little notice for the students. She didn't know why she felt annoyed at explaining the situation to this particular man.

"We were all curious," she said evenly. "Lara Trudeau was amazing. She wasn't into alcohol or drugs, prescription or otherwise. None of us knows what happened that day. She was brilliant, and she, and her talent, will be missed. But dancing is hardly dangerous. Obviously, it's a physical activity. But we've had a number of heart patients here for therapy. It's dangerous to sit still and become a couch potato, too." She was suddenly angry, feeling as if she was personally under attack, and didn't understand why. She was about to get up and assure him that she would return Doug's money for the guest pass, but then he spoke.

"Rhythm," he said.

"Pardon?"

"I think I said the wrong thing. I'd like to be able to go to a club like Suede, the one right below you, and not look like a total horse's a—idiot. Salsa, right?"

"They do a lot of salsa. Mambo, samba, merengue... Tuesday nights they have a swing party."

"But they waltz at weddings, right?" He gave the appearance of seriously considering his options.

"Yes."

"Do I have to pick certain dances?"

"No, but it would be nice to know where you'd like to start."

"Where do you generally start?"

She rose. "At the beginning. Come on. If you've no real preferences, we'll do it my way."

"You're going to be my instructor?" He was surprised, but she didn't think he was pleased.

"Yes. Is there a problem?"

"No, I just…Doug said you didn't take new students."

"I don't usually. But the way it works is, unless there's a problem, the teacher to sign on a new student becomes their regular instructor." She hadn't meant to actually take him as her student, but now…she meant to keep him. There was just something about him that…

A voice in her ear whispered that he was the most arresting man she'd met in a long time. Best-looking, definitely most sensual, man.

Yes, yes, all acknowledged from the start.

But that wasn't the point. It wasn't his appearance, which was, admittedly, imposing.

There was something else.

It was ridiculous that she was feeling so paranoid.

But the man bore watching. That feeling of wariness would not go away.

Maybe.

That was her thought thirty minutes later.

Maybe she hadn't been teaching enough lately. Maybe she couldn't teach and keep an eye on him at the same time. Her patience just wasn't where it should be. There was no chance of anyone stepping in and actually leading him— placing a hand on his arm had assured her of that. It was like setting her fingers on a solid wall. It didn't help that he was stiff, no matter how much she tried to get him to relax.

He actually seemed to be confused between left and right.

They were doing a box step, for God's sake. A simple box step.

"No, Quinn, your left foot goes forward first. The same foot we've used the last twenty-five times." Was her voice showing strain? Once upon a time, she'd been known for her patience.

He hadn't lied when he said he had two left feet.

"We're just making a square—a box. Left foot forward, right side…a box."

"Yeah, right. A box. So how many teachers are there here, actually?"

"Are you afraid that I can't teach you, Mr. O'Casey?"

"No, no, I just wondered. You're doing fine. I was just curious as to how many teachers you have."

"Ben Trudeau is teaching full time now."

"Trudeau?" he said.

"He used to be married to Lara. They've been divorced for several years. He was mainly doing competitions and coaching, but he decided a few months ago that he wanted to take up residence on the beach. He's an excellent teacher."

"He must be devastated."

"We're all devastated, Mr. O'Casey."

"Sorry. I can imagine. She must have been something. So accomplished, and such a friend to everyone here, huh? Doug told me she taught here sometimes."

"She coached," Shannon told him.

"Must be hard for all of you to have the studio open and be teaching already."

"Work goes on."

"So all the teachers have come back?"

"Yes."

"Who are the rest of them?"

"Justin Garcia and Sam Railey, and Jane Ulrich, who teaches your brother, and another woman, Rhianna Markham."

His foot landed hard on hers once again.

"Sorry—I told you I had two left feet," he apologized.

Shannon drew a deep breath. "We do want to get you to where you can converse while you're on the floor, but maybe if you didn't ask so many questions while we were working, it might be better."

"Sorry. Just want to get to know the place, feel a little more comfortable here."

"That's what the practice sessions and parties are for," she murmured.

"Parties?"

"And practice sessions," she said firmly. "Beginners come on Monday, Tuesday and Friday nights, sometimes even the other weeknights if we get busy, and learn more steps in groups. Then you hone those steps with your teacher."

"Do students have to come?"

"Of course not. But individual sessions are expensive. The group sessions are open to all enrolled students. You learn a lot faster and make a lot better use of your money by attending the group classes."

"And the parties? When are they? Are they for all the students?"

"Wednesday nights, eight to ten, and yes, beginners are welcome. You should come."

"I will."

His foot crunched down on hers once again. Hard. She choked back a scream. How much longer? Fifteen more minutes. She wasn't sure she could take it.

She looked around. Jane still hadn't returned from her appointment. Rhianna was working with David Mercutio, husband of Katarina Mercutio, the designer who shared the second floor of the building with them. She was wonderful—specializing in weddings, with one-of-a-kind dresses for both brides and wedding parties. She had also learned the special requirements for ballroom-competition gowns, and had made some truly spectacular dresses. Just as it was great for the studio to be right on top of the club, it was a boon to have Katarina right next to them.

David was a regular who came twice a week to work with Rhianna. He had also known and worked with Lara. He and Rhianna were deep in conversation as they twirled around, working on a tango. She knew they were probably discussing Lara. Sam Railey, however, didn't have a student at the moment. He was putting his CDs in order.

Quinn O'Casey's really large left foot landed on her toe once again.

"Sam!" she called suddenly, breaking away from her partner.

"Yeah?" he looked up.

"Can I borrow you for a minute?"

"Sure."

Shannon headed toward the stereo, waiting for the tango to play out, removed the CD and replaced it with an old classic—Peggy Lee singing "Fever." Sam walked over to partner her as she spoke to her new student. "Right now, you're just trying to get the basic box. But if you think of the steps to the music, it might help you."

Sam led her in the basic steps while she looked at Quinn. She was not at all convinced he was trying very hard.

To her surprise, Sam spoke up. "It looks like a boring dance," he said to Quinn. "But it can be a lot of fun."

The next thing Shannon knew, Sam had taken the initiative. They moved into a grapevine, an underarm spin and a series of pivots. Steps far advanced from anything their new student could begin to accomplish.

"Okay, Sam," she said softly. "We don't want to scare him off."

"Well…he should see what he can learn," Sam replied.

She couldn't argue. They did lots of demonstrations to

show their students what they could learn. She just wondered about this particular student.

But Quinn was nodding and looking as if he had suddenly figured something out. He stepped in to take his position with her again. The guy had a great dance hold; he also wore some kind of really great aftershave. He should be a pleasure to teach.

Except that he was always watching.

But weren't students supposed to watch?

Not the way he did, with those piercing blue eyes.

She looked back up into them, reminding herself that she was a teacher, and a good one.

"Listen, feel it, and move your feet. Remember that you're just making a square."

To her amazement, he had it. He finally had it. A box. A simple box. It felt like a miracle.

"Head up," she said softly, almost afraid to push her luck. "Don't look at your feet. It will only mess you up."

His eyes met hers, and he maintained the step and the rhythm. His dimple showed as he smiled, pleased. His hold was just right. There was distance between them, but she was still aware of hot little jolts sweeping through her, despite the lack of real body contact. Not good.

Dance teachers needed to be friendly. Accustomed to contact. The more advanced a student, the closer that contact. She was accustomed to that.

But it had never been like this.

She suddenly wanted the lesson to be over for reasons other than her sore feet.

When they were done, he seemed actually enthused.

"When do I come again?" he asked.

"Whenever you schedule."

"Tomorrow?" he asked.

"You'll have to see Ella, our receptionist."

They were standing near the little elevated office. Ella had already heard. "He can have a two-o'clock."

"I thought I had an appointment with the hotel about blocking out rooms for the Gator Gala?" Shannon said frowning. "And I know I have Dr. Long coming in for his regular class."

"The hotel pushed the meeting to Wednesday," Ella said cheerfully. "And they want you to call them back. Dr. Long isn't in until five-fifteen."

"Two o'clock, then," Shannon said.

"Thanks. I'll see you then."

Their new student departed, and Shannon stared after him.

Jane, returning from the dentist, passed him at the door. "Who the hell was that?" she demanded when she reached Shannon.

"Doug's brother."

"Doug's brother...wow. Look what a few more years are going to do for that guy. Of course, the eyes...shit! Who taught him?"

"I did," Shannon said.

"Oh. And you're keeping him?" She tried to sound light. Shannon hesitated. "Yes."

Sam went dancing by, practicing a Viennese waltz on his own. "Hey," he teased Jane. "You've already got the one brother."

Jane gave him a serious glare. "Yeah, and I also have nasty old Mr. Clinton, ninety-eight, and decaying with each move we make." She looked at Shannon. "I thought you weren't going to take on any new students."

"I wasn't. But you know how it goes."

"You're the manager," Jane reminded her. "You don't have to keep him."

"I know, but that forty-five-minute investment of time felt

like ten hours. The guy is a challenge I don't think I can refuse. Hey," she added quickly, teasingly, "careful—your old-timer just walked in."

Jane glanced at her white-haired, smiling student.

Ben had already walked forward to shake his hand. That was studio policy—all employees greeted all students when not otherwise occupied. Courtesy and charm to all students, regardless of sex, age, color, creed or ability.

They were a regular United Nations.

And more. Being in South Florida, gateway to Latin America, they were also a very huggy bunch. People hugged hello and hugged goodbye. Cheek kissing went on continually. It was nice; it was warm, and it was normal behavior for most people who had grown up here.

Mr. Clinton was actually a dear. They all kissed and hugged him hello all the time. He wasn't really decaying, and he wasn't nasty. He was just a little hard-of-hearing, so it sounded as if he was yelling sometimes.

Jane sighed. "Yep, here's my old-timer."

"Jane, he brings you gourmet coffee," Shannon reminded her.

"He's a sweetie, all right."

Jane stared at her. She didn't say anything more. They both knew what she was thinking.

Sure, the old guy was a sweetie. He just wasn't Quinn O'Casey.

Jane forced a smile.

"You are the boss," she murmured lightly, and moved away. "Mr. Clinton, how good to see you. What did you say you wanted to do today. A samba? You're sure you're up to it?"

"You bet, Janie," he assured her with a broad grin. "I got the best pacemaker ever made helping this old ticker. Let's get some action going."

Watching them, Shannon smiled. No, Mr. Clinton wasn't a Quinn O'Casey, but then again…

Just what did Quinn expect to get from the studio?

Suddenly, for no reason that she could explain, she felt a shiver trickle down her spine.

CHAPTER 4

In the afternoon, the beach wasn't so bad, Quinn thought. It was slower. Weekends, it was crazy. If he suddenly heard there had been a run of cab drivers committing suicide on a Friday or Saturday night at the beach, it wouldn't be shocking in the least. Traffic sometimes snarled so badly that a lifetime could pass before a vehicle made it down a block.

But in the afternoon...

Though they were moving into fall, temperatures were still high, but there was a nice breeze coming off the ocean, making the air almost cool. Walking from the studio, which sat between Alton Road and Washington, he passed some of the old Deco buildings and houses that had undergone little or no restoration, appreciating their charm. There were also a number of small businesses, including a coffeehouse that wasn't part of a big chain, a pretty little flower shop, some duplexes, small apartment houses and a few single dwellings. The beach itself was barely three blocks away, and he was tempted to take a quick stroll on the boardwalk and get a real feel for the area.

The stretch of sand facing the bay was dotted with sun

worshipers. A volleyball game was going on, and down a
bit, a mother was helping two toddlers build a sand castle.
The little girl wore a white eyelet cap, protecting her delicate skin, while just a few feet away, a young couple, both
bronzed and beautiful, applied great gobs of something from
a tube labeled Mega-Tan to each other's skin. During the
week, the beach could be great. He had to admit, the Keys
didn't offer huge expanses of beach. Just more privacy.

On the stretch in front of a chic Deco hotel, the bronzed
and beautiful were joined by the more mundane. A huge
woman wearing a skimpy suit that was totally unsuitable for
her ample physique was strolling along with a scrawny man
in a Speedo. They were smiling happily, and nodded as they
passed him. Quinn offered them a hello and decided that the
mind's perception of the self was really what created happiness. The couple looked completely content. More power
to them. Who the hell was he to judge? He was walking the
beach in dress shoes, chinos and a tailored shirt.

A bit farther down, a group of kids seemed to be dis-
persing. Gathering towels, chairs and lotion bottles, they
were calling out to one another, saying their goodbyes. He
kept walking, watching as one by one they all disappeared—
except for one little waif who was tall when she stood but
slim to the point of boniness. Beyond model slim. She had
long brown hair and huge eyes, and as she watched her
friends disappear, she suddenly wore a look of loneliness and
pain. She looked so lost he was tempted to talk to her, but
hell, this was South Beach—she could be anyone, including an undercover cop.

Not old enough.

She heard his footsteps in the sand and swung around,
looking straight at him. She sized him up and down, and
swallowed.

"Hey, mister, you got a dollar?"

"You a runaway?"

She flushed but said, "Not exactly. I'm eighteen. Honest."

"But you ran away?"

"I left. I've graduated high school. I just haven't been able to find a job. A real job."

"So you're living on the streets."

She actually grinned. "The beach isn't as bad as the streets. Really. If you're going to be homeless, this is the place to be."

"But you've got a home?"

"What are you, a cop?"

"No, just a concerned citizen who doesn't want to see your face in the news. 'Does anyone know this girl? Her body was discovered Saturday night.'"

The girl shook her head vehemently. "I'm careful. You got a dollar or not? I don't need a third degree."

"Hey, wait." He pulled out his wallet and found a five.

She blinked and walked toward him. "What do you want?" she asked uneasily. "I'm not a cheap hooker."

He shook his head. "I just want you to tell me that you're going to buy food, and that you're not a junkie, either."

"Hey, you see any punctures in these arms?" She was wearing a tank top over cutoff jeans, and she spoke with pride as well as conviction.

"Get yourself something to eat, then. And hey, listen. If you do need help, you can get it, you know. Find a cop. The guys on the beach are pretty damned decent, and if not, head for the South Miami station. There's a woman there who is a victims' advocate, and she's an absolute gem. Wait, I'll give you her card."

She looked as if she was going to run with the five at first, but then she waited and even took the card.

"I thought you said you weren't a cop."

"I'm not."

"Kind of overdressed for the beach, aren't you?"

He started to shrug. Her eyes widened. "I'll bet you were at that dance studio."

He didn't answer, and she laughed. "Hey, I'd be there, too, if I had the bucks. God, I love to dance." She flushed again, then wiggled the five in her hand. "Thanks."

"Be careful, huh?"

"Hey, don't I know? Don't worry, I'm tougher than I look. And I know that you can get into a lot more out here than just sea and sand."

She turned and sprinted off, then paused a good thirty feet away and called back to him, "Hey, you're all right, you know? My name is Marnie, by the way." Then, as if she had given away far too much, she turned again, this time running toward the street at full speed.

He watched her go. He hoped she was as tough as she thought.

Miami Beach was a gateway to every vice in the western hemisphere.

He noted the position of the sun in the sky and glanced at his watch. Time to get moving.

He headed back for his car, which was parked over on Alton. He wasn't sure why, but he hadn't wanted to park closer to the studio. He returned to his car, took a look at his watch again and figured he had time. It was a short hop from South Beach to pay a visit to the medical examiner's officer.

The newly revamped and renamed hotel where they were hoping to hold the Gator Gala had called while Shannon was giving Quinn O'Casey his first lesson. When she returned the call, she was happy to learn that she had played hard-ball with them to just the right degree—they were calling to agree to a per-night room charge that was completely reasonable and would surely help draw northern entrants to the competition, which was planned for the second week in February. Despite the heavy pall that had seemed to hang over her since Lara's death, Shannon was delighted. They would wrap up the deal at their meeting later in the week. She hurried into the main office to tell Gordon.

"Great," he told her, really pleased. "That should make a difference for us. I mean, who wouldn't want to come to Miami Beach in the middle of winter? Especially at such a great price. What about the meals?"

"We're still negotiating," she said.

"What are we negotiating?" Ben Trudeau asked, poking his head in.

"Meals," Shannon told him.

"Ah." Ben was one of those men who was so good-looking he was almost too pretty. Of course, once upon a time, it hadn't seemed that way to Shannon. Once he had been like a god to her—tall, lithe, elegant, able to move with the speed and electric power of lightning or as smoothly as the wind.

He was an incredible dancer and always a striking competitor. His hair was ebony, his eyes dark as ink, and his features classically flawless. He had amazing technical ability and was a showman to boot. For several years he had competed with Lara, but then it had all fallen apart. They'd been divorced for almost five years before her death. In that time, she'd taken a number of championships, working steadily with Jim Burke. Ben, in the meantime, had grabbed any number of best in shows and number ones and cash prizes, but he hadn't gone as far as Lara. He'd changed partners too many times. Now his eyes moved over Shannon as he stood in the doorway.

"It's a waste," he said.

"What?"

"All the time you're spending on business."

"Hey!" Gordon said.

"Well, she should be competing."

Gordon looked at Shannon, a slight smile curving his lips. "She can go back into competition any time she wants."

"Gentlemen, I'm well aware of that. And I don't want to compete."

"You know, that's just silly," Ben said, smoothing back a thatch of hair from his forehead. "You get out there in the Pro-Ams with your students all the time. What's the difference?"

"They're my students."

"Lucky students," Gordon noted, still amused. "You make them look great."

"And I'm really proud of them when they do well. Why can't you two understand that? Everyone isn't ruled by blinding ambition."

She sighed. "Look, since I broke my ankle all those years ago, it's never been the same. I never know when it's going to give, and after too much practice, it hurts like hell. It's not good enough to work as hard as I'd have to if I wanted to compete professionally. The good thing is, I really love to teach. I get my thrills by working with the students."

"Beginners," Ben said, a note of contempt in his voice.

"Everyone is a beginner at some point."

Ben laughed. "Right. So you gonna talk that new student of yours—that tank—into entering the newcomers division at the Gator Gala? That the kind of challenge you're up to?"

"Maybe I *will* talk him into it," she said.

"It's all just an excuse for cowardice," Ben said.

She didn't have a chance to respond. A buzzer sounded on Gordon's desk, and he hit the intercom button.

"Dr. Long is here for his lesson with Shannon," Ella's voice informed them.

"I'm on my way." Before she left, she addressed the two

men one last time. "Both of you—I'm happy with what I do. Jane and Rhianna are both young and beautiful and talented. Let's support them, huh?" She glared at both men. Neither responded.

Shannon started out of the office. Ben slipped up behind her, catching her shoulder the minute they were out of the doorway.

"We were good, you know," he reminded her.

"Once."

"You really are afraid, you know. Maybe you're afraid of me."

"Ben, I promise you—I'm not afraid of you."

"We could be really good together again," he whispered huskily.

"Not in this lifetime, Ben," she said sweetly, then edged her shoulder free. "Excuse me. My student is waiting."

"Time has gone by, you know. A lot of it."

"My student is waiting."

"You don't have to hurt us both by being bitter. You could forgive me."

"I forgave you a long time ago, Ben."

"Then don't play so hard to get."

"Are you trying to come on to me again—or do you just want to dance with me?"

"Both?" He laughed with a certain charm, but it just didn't strum the same heartstrings for her it once had.

"I'm sorry. I know this must be amazing to you, but I'm not hateful, bitter or playing hard to get. I'm just not interested."

"You'll be sorry," he said, his voice teasing.

She stopped, staring at him. "Ben, you have a new partner. What's her name, from Broward. Vera Thompson."

He shook his head. "She's okay. She's not the caliber I need."

"Have you told *her* that?" Shannon inquired.

"Of course not. Not yet."

"Why not?"

"You haven't agreed to dance again."

She shook her head. "Ben, if I ever *were* to dance professionally again, it wouldn't be with you."

"Why not?"

She could have told him that the reasons should have been obvious. But then, maybe nothing was as obvious to Ben as it should be.

So she shrugged. And then she couldn't help the reply that came to her lips. "You're just not the caliber I need," she said, and hurried out to meet Richard for his class.

Quinn had already read the police report that had been provided by Doug. He'd read the M.E.'s report, as well, which had provided a stroke of luck. There were eight M.E.s under the direction of the chief, but Anthony Duarte had performed the autopsy on Lara Trudeau.

Just as he had performed the autopsy on Nell Durken.

And though Dixon might not be a ball of fire in the homicide department, Duarte was tops in his field, a man with a natural curiosity that gave him the propensity to go far beyond thorough, even in the most straightforward circumstances.

At the desk, Quinn produced his credentials, though he knew the receptionist and she waved away his wallet as she put through the call to Duarte.

Despite it being close to five, Duarte came down the hall, smiling as he greeted Quinn. "Hey, thought you were heading off on vacation."

"I was."

"What are you doing down here?"

"Right now? Feeling damned lucky to see you."

"Most people don't feel that way—when I'm at work, anyway," Duarte said with a touch of humor.

"Let me rephrase. Since I have to see a medical examiner, I'm glad it's you. You performed the autopsy on Lara Trudeau."

Duarte, a tall, slim black man with the straightest back Quinn had ever seen, arched a graying brow. "You're working an angle on Lara Trudeau?"

"That's surprising, I take it?"

Duarte lifted his shoulders in a shrug. "Nothing surprises me. I've been here far too long. I ruled the death accidental because I sure as hell couldn't find any reason not to. Due to the circumstances, though, Dixon is still doing some work—though nothing more than paperwork, I imagine."

"What do you mean, the circumstances?"

"A healthy woman popped too many nerve pills, swallowed some hard liquor and dropped dead. It isn't a daily occurrence. Not even in Miami." The last was spoken dryly and a little wearily. "Although, in all honesty, the number of people who do die from the misuse of prescriptions and even over-the-counter drugs is a hell of a lot higher than it should be."

"Really?"

"People mix too much stuff. And then they think, like with sleeping pills, hey, if one helps, I could really get a good night's sleep with a bunch of them. As for Lara Trudeau, who the hell knows what she was thinking? Maybe she just thought she was immortal."

"I'm surprised the stuff didn't affect her dancing."

"That too—she must have had a will of steel."

"She dropped dead in front of an audience."

"Not to mention the television cameras. And no one saw anything suspicious."

"There was no sign of…?" Quinn said. Though what the hell there might be a sign of, he didn't know.

"Force? Had someone squeezed open her cheeks to force pills down her throat? Not that I could find. The cops, naturally, checked for prints on her prescription bottle. Not a one to be found."

"Not a single print?" Quinn said with surprise. "Not even hers?"

"She was wearing gloves for her performance."

"And that would normally wipe the entire vial clean?"

"If she was rubbing her fingers around it over and over again, which a nervous person might do."

"Still…"

Duarte shrugged. "I guess it's one of the reasons the cops kept looking. She was famous and apparently not all that nice, so…there might have been any number of people who wanted her dead. Trouble is, they just haven't got anything. There were hundreds of people there. She went out to dance with a smile on her face. No apparent argument with anyone there…well, I'm assuming you've read the report." He stared at Quinn. "She's still here. Want to see her yourself?"

"I thought you'd released her body."

"I did. The funeral home won't be here until sometime tonight. Come on. I'll have her brought out."

They walked down halls that, no matter how clean, still somehow reeked of death. Duarte called an assistant and led Quinn to a small room for the viewing. Loved ones weren't necessarily brought in to see their dearly departed. A camera allowed for them to remain in the more natural atmosphere of the lobby to view the deceased.

She was brought in. Duarte lowered the sheet.

Lara Trudeau had been a beautiful woman. Even in death, her bone structure conveyed a strange elegance. She truly gave the appearance of sleep—until the eye wandered down to the autopsy scars.

Quinn stared at her, circling the gurney on which she lay.

Other than the sewn Y incision that marred her chest, there was no sign of any violence. She hadn't even bruised herself when she'd gone down.

"I couldn't find anything but the prescription pills and alcohol. She'd barely eaten, which surely added to the pressure on her heart. That's what killed her—the heart's reaction to drugs and alcohol."

"Like Nell."

Frowning, Duarte stared at him. "Not exactly. No alcohol in Nell. Why, what do you think you're seeing?"

"I don't know."

"Is that why you're on this?"

"Maybe. I found out that Nell Durken had been an amateur dancer and took lessons at the same studio where Lara Trudeau sometimes practiced and coached."

"But the police arrested Nell's husband. And his fingerprints *were* all over the pill bottle. You were the one who followed the guy, right, and gave the police your records on the investigation?"

"Yep."

"Art Durken has been in jail, pending trial, for over a week. He sure as hell wasn't at that competition."

"Yeah, I know."

"So?"

"I don't know. There's just…something. That's all."

"Durken still denying that he murdered his wife?"

"Yes." Quinn met Anthony Duarte's eyes. "Admits he was a womanizing bastard, but swears he didn't kill her."

"You think a dancer is the killer?" Duarte shook his head. "Quinn, the circumstances were odd enough for the police to investigate, but you've got to think about the facts again. Lara Trudeau didn't argue with anyone at that competition, and she walked out on the floor to dance without the least sign of distress. When she fell, she did so in front of a huge audience. The pills she took were prescription, the vial had no prints, and the prescription was written by a physician she'd been seeing for over ten years—and to the best of my knowledge, he wasn't a ballroom dancer."

"Yeah, I know. I read the report. I'm going to pay a visit to Dr. Williams, though I know he was already interviewed and cleared of any wrongdoing."

Duarte grimaced. "If the cops blamed a physician every time a patient abused a prescription, the jails would be spilling over worse than they are now. This is a tough one, Quinn. Strange, and tough. I just don't see where you can go. There's simply no forensic evidence to lead you in any direction. If it is a crime, it's just about the perfect one."

"No crime is perfect."

"We both know a lot of them go unpunished."

"Yeah. And this time, I agree, there's nothing solid to go on. Unless I can find someone who knows something—and that person has to be out there."

"Wish I could be more helpful," Duarte said.

Quinn nodded. "Nell Durken hadn't taken a lesson in the sixth months before she died. With Nell…there was nothing else, either, right? No…grass, speed…anything like that?"

"No, sorry. There were no illegal substances in either woman. Just massive overdoses of prescription medications and, in the Trudeau case, alcohol."

"Well, thanks," Quinn said. "Sorry to take up your time."

Duarte offered him a rueful smile. "You never take up my time. I really believe in the things you read and see on television. The dead can't speak anymore. We have to do their talking for them, but sometimes we're not as good at interpreting as we want to be. If I've missed something, or if I haven't thought to look for something, hell, I want to know."

"Yeah. Thanks."

"You going back to the Keys tonight?" Duarte asked.

"No. I have my boat up at the marina by Nick's, doing some work. I'm still there."

"Maybe I'll see you later. I'm starving—it was a long day. I got busy and forgot to eat. I'm dying for a hamburger."

Quinn nodded, but at the moment, he didn't feel the slightest twinge of hunger. He'd stood through a number of autopsies and he'd never gotten sick or fainted—as some of the biggest, toughest guys he knew had done—but he'd never gotten over a certain abdominal clenching in the presence of a corpse. Time and experience didn't change some things.

Duarte was one of the best of the best. But he could chow down with body parts on the same table. Survival, Quinn thought, in a place where the houses of the dead were as big as they were in Miami-Dade County.

"You'll be around later?" Duarte said.

"Sure," Quinn agreed. It would be a lot later, he knew.

Lara was covered and rolled away by the assistant as the two men started out the door and back down the hall.

A trip to the main station on Kendall was pretty much as worthless as Quinn had suspected. Detective Pete Dixon worked nine to five.

No overtime for Dixon these days.

He said a quick hello to a few old friends and started out. In the parking lot, he ran into Jake Dilessio, with whom he'd worked prior to leaving for Quantico. He wished that Dilessio had been assigned to the Trudeau investigation. He was certain he wouldn't be taking dance lessons if the chips had fallen that way.

"Hey, stranger, haven't seen much of you," Dilessio greeted him. "Seems we're living only a few feet away from one another, too. You're moored at the marina by Nick's, right? Thought you were taking off for the Bahamas."

"I was." Quinn shrugged. "I'm investigating the Trudeau case."

"Trudeau?" Dilessio arched a brow. "Sounds familiar."

"The dancer who died."

"I thought that was ruled accidental. Last I heard, Dixon was just tying up the reports to close the case."

"It *was* ruled accidental."

"But someone thinks it wasn't?"

"Something like that."

"So who are you working for?"

"The word 'work' would imply pay."

"Oh, yeah, that's right. They're calling your brother twinkle-toes on the beat. Not without some envy, I might add. I hear the kid is really good."

"I wouldn't know. I haven't seen him dance yet."

"No?"

"I didn't even know he was dancing until this all came up."

Jake shrugged and nodded. "I saw him not too long ago. He said you'd been really wrapped up in work. Congratulations, by the way. I hear your surveillance reports on Art Durken gave the cops what they needed to arrest him and enough for the D.A.'s office to charge him."

"Not really. If I'd been good enough, she wouldn't be dead."

"How long have you been in this business? You can't blame yourself for all the bad shit that goes down."

"Yeah, I know. But I can't stop it from bugging me, either."

Jake shrugged and said, "That's true. But at least it's better than the shit that goes unpunished."

"I guess you're right. Anyway, the dancer who died was connected with Doug's studio. I'm doing a little follow-up of my own."

"Well, Dixon is known to show up at Nick's in the evening. No wife, no kids, no kitchen. He eats a hamburger there almost every night. I'm heading home now. In fact, if you're free, I'll buy you dinner."

"If you're buying me dinner, I'm not exactly free, but at least, at Nick's, I'll be cheap. Sounds good to me. Where's your wife? Is she joining us? I saw her when I tied up the other day. That baby's due awful soon, isn't it?"

"Too soon. Three weeks. And she went up to Jacksonville anyway, with a special dispensation from the airline. They wanted her to do some sketches of a homicide suspect."

"I thought that she left forensics and graduated from the academy."

"She did graduate from the academy, but she stayed in forensics. She's one of the best sketch artists in the state, in the country, maybe. They asked her to go, and she thought she could help, so she went."

"You know, you marry a cop, and that's what happens," Quinn said lightly.

"Yeah, I know."

They arrived at Nick's right before six.

It was a great time of the day at the marina. Darkness was falling, coming fast, but the sky over the ocean was in the midst of its last majestic frenzy of color. Magenta, oranges, trails of gold, all sweeping together across the heavens over the shadowed ocean. The breeze at night was cool, pleasant after the heat of the day.

As Jake had suspected, Pete Dixon was there, already on his second cheeseburger, it appeared, since one empty basket was pushed behind the one in front of him.

Quinn pulled out a chair at Dixon's table without being asked, turning it backward and straddling the seat. "Jeez, Pete, you might want to opt for something green now and then, watch out for the fat and cholesterol once a week, maybe," he said.

Dixon wiped his mouth, looking at Quinn as if he'd just been joined by a barracuda. His eyes, small in the folds of his face, fell on Jake Dilessio next, riddled with pure accusation. "Sit down, Quinn, Jake. Come on, join me. And while you're at it, give me grief about my eating habits."

"Thanks," Jake said, sitting.

"You're close to retirement. You might want to live to enjoy a little of it," Quinn said.

"Like you're a vegetarian or something," Pete muttered.

Quinn grinned. "No, I think I'll have a cheeseburger, too. But just one."

"You brought him here," Pete said to Jake. "Make sure his food goes on your bill."

"I'll even pick up *your* bill," Jake said. "Quinn has a few questions for you."

Pete groaned aloud. He was a big man. His belly jiggled as the sound escaped him. "Hope Nick has some Rolaids back there. Shit. I'm off duty. You had to bring a P.I. here to bug me?"

"Hey, I've got my boat up here," Quinn protested. "This is the most convenient place for me to eat."

"What do you want?" Pete asked him flatly. Before Quinn could answer, he looked at Jake again. "You really picking up my tab? If so, you can order me another beer."

"Sure thing," Jake said, grimacing at Quinn. He looked around and saw one of the waitresses at the next table. "Debbie, when you get a minute…"

The girl turned to him, scratching on her pad. "Pete—another cheeseburger?"

"Funny," Pete said.

"No, but two for Quinn and me, and three Millers," Jake said.

"Coming up." Debbie was young and cheerful, bronzed and wearing tiny white shorts. Pete watched as she walked away.

"Pete, pay attention over here. What's the story on Lara Trudeau?" Quinn asked.

Dixon frowned. "Trudeau? You're here to ask me about that?"

"Yeah. Why?"

"I closed it up today."

"You closed the case already?" Quinn said.

"What case? There is no case. You want to see what happened yourself, the tape is in my office. Come by anytime. She went out on the dance floor smiling like a little lark. Moments later, she drops. A doctor is right there and tries to revive her. The ambulance arrives, and the med techs try to revive her. She gets to the hospital, and she's pronounced dead on arrival. She's turned over to the M.E., who discovers that she did herself in with booze and pills. Or her heart gave in 'cuz of the booze and pills. She ordered a drink at the bar herself—a dozen witnesses will tell you so. And the pills were a prescription from a physician with a flawless reputation. No prints on the vial. Our lady was wearing gloves. Of course, we checked anyway. We questioned waiters and waitresses, judges, dancers and the audience. Dozens of people talked to her. No one saw her argue with anyone. Hell yes, I closed the case. There was no damned case."

Debbie arrived with the three beers as he finished. They thanked her, and she nodded, moving on quickly. It was casual at Nick's, but the place was getting busy, and Debbie seemed to be working the patio area alone.

When she was gone, Quinn asked, "You don't think her death was odd?"

"Odd? You should see my caseload. It's odd that a man shoots his own kid, his wife, and then himself. It's odd that out of the clear blue, a shot rings out in North Miami and a kid in all honors classes falls down dead. Hell, there's odd out there. You bet. But as far as this Trudeau thing goes, what the hell do you want? There's nothing there. So it's odd. So what? Everyone down here is frigging odd. And guess what? It ain't illegal to be odd."

"If I understand the situation," Quinn said evenly, "there were lots of people out there who hated Lara Trudeau."

Pete Dixon stared at him, lifted his beer bottle and took a long swig. "Maybe lots of people hate *you*, Quinn. It's America. It's allowed."

"I'm not dead," Quinn reminded him.

"Yeah, well, hell, you're not in the position we're in at the force, either. People hire you, pay you by the case, and you've got the luxury of lots of time to investigate 'odd' and nasty things. My plate is full with stuff that definitely has murder written all over it. You feel free to spend your time chasing 'odd.' I can't do it."

"Hey, we're all on the same side here," Jake reminded him. "You know, fighting crime. That's the idea."

"Yeah, that's right, and our big man Quinn here comes straight from the FBI. How was it, then, Quinn? What the hell made you leave, anyway? Or did being with the Feds just make you think you could come back and be better than anyone else?"

Quinn might not have expected a lot of help from Dixon, but he hadn't expected total animosity, either. He watched his fingers curl too tightly around his beer bottle, and he forced himself to control his temper.

"You're right, Pete. You've got lots of cases. Right now, I've just got one. If you do think of anything that can help me, I'd appreciate it if you'd let me know."

Maybe he should have spent a little more time with the Bureau shrink—the control thing seemed to work. To his amazement, Pete flushed. Being such a big man, he went very red.

"Yeah, sure." He swallowed more of his beer. "Hell, the whole damned thing was odd, you're right. The oddest thing is, how the hell did she down all that stuff and get out on the floor and dance so damned well, then…drop? She must have been totally oblivious to what she was doing beforehand. Come by and get the tape. Maybe that will help you. Who the hell knows? I looked at it over and over again, and it didn't give me a thing. I gotta go. My brother's kid is playing the saxophone at some dumb school thing." He stood. "Thanks for the meal, Dilessio."

"Sure thing," Jake said.

"He gets discounts here anyway, you know?" Pete said to Quinn. "Married the proprietor's niece. When's that kid due, Dilessio?"

"Soon."

"Hope you have a boy."

"Oh, why?" Jake said.

"'Cause women are trouble. Right from the get-go.'"

The both stared after him as he walked away toward the parking lot. Then Jake laughed out loud. "Quinn, you've come a long way."

"Oh yeah?"

"For a minute there, I thought you were going to get up and deck him."

Quinn shrugged. "Psychology one-oh-one," he said lightly, except that he had a feeling Jake knew better. "You know, I think he believes there's more there than meets the eye, but he's got the same problem as everyone else."

"And what's that?"

"Figuring out just how 'odd' fits in with illegal. And murder."

"Well, if you need help, I'm around," Jake told him.

"What, you've got a small caseload?"

Jake shook his head, scratching the paper off the beer bottle. "Nope. Murder is murder, though. Whether it's obvious or not. You find something, I'll step on a few toes for you."

"Great. Thanks."

"We're playing poker later, out back in Nick's house, if you want to join us."

"I think I'm going clubbing."

"You're going club hopping?"

"Not hopping. Just clubbing."

"Heading down to Suede?"

"Yep. Want to blow off the poker thing and come with me?"

Jake shook his head. "Someone down there might know me."

"How come?"

"I got called in when a dead hooker was found not far from the place."

"Was that one ever solved?"

"No." Jake looked up at him. "The kid had no track lines, but she managed to overdose."

"So it was, or wasn't, a homicide?"

"I haven't closed the case," Jake said flatly. "Haven't found anything, but I haven't closed the case. I haven't put it into cold cases yet, either. Sometimes, the drug cases are the easiest. The perps are known to the narcotics guys. Not in this instance. They ran the ropes for me on it, checking into every club with a name. No one has come up with anything. She had a name, Sally Grant, and she picked up tricks on the street, no known regular johns. There were no witnesses, no one who could be found who admitted to seeing her in days, just a dead girl with a needle next to her."

"Prints on it?" Quinn asked.

"Her own—but that could have been staged."

"Hell of a lot overdoses going on," Quinn commented.

"The M.E.s will tell you their tables are full of them. Legal substances, illegal substances. But it sure does add up to 'odd,' doesn't it? Two dance students, too much Xanax. One dead hooker, too much heroin. They shouldn't connect. But maybe they do. Hell, maybe dancing is dangerous for your health."

"The prostitute was a dancer?"

"Not that I know of. She was just found not too far from the studio. Not that that necessarily means a damn thing."

"Did they question anyone at the studio, find out if she had ever been in?"

"Yep. None of the teachers had ever seen her."

"Thanks again for the dinner, Jake."

"Keep me informed."

"Will do."

Quinn left Jake at the table and headed for his boat to change. It had been one hell of a long time since he'd been to a club on the beach.

What the hell were people wearing to clubs these days?

CHAPTER 5

"Want to make me look good?"

"Pardon?" Shannon said.

She was definitely off today. First there had been the strange lesson with Quinn O'Casey, which she had wanted to scream through, her patience nonexistent.

Now Richard.

She didn't need to scream when she danced with Richard. He was good. Excellent. A doctor, he had found that dance took his mind off the strain of his day. He wasn't performing brain surgery on a daily basis, but something far more demanding—at least in the eyes of his customers, he had once told her humorously. He was a plastic surgeon. Trusted with looks—the most important thing in the world, to the players in the area. He'd "fixed" or repaired the old, the young, the famous, the rich. He was written up constantly in magazines and had even been touted as the "Botox king of the western world" by one popular publication.

Shannon wasn't sure about his age but assumed he was around forty. He was in great shape, a golf enthusiast when he wasn't in the studio or working. He maintained a great tan, had a full head of almost platinum blond hair and fine gray eyes. He was married, and his wife, a pediatrician, came in now and then, as well, but she wasn't as enamored of dancing as Richard was. She preferred diving and spent most of her free time out on a boat. They seemed to have a perfect relationship. When they could be together, they were. When one had an opportunity that didn't work for the other, they just went their separate ways. Mina Long was petite and, like her husband, fortyish, platinum blond, bronzed and in great shape. The only difference was that she had brown eyes. After all their years of marriage, Shannon thought with some humor, they almost resembled each other.

He was a nice guy, and she enjoyed teaching him. He learned quickly, and in the year since he had been coming to the studio, he had advanced rapidly. But then again, he could afford all the private lessons he wanted. Most people, with more moderate incomes, took one or two private lessons a week and attended group lessons whenever they could.

"Earth to Shannon."

"Oh, sorry. Make you look good? You don't need anyone to make you look good, Richard. In fact, you've gotten so good, I have to admit, I did just drift off in thought. Forgive me. That's not at all a good thing for a teacher to admit."

He smiled. "You're still upset about Lara."

"Of course," she admitted.

"You do know I did everything that I could," he said quietly. "I may be a plastic surgeon, but I was top of my class at med school and spent plenty of time interning in the emergency room."

"Oh, Richard, of course, I know you did everything. It's just still so…sad."

"Yes. We'll all miss her tremendously. I mean, you *will* miss her, right?"

"Of course." Shannon frowned. "Why do you say that?"

"No reason."

They had been waltzing. She stopped near the stereo, frowning as she looked at him.

"Richard, why did you say that?"

"Oh, Lord, now I'm really sorry."

"Richard."

"A little bird told me once—a while ago—that you and Ben Trudeau had been partners and a very hot duo—before Ben married Lara."

"I see."

"You *were* partners, right? I hear you stormed the floor in competitions, that no one even came close to being as good."

"We won a few competitions, but that was ages ago. And I do mean ages."

"Sorry, I shouldn't have said anything."

"Who told you about it?"

"Now, I swear, my lips are sealed."

"It doesn't matter, Richard. It's not like it was a deep, dark secret or anything. I was just curious."

"I told you, my lips are sealed. And hey, you didn't answer my question."

"What question?"

He sighed with a pretense of mock impatience. "Do you want to help me look good?"

"I did answer your question. You do look good."

He shook his head, smiling. "There are some hotshots down from the board. I'm bringing them out to Suede tonight. Would you show up for a few minutes?"

"Richard, I was going to try to head home early. Someone will be down there, though. Rhianna or Jane."

He shook his head. "You're my teacher. We both know that even the top professionals work with their partner over and over again. I look best with you. Show up for one dance and one drink? I'll get you out of there by ten-thirty, I swear it. Please?"

"Richard, don't beg."

"I am begging."

"All right—you tell me what little bird told you about Ben and me, and maybe I'll come."

"That's bribery!"

"You bet," she said, smiling.

"I can't tell you. And I don't fold easy."

"If you want me to show up…"

"Gordon," Richard said.

"Gordon?"

"Yes, I said Gordon, didn't I?"

"Yes…and quickly. You folded like a bad poker hand," she said, laughing.

"Right. So now you have to show up."

"I will, I will," she told him. "Right after I strangle Gordon."

"Why? You just said that it wasn't a deep, dark secret or anything."

"But still…we're not supposed to bring our personal lives into the studio."

Richard let out a snort. "That gets ridiculous, you know."

"It's only professional."

"Not professional—silly," Richard said. "And you're getting that prim look on your face again. I'll let it go, but let's concentrate on something wild and sexy. I want to be known as the salsa king of Miami, not the reigning Botox monarch, okay?"

She laughed.

"We'll give them a show," she promised.

"And, Shannon?"

"What?"

"What happened was terrible. But it wasn't your fault in any way. We're all stunned, and so sorry, but…please. It's okay to grieve. Lara was tremendously talented, a force…. We'll all miss her, maybe forever. But…well, you've got to move on. It hurts to see you so unhappy."

"I'm fine. It's just…the whole thing was so absurd. I can't believe it. I can't believe Lara would drink on top of drugs before a performance."

"You've got to accept it. It happened. You can't keep questioning fate—you have to let it go, however much you don't want to."

"Thanks. Moving into psychiatry, are you?" she teased.

He put up his hands in mock surrender. "Okay, I quit. Come on, let's play some salsa, huh? I really want to wow 'em tonight."

She walked over to the stereo system. "Salsa it is."

What did they wear to clubs these days?

Next to nothing, it seemed.

It was still early—for clubbing—when Quinn returned to the beach. Luckily it was a weeknight, and he was in time to get a meter right on the street and a seat at the sidewalk café across from Suede and Moonlight Sonata. He sat staring at the Deco building that housed the club and dance studio. He'd watched people arrive for dance classes—taking the stairs up to the second floor at the side of the building—along with the few who were already arriving for a night on the town. Several people had entered the lower level dressed in shorts and T-shirts with lettering that advertised "Suede." Apparently they were employees. In between arrivals, the café was one of those perfect spots for people-watching.

A gothic group cruised by, one girl, two guys, all three with nose rings and enough silver in their ears to weight down a cargo ship. Despite the balmy quality of the weather, they wore dark jeans and long black jackets, along with makeup that left them looking like walking cadavers.

They were followed by an elderly couple, moving very slowly. Harvey, as the wife addressed the man, wasn't holding the bagel bag securely enough, according to Edith, the woman.

Three bathing beauties strolled past him next. One had on a short jacket, which pretended to cover up the expanse of ample breasts displayed by the strings of her bikini top. The jacket, however, ended at her midriff. The bottom of her bathing suit was a thong. She was wearing three-inch heels, as well.

Interesting ensemble.

As night came on, so did more of the bold, the beautiful and the downright ugly.

A doorman came out to guard the entrance to the club.

A lithe Latin girl in see-through white entered with a tall dark man, followed by three obvious rockers, speaking so loudly that their English accents were clearly discernible across the street.

Quinn sipped a mineral water, somewhat amused as he turned a page in the notebook before him—compliments of Doug. His brother was meticulously thorough. This file described the teachers at the studio. Interesting group. He'd started with Gordon Henson, who had bought the business in the early seventies. He no longer taught, but in his day, he had apparently instructed some of the top champions in the world. He still showed up at the studio and did some overseeing of the day-to-day business. He had basically turned things over to Shannon Mackay, though. She had some students but also saw to the running of the studio. She was a native Floridian, born in Winter Haven, moved with her folks to the Miami area when she was three, had graduated from the area's specialized high school, then gone to an arts school in New York City. She was five feet seven inches, one hundred and twenty-five pounds, a green-eyed, dark blond dynamo, with a capacity for pure professionalism. Doug, it seemed, had waxed a little poetic on the last.

That didn't surprise Quinn.

Everyone he had seen in the studio was attractive. Well-dressed, well-groomed. The men wore suits, the women dresses or feminine pants ensembles. The girls were pretty, the men, if not exactly handsome, certainly presentable. But Shannon Mackay was a standout. Features delicate but precise, hair soft in a stunning color of sunlight, and eyes deep, direct and thoughtful. More, she seemed to radiate a sensual energy, her every movement unintentionally seductive, her smile somehow open and secretive in one. Beguiling.

She wore one of the Versace scents—he knew it because his mother loved perfumes and he'd learned the names. Shannon had the ability to touch gently but still steer and manipulate a student as she wanted. At his stage, he stood somewhat awkwardly apart from her when they danced. Close enough, though. She was something. Maybe that was why he had done so badly—it was difficult to concentrate when he was so close to her. Hell, yes, difficult to concentrate, but he just wasn't cut out for dancing. Didn't matter. He wouldn't be taking lessons long.

He wondered idly what he would have felt if he'd met her under different circumstances. Severely piqued interest, at the least. She had a chemistry that instantly aroused interest at an instinctive level. He would have liked to ask her out, listen to her voice, get between the light and shadow of her eyes.

She was as suspect as anyone else in a possible murder, he reminded himself.

A damned sexy suspect.

And yet…what if he'd met her elsewhere? He suddenly

found himself pondering his last night with Geneva and wondering what exactly was wrong with him. They'd been together five years, and that night, she had just exploded. He was never with her, she'd said. Not ever really with her. Not even when they made love. He lived work, breathed work and had become his work. She'd been crying. He had wanted to assure her somehow, but every word she'd said had been true. To others, it had been a perfect relationship. He was FBI; she was an assistant D.A. Tough schedules, the same parties. She teased that she always looked great on his arm; she was bright and beautiful. But somehow, it was true. The work—and the way it didn't always work—had begun to obsess him. He had been able to leave the office but never to let go. His workouts at the gym were no longer exercise but him beating up an enemy he couldn't touch, a vague force that was beating him, creating an inner rage.

Over. Over and done with. He was further disturbed by the knowledge that he hadn't felt any lonelier when she was gone. He had merely felt the strange darkness, the frustration, and, finally, the feeling that he wasn't where he should be, that he was no longer effective. Time to change his life, maybe even come home.

Then there had been the Nell Durken case.

The bastard who had killed her was in jail. Largely because of *his* work, his records, and what he'd given the cops. A killer was caught. He would face trial.

But *was* he the killer?

The question nagged at him, and he gritted his teeth.

Back to the files. The business at hand.

Shannon Mackay. She ran the business, taught, didn't compete. Apparently a broken ankle several years ago had caused her to step out of the arena of professional competition. She'd been at the top of her form, and the trophies she'd won were part of what gave the studio its reputation.

So what had she felt about Lara Trudeau? Doug's files didn't say.

He stared across the street, reflecting on his instructor. She'd been tense. His questions had made her nervous. Or maybe she was always tense. No...she was on edge, something more than usual.

Rhianna Markham, Jane Ulrich. Both pretty, unmarried, no solid relationships, no children. Rhianna was from Ohio and had a degree from a liberal arts college. Jane had never gone past high school but had worked three years as a dancer at one of the central Florida theme parks before coming south. Both were ambitious, wanted to advance in the professional world. Lara Trudeau would have been their competition.

Of course, every female competitor in the dance world would have been in the same position. Assuming that Lara Trudeau had somehow been helped to her demise, she had done so before a crowd of hundreds—a large percentage of them competitors. He could be barking up the wrong tree entirely.

But he had to start somewhere. If Lara Trudeau had been murdered, it had been by someone with whom she had a close relationship. To have her die the way she did, before a crowd of hundreds, a murderer would have had to plan very carefully. And it certainly did seem odd that a woman who had been a student at the school had died from an eerily similar overdose just weeks before, even if she hadn't been at the studio in some time.

So...

Love. Hate.

The male instructors. Ben Trudeau. The ex-husband. Always a good suspect. Late thirties, tall, attractive, talented, a bit hardened, and, like Lara, growing old for the field of competition. He'd taken a steady teaching job rather than just coaching. Sam Railey, Jane Ulrich's partner, deeply loyal, determined that they would rise to the top—they had come close together, many times. Justin Garcia, salsa specialist, newest teacher at the studio.

Then there was Lara's partner, Jim Burke. Not a full time teacher at the studio but a coach, as well. Again, a tall, striking man of thirty, lucky to be chosen to be Lara's partner. Now alone. With Lara, he flew like an eagle. Without her…he had no partner. He was back to square one. No matter what his talent, Lara had been the driving force of the pairs, the true prima donna of the dance floor. Jim Burke seemed an unlikely candidate as a murderer.

Gordon Henson?

Quinn shook his head. It wasn't difficult finding motives for most of Lara's acquaintances and associates. Gordon had gotten Lara started; he gave her space, taught her to move. Had she spurned him, rejected him, made fun of him… threatened him?

He looked across the street again. He had only glanced through the files on the teachers and he had half a dozen scenarios already. He hadn't even begun to study the student lists.

It was now beginning to get busier over at Suede. He checked his watch. After ten. He was surprised to realize that the waiter at the little café had politely let him sit here, nursing a water, for so long. He started to rise, then paused, watching.

Shannon Mackay was coming down the steps from the side entry to the studio. She had apparently left in a hurry and rushed halfway down, looking behind her as she did so.

Then she stopped, took a deep breath and squared her soldiers.

For a minute she simply stood there. At last she turned and slowly walked back up. She took out a set of keys and made quick work of locking the door, then started down the steps again.

She walked slowly at first. Then, as she neared the bottom, she began rushing again. She reached the sidewalk and took another deep breath. She stared back up the steps, then shook her head.

The doorman at Suede saw her as she stood on the sidewalk. He called out a greeting, and she swung around, greeting him in turn.

Then she disappeared into the club as he opened the door for her.

Very curious behavior, Quinn thought.

He left the café, making sure to leave a generous tip. He would undoubtedly be wanting his table back in the days to come. He stopped by his car long enough to toss in the files he'd been reading, then headed across the street.

The doorman at Suede was jet-black, a good six-three, and pure muscle. He looked at Quinn, frowned, sized him up and down, and decided to let him pass.

Inside, the music was loud.

The bar was to the rear of the building, the dance floor about ten feet from the entrance. The place advertised live music and lived up to the advertising. The room was handsomely appointed, with the walls painted to imitate a sunset. Floor lighting gave the place just enough illumination to make the tables navigable, while spotlights gave a burst of life to the polished dance floor. A Latin trio was playing, and the beat was fast. Tables surrounded the floor on either side, and despite it being a weeknight, most of the tables were filled, though the place wasn't overcrowded. Scantily clad women on the dance floor gyrated at shocking speeds, some looking good and some not.

Toward the rear of the place, to the left of the bar, he caught sight of Gordon Henson. The thick thatch of white hair on his head was caught in the light, drawing attention to him. Skirting around the dance floor, Quinn saw that his brother was in attendance, along with Bobby Yarborough, one of his classmates from the academy, and Bobby's new wife, or at least, Quinn assumed it was his wife. He'd never met her. Shannon Mackay was next to Doug, on her other side a tall man in a white tailored shirt and sport jacket, who, in turn, was next to a small woman of about forty, perfectly elegant, but with features so taut they screamed plastic surgery.

Doug, looking across the floor, saw him and, with some surprise, called his name. "Quinn!"

Quinn continued across the room, excusing himself with a quick smile when he nearly collided with a waitress.

"My brother with the two left feet," Doug teased, rising to greet him with a handshake.

"Hey, now, that's not really true," Shannon said, defending him. The words, however, seemed to be a natural reaction; she smiled, but she seemed distracted.

"That's right. You had your first lesson today, so you've met Shannon and Gordon, and of course, you know Bobby."

Quinn nodded, reaching out to shake Bobby's hand. Bobby grinned broadly. "Hey, Quinn. You haven't met my wife, Giselle."

"Giselle, nice to meet you. Congratulations on your wedding."

Giselle smiled. "Thank you. It's amazing. I thought it would never come. Now, I feel as if we've been married forever."

"Ouch," Bobby said.

She squeezed his arm. "I meant that in the best possible way."

"Hmm," Bobby mused, feigning a frown.

"Quinn, these are the doctors Long," Doug continued. "Richard and Mina."

He shook hands with the couple. "How nice. Do you work together?"

The petite blonde laughed. "Good heavens, no. Richard is a dermatologist and plastic surgeon. I'm a lowly, hard-working pediatrician."

"She's far more noble," Richard said, grinning.

"You're the artist," his wife teased back.

His arm, casually around her shoulders as they sat in the expansive booth, tightened affectionately. "We simply thank God we don't work together. That way, we get to enjoy the time we do share."

"Great," Quinn said.

"Here, please, sit," Mina Long said, inching closer to her husband.

"I don't want to crowd you."

"Oh, please, don't worry," Richard said. "We're only here for a few minutes longer. We have to join some other friends across the room. In fact...we were about to dance?" He wasn't looking at his wife but across the table at Shannon.

"That's the music you want?" she asked.

"That's it," he told her.

"Excuse me, then...?"

Bobby and Giselle moved out, allowing Shannon to slip from the booth. She brushed past Quinn, who excused himself, moving backward again to allow her more room.

"Sit, bro," Doug said, as the others slid back in. "So how did you like your lesson?"

"It was...great," Quinn said. He watched as Shannon took the floor with Richard Long. A moment later, they were moving with astonishing grace, taking up the floor, entwined in seemingly impossible ways, and doing it so well that many of the people on the floor moved back, cheering.

"That's salsa?" Quinn said.

"Samba," Gordon told him.

He looked across the table at Mina. "And do you dance, too, Dr. Long?"

"Oh, yes." She laughed pleasantly. "But not like Shannon." She grinned. "Richard and I dance together at social functions, of course. But frankly, he prefers Shannon—and I prefer Sam. Sam Railey. He's my teacher. Two amateurs naturally dance better with two professionals." She leaned closer across the table. "I'm afraid Richard is showing off tonight. We have to join a few of his professional associates in a minute."

"Ah, I see," Quinn said.

She smiled again. It would have been a great smile—if it hadn't appeared that her entire face might shatter. "You *will* see. Wait until you get into it more. Hey, have you seen your brother dance?"

"Believe it or not, I haven't."

Mina Long looked at Doug. "I'm not exactly Jane or Shannon, but we can give your big brother a bit of show, if you like?"

"Absolutely," Doug agreed. "Sorry," he said apologetically to the others again.

"Hey, we might as well dance, too," Bobby told his bride.

"Might as well?" Giselle said with a groan. "See, Bobby, it *is* as if we've been married forever."

Bobby laughed. "Sorry. My beloved wife, would you do me the honor of dancing with me?"

"Good save," Doug muttered, and they all laughed.

"Pretty darned good, yes," Mina agreed, and she took his hand, heading for the dance floor.

"How did you enjoy your lesson?" Gordon Henson asked Quinn.

"You know, quite frankly, I went because Doug bought me the guest passes and he was so into it himself. But I was surprised. I *did* enjoy it," Quinn said, his eyes on his brother and Mina.

His brother, he noted, was good. Bobby and Giselle, both beginners, weren't as smooth but obviously enjoyed themselves.

"Those two only came in to take some classes before their wedding. They keep coming back," Gordon told him. Then he leaned against the table. "So, what do you do, Mr. O'Casey?"

Quinn didn't have a chance to answer him. A man approached the table, calling out cheerfully, "Gordon! I'll be damned. They actually got you in here?"

The man was tall, dark, good-looking, casually dressed in an open-neck black silk shirt, tan trousers and a dark jacket. His eyes were dark, too, his face deeply bronzed.

"Yeah, they dragged me down," Gordon said, half rising to shake the newcomer's hand.

"Gabe, this is Quinn O'Casey, Doug's brother, a new student. Quinn, meet Gabriel Lopez, entrepreneur extraordinaire! Suede is his club."

"How do you do?" Quinn said, shaking hands with Lopez.

"Great, thanks. And welcome. You ever been in here before?"

Quinn shook his head. "Never. I'm a total novice."

"You'll like it. I get the best musicians, even during the week. We keep up the floor, and our kitchen turns out amazing food."

"So far, so good," Quinn said.

"You haven't been on the dance floor yet?"

Quinn grinned. "No. And you won't see me on it for a very long time, I assure you."

Lopez had slid into the booth next to him. "My friend, you'll be surprised, don't you think, Gordon?"

Gordon nodded. "Dancing gets in your blood. You hear the music, you have to move." He shrugged, staring at the floor. "Maybe you don't get to be a Shannon Mackay right away, but look at Doug. Six months, and he's quite impressive. Most importantly, he's having fun."

"Yeah, he really enjoys it. And hey, what a setup you two have here," Quinn said, including Lopez. "You learn upstairs, you dance downstairs. Couldn't have been planned better."

"True," Gordon agreed. "And it wasn't even planned."

"This wasn't a club before?"

"It's always been a restaurant—with an excuse for a dance floor," Lopez said. He shrugged. "When I came down, a year or so ago now, I saw the potential in the place. The other owners weren't making use of the gold mine they had."

"We have a great relationship," Gordon explained. "We have the same people come in to take care of the floors, and we both get a deal that way."

"They send me their students all the time," Lopez said.

"And we have a place to send our students, so that they have a good time and want to take more lessons," Gordon said, then pointed toward the ceiling. "The other tenant in the building is a designer and costumer. She's great, too. Katarina. When someone is looking for a dress—for a night out on the town, or for a competition—they just go right across the hall. You couldn't get a better setup."

Lopez nodded and stood. "Well, back to business. Welcome, Mr. O'Casey." He cocked his head, smiling. "Are you a cop, too? With your brother and his friends around now, we feel safe all the time."

Quinn shook his head. "No, sorry, I'm not a cop. I'm into boats. Charters, diving, fishing," Quinn said. Absolutely true, just not the whole story.

"Ah, I see. Well, then, you're a lucky man, too. There's nothing in the world like the sea."

"Nothing like it," Quinn agreed.

"Enjoy your night," Lopez said.

"See you, Gabe," Gordon said.

Lopez walked away, toward the kitchen.

"He's a great guy," Gordon said.

"Seems to be," Quinn agreed.

"Hey, you want to see your brother really look good?" Gordon asked. There was a note of pride in his voice.

Quinn looked back to the floor. The couples had all switched around. Doug was dancing with Shannon Mackay, and there were only a few people on the floor now. The music had changed, as had the dance. It was sweeping and incredibly graceful.

"Bolero," Gordon told him briefly.

The dance was beautiful. And Doug *was* good, made all the better by the elegance of his partner.

"I don't think I've ever seen anyone move so…"

"You mean your brother?" Gordon teased.

Quinn shook his head, grinning. "Ms. Mackay."

"She's the best," Gordon said.

"Hey, Quinn, can we slip back in?"

His head jerked up. Bobby and Giselle had returned. Panting. Quinn hadn't realized he had been almost trans-fixed, watching the dancers.

"You're not doing the bolero?" he asked the pair.

Bobby snorted. "Every time we try it together, we trip each other. I'm actually kind of hopeless."

"You're not!" Giselle protested.

Bobby made a face at Quinn. "You should see her in group class. She subtly—lovingly—tries to make sure she's in front of some other guy all the time."

"I do not. I would never." She shrugged sheepishly at Quinn. "We change partners every few minutes anyway. What good would it do?"

Doug came up to the table, drawing Shannon by the hand. "Well?" he asked Quinn. It was strange. Doug had been totally serious about his suspicions regarding Lara Trudeau's death, but right now, he was like the anxious little kid brother Quinn had known all his life, wanting his approval.

"You two blew me away," he said.

Doug was pleased. "Now it's your turn."

"You're out of your mind," Quinn said, laughing.

"No, no, you'll be fine," Bobby encouraged. "It's a merengue. You can't mess it up."

"Trust me, I can."

"Come on, Mr. O'Casey," Shannon said to him. "It's step, step, step. March, march, march. I know you can do it."

She was extending her elegant hand to him, those eyes of hers directly on his, challenging. It was as if she didn't believe for a second that he had really come for dance lessons.

He shrugged. "All right. If you're all absolutely determined to make me look like a fool…"

"You'll never look like a fool—not with Shannon," Gordon said.

"Doesn't look like they're just doing march, march, march to me," he told her ruefully as they stepped onto the dance floor.

"They are—they're just adding turns."

She was in his arms, showing him the hold. "Just follow my movements. Men always—always—lead in dance," she told him, "but since you haven't done this yet…left, right, left, right…feel the beat?"

He did feel the beat. And more. The searing touch of her eyes, probing his. The subtle movement of her body, erotic along with the music.

"March, march," he said.

"You're doing fine."

"Thanks. And how about you?"

Her brows hiked. "I'm impressed. You really do have a sense of rhythm. We can try some of those arm movements if you want. Just lift them…and I'll turn, then you turn. Merengue is a favorite, because no matter what, it's march, march."

"I'm not wiggling like those guys."

"Because you don't have your Cuban motion yet. You'll get it."

Cuban motion, huh? She certainly had it. The way her hips moved was unbelievable.

He lifted his arms as she had instructed. He was a little too jerky, but she could deal with it.

"Now you," she told him, and he repeated her motion.

Step, step, march, march. Okay…

"Was something wrong earlier tonight?" he asked her.

"What?" She frowned.

"I saw you coming down the steps. You looked…uneasy," he said.

"You saw me? You were watching me?" Her tone was level, but he heard a note of outrage. "Are you following me or something, Mr. O'Casey?"

He laughed, keeping the sound light. "No, sorry, and I didn't mean to imply such a thing. I went over to the place across the street for a hamburger before coming here," he said. Okay, so the hamburger was a lie.

"Oh." She flushed. "Sorry. I just… It's an uncomfortable feeling, to think you're being watched."

"No, no…sorry. It's just that…you looked scared."

Maybe women weren't supposed to lead, but she pressed his arms up and moved herself into a turn, shielding her eyes from his for a moment. Facing him again, she said, "Gordon was already down here. I was locking up alone. One of the books fell or something right before I walked out. It startled me."

His hamburger story was a lie, and her falling book story was a lie, as well. Something much bigger had definitely frightened her.

"Unfortunately, Miami deserves its reputation for crime. You do need to be careful if you're locking up alone," he told her.

"The club is open every night. There's a doorman on Thursday through Sunday. We park in the lot in the back, but it's right across from a convenience store. There probably couldn't be a safer place. And there are only three of us in the building—the club, the studio and the design shop. I know everyone."

"But you can't know everyone who comes into the club," he said.

"No, of course not. But still I've always felt safe. Not only that, but I'm tougher than I look."

"Really?" He had to smile.

"Don't doubt it," she told him, and there was definitely a warning in her voice. "Trust me. I can be tough."

"A tough dancer," he mused.

"That's right. I love the studio—and I hate lies."

"Do you, now?" he demanded. He thought that he saw the slightest hint of a flush touch her cheeks before she drew away from him.

"The music has changed. You're not ready for a mambo," she told him.

And turning, she walked away, leaving him on the floor.

CHAPTER 6

Shannon made a point of getting to the studio by nine the following morning. She had agreed to coach Sam and Jane at ten, and at eleven, Gordon wanted to go over more of the Gator Gala figures and plans.

Reaching the studio wasn't difficult—she walked fifty percent of the time. Her house was just a few blocks away—thanks to Gordon.

Years ago, he had found the old place for sale. At that time, the block had been very run-down, and her house had come with horrible plumbing, no central air and the ugliest wallpaper known to man. The carpet could actually cause one to gag.

But the house had been the deal of the century. Small—there were only two bedrooms, and the yard was the size of a postage stamp—but she lived three blocks from the beach, and in the years since she had owned the house, the value had quadrupled. And it was hers. There weren't that many private homes in the area, and she knew she was very lucky to have the space. And she wouldn't have it, if it weren't for Gordon. He'd loaned her the down payment.

Sometimes, when she realized that she'd been in the studio for probably eighty hours in one week, she liked to tell him that he'd gotten his investment back from her in blood and sweat. He told her that of course he had, he wasn't a stupid man.

This morning, though, she was anxious to be in the studio—by the light of day. She was determined to convince herself that she was either overwrought or a little bit crazy—or both.

She climbed the stairs to the front door and waited, then inserted the key in the lock. Hesitantly she pushed the door open, then paused, listening.

Not a thing.

She entered the studio slowly, scoping out the polished wood floor and gazing around the room. Two sides were composed of floor-to-ceiling mirrors. Facing the street, giant picture windows looked out on the day. The "conference room" was to the front, while the reception area and offices lined part of the wall nearest the door. Toward the rear were four doors, the first opening to the instructors' room, the next opening to the men's room, the third to the ladies', and the fourth—with a counter section next to it—leading to the mini-kitchen. A small hallway between the bathrooms led to the rear door, where, just outside, there was a little patio shared by both upstairs establishments. To the left of the rear door was an expanse of wall with a door that led to the storage space. There was also access from the outside, since originally the storage space hadn't come with the studio. Now, all of them had keys to it. Katarina kept a few costume dummies and supplies there, the dance studio kept records and various other items at different times, and while the club actually had much greater space downstairs, they sometimes needed a little extra now and then. There had never been any problems over sharing.

Across the patio were stairs leading up to a newly re-vamped third floor. Previously, it had pretty much been wasted space, but Gabriel Lopez had gotten permission from the corporate owners of the property to finish it and create an apartment. He and Gordon joked about it all the time—the apartment was terrific, and Gordon was jealous. He wished he'd come up with the idea. He had a great condo farther up on the beach—he just hated driving.

Shannon knew the studio and the building like the back of her hand. And that was why she had been so unnerved the night before.

With everyone else gone and the stereo silent, she had been in her own office, glancing over the student records. They all did their best to keep their students coming. The students were their livelihood. She had an excellent staff—dedicated professionals who were determined to really teach dance and give the clients their money's worth for every minute on the floor—and everyone took responsibility for keeping the students happy. Still, when a student with a regular schedule suddenly became a no-show, something was wrong, and as manager, it was her responsibility to call that person, chat with them and make sure they hadn't been offended in some way.

After Lara's death, she thought she might have to make a number of personal calls and give people the best reassurance she could.

And so she had sat there with the files. Though the building was old, it had been well maintained. The soundproofing down at the club was excellent, and noise from the street never seemed to filter into the studio.

She could have dropped a pin and heard it fall as she worked.

And that was when she'd heard the noise.

A grating.

It had sounded as if it were coming from inside the studio itself.

It was a quick sound. Like nails scraping against a blackboard. Eerie, creepy, quick—gone. Gone so quickly she might have imagined it. Except that she hadn't.

She'd jumped to her feet, dropped the books, and burst out of her office and into the main room. Maybe Gordon had forgotten to lock the doors when he'd left. Or maybe he hadn't forgotten but had just decided he didn't need to bother, since she would be coming down right behind him.

The dance floor was empty. When she walked to the front door, she'd found it locked. She'd wanted to walk through the bathrooms, kitchens, teachers' room and Gordon's office, but she hadn't. For some reason, the silence, and the strangeness of the noise that broke it, had unnerved her too badly. Grabbing her purse and overshirt, she'd sprinted out the door, not at all certain why the noise had made her feel as if she was in imminent danger. She'd been so anxious to get out, she'd nearly forgotten to lock the door and then had forced herself to go back. Silly.

Now she was slightly embarrassed by her reaction.

Especially since it had been seen. Quinn O'Casey had somehow just happened to be having a hamburger across the street. Mr. Twenty Questions, himself.

So what?

The idea made her feel on edge, just as the man himself did. Far too good-looking. Not pretty, though his features were aligned exceptionally well. Just arresting. Two left feet, too tall, arms like steel. He wasn't an ordinary man. He both compelled her and irritated her beyond reason.

He hadn't just happened to be across the street, she was certain.

Either that, or she was paranoid. She had never been

paranoid before, but ever since Lara had died, everything seemed to have taken on a new and evil connotation.

You're next.

Those words, spoken when obviously someone would be going up next, should have been entirely innocent.

But she didn't believe they were. Okay, that had to be paranoia. Lara had died. In her warped little mind, she was taking the words to somehow mean that she was supposed to die next.

She gave herself a firm mental shake and walked purposely around the studio as she should have done the night before. Kitchen, bathrooms. Teachers' room, conference room, Gordon's office, her own. She found the books she had dropped and picked them up. Finally she opened the back door and went out, going so far as to check the lock on the outside storage-room door. On a whim, she went back inside, got her keys and opened the door to the storage room.

Everything was in order. Rows of shelves held all kinds of records, a few small appliances, lightbulbs, boxes of material. She moved among the shelves. In the back of the room, she started, freezing for a moment, suddenly convinced she was not alone.

She had merely come face-to-face with one of Katarina's dressmaker's dummies.

"Stupid," she said aloud to herself. Then, turning purposefully, she walked back to the door. Odd, the dressmaker's dummy had given her another wave of unease. She felt that if she turned around, the mannequin was suddenly going to have gotten a face and found movement.

She spun around to look. The dummy stood just as it had, swathed in a spandex body suit with a sweeping skirt. No face. No movement. The mannequin gave that appearance because a huge feathered hat—of a sort that would never be worn on a dance floor—had been tossed on top of its neck.

It was just a dummy, and there didn't seem to be a thing in the room out of place. She exited, closing and locking the door behind her, and returned to the studio.

As she walked through the back hallway, she reminded herself that a person's own mind could be their greatest enemy, and she was letting what had happened to Lara take root in her far too deeply. She couldn't help it. No matter what her personal feelings had been toward Lara at times, she could at least say that she had known her well. Nothing had mattered to Lara more than dance. She might have a drink now and then. She might even take *a* Xanax to steady her nerves. But she would never, never, overindulge to the point of affecting a performance.

A sudden clicking sound caused her to jump, her hand flying to her throat. Then she realized that the front door had opened and closed. Jane was standing in the entry, staring at her with a serious crease furrowed into her brow.

"Hey. What's wrong?"

"Nothing."

"You look as if you've seen a ghost."

"No, no, sorry. I guess I was kind of deep in thought, and you startled me."

"Oh, sorry. I just…opened the door," Jane said.

"I know."

Jane offered her a small smile. "People will be opening and closing the door all day, you know."

"Yep."

Jane walked across the room to her, looking around the studio. "We're alone?"

"Yes. Sam hasn't come in yet."

"He'll be here any minute. He won't be late for a coaching session."

"I'm sure he won't be," Shannon said. She arched a brow to Jane questioningly. She might have jumped when

Jane entered, but Jane was definitely acting strangely. "What's up?"

"I don't know. I'm still nervous, I guess."

"Why? Did something happen?"

"To me? No," Jane said.

"Because of Lara."

Jane nodded, looking directly and somberly at her. "You think there was something fishy about it. I know it. I mean, I know you think somebody killed her for some reason. Let's face it, lots of people might have wanted to. We'd both be suspects, you know. Me—she beat me in everything and loved to gloat about it. You—maybe you're entirely circumspect and so blasé that most people don't know, but anyone who goes back several years knows about Ben Trudeau and you."

"Jane, I'm not blasé. It was so long ago that it means nothing."

"You're so professional, to be able to work with Ben."

"I'm not sure I'm all that professional. I simply have no real memory of being attracted to Ben romantically in any way whatsoever. We have different goals and beliefs in life, and…there's just nothing there. Nothing at all. He's a good teacher and an excellent dancer. He should be a competitor, and he should have a great partner. He's that good."

"And she blew him off," Jane said, whispering for some reason. "That's what I mean, Shannon. Anyone might have wanted to kill her. Even Gordon, say."

"Gordon was proud of her. She was a big part of this studio's reputation, since this is where she started and did a lot of coaching."

"And as good as he was to her, she was rude to him."

"People don't usually commit murder simply because someone was rude, Jane," Shannon said. She was actually feeling a little bit ridiculous herself, now that it was daylight and she wasn't alone.

"You say that, but you don't mean it," Jane said.

"I don't know what I feel, exactly," Shannon said. "We've just got to go on and get past this."

"There was so much going on with her," Jane murmured.

"Like what?"

"Well, for one thing, she loved to flaunt the fact that she didn't actually work for the studio, so she wasn't bound to any of that nonfraternization stuff." Jane's voice lowered even more. "You know what I think? I think she just liked to hurt people. Remember how excited I was, pleased with myself, when Doug O'Casey started to learn so much so quickly? Well, Lara knew it. The first coaching session that I arranged for him with her, she seemed to catch on that he was kind of a prize to me, someone very special. She hardly included me in the session at all. And then, later that night, she was dancing with him down at Suede."

"Jane, we all dance with people down at Suede."

"I know, I know, but this was different. It was as if she had her claws in him or something. She looked at me and smiled, and it was like she was gloating, telling me she'd taken over my student."

"Jane, he's still your student."

"Yes, he's my student. But I'd swear she had something going on with him. And not just him. All my students, I think."

"Even old Mr. Clinton?" Shannon said, trying to interject a light note into the conversation.

Jane wasn't amused. "That should be funny—except that Clinton is rich. She was always an angel to him. She knew how to hedge her bets. If she wanted to enter something, she wanted to feel that she had lots of people with money waiting in the wings, in case any of her sponsors fell through."

"Jane, come on, she wasn't having any kind of a thing with Mr. Clinton."

"Maybe not, but I'm willing to bet she would have, if she felt it would further her career."

"She had a great career. Jane, face it, she was good. No, beyond good."

"But she was a witch!"

"She liked to use people, and she liked to jerk their chains. But she's gone now."

Jane nodded, then looked at her again. "I think you should be careful."

"Me? Why?"

"Because too many people know you're convinced that Lara would have never done herself in."

"No one said it was suicide. Just an accidental overdose that caused her heart to stop."

"You don't think it was an accident."

"Neither do you, so it seems."

"But…" Jane paused, her beautiful dark hair sweeping around her delicate, gamine's face as she assured herself once again that they were alone. "People know what you think and feel. You were honest with the police. You've said a few things around her. I think you need to be careful."

You're next.

Shannon forced a smile, refusing to psych herself into a worse state of paranoia. "No matter what anyone thought, Jane, Lara's death was ruled accidental. She's being buried tomorrow. It's over. It's hard, and of course we're not going to forget it right away, but we're going to move on. We have our own lives to live. Okay?"

Jane nodded solemnly, reaching for the hand Shannon offered her, squeezing it.

Then they both jumped a mile when the door opened again.

"What the heck is up with you two?" Sam Railey demanded as he walked in. He frowned at them, then looked over his shoulder.

"What? I have a huge zit on my forehead? Spinach in my teeth?"

Shannon and Jane laughed, looking at each other a bit guiltily.

"Nope, you look great, Sam," Shannon said. "Hey, both of you, get your shoes on. Let's get going. Your CD's over by the stereo, right? When you're ready, go through the whole routine, then we'll break it down. Come on, come on, let's move, before the day gets really busy."

"Yes, ma'am," Sam said. Shaking his head, he started for the teachers' room to get his shoes. "What a tyrant," he muttered, but the words were quite intentionally audible. "Not, gee, Sam, take your time, we'll throw some coffee on and talk a minute or two. Not, good morning, Sam, how are you doing, everything all right? I'll just ask myself, then. Sam, how are you? Not too bad, but somehow, I am getting one mother of a blister on my left heel."

"Shoes, Sam. Chop, chop," Shannon told him.

Giggling, Jane hurried after him to get her own shoes.

Shannon looked around. The day outside was bright and beautiful. Light was pouring in. Sam and Jane were chattering away as they slipped into their smooth shoes.

Everything seemed good, clean, bathed in sun, normal.

It remained so until Gordon came in, informing her that they needed to break any appointments for that evening and cancel their group classes.

Lara Trudeau was being buried Saturday, and that night there was going to be a viewing at the funeral home, and they all had to be there.

"I have to admit," Sam whispered to Shannon, "she looks beautiful. I mean, you know, most of the time when you come to a viewing with an open coffin, the person looks dead. Bad. Stiff. Everyone tries to say that someone looks beautiful, but they don't. But Lara, for real, looks beautiful. Like she's sleeping, huh? She looks young, too. This is so tragic."

Tragic.

Beyond a doubt.

Down on the kneeling pad in front of the coffin, Shannon felt a million emotions rush through her. No, Lara had not been particularly nice. But she had been talented and, more, so full of life that she had exuded energy at every turn. She had entranced her own private world and given dozens who had come after her a height of professionalism and beauty for which to strive.

But not nice.

Sam sighed deeply. "Not that she would ever have been eligible for a community-spirit award."

"Sam!" Shannon nudged him. "You're supposed to sit here and pray for the deceased."

"Think she needs our prayers?" he asked. "Okay, she wasn't Mother Teresa, but she wasn't a murderess or anything. She's probably dancing in the clouds right now. Or maybe…if there is a purgatory, she's there, trying to teach steps to a bunch of dunderheads."

"Sam," Shannon groaned.

"Oh, right, and you're praying that she's sitting on the right hand of God?" he whispered back.

Shannon sighed and gave up. She hadn't been praying. Or maybe she had. It was sad, it was tragic, Lara was gone. And she hoped that her beliefs were right, that there was an afterlife, and that, indeed, Lara was dancing in the clouds. But what she had really discovered was that more and more, with her whole heart, she just didn't believe the ruling of accidental death. Lara had loved life. She had loved the simple act of waking up and living, moving, using the tool of her body to create beautiful, bewitching motion. She simply couldn't have done herself in—not even accidentally.

She rose, Sam taking her elbow to rise with her.

There was a long line behind them. The funeral home was filled to capacity and beyond. People who had known her, professionals, amateurs and the just plain curious, had come to pay their respects.

She walked over to where Gordon was standing, talking quietly with Gunter Heinrich, one of the champions from Germany. Gunter greeted her with a sad smile and a kiss on the cheek.

"Gunter, you made it here. I'm amazed to see you. This was all arranged so quickly."

Very tall, blond, an elegant man with strong facial features, Gunter shrugged. "I was in the States—Helga and I stayed after the competition on the beach. We're going on—we'd planned on doing the competition in Asheville next week. I was just speaking with Gordon about using the dance studio for some practice sessions next week," Gunter continued. "Are you available for some coaching?"

They were at a wake, she thought, and yet Gunter was scheduling. Maybe she hadn't been to enough wakes. She could hear soft conversation all around her. Maybe that was part of it. Life went on.

"I think so," she murmured.

Mr. Clinton was at the coffin then. Looking grave, he went to his knees, said a little prayer and crossed himself. Jane came up to him as he rose again, slipping an arm around his shoulders. The Longs were there, quietly standing at the back of the room, engaged in conversation with the young couple who had come to learn to dance for their wedding. Rhianna Markham, who had taught the couple, stood with them.

Ben was on the other side of the coffin, standing alone, looking somber, and almost as if he were in another world.

Mary and Judd Bentley, owners of a franchise studio down in South Dade, came up to the coffin and bent down together. They were good people, and good friends. Mary was actually crying—one of the few in attendance doing so.

"You're next."

"What?"

Shannon's attention was drawn sharply back to Gunter.

His brow arched. She hadn't realized how sharply she had spoken, or how loudly. She flushed. "Sorry. I'm afraid I was distracted."

"I was telling Gordon, he has to find the right words to get you out there. You're the best coach we've ever had—and one of the best dancers I've ever seen. If you went back out there, you could be next."

"Oh, I…thanks," she murmured. "That's very sweet. Excuse me, will you?"

She suddenly knew she had to get out of the building, if only for a moment. She turned and started down the center aisle between the rows of chairs. The smell of the multitude of flowers lining the room, set against every available wall, in stands and over the casket itself, was overwhelming. She closed her eyes and nearly crashed into Ella Rodriguez and Justin Garcia as they took their turn heading to kneel down before Lara.

In the antechamber, she moved through a milling crowd. More dancers. She saw one of last year's local salsa champions, a beautiful, petite girl with a body to kill for. She was in black—a tight black dress that hugged her every curve. She was in deep conversation with one of the officers of the national dance association.

Katarina was in the antechamber, looking sedate in a navy suit and apparently saddened by the occasion. But before Shannon could even approach her, another woman stepped in front of her, loudly asking if she could come in for a fitting the following day. When Katarina informed her that she would be attending Lara's funeral, the woman insisted on seeing her Monday.

Shannon lifted a hand to Katarina, then rushed out the front door.

The funeral home Gordon had chosen was almost dead in the center of Miami proper. He'd paid a great deal to buy a plot for Lara in one of the area's oldest cemeteries, Woodlawn, a beautiful place made more beautiful by the heavy respect that the Latin community paid to their dead.

The street in front of her was busy with traffic racing by. A horn blared. A driver shouted out his window at someone who didn't move fast enough in front of him. There was a convenience store across the street, and a group of teens sat in front of it on the hood of a restored Chevy, chatting, laughing.

The air wasn't exactly fresh and inviting—a burst of exhaust fumes came her way. But she felt better away from the overwhelming scent of the flowers. And away from the strange state of hypocrisy that existed inside.

People exited as she stood there, lifting their hands in solemn salute to her as they headed for the parking lot. Some she knew well, some she had at least seen before, and in some cases, she didn't have any idea who they were. She waved back anyway.

Then, weaving through a group that was leaving, she saw two men on their way in. The brothers O'Casey.

Doug came straight to her, giving her a hug, kissing her cheek. He looked truly distraught. His usually neatly brushed wheat hair was rumpled in front, as if he'd been running his fingers through it. His features were strained.

"This is it, huh?" he said, his voice husky. "This makes it real."

She nodded, touching his cheek, and felt suddenly glad,

because here was someone who had really cared about Lara Trudeau, if only as her student and a friend. Except, according to Jane, he might have cared about her as much more.

"It *is* real, Doug, I'm afraid. Very real."

"How does she…look?" he asked.

"This sounds trite, of course, but it's true. She's beautiful. As if she's sleeping," Shannon told him.

He lowered his head. "I'm going in."

He turned and walked toward the door. Quinn remained. Tall, dark, striking in his suit. Watching her. In the shadows of the street, his eyes appeared almost black. Like dual abysses of some deep, dark knowledge that somehow accused her, or saw more than they should.

She crossed her arms over her chest, returning his stare. "It's interesting to see you. You didn't know Lara, did you? Had you ever seen her dance?"

"I came with my brother," he said.

"Ah, I see."

"Do you?" He looked toward the door. "It's interesting to see lots of the people who come to a wake, isn't it? I mean, seriously, how many people are here because they care—and how many are here just to see her and be seen themselves?"

"People often come to see someone well-known," Shannon said. "Gordon didn't specify anywhere that this was to be private. He wanted anyone who wished to see Lara and pay their respects to her talent to feel free to come."

"Noble," Quinn murmured. She couldn't tell if it was in mockery or not.

"Are you going back in?" he asked.

She stared at him and shook her head. "No, I don't think so. I came early with Gordon and Ben to see that everything was set up properly."

"Of course. And then there's the strain of the funeral tomorrow." Again she couldn't pinpoint the tenor of his voice. Was he mocking? Did he somehow see that so much of this was a sham, a performance for Lara or, perhaps, for all of them?

"Do you need a ride home?"

She hesitated. Actually, she did. She had come with Ben, and he and Gordon would be staying to the bitter end.

"Don't worry—I won't fraternize," he told her, definite amusement in his eyes then. "Just give me a minute to go in and pay my own respects."

"It's not necessary."

"I don't mind."

She lifted her head slightly. "Doug is already in there. And you didn't know Lara. So…just what is your intention in going in?"

His lips curled slightly. "Well, to see, of course. And maybe to be seen, as well. Wait for me. I'll be right with you."

He turned and headed for the entrance. She watched him go, wishing that, in the midst of all that was going on—and despite the definite mistrust she felt—she weren't admiring the way his shoulders carried the sleek lines of his suit, or noting again the subdued but rich, evocative scent of aftershave that seemed to linger when he had gone.

Lara was dead and would soon be buried.

She had to admit, she was afraid herself. Afraid of something vague that she knew but couldn't touch.

And Quinn O'Casey?

The man was after something. She just wasn't sure what.

CHAPTER 7

Doug was by the coffin and Quinn decided, for the moment, to let him be. He strode up the aisle and waited off to the side.

People were filling the chairs and lining the walls. Bits and pieces of conversation came to him. One group talked about the weather, and someone chimed in that it was a stroke of genius for Moonlight Sonata to plan the Gator Gala for February, the dead of winter, when everyone would want to be in Florida.

Two others were talking technique, comparing notes on footwork. He was pretty sure that most of the people here were in the world of dance.

Doug remained on his knees before the coffin.

Gordon Henson saw Quinn and lifted a hand in acknowledgment. Jane walked over to Doug, kneeling down beside him.

Ben Trudeau was standing at the coffin, arms crossed over his chest as if he were a sentinel, guarding the remains.

Quinn moved closer, waiting his turn, listening. At last Doug rose, arm in arm with Jane, and the two moved away.

Quinn walked up to the coffin. The woman inside had been beautiful, of course. Now her hair was styled, makeup had been applied. She had been dressed for burial in a sky-blue dance gown with elaborate beadwork on the bodice. Her hands were folded. She held a flower. She really did look as if she were a modern day Sleeping Beauty, awaiting the kiss that would awaken her. Except that it wouldn't come. The telltale autopsy scar was, of course, not visible, and so Lara Trudeau lay like a whirl of grace and motion that had been paused in an eternity of time.

He'd seen the tape of that day. Seen her fly and touch the clouds. Seen her die.

He'd gone to Sunday school every week when he'd been growing up. He still attended church with Doug and his mom now and then. He automatically signed a cross over his chest, bowed his head...

And listened.

Someone was standing with Ben Trudeau by the huge flower urn at the head of the coffin. He recognized the voices—it was that of Gabriel Lopez, the sleek owner of Suede.

"Are you all right, Ben?" Lopez sounded like a true friend, concerned.

"Of course I'm all right. We'd been divorced a long time."

"Still, I didn't know her anywhere near as well, but...she made an impression," Gabriel said.

There was a hesitation. "I guess I never did stop loving her, in a way. Like you love a selfish child. I hated her, too, though, sometimes."

"You might want to be careful what you say," Lopez warned Ben, his voice quiet.

"Why?" Ben demanded.

"Well, the circumstances were pretty strange."

"Oh, jeez, that again. The cops questioned everyone. They

did an autopsy. They studied the tape. The circumstances were strange because Lara was such an idiot for killing herself that way. Accidentally. Idiotically." He sounded angry. "I wish everyone would just stop with this. God knows—we could all point fingers at one another."

"I don't know…is it really over? I heard that Shannon Mackay isn't convinced."

"Shannon doesn't want to face reality. And hey, if someone wanted to start pointing fingers, they could point right at her," Ben said irritably.

"Is everything all right?"

A third voice had joined in. A woman's. Memory clicked. It was Mina Long. *Dr.* Long, the pediatrician.

"Well," Lopez murmured, a trace of humor in his voice, "this *is* a wake."

"Of course, of course. You know, Ben, I meant… You *do* believe Richard did everything he could, don't you? He may be a plastic surgeon, but trust me, he knows CPR and emergency measures."

"Mina, please, of course we know Richard did everything he could," Ben said. "It's just hard to accept that she's really gone. Excuse me, will you? An old partner of mine just walked in. I think I'll say hi."

Ben moved away. "He looks upset," Mina said to Gabriel, concerned.

"Sure he's upset. But I think he sees a chance to find himself a new partner, rather than an old one. Ben hasn't danced professionally in a while now, and he's anxious to get back to it." There was a long sigh. "I've got to get going. I didn't know Lara that well, but the club and the studio have a great relationship, so I wanted to be here. Still, I couldn't close the club, and it's a Friday night. Give Richard my best. How is he holding up, by the way? I know he considered Lara a big part of his success as a dancer."

"Well, of course, his sessions with Lara were important, but I believe Richard knows that Shannon is the one who really taught him. He did admire Lara, though. And being the first one to reach her when it happened… He's all right, though. Good night, Gabriel. We'll be seeing you."

"I count on it," Gabriel assured her, and left.

A woman came up to Mina. "Hello, dear, how are you?"

"Gracie, nice to see you. Sorry for the circumstances, though. And congratulations. I understand that Lara was posthumously awarded the trophy for the night she died, but that you came in second."

"It was a rather hollow victory," the newcomer said. "I wonder why on earth Gordon and Ben chose that dress. She has so many others that would have been…more appropriate. I mean, it was perfect on the dance floor, but in a coffin…it's rather garish, don't you think?"

"I would have chosen that pink gown she wore for her last Viennese waltz," Mina said. "And the delicate little diamonds she wore with it." Mina sighed. "I helped her into it the last time she wore it."

"Really?" the woman named Gracie said, then changed the subject. "We'll be seeing you at the Gator Gala?"

"Of course."

"I've got to find Darrin. You and Richard take care, now."

Mina Long was left standing alone but not for long. She saw Doug standing with Bobby and Giselle, not far away. "Doug, Bobby, Giselle, sweetie. How are you doing?" she called as she walked off.

Quinn didn't hear their replies, distracted when someone knelt next to him. He knew before turning that it was Shannon. He recognized the scent of her cologne.

"Seriously religious, are you?" she asked softly.

"I have been known to go to mass," he replied.

She was staring at the coffin, her expression tense.

"What's wrong?" he asked.

"Well, she *is* dead," Shannon pointed out irritably.

"Yes, but you look a lot more than just sad."

She shook her head. "She shouldn't be dead, that's all. She was only in her thirties. She was stunning. She didn't smoke. She drank power shakes all the time…. She just should not be dead, that's all," Shannon said. "Has everyone seen you yet? Have you seen everyone? I need to get home, but I can call a cab."

"No, I'd be delighted to drive you home. As long as you won't get fired for it or anything."

She cast him a glare. "You know, we're not that ridiculous. It's not a good thing for teachers and students to get too close. It can cause professional difficulties."

"Then again, you have to try to get your students to feel a sense of closeness, right? Dancing is a social activity. The longer you do it, the closer you get."

She rose, saying, "We're hogging the prayer bench."

Then she was gone.

Quinn rose more slowly and found Bobby standing to his side. He offered Quinn an awkward smile. "She was a beautiful woman, huh?"

"You worked with her?"

"Only a few times. Giselle and I wanted a picture-perfect wedding. And we had fun. Doug's the one who got so involved in the dancing." Bobby shrugged. Quinn realized that Bobby didn't know that Doug had not just gotten into dancing, but that he had gotten into Lara Trudeau, as well. Bobby frowned, though, and lowered his voice. "He didn't drag you down here just to get you into dancing, though, did he?"

Quinn shook his head. "But they don't know that at the studio."

"Hey, I wouldn't say anything." He shrugged again. "But

I don't know what you're going to find. I was there when it happened. She just dropped."

"I know. I saw the tape today."

"Well, if I can help, I'm there."

"I know. Thanks."

By the time Quinn walked away down the aisle, Shannon Mackay was almost out the front door. He stepped up behind her as she walked out to the street, ready to hail a taxi.

"Sorry. I'm here."

"Look, it's okay. The beach isn't on the way to the Keys."

"I brought a boat up to Coconut Grove. You're only a five-minute detour."

"You can get to the Grove by driving straight south."

"But I like to drive on the causeway out to the beach. Especially at night. All the lights are on. The shadows hide all the city's dirty little secrets. Night on the water is the most beautiful time. Come on. Let me drive you home. It's really no big deal."

"All right, thank you."

She walked along beside him, then stopped suddenly. "How did you know I live on the beach?"

"I didn't. I assumed. I guess because of the studio."

"You assumed?"

"My God, you're suspicious. I figured if you lived somewhere else, you'd tell me so. Just so I could drive you to the right place."

He must have sounded exasperated, because she actually smiled. "I live on the beach. Just a few blocks from the studio."

The night was balmy. As they walked along, however, she shivered slightly.

"Cold? Would you like my jacket?"

"No, thank you. I'm fine."

She spun around suddenly. A couple who had attended the wake was walking behind them. Quinn glanced at them, then at Shannon, arching his brow. "You seem a little jumpy."

"Not at all."

"Okay. If you say so. That's my car."

He hit the clicker, and his Navigator beeped. Stepping ahead, he opened her door. She gave him a brief thanks and climbed in. She was quiet as they left the parking lot, then headed north and east, toward the expressway entrance.

"You really are nervous. You going to feel safe once you get home?" he asked.

"I live in a nice, safe area."

He sniffed. "Sure. I heard they found a dead prostitute near you, not long ago."

She frowned. "Yes, they did, but that was unusual. Most of the people who live and work around there all know one another. She must have gotten in with the wrong element."

"Easy to do on the beach. Face it, South Beach is where people go for action. Sure, for some that means dancing and restaurants, but some people go for the sheer excitement. Some people love alcohol and drugs—like ecstasy. And some of the people there aren't exactly honest. There are big bucks to be made in the drug trade. You know that."

"Of course. But dancers tend to be health freaks."

"Some of your students might not be so dedicated, right?"

"Of course. But Gabriel runs a clean establishment. You can trust me—the cops have checked him out."

"I can imagine. So why are you so jumpy?"

"I'm not jumpy!"

"Hey, you know, you can ask me in for coffee when I drop you off. I can check out the closets and under the beds before I leave."

She stared at him, her emerald eyes bright in the neon glow of the local businesses. "*That* would be fraternizing."

"No, that would be professional courtesy. You teach me to dance, I check out the hidey-holes in your house."

"Gordon doesn't allow any free lessons."

"Not after the customers are sucked in, huh?"

"Sucked in? I resent that. We can give your brother a refund—I told you that."

"But I'm sucked in already," he said.

She turned away from him, looking out the window. "You know, you're right. I forget sometimes how beautiful it is," she said.

Across the water, the skyscrapers of downtown Miami were decked out in their night lights—blues, greens, shades in between. Moonlight glowed down on the water, as well. The breeze was light, the waves small. They lapped gently in a captivating pool of deep color beneath the kaleidoscope of glowing pastels.

"Yeah," he murmured. "The beauty was one of the first things I noticed when I got here."

"You've just moved here?"

"I was born here. I just moved back."

"Where were you before?" she asked. There was a suspicious note in her voice again. It made him smile.

"Northern Virginia. Which is beautiful, too. Virginia has the sea and the mountains and everything between. But this is home. I missed it."

"Did you run a charter service in Virginia, too?"

"What?" He frowned. "Oh, yeah. Boats. I love boats. I can't stay away from a boat very long, or the water. Do you like the water?"

"Sure."

"Do you fish? Dive?"

"I fished when I was kid. And I did some diving in the middle of the state when I was a teenager. I did a few of those dives where you go in with the manatees."

"You didn't like it?"

"I loved it."

"But you don't dive anymore?"

She shrugged. "I don't think I do anything anymore. I've gotten too involved with work."

"But you don't compete."

"I do a lot of coaching. I'm sure I told you—I'm a good teacher." She smiled and added ruefully, "Really good. Come to think of it, I wasn't joking. I really don't have a life other than the studio." She turned back to the window suddenly, as if she had said far more than she intended. She swung back to him. "What an idea, though. A boat would be great."

"You want to go out with me on my boat?"

"Yes. No, not exactly. I wanted to do something special for the group that's registered for the Gator Gala. Let me see, with the teachers and students from the local studios, we'd be talking about a group of about fifty. Can you get a nice boat for an evening out? It doesn't have to be a gourmet meal with a sit-down dinner or anything. In fact, I'd prefer something more casual. A buffet, plastic plates, room for a small dance band, of course. Can you set up something like that?"

"Sure," he said quickly.

"I'll get you some figures...you know, what I can afford to spend. You can arrange it, right? I mean, you really do charters?"

"I can arrange it."

He looked straight ahead as he pulled off on Alton. "Okay, where am I going?"

She directed him. When they pulled up in front of the house she indicated, she frowned.

"What's wrong?"

"I could swear I left the flood light on."

Her porch was dark. He drummed his fingers on the wheel. "I told you, I can look under the beds."

She glanced at him and exited the car quickly on her own, digging into her purse for her keys as she strode up the tiled path and across the porch and the door. The little house was charming, with a bit of the old Spanish style nicely incorporated with some cleaner Deco features.

He followed her. "Really, if something might be wrong, maybe I should look around."

"Come on in," she said.

He did, curious not just about her and what she knew, but about her home, as well. He wondered if he would see her old trophies and pictures of herself dancing, with or without a partner.

Not in the living room, though there was a dance scene above an old coral rock fireplace against the far wall. It was a painting, and the dancers were ballerinas in traditional tutus, floating in a sea of soft blue and pink. It was a beautiful painting, complemented by the warmth of the room. Heavy wood furniture was offset by the lighter colors of the carpeting, draperies and inviting throws tossed over the sofa and love seat, both facing not a television but the fireplace. The floor was light tile, except for the hooked rug before the hearth.

"I can see there's no one hanging around in the living room," she said dryly.

"I figured you'd try to deck me if I went straight into your bedrooms," he told her.

Eyes of green ice swept over him. "You just sized up this place with the same swift once-over you gave me at the studio."

"I gave you a swift once-over?" he queried, feeling a smile as he stepped in farther. "The kitchen?" he asked, striding through the living room.

"The kitchen and dining room are on this side of the hall, behind the living room. The bedrooms and family room are on the other."

He nodded, flicking on the light as he entered the kitchen. Copper pots hung from a rafter above the island workstation in the center. A counter separated the kitchen from the dining room, which was furnished with an antique table, six chairs and a matching hutch.

"Very nice," he commented.

"Glad you approve."

He turned on lights as he went, crossing from the dining room to the family room, where she had an overstuffed sofa, ottoman, recliners, and a television and stereo system. And a closet. He quirked a brow to her before opening the door. There was nothing but an assortment of gowns in plastic bags, tennis rackets and two pool cues.

"I thought you had no life?"

"Not now," she informed him. "I simply don't like to throw things away."

"Are you good?"

"At what?"

"Either pool or tennis."

"No, I suck at both. But I do enjoy them. Or I did. Once."

"All work and no play, you know."

"I never tried to convince you that I wasn't dull."

He brushed past her, heading down the hall to check out the bedrooms. The house was quiet, and the contact between them seemed to scream. He caught her gaze for a moment and wondered if she'd heard it, too.

"Bedroom," he murmured.

"What?" Her eyes widened.

"Bedrooms. I'll check out the bedrooms."

"Yes. Right."

She followed him as he came to the first door. Light flooded the space. It was perhaps twelve feet by fourteen. Not a stick of furniture. The walls were mirrored; the floor

was shiny wood. This, he thought, was her own private little studio. Her haven, maybe. He stood, staring, thoughtful.

"There's a closet," she said.

He walked across the room and threw open the closet
door. Clothing and tons of shoes. "What did you do? Rob
Imelda Marcos?" he asked.

"They're all old dance shoes. I'm hard on them."

"Why do you keep them?"

"Well, some I mean to get fixed. They'd be good again
with new soles and heels."

"I see. Interesting."

"Why? I'm a dance teacher. It's a practice floor."

"And you have no other life. But you're three blocks
from the studio?"

"I'm three blocks from the ocean, and I wish I had a
pool," she said.

"Ah," he murmured. "Well, last room."

He passed by her again, wondering why there could be
something almost like open hostility between them at times,
then brief encounters where he felt a surge of pure electricity just being near her. Scent, he thought. Or the whisper of
gold spun silk against his flesh when his chin and cheek
brushed against her hair.

"Bedroom. A real one. With a bed. And look, will you?
Great bed—love the canopy. Rug looks as soft as can
be...and there, right on the dresser, the computer."

"Everyone has a computer."

"Not in their bedroom."

"I'll bet lots of people keep their computers in their
bedrooms."

"Not when they have a whole house."

"Oh, and where do you keep your computer?"

"I'm living on a boat right now. It's in the dining area, by
the galley."

"Where did you keep it when you weren't living on a boat?" she demanded. "Or did you live on a boat in Virginia?"

"No, I had an apartment."

"And where was your computer?"

"*Not* in the bedroom. Okay, suppose you did have a life. Suppose you had someone over, and he was the best thing in the world, the greatest lover since Casanova. And there you are, in heaven beneath the canopy, but you've forgotten and left the damned thing on, and right in the throes of a magical moment you hear not how beautiful you are, you hear 'You've got mail.'"

She stared at him with surprise and indignation, but her lips were twitching as well.

"It could happen," he persisted. "Ah, I see. The greatest lover since Casanova hasn't cruised by yet."

"Maybe he has," she informed him.

"You see the problem, then."

"No. I never forget to turn anything off," she said, then spun and started across the hall. "Don't forget the bathrooms. There are two of them, one in there, one on the other side of the studio."

"Sure. As soon as I've looked under the bed."

There was nothing under the bed. Not even dust.

They were small bathrooms; it was a small house. He dutifully checked behind the shower curtains in each. He should have felt as if he was being intrusive. He didn't. He was fascinated, instead, by this strange insight into her intimate life.

"Hey!"

He had opened a medicine cabinet. She was standing behind him, a steaming cup of coffee in her hand.

A cardboard to-go cup.

"Coffee already?" he said. "That was quick."

"It's a state-of-the-art machine. Thanks for making sure the place was secure. However, I don't think there's an intruder hiding in my medicine chest."

"If you're going to search a place, you might as well make sure it's free of aliens, gremlins—you know."

She lowered her head, smiling. "Right. Well, anyway, thanks. I do feel more secure now."

"No problem." He accepted the cup of coffee, studying it. "I guess I'm leaving."

"You're welcome to sugar and milk first."

"Thanks, I like it black."

"Actually, you're welcome to have a seat. I wouldn't want you to spill it on your lap or anything. Get burned, sue the studio, anything like that."

He leaned against the door for a moment, watching her. Those clear bright eyes were on him. She wasn't touching him in any way, but the electricity seemed to sear right through empty space. There was nothing overtly sexual about her; it was all beneath the surface. But in that subtle manner, she was certainly the most sensual creature he'd ever met. He'd done some teasing before. Now just a glance at the bare flesh of her upper arm created mental visions of other parts of her anatomy, equally bare. Libido was kicking in with a sudden vengeance, as it hadn't since before he'd left his teens.

He swallowed his coffee quickly, heedless of whether he burned his mouth or not. He handed the cup back, his eyes locked with hers.

"I'd better go." The depth of his voice was startling to himself, along with its husky tenor. "If I stayed, it would be fraternizing," he said quickly. "Good night."

"Good night, and thank you," she said.

On the porch, he gave himself a serious mental shake and turned back to her. "Do you think…are you nervous because you don't believe Lara Trudeau's death was accidental?"

"I don't know what you're talking about," she said, but her eyes narrowed, and it was almost as if a mask had slipped over her face.

"You think Lara Trudeau was murdered. If you know something, if you are afraid of something, you've really got to say it, tell the police."

"I talked to the police the day she died," she said flatly. "I never, ever, told anyone I thought Lara had been murdered."

A lie.

Maybe she hadn't said it in so many words, but still…a lie.

"Really? Maybe you should be careful. A lot of people seem convinced you're the main one suggesting Lara didn't pop those pills herself. And if Lara *didn't* just pop those pills—"

"Lara died because she abused a prescription and drank on top of it, Mr. O'Casey. That's what the medical examiner said. And that's all there is to it."

"I'm not the one you need to convince," he said softly. "Make sure you lock your door."

"I always lock my door."

"Good."

He turned and walked to his car, aware that she was still on the porch, watching him.

He turned back. "Now would be a good time to lock it."

She disappeared inside. He could hear the force of it slamming from where he stood on the street.

Smiling, he slid into the driver's seat and twisted his key in the ignition.

Shannon leaned against the door after he had gone. The night had been long. She was so tired it hurt.

She was glad she'd had him in, glad she wouldn't be adding to her ridiculous new paranoia by wondering if someone was hiding in her closet.

And yet...

Damn, he was attractive. She shouldn't find a student so compelling. Maybe she should take a step back. Turn him over to Jane. This was absurd.

Maybe not so absurd. She was twenty-eight. She joked about the fact that she had no life, but...

It was true. She had no life. She saw the same men day after day. Anyone new was a student, and seldom, if ever, had such a student walked into her life.

Most people would think her life was exciting. She danced all day and was guaranteed entry to one of the hottest spots in the city at night. Gabriel was attractive. He'd even asked her out. But Gabriel was a player. He was fun to dance with, and a great man to have as a friend. She would never want anything more with him, though. So this wasn't just a sexual thing, because she did know attractive men.

Just not like this one.

She would never trust a man like Gabriel—he needed too much excitement and variety in his life. And Ben...she had fallen out of love with Ben long ago. He was like a childhood mistake. Sam and Justin were like younger brothers. Sometimes she was mad at them, and sometimes she was proud of them.

It wasn't that no one ever touched her life, or that there weren't possibilities. Just none that had touched her, not in a very long time.

And this man...

Was a liar. He wasn't taking dance lessons just for the hell of it. And he wasn't interested in her just for the hell of it either.

She pushed away from the door. A man like Gabriel was obvious. This guy was more devious.

She suddenly heard something from outside. Like a branch breaking.

She froze against the door, listening. Nothing…no, something. Like footsteps, falling fast and soft, heading from somewhere right by the house out to the street.

And then…

Nothing. She stood there for what felt like forever. She didn't breathe. She didn't move.

And still…

Nothing.

At last she moved away from the door and stared at it. Her throat felt constricted. She tried to reason with herself. If she *had* heard footsteps, they were moving away from the house. And maybe she hadn't really heard steps. There had been a cat out there; it had gotten spooked, and it had run off at high speed. She'd lived in this house for years now. She was in a good neighborhood.

Right. So good she didn't even have an alarm system.

She backed away from her door, staring at it. If she opened it, she was probably an idiot. If she didn't open it just to make sure no one was hanging around the place, she would never get any sleep.

She hesitated for a long time, seconds ticking by, as she stared at the door.

Then she reached for the bolt, slid it, hesitated again and threw the door open.

CHAPTER 8

Back at the marina, Quinn noted the large group of cops still gathered at the patio tables outside Nick's. His brother was among them. He'd thought he was dead tired, ready to call it quits, but on second thought, he headed for the tables.

Dixon wasn't there that night, but Bobby, Giselle and Doug were sitting with Jake Dilessio. Jake greeted him with a wave, drawing out a chair as Quinn approached. At another table, Quinn saw some of the guys he knew who were with narcotics. Waves and casual greetings went around as Quinn sat.

"So, what do you think?" Doug asked. "She looked good, didn't she? Lara, I mean. Even dead. Still beautiful, huh?"

"Yeah, she looked good," Quinn said. His brother had obviously had a few. He looked morose. Okay, so they'd come from a wake. But since Quinn was certain that not even Doug's best friend Bobby knew he'd been sleeping with the deceased, it wasn't like Doug to give himself away like this.

"You've been fraternizing, huh?" Bobby teasingly asked Quinn.

He shrugged. "Not with any intent on the part of Miss Mackay. I'd told her I'd give her a lift, that's all."

"She doesn't know you're a P.I., huh?" Bobby said.

"It's easier to ask questions when people aren't instantly suspicious and defensive," he said.

"Don't worry—I don't intend to mention it," Bobby assured him.

"It's an interesting crowd, isn't it?" Giselle said, smiling. "And it's very strange. You go into the studio, and they're all as friendly as can be. But then, when they come down and dance and have drinks at Suede, you realize that you don't really know any of them. You know, like what they do with their spare time, what makes them tick."

"They don't have spare time," Bobby said. "They dance. The competitors, anyway." He grinned. "You should have been at the championships, Quinn. They change in and out of those outfits in seconds flat. They have to be perfect. There're hairspray cans all over the place. Different shoes, different jewelry. They gush all over each other. Some of them act like they're Gods, and when you listen to them talk, it's as if you walked into a sitcom. Some of them are actually warm and cuddly, as well," he admitted.

"A lot of them are too warm and cuddly." Giselle laughed. "A couple of the gentlemen were a little too impressed with Bobby—if you get my drift."

"If you're talking about sexual orientation," Jake said, leaning forward, half teasing, half serious, "some of the best cops I know are gay."

"I guess," Bobby agreed.

"What are you—homophobic?" Giselle accused.

"Hey! You brought it up."

"Yes, but I'm allowed to. Several of my best friends are of a different persuasion."

"Hey, most of your best friends are my best friends!" Bobby said.

"Trouble in newlywed paradise," Doug moaned. "I gotta take a leak. Stop them if they start to get too crazy, huh?" He rose and walked off, wobbling a little.

"Don't let him drive home," Jake warned Quinn.

"Bobby, he ought to sleep on the boat," Quinn said.

Bobby nodded. "Yeah, I know. He's been kind of weird tonight. A wake isn't any fun, I know, but he's really taking Lara's death to heart. What do you think, Quinn?"

"I haven't had enough time to come to any conclusions," Quinn said. "As far as the actual death went, the M.E. called it as he saw it."

"Hey, O'Casey!" Nick himself stepped out of the bar, bearing the house phone. "Call for you."

"Thanks, Nick."

"Sure thing. Make sure you bring it back in. It'll be the fourth phone I've lost in three months, if you forget," Nick said. "Watch him for me, Jake, huh?"

"Absolutely," Jake promised.

Quinn glared at Jake, shaking his head as he took the receiver. "O'Casey here."

"Hi. I'm sorry to bother you. I had this number in your file, and I accessed it from home. I shouldn't be doing this, calling you like this, taking advantage, but…"

"Shannon?" Quinn said.

"Yes, I'm sorry. I feel like an idiot, but I think there was someone out in my yard. Hanging around the house. I thought maybe you'd know someone who could take a cruise by the house and just look around a little. Or should I just try getting hold of the beach police? You're a cop. What do you think?"

"Shannon, this isn't Doug. It's Quinn."

"Quinn?" Her voice hardened suddenly. "Oh, so you hang around Nick's, too. I thought you weren't a cop?"

"I'm not. They don't require you to be a cop to serve you here. It's a fun place. Have you ever been? No, of course not. I forgot—you don't have a life."

"Funny. Look, never mind. I'm sorry I bothered you. I just thought Doug might have a friend on duty, or...never mind."

Her voice was tight, and she was obviously defensive. He instantly knew what she was thinking. He had just been at her house, just checked it out thoroughly. She was surely thinking that he must think her the most paranoid whiner in the world.

"What happened?" he demanded.

"Nothing."

"So what freaked you out?"

"I..." She hesitated. He thought for a minute that she was going to hang up. He heard a long sigh. "After you left, there was a noise. As if someone had been leaning against the house, listening or something, then ran across the yard. I opened the door—"

"You what?"

"I opened the door."

"Why on earth would you do that?"

"To convince myself there was no one there," she snapped back.

"And?"

"Well, it's dark out, you know."

"Yes, but...?"

"I think someone *had* been there. There was someone moving down the street. Away from the house. Hunched over, in shadow. It's perfectly possible it was just someone walking down the street. And we do have stray cats around here, and it's likely if I'm hearing things, it's one of them. Look, I'm sorry I called. It's just my imagination, I'm certain. A wake tonight, a funeral tomorrow... sorry, really. I'm going to hang up now."

"Don't go to sleep. I'm on my way out."

"No! Don't be ridiculous. It's all right. Really. Don't come back out here."

"I'm on my way," he said, hanging up.

He hit the button to end the call. The three others at the table were staring at him.

"Shannon Mackay. A case of nerves, probably. But I'm going to drive back out. Check things around her place." He set the phone down as he rose. "Bobby, get Doug to sleep on the boat, all right? Jake—"

"I'll see that the phone is returned to the bar," Jake said dryly. "Call if you need anything."

"You bet."

Quinn left them and hurried back to his car.

Shannon paced her living room, swearing to herself, feeling on the one hand like an absolute idiot and then, on the other, wondering how long it would take for Quinn to drive back out to her place.

Why had she opened the door? To assure herself, naturally. She wasn't afraid of the dark—at least, she'd never been afraid of the dark before. She came home late every night of her life, except for Saturdays and Sundays. They were only open mornings on Saturdays, and Sunday the studio was closed. But Monday through Friday, it was usually nearly eleven when she reached her house. She never thought twice about parking her car, hopping out and walking to her door. Sometimes her neighbors were around, walking their dogs in their robes just before bed, throwing out their garbage or recycling, or taking a breather to look at the night sky. It was a friendly area. She had never felt the least threatened before.

With a groan, she sat on the sofa, running her fingers through her hair. This was ridiculous. Lara had died right after a waiter had said to Shannon herself, "You're next."

And since then…

She had once been sane, confident and secure. Life had taken her through a few ups and downs, but she was mature and in charge. She knew she excelled at her chosen profession; she enjoyed the people she worked with; she was meant to take over the reins of the studio. Life was good.

Had been good, even if a little empty.

But then Lara had died.

No, that was just it. She didn't believe that for a minute. Lara *hadn't* just died. And those words… *You're next.* So now…

So now, was it ridiculous to think she was being stalked?

She winced, thinking about her conversation with Jane. Had she let too many people know that, no matter what conclusion the police and the M.E. had come to, she wasn't convinced Lara had brought about her own demise?

There was a noise in the front again. She jumped off the sofa, her heart thundering. She forced herself to walk to the door and stare out the peephole.

She smiled, leaning against the door, actually laughing out loud. Harry—her next-door neighbor's golden retriever—was marking one of the two small palm trees she had recently planted at the front of the walk.

But even as she laughed at herself, a thud against the door brought a scream to her lips.

"Shannon?"

"Idiot, you *are* losing your mind," she whispered to herself, hearing Quinn O'Casey's voice.

"Yes. Hi," she said, unlocking the door and opening it.

"What happened?" he asked sharply. "I heard you scream."

"You knocked," she said ruefully.

"You screamed because I knocked?" he said.

She lowered her head. He must really think she was an idiot.

"Never mind, long story. Hey, you must be sorry Doug bought you those lessons, huh? I swear to you, most dancers are sane."

"I'm here, think you might want to invite me in?"

"Sure, sorry."

He stepped in. "Might as well hear a long story."

"Actually, it's not that long."

"Tell me."

She sighed, suddenly almost as unnerved having him there as she had been when she'd been alone. But for a different reason. Despite the fact that she was wearing a floor-length Victorian nightgown, she felt less dressed than she might have in a bikini. The night was too quiet. He was too close, and the bit of world between them seemed far too intimate.

"It was the dog." She laughed. "I'd better start at the beginning. I guess it's just tonight. The wake and all. It's been a wretched week. Lara wasn't my best friend or anything, but I have known her forever, and her death really was a tragedy. Anyway, I thought I heard something again, so I looked out, and I was just laughing at myself because what I had heard was Harry, the neighbor's dog."

"Big shaggy golden retriever?"

"That's him."

"Anyway, I'd leaned against the door, feeling like an idiot for going into a panic, and then you knocked. You startled me. I screamed. There's absolutely nothing wrong, and I am truly an idiot for having made you come back out here. It's late, you were with friends. I didn't mean to interrupt."

"It's all right. I'm wide-awake. I'll go take a cruise around the house."

"Thanks. Hey, do you want more coffee? Wait, not a good idea—we'd both be up all night. How about tea? Iced tea? Hot tea?"

He hesitated, looking at her.

"Have you got any microwave popcorn?"

She arched a brow. "I think so."

"Have you got a DVD player?"

"Yes."

"Got a movie you've been wanting to see?"

"Actually, I have dozens of movies. I keep buying them and never watching them."

"Throw in some popcorn, make it iced tea and pick a movie. I'll be back." He started to step back out the door, then popped his head back in. "I guess this would definitely be considered fraternization, huh?"

"I'm afraid so," she agreed.

"I could sit on one side of the room, and you could sit on the other. But then again, I'm just temporary, not really a student."

"Yes, you are. You're taking lessons."

"I'm still so bad surely it can't count."

She laughed. "You're not that bad, and it does count, but I don't intend to tell, and I hope you don't, either. If you're sure you don't mind being a baby-sitter for a few hours."

"Dancer-sitter," he said with a shrug. "And since you probably won't have any toes left after me, I'm sure I can afford the hours."

She hated herself for the thrill of absolute happiness she felt.

Quinn woke, aware of voices on the television and daylight filtering in through the windows in the back. It was a gentle awakening. He didn't move at first, simply opened his eyes.

In a few hours, he would be aching all over. He'd fallen asleep in a sitting position, his head twisted downward at an angle. Shannon was next to him, her head on his lap, her knees tucked to her chest, her arms encircling a throw pillow. Tendrils of golden hair were curled over his trousers, and the warmth of her weight against him was both captivating and arousing. Beyond anything, though, the feel of her against him stirred a sudden sense of memory, of nostalgia. He found himself remaining there, thinking of a time when a wealth of both passion and affection had been so easily his, and he had barely noticed, his mind so consumed with his job. And even when it had all slipped away, he hadn't really noticed, because somewhere inside, he had become deadened. And in the weeks and months that had followed, he hadn't wanted anything more than a brief encounter with the gentler sex, moments of human contact and nothing more. The numbness had remained. He hadn't known how to shake it. He'd been walking through life by rote, wondering where he had lost his senses of humanity and need, and his ability to have fun. Then Nell Durken had been found dead. And the numbness had been pierced with fury and impotence and a need to question every facet of life.

And then had come Shannon Mackay.

He was loath to move her. The softness of her hair against his flesh was like a breath of sweet, fresh air. The sight of her hand dangling over his knee. Fingers elegant, nails manicured, flesh so soft. Just the warmth of her, the weight of her, made him want to stay, drown in these sensations. It was this casual, intimate closeness that had been something so lost to him, something he hadn't known he missed, needed or felt a longing for, somewhere deep within.

She wouldn't be happy, of course, that they had fallen asleep and essentially spent the night together. Definitely fraternization.

At last he rose very carefully. As he moved, she stirred slightly, seeking the same comfort she had known against him. He quickly put a throw pillow beneath her head, settled her weight and backed away. The Victorian lace of the gown framed her chin, and her hair spilled everywhere, caught by the light, a splendid halo. The fabric was thin, hugging the length of her ultratoned form. She was supple, curvaceous, and swathed in that Victorian purity, she seemed somehow all the more sensual and vulnerable.

It was time for him to get out.

He walked away, found the jacket he had doffed, turned off the television and headed for the front, through the kitchen. He found a notepad and wrote a few quick lines. "Thanks for the popcorn, tea and movie. It's light, and you're locked in. Quinn."

He walked quietly to the front and exited, making sure he hit the button lock, since he didn't have a key. He checked it twice, then headed for his car and drove away.

The cemetery was even more crowded than the funeral home had been. The dance world had come in high numbers: Lara's students, friends, associates and lovers all came to say their final goodbyes. And once again, there were reporters and news cameras and scores of the curious.

Shannon had a seat next to Gordon in the row of folding chairs arranged on the little piece of green carpet before the coffin. As the priest talked about life on earth and life in the sweet promise of eternity, she bowed her head but found her mind wandering. It seemed a terrible shame to her that so many people had come, because others with loved ones in this cemetery tended to the graves, and their tributes of beautiful flower bouquets had ended up strewn across the landscape, kicked around by the unnoticing mob that had come to attend a "celebrity" funeral.

Lara was going into a spot not far from the mausoleum, surrounded by majestic oaks. A large angel-framed stone nearby honored a family named Gonzalez, while an elegant marble crypt belonged to Antonio Alfredo Machiavelli, who had passed away in the late 1940s.

Birds soared across an amazingly blue and beautiful sky, not touched by so much as a hint of a cloud. She was glad Gordon had planned the ceremony early. In a few hours it would be roasting, whether it was officially autumn or not. Somewhere not far away a bee buzzed. In the distance, she could hear the barking of a dog. A residential neighborhood surrounded most of the cemetery. Children played on the lawns nearby; cars impatiently moved at slower speed limits, and horns honked. Life went on, even on the outskirts of a cemetery—maybe more so on the outskirts of a cemetery.

Someone touched her knee. She lifted her head. Ben Trudeau, grimly passing her a rose to toss onto the coffin. The service was over.

She stood and walked to the grave site, then threw the rose in. Gordon took her elbow, and they walked away from the grave.

"Mr. Henson! Miss Mackay!"

Shannon turned with annoyance to see Ryan Hatfield, a reporter she particularly disliked from a local paper. He was tall and skinny and needed a life worse than she did. When he attended events, he liked to make fun of the amateurs *and* professionals. He'd once written a truly cruel comment on a less-than-slender couple who'd won an amateur trophy in waltz. She'd furiously—and pointlessly—tried to explain to him that people were judged on their steps and the quality of their dance, and that for amateurs, dance was fun, and it was also excellent exercise. As far as professionals went, according to him, they were all affected, ridiculous snobs who looked down their noses at anyone with a new twist to anything. In response, she'd pointed out the different categories of dance, even the subcategories. He'd printed her explanation and still made her sound like an affected witch, living in a make-believe world.

"What do you want?" she asked sharply, before Gordon could speak.

"Come on, just a few words," Hatfield said.

"So you can twist them?" she asked.

"Lara was an acknowledged goddess in the world of ballroom dance. How are you feeling?" Ryan demanded, sounding as if he were actually sympathetic.

"How the hell do you think we feel?" she demanded angrily. "She died far too young. It was tragic. What do you think people feel? *Pain.* It's a loss. Now, if you'll excuse us, please?"

"Where are you going? Are you all getting together somewhere? I didn't hear the priest invite the crowd back anywhere," Ryan persisted.

"The wake was open to the public, as the funeral was," Gordon said firmly. "Now it's a private time for those who knew her. Come on, Shannon."

With Gordon's arm around her shoulder, she started for the limousine, but Ryan's words followed her. "Look at that, will you? Ben Trudeau, still standing at the grave. She divorced his ass a long time ago, huh?"

Shannon couldn't remember feeling such deep-seated fury in a long time. She was afraid she was going to lash out, lose control, hurl herself at the reporter with teeth and nails bared, and take out all her concerns, frustrations and, yes, *fears* on the man.

But when she turned, he wasn't alone. Both O'Casey brothers were there, flanking Hatfield, ready to escort him away.

"What on earth are you doing?" the reporter demanded indignantly. "Let me go this minute or I'll go to the police. I'll have you sued until you have to sell the clothes off your back. I have the cops on speed dial."

"I *am* a cop," Doug said flatly.

"Let's go," Gordon said, taking Shannon's arm.

"Go," Quinn said to her.

"Hey, this is like kidnapping or something," Ryan complained.

"They might want to charge you with harrassment," Doug said.

Shannon didn't hear any more. Gordon was moving; he had her arm, so she was moving, too. In another minute, she was in the limo.

Just before the door closed, they were joined by Ben Trudeau. He shook his head as he stared out the window.

"Fucking reporters," he muttered.

"Ben," Gordon admonished quietly.

"There aren't any students around," Ben said distractedly.

"It's still—" Gordon began.

"It's a rat-shit day. Leave him alone, please," Shannon put in.

The limo moved out of the cemetery. Ben looked downward between his hands, then up, letting out a long breath. "It's real. She's really gone. Into the ground. I don't believe it."

Gordon set an arm around his shoulders. "Yeah, it's hard to accept."

You're next.

The memory of the words came to Shannon with a sharp chill. She shivered.

Ben looked past Gordon, who was in the middle. "I'm sorry, Shannon. Are you all right?"

"Of course. I'm fine."

He looked out the window again thoughtfully. "Interesting. That stinking rag writer would have driven us all nuts. I guess it's a good thing we have one of the county's finest

among our students. Doug. You know, though, his brother
is the one who saw the guy and went after him first. Are we
sure he's not a cop? He's in awful tight with them."

"No, he's not a cop. Maybe he was once, but not anymore," Shannon said.

"He still acts like one," Ben noted.

"What do you mean?" Gordon demanded.

Ben shrugged. "I don't know. He's always…watching.
You know, I was at lunch yesterday, and he was in the same
café. In the back…"

Gordon shrugged. "I run into people all over town. At the
bank, at the movies, wherever."

"Yeah, I guess you're right. Hey, is he coming to this
thing?"

"No. I didn't ask any of the students. Only some of the
pros Lara worked with, and the people from our building."
Gordon pressed a hand to his forehead. "The public had the
wake and the funeral. Time to be alone."

The spot he had chosen for the after-funeral tribute was
a small place on Lincoln Road where they'd gone many
times for special occasions. Gordon had kept the attendance
down to about twenty.

They gathered around four tables, and Gordon gave his
personal eulogy to Lara. Then Ben spoke, and, to Shannon,
his emotions seemed honest. He spoke of their relationship
as passionate and sometimes as emotionally violent as the
dances she had performed, but said in the end that her spirit
was one that had touched them all, and that their loss was
tremendous. They would all remember things she had told
them—bluntly, at times, but each and every word one that
would make them better at their craft, their vocation, the
dancing that was not just work but part of their very being.

Shannon was glad to see that the people who attended
included not just friends from the area but all over the

country and even from Europe. She agreed again to see Gunter during the week, but broke away when he told her she created the best choreography he'd ever seen and they were all lucky she didn't use it for herself—but she should.

At one point she found herself talking with Christie Castle, five time National Smooth Champion, and now both a coach and a judge at competitions around the world.

"How are you holding up?" Christie asked her. Christie was slender as a reed, about five-five, with huge dark eyes and ink-black hair. Her age was indeterminate, but at ninety, she was still going to be beautiful.

"Fine. It's a shattering event, but Lara and I didn't hang out," Shannon reminded her.

"Gordon says you've been nervous lately." She lowered her voice. "And your receptionist told me that you're convinced there's more going on than we know."

"Ella shouldn't have said anything to you."

"Do you really think Lara might have been murdered?"

Shannon noticed that Christie was whispering. Gordon, Ben, Justin, Sam Railey and several others were right behind them. Shannon thought that Ben turned slightly, as if he were more interested in what they were saying than in the conversation in which he was taking part.

"I don't really think anything," Shannon said.

Christie set a hand on her knee, dark eyes wide with concern. "You look really tired. Are you sleeping all right?"

Last night, ten minutes after the movie had started, Shannon had been sound asleep, but that had been the first time in a week she had really slept.

"Not really. I don't know why. I'm just a little tense."

"You need a dog," Christie said, nodding sagely.

Shannon smiled, looking downward. Christie had Puff, a teacup Yorkie. The little dog went everywhere with her. In fact, Puff probably had more airline mileage stacked up than most CEOs.

"Christie, I'm gone almost fifteen hours a day. And honestly, if I had a little Puff, and someone was after me…"

"Excuse me, he may be small, but Puff has a killer bark."

"What's that about a killer bark?"

Gabriel Lopez slid into the seat next to Christie. He had a look in his eyes, a flirtatious look. He never actually leered. He had a way of looking at a woman that simply indicated total appreciation and therefore managed not to be offensive.

"Puff, of course," Christie said.

He laughed. "I thought that you were referring to killer cute and meant me."

"Thankfully, Gabriel, neither of us is foolish enough to take you seriously. We're both well aware that you've dated every single celebrity who has ever come to town. And then some," Christie told him.

"Not true!" he protested. With a shrug, he smiled ruefully. "You know, there's an image a club owner needs to keep up."

Ben had apparently tired of the conversation behind them. He slid into the empty chair on Shannon's other side. "You seem to keep it up okay," he assured Gabriel, grinning at his own double entendre.

"And what about you? As charming as Fred Astaire, with women ready to follow your every step." He spoke lightly, but then his face changed slightly. "I'm so sorry, Ben."

"We're all sorry. I guess we have to accept it." Ben stared at Shannon. "God knows we've got the students to set our minds at rest. Doug O'Casey admired Lara, and he's in a position to make sure the police checked out every possibility."

"Ah, yes, the young patrolman," Gabriel murmured. "He watched her like a puppy dog. You could tell he hated it when she danced with others, and he looked as if he'd died and gone to heaven when she danced with him."

"He's a terrific student," Christie said. "She certainly made a difference for him."

"Jane is his instructor, and she's excellent," Shannon put in.

"Yes, but he signed up for a lot of coaching sessions, didn't he?" Christie asked. "I understand he signed up for half the day when Lara was around." She shrugged as she looked at Shannon. "She was still competing and I'm not. That makes a difference to some people."

"Interesting," Ben noted.

"What?" Christie asked him.

"It's so expensive…paying for coaching when you're an amateur. And Doug is just a patrolman. Where do you think he got the money?" Ben mused.

"Dirty cop?" Gabriel said.

"Hey!" Shannon protested.

"Well, he has spent a lot of money at the studio, right?" Ben said.

"Maybe he has family money," she suggested.

"Well, maybe. And now his brother's there. He says he's not a cop, that he runs charters or fishing boats, or something," Ben said.

"Maybe he's a drug lord with a great cover," Gabriel suggested.

"Who's a drug lord?"

They had been joined by Jim Burke, Lara's last partner. He looked like hell. Shannon had the feeling he'd spent the week crying. His hazel eyes were red rimmed. He was in a sleek suit and a subdued blue tailored shirt, but he looked haggard despite the fact that his clothing was immaculate.

"Shannon's new student," Christie said. "Not really—we were just speculating."

"He runs a charter business," Shannon told Jim. She smiled at him. "You all right?"

"Yeah, yeah, I'm doing fine. Feeling a little lost, but... I should be getting ready for Asheville. The competition there. Lara and I were signed up for it. Instead..."

"Take some time," Shannon suggested.

"I can't afford to take too much time," he murmured. "I don't have Lara's deep pockets. I survived on the purses from our winnings most of the time."

"You'll get a new partner," Christie told him.

"Yeah," Ben muttered.

Christie turned to Shannon. "Someone should be cultivating Doug Quinn. I know he's on the police force, but that young man could have a career in professional dance."

"Maybe he likes having a life," Jim muttered.

"And he'd have to go back to making zilch if he wanted to teach, so he could spend time getting the training he'd need," Gabriel pointed out.

"Maybe his drug-dealing brother could help him out," Ben muttered.

Shannon groaned. "Oh, please. Maybe everything is just what it seems. Come on. We're all going to be ripped to shreds in the papers tomorrow—let's not do it to ourselves." She stood. "Excuse me, you all. I think this has been the longest week in history. Christie, you'll be down for at least a week before the Gator Gala, right?" She wanted to kick herself the minute the words were out of her mouth. This was the last tribute to Lara, and she was bringing up business.

"Hey, how about me?" Ben asked her.

"Of course, Ben. We'd love to bring you in to coach," she told him.

Gabriel stood. "You came in the limousine?" he asked her.

"Yes."

"I'll give you a ride home. I need to get to work."

"Great, thanks," she said. She walked around the table,

saying her goodbyes, kissing cheeks. Leaving always took awhile—they were an affectionate group. It was like leaving an Italian family dinner.

"I'm sorry, I had a lot of goodbyes," she told Gabriel when they at last exited into the late afternoon.

"It's all right. I like following you around," Gabriel said. "Everyone kisses me."

She laughed. "You're so full of it. Everyone walks into your club and kisses you, too."

He shrugged. "It's a good life. I work hard, but it is a good life. Don't you feel that way?"

"Yes, of course. I absolutely love what I do."

"But it doesn't leave room for much else. At least," he teased, "what I do is social."

"Oh, come on. You can't get much more social than dancing."

"But you put up walls. I don't."

She laughed suddenly. "What is this? All of a sudden everyone has decided that they have to be my psychoanalyst. I'm fine."

He arched a brow. "Everyone is telling you this?"

She shook her head, suddenly not wanting to tell him it was her brand-new student—Quinn, the cop's brother, the one they were teasingly suggesting might be a drug lord—who had made a similar observation.

"Never mind. There's my house."

He let out a sound of mock disgust. "I know where your house is."

He pulled up in front and started to get out. For Gabriel, it was natural. A man opened a door for a lady.

"Gabe, I'm fine," she said, reaching for the door handle.

"Hey, you taught me—in dance, a man always leads. I will teach you that, in life, that same man likes to open doors for a lady and walk her to her door."

She laughed. "Okay, Gabe."

He came around and opened the car door, taking her hand in an elaborate show of attention. "If you had any sense, you'd fall madly in love with me. We'd rule the world."

"I have plenty of sense, and that's why I'll never fall madly in love with you. And I don't want the responsibility of ruling the world." She slipped the key into her lock and opened the door, then turned to say goodbye.

"You could still invite me in. We'd be two lonely souls making wild passionate love on a stolen afternoon so that we could go back to our all-business lives with secret memories of what might have been," he said.

"Gabriel, that's the biggest crock I've ever heard."

"Okay, but it would still be fun, huh?"

"I'm sure there are dozens of women out there who would willingly give you an afternoon," she assured him.

"They don't have your body."

"Thanks. I think."

"I've got it. You're already having a secret affair with someone."

"No, I'm afraid not."

"Then come on. My body is pretty good, too."

"Gabriel, you're practically perfect in every way."

"Then why not?"

"You're my friend. I want to keep it that way."

"Okay. Want to go to a movie?"

She burst out laughing again. "You know, that would be fun. Ask me again. But not today. It's just been far too long a week. And, hey, I thought you had to go to work."

"I'd call in sick for you." He sighed. "All right. Spend your lonely Saturday night by yourself."

"Thanks for the ride, Gabriel."

He swept her a little bow and gave her a mocking grin. "Any time. Goodbye. Lock up, now."

She nodded. As he walked down the path to his car, she noted that it had gone from dusky to dark. She wished it was summer. She loved it when the daylight hours extended late.

After closing and locking the door, she hesitated. The shadows had invaded the house. She walked around, turning on all the lights in a sudden flurry. Better.

Ridiculously, she had another creepy feeling. Not creepy enough to make her wish she had invited Gabe in, but uncomfortable.

There was, she thought, absolutely nothing in her house that resembled a weapon. Until recently she had never been afraid in her own home.

The best she could come up with was one of her old tennis rackets. Brandishing it in one hand, she began a methodic check of the house.

Beyond a doubt, it was empty.

She sat down in the back, staring at the TV, despite the fact that it was off. The room was bright. The back windows were large, looking out on her little bit of yard. It was rich with foliage. She suddenly realized that if you were worried about people looking in at you, it wasn't smart to have bright lights on inside, darkness outside and the draperies opened. She jumped up to close the drapes.

As she did so, she thought she saw a flash of movement through the trees.

No.

She *did* see it.

Palms bent, bushes swayed. And a sense of cold deeper than any fear she had ever known coursed through her veins.

He watched and cursed himself.

Close call.

Close call? No, not really. She wouldn't have come out into the yard. And if she had…?

Pity.

But she was nervous. Really nervous. Why? Because she just didn't believe? The little fool. What the hell did she owe Lara Trudeau? Why should she care?

But she wasn't giving up. Everyone talked about the way Shannon kept insisting that Lara hadn't accidentally done herself in. Was it because she knew Lara?

Or because she knew something else?

He stared at the house for a moment longer. Then he turned, disappearing silently around the back. He knew the house well. There was no alarm. If it was ever necessary...

He paused, looking back.

Let it go, Shannon, he thought.

Let it go.

Or...

You'll be next.

CHAPTER 9

Quinn rubbed his forehead and looked over his notes. Students, teachers, competitors. Possibilities, motives. He had a sheet with the names of everyone who had attended the competition, and there were hundreds of names on it. Many, of course, he had come to know.

He had started a list himself. Similarities, dissimilarities. The death of Nell Durken, the death of Lara Trudeau. Nell, her death classified a homicide. Lara, her death classified an accident, an overdose, self-inflicted.

Two different physicians, both of them respected in their fields, their prescriptions for the tranquilizers perfectly legitimate, proper dosages duly specified. Nell's husband had been caught cheating. His fingerprints had been all over her bottle of pills.

Lara had been drinking as well as pill popping. She had still managed to go out on the dance floor and perform perfectly—until she had dropped. Nell had taken classes at the studio but had quit six months before her death. There had to be a connection, but what? Nell's husband was in jail. And even if someone had killed Lara because she was competition, why would they have killed Nell? Say Ben Trudeau was the one who'd done Lara in—what on earth would be his connection with Nell? Teachers didn't just off students and make it appear that their husbands had done the deed.

He groaned, having spent the afternoon on a paper chase that went in circles. He glanced at the clock, wishing Gordon Henson and Ben Trudeau hadn't chosen to make their after-service get-together a private one. Someone had a key to this. And it was someone associated with the studio, he was certain.

Water lapped against the boat. He glanced at his watch and noted that the day had gone to dark.

Laughter filtered to him from the restaurant and bar.

Hell, he needed a beer. And maybe his brother or some of the other guys were at Nick's.

His brother, who had gotten him into this.

Impatiently he rose.

He was getting obsessive again.

Doug had better be there, he thought. His brother owed him. Leaving things as they lay, he left the boat.

Shannon stared out the window as time ticked by. Then, at last, she gritted her teeth and arched her back, unknotting her shoulders.

"This is so ridiculous," she said aloud to herself. "Why would anyone run around my yard night after night, staring in?"

If someone really wanted to break in, they would have done so already.

And yet...

She could have sworn that, last night, she had left the porch light on. How had it gotten off?

"Right. Someone broke into my house, touched nothing

at all, but turned the porch light off. Sure," she muttered, her words seeming ridiculously loud in the quiet of the house.

She suddenly, and desperately, wanted to get out. She didn't want to be alone, which was absurd. She loved her house, loved her quiet time. Loved nights alone when she worked on steps on her own little dance floor. And, sad as it might seem, she did like those moments when she threw a bag of microwave popcorn in, then caught up on a movie on DVD, since it seemed she never quite made it to a theater.

But not tonight.

On a sudden whim, she raced into the bedroom and quickly changed into more casual attire. She didn't know where she was going, or at least didn't realize where until she got out to her car.

She could have gone to the club. Gabriel would always find her a place, and she might find her friends there. But she wasn't going to the club. A strange idea had actually been brewing in her mind throughout the past several minutes.

There had been so many questions that day. And suppositions. So...

Exactly what was the real story with Quinn O'Casey?

He wasn't a drug lord. She couldn't believe that. Way too far-fetched.

But...

Neither was he what he claimed to be. She was sure of that.

She started to drive, not even sure where Nick's was.

"Wouldn't happen. Would never happen. You can just tell," Doug was saying.

He was sitting across from Bobby. The two of them were alone at the table, remnants of the fish and chips they had eaten pushed to one corner. Doug had an iced tea; Bobby had a beer.

"I don't see why not," Bobby said. "The guy needs a partner." Bobby looked up and saw Quinn coming toward them. "Hey. Are you joining us?"

"Yep." Quinn sat down. A girl named Mollie was working the patio that night. She waved to him. "Miller, please," he called to her. "You're buying," he told Doug.

Doug grimaced. "Sure."

Quinn looked at Bobby. "What wouldn't happen?"

"Shannon. She'd never dance with Ben Trudeau."

"She dances with him at the studio, doesn't she?" Quinn asked.

"Bobby is talking professionally," Doug said.

"She doesn't compete at all, does she?" Quinn asked. Mollie brought his beer, and he gave her a thanks, then stared at the other two.

"No. She did once, though. And according to a few of the conversations I overheard at the wake, she was great. Maybe better than Lara," Bobby told him.

"I watched the tape," Quinn said. "I saw Sam and Jane out there, but no one else from the studio."

"Ben hasn't competed since his last partner got married and decided to have a baby," Doug said. "He's been looking for a new partner for about two years."

"But he's been back at the studio working for a while, too, right?" Quinn asked.

"About a year, I believe," Bobby said.

"So why would Shannon suddenly dance with him now? He wasn't with Lara anymore, anyway," Quinn said.

Bobby looked at Doug. "You never filled him in on Shannon's past, huh?"

"No, he didn't," Quinn said, irritated as he stared at his brother. Doug had gotten him involved. He shouldn't have left out any information that might have been pertinent.

"When she was younger, Shannon was nuts about Ben,"

Bobby said. "He's the one who found her. She was working some small professional gigs and teaching in a little mom-and-pop place up in the Orlando area. He saw her potential, and whether they started an affair and he brought her down, or he brought her down and then they started an affair, I'm not sure. What we know is really gossip, of course, because I only went for lessons about six months ago—getting ready for Randy's wedding and of course my own— and then I dragged your brother in right after that. But anyway, some of the people there have been taking lessons for years, and they talk. Anyway, one night when I was watching Ben and Shannon do a waltz together, I said something about how incredible they looked together. It was old Mr. Clinton, I think, who said 'Well hell, they should look great together. They competed together for two years.' Then Shannon had broken her ankle. Lara had been hanging around, and the next thing you knew…well, Shannon needed a lot of therapy, and Ben wasn't about to wait around for her to get better. He started working with Lara. Then…"

"Then they wound up married," Doug said flatly.

Quinn stared at Doug. "Suppose," he said evenly, "something involving foul play did happen to Lara Trudeau. Shannon Mackay might be a prime suspect. Jealousy, passion, anger—the motives are all there."

Doug shook his head. "All you have to do is meet Shannon, speak to her once, and you know she's not a killer."

"The right motives are there, Doug," Quinn said irritably. He didn't think Shannon Mackay could be a killer, either. If she were, she also had to be the best actress in the universe. But then again, murder often proved that all things were possible.

"Hell, everybody had a motive. We all know that," Doug said, sounding a little defensive. "Most women hated Lara— she was gorgeous."

"Wait a minute," Bobby protested. "All women do not hate all other women who are gorgeous."

"You sure?" Doug asked. A slow smile was curving his lips.

"Yes, I'm sure," Bobby said.

"Did Giselle teach you to say that?"

"Bite me," Bobby told him.

"Hey," Quinn protested.

"Okay, seriously?" Bobby said. "She was competition, sure. But they're all competition for each other. Most people don't kill people just because they're in competition with them."

"Ah, but let's see, Jane has gone up against her dozens of times—and lost," Doug said. "Half of the professional dancers out there have gone up against Lara—and lost. That creates hundreds of suspects."

Quinn shook his head. "Whoever did it had to be there that night."

"True," Doug agreed. "And they would have had to figure out how to force all that stuff into her without her protesting, saying anything to anyone…ah, hell. Maybe she did just take too much stuff. I keep thinking that I knew her. Maybe I didn't."

"What about Gordon Henson?" Quinn asked, taking a swig of his beer.

"Lara was kind of a cash cow for Gordon. A prize—even if she could be just as bitchy to him as she was to everyone else," Bobby said.

"Ben could easily have had a motive," Quinn said.

"You bet," Doug agreed, and it sounded as if he was growing angry. "In fact, they argued a lot."

"Really?" Bobby said. "I've never seen *any* of them argue."

"They're not allowed to argue in the studio. But I went

back to get coffee one day, and they were both there. Though they shut up when they saw me, I heard him speaking really sharply to her, and she said something like, 'In your dreams, asshole,' to him."

Quinn's chair was facing the pathway that led around to the patio from the parking lot. Glancing up, he was amazed to see Shannon Mackay—in form-hugging jeans, a tube top and an overshirt—walking tentatively along the trail to the back tables. "I don't believe it," he breathed.

"Why don't you believe it? I'm telling you the truth," Doug said irritably.

He glared at his brother. "No. I don't believe that Shannon Mackay is here. Now."

Both Bobby and Doug swung around. At the same time, she saw them. She looked startled at first, then waved. Bobby waved back, beckoning her over.

She approached the table, smiling. She kissed Doug and Bobby on the cheek, then got to Quinn. Her fingers felt cold and tense on his shoulders. Her lips brushed his face with less than affection. Her smile, he thought, was insincere. Yet her scent, and the way she felt, brushing against him...

"This is a surprise," he said. "A real surprise. I thought your group was all tied up with itself this evening."

She looked intently at him, then shrugged. "I needed to get away. I know too many people on the beach, though, and I'd heard everybody talk about this place, so..."

"So here you are. Running into us," Quinn said flatly.

"Uh, yeah," she murmured.

"Quinn, man, that was rude," Doug said, glaring at him. "Sit down, join us. I mean, I know you're not supposed to hang around with students, but hell you're the boss. And this is definitely a strange occasion, huh?"

"Yeah, I guess it's a strange occasion," she agreed, taking the fourth chair at the table.

"Are you hungry?" Bobby asked her. "The fish is as fresh as it gets. And the burgers are good, too. Or are you a vegetarian? Jane is, right?"

"Jane is a vegetarian. I'm a carnivore. I think a burger sounds great," she said.

"Hey, Mollie!" Bobby started to turn around, but Mollie was already there.

"Hi," she said cheerfully. "What can I get you?"

"Iced tea, please," Shannon said, smiling. "And a hamburger."

"Cheese?"

"Plain, thanks."

"Fries okay? Or would you prefer slaw."

"The fries are wonderful here, too," Doug said.

"Fries."

"You sure you want tea?" Bobby asked her. "You look as if you could use a drink."

She smiled. "I think I could use a lot of drinks. But I drove."

Quinn leaned forward. "Have a drink. You can leave your car here. I can drive you home and get you tomorrow so you can pick it back up."

She was going to say no, he was certain. That would constitute much more than an accidental meeting between a teacher and some students at a restaurant.

"We won't have to talk while I drive," he teased. "I swear, I won't fraternize. Well, unless you fraternize first."

"I can't, I mean I really shouldn't."

"Oh, have the damn beer," Mollie piped in, then grinned. "Sorry, I guess I've worked here too long. I just thought I should solve this thing. Honey, I don't know the situation, but you do look like you need a drink. This one here…" She paused, pointing at Bobby. "He's a newlywed, not dangerous in the least. I'd swear it on a stack of Bibles. And these two…well, if they say they'll get you home safe and sound, they'll do it."

Shannon had looked surprised at first, almost offended. But by the time Mollie finished speaking, she was laughing. "Great. Bring me a beer. Something on draft, and very big."

"You got it," Mollie told her, and moved on.

"I get to pick up the tab, though," Shannon said firmly. "I owe you guys, after this morning."

"After this morning?" Doug said.

"The reporter," Quinn reminded him. "That guy is a real pain in the ass."

"His paper has been sued a dozen times," Shannon assured him. She sat back in her chair, looking around. "Great place," she murmured. "It's so rustic—and nice."

"Dancers are used to white tablecloths and diners in gloves and beaded gowns, huh?" Quinn asked.

"I seldom leave home without my beads, you bet," she said seriously. "I wasn't taking a crack at your special place. I like rustic. I live on the beach. My favorite vacation spot is the islands. This patio is outside, and there are boats and oil and fish all over the place down on the pier, and it's still unbelievably clean. I'm not sure I could manage that."

"Nick is a great guy," Doug said. "He runs a tight ship."

"And it's a big cop hangout, huh?" she said.

She was definitely after something, Quinn decided.

"His niece is a cop. Married to another cop," Bobby said. He stood abruptly, looking uncomfortable. "Thanks very much for dinner, Shannon. I'll let you buy, since we did invest pretty heavily to look good for the wedding."

She grinned. "And you two *did* look good."

"Yeah, we did. Thanks again for dinner. Since I'm still pretty much a newlywed, I've probably hung out long enough. Night, all."

He received a chorus of good-nights in turn, not just from their table, but from others. As he left, Mollie returned with Shannon's meal.

Shannon thanked her and bit in, chewed, then said, "Wow, this is a great burger."

"Naturally," Doug told her. "We wouldn't lie."

"No?" she said, smiling. Doug looked at her gravely and shook his head.

"You nervous to be at your house?" Quinn asked her abruptly.

"Nervous? No," she said quickly.

"Why would she be nervous at her own house?" Doug asked.

"No reason," she assured him.

"Everybody's nervous now and then," Quinn said. "Houses creak. Especially old houses with old floorboards."

"What's it like living on a boat?" Shannon asked. "You have one up here, right? Isn't that what you said?"

He pointed down to the pier. "She's right there."

"You should see her," Doug said. "Sweetest little thing in the bay."

Quinn glared across the table at his brother.

"I'd love to see your boat," Shannon said.

"Would you?" Quinn murmured. She was nervous, he thought. She wanted company and had actually chosen him. He rose abruptly. "Let me take a look at her first, then—pick up a little."

"Don't be silly. I don't want you to go to any bother," she told him.

"I'll just take a peek and see if the place is presentable. Doug, don't even think about leaving Miss Mackay until I get back."

"Hey, no problem."

Quinn left them at the table, ready to strangle his own

brother. Doug had forced him into the game and hadn't given him the full deck.

He hurried down the pier to his boat and jumped aboard, quickly heading into the cabin. The tape of Lara Trudeau's last performance was sitting on the counter between the galley and dining area. His files, with the copies of the autopsy reports on Nell Durken and Lara Trudeau and various other papers, were next it. He quickly stashed them in one of the cabinets by the small desk. Taking a quick look around, he ascertained that he'd left out nothing else incriminating.

Incriminating? Shit! If she'd seen that stuff, she would have been furious.

He went topside again, leaped to the pier and hurried back to Nick's patio. Shannon hadn't lied when she'd said she wasn't a vegetarian—she'd consumed everything on the plate. Apparently she didn't starve herself to stay so perfectly in shape. But then again, in her line of work, she must burn energy by the barrel.

"Am I allowed to see the sacred ground now?" she teased.

"It's still not great, but…hey." He arched a brow. "You're sure you won't be fraternizing if you come to my boat?"

She'd finished her beer, as well. She looked more relaxed than he'd ever seen her. "I'm coming to see if you're capable of arranging the charter I need for my get-together before the Gator Gala."

Doug rose. "If you'll excuse me, I've seen the boat. And I'm on at eight tomorrow morning, which means I try to get into the station by seven. Good night, and, Shannon, thanks for dinner."

"My pleasure, Doug," she said, rising as well.

Quinn realized she had apparently paid the bill in his absence.

"You really didn't have to pick up all our dinners," he told her.

She flashed a smile. "You were really cheap dates, and I was glad of the company. Besides, I didn't pay for *your* dinner. Just a beer. You didn't eat."

He smiled. "I just came out and found those two talking. I ate in."

"You cook?"

"Not a lot, but enough to survive. I'm not bad. And you?"

"I'm pure gourmet."

"Really?"

"No, I'm horrible. But I can manage the basics, like boiling pasta and heating sauce. And hey, can I break a head of lettuce!"

She spoke lightly as they walked along the pier. He glanced at her. It was almost as if a wall had come down.

One beer. And she hadn't really wanted that. He had a feeling she didn't drink very often.

"Lettuce is good," he murmured. "Well, here we are."

She was wearing sneakers and easily leaped the foot that separated the dock from the boat. On deck, she looked around, closing her eyes briefly as she felt the night's breeze. "She's lovely," Shannon said.

"Cabin is that way," he told her, pointing. "Pretty obvious, huh?"

She nodded and turned toward the steps leading down to the cabin.

"Tight, but oddly spacious," she told him.

"There are two bedrooms, one forward, one aft. Galley, as you can see, and the head is there, on the left, right before the master bedroom. She's not all that small, but then again, on a boat, a tour is pretty quick," he said dryly, then switched topics, hoping to surprise her into an honest answer. "You're afraid to be at your house, aren't you?"

"No!" she protested quickly. She turned as if she were inspecting the inside of the cabin. "No, I came home before it was too late." She glanced at him wryly. "I did the inspection thing myself, looking under beds and in closets and all."

"So you just wanted to get out and have some fun?"

"Yes."

"Well, have a seat."

There was a small sofa, which could be used as a sleeper, across from the dining table. She gingerly sat.

"Can I get you something?"

"No, thanks."

"Well, then, excuse me, I'll get myself something."

He walked the few steps into the galley and got a Miller out of the small refrigerator. On second thought, he took two, twisting the top off one and handing it to her.

"Really, I'm fine," she said.

"Really, you need to relax. Forget the last week."

She hesitated, then took the bottle from him. "Thanks," she said, and shrugged. "You're driving."

He sat down next to her, watching her as he sipped his own beer. "So, you do own a pair of jeans."

"Actually, I own several."

"They weren't in your closets."

"You didn't go through my drawers."

"True."

She was downing the beer a little fast, especially for a woman who had originally refused a drink. But it was nice to see her without the guard that was customarily so carefully wrapped around her. Not a guard that repelled—she was warm and friendly with people; he'd seen it. It was a guard that kept something back. He wondered if it would have been there if he'd met her before Lara's death.

Tonight the smiles she flashed were genuine, warm. And despite her casual attire, he didn't think she'd ever been more appealing. The color of her hair was like wheat touched with gold. Her eyes flashed with a true emerald depth. Her skin was pure ivory, barely touched by the sun. Smooth, silken. And that scent she wore…

He should move. He didn't want to. And suddenly he wasn't sure why he should. He was tempted to reach out, smooth back a lock of that golden hair, so he did. She looked at him, startled by the touch.

"Sorry, you look a little lost there."

"Oh, I'm not lost. I know where I'm going," she murmured.

"Why didn't you tell me you'd had a thing with Ben Trudeau?"

She stiffened instantly, looking as if she was about to rise and find her own way home.

"Hey…" He gently laid a hand on her shoulder. "Innocent question."

"Really? And none of your business," she said.

"Sorry. I guess I just heard the talk about it."

"Oh, great, so people are talking about it. It was a long time ago."

"You might have mentioned it."

She stared at him, and her gemstone eyes were hard. "Why should I have mentioned it? It's not as if we've suddenly become deep friends."

He shrugged. "I guess you're right."

"I don't remember you sitting on my couch spilling secrets about your love life," she said.

He smiled, almost laughing. "Shannon, you fell asleep ten minutes after I sat on your couch. By the way, though, I did enjoy the movie."

She blushed, staring across the room. "Sorry. It was nice of you to stay. You're being awfully decent. I really don't want anyone else to know how ridiculously paranoid I've gotten."

"So you *were* nervous at your house. Why?"

She shook her head. "No reason. Well, all right. I thought I saw something moving in the backyard. And being scared of that is kind of ridiculous. There's the neighbor's dog. And we've got cats aplenty in the neighborhood. And now and then a possum or a raccoon. I know I'm being ridiculous. I just can't seem to help it."

"It's all right," he said.

"I'm sorry. I'm probably keeping you from something," she said.

"I offered to drive you home."

"Yes, you did. Still…"

"I'm not married and not involved," he said flatly.

"I didn't ask for that information."

"You said I hadn't told you anything."

"Only because you sounded as if I should have told you about Ben. Why would you think that?"

"No reason, I guess."

She looked at the empty beer in her hand, then at him. "One more. Then I'll sleep like the dead when I get home." She winced. "I'll sleep well, I mean."

He took the empty bottle from her, walked to the galley and got her another. "You're sure?"

"I'm twenty-eight, and I'm sure."

"I don't want you saying I took advantage of you because you'd been drinking."

Her brows arched and she looked down, a little smile teasing at her lips. "You're planning on taking advantage of me?"

"There's nothing planned," he told her. He handed her the new beer and sat next to her. "Okay, sorry, I have to ask. The Ben Trudeau thing is really over?"

She looked irritated. "Years over. I can't believe anyone even brought it up."

"He sounds like a real jackass, but he's working for you. Why?"

She shrugged. "He's good at what he does. I don't hate Ben."

"Did you hate Lara?"

She laughed suddenly. "That would be kind of like hating a bee for having a stinger. I didn't particularly like her. Like I said, we didn't hang out, have lunch or go shopping. But I admired her talent. I even felt sorry for Ben when she broke up with him." She hesitated a minute. "Ben is a really good dancer. Their problems were professional, at first. Ben started getting angry with the way they worked—it was her way or the highway, that kind of thing. The fights spilled over into their marriage, and she walked out. Jim Burke was a perfect partner for Lara. He let her lead. Well, you know, men lead, but…he let her call all the shots, so they worked well together."

"You must have been angry when he walked out on you—all because of a broken ankle."

"I was too young to be really angry. Too naive. He was long gone before I ever realized he'd reached the door. But, like I said, it was ages ago. Whatever our differences, Ben gave me my life, and I love my life. Mostly. He brought me down here. I started working in Gordon's studio, and now I manage the place. I'm the heir apparent to own it, when he decides to retire." She looked at him, grinning. "And now Ben works for me. So…your turn. What about your love life?"

"She left me," he said lightly.

"Why?"

"I was a workaholic."

"But you don't seem to be. Not now. In fact, it seems as if you have tons of leisure time."

He took a long swallow of his own beer. "Not always,"

he said, not looking at her. "It's slow right now in the Keys, won't pick up until we're closer to real winter. You know, when all the snowbirds fly down."

"Oh, right, of course." She was looking at him, intently. "Were you bitter?"

"Bitter?"

"About being left."

He stared at his bottle. "No…she was right to leave."

"Why?"

"I'd let too many things get in the way. I can get obsessive, I'm afraid."

"An obsessive workaholic," she murmured, still studying him carefully. "But you are here, whiling away the time with a silly woman who's nervous because of a cat in her backyard."

He smiled, and this time took care when he smoothed back the straying tendril of her hair. "I can't think of any place I'd rather be right now, or anyone else I'd rather be with." He was amazed by his own sincerity. Not just because she was beautiful, with the greatest cleavage he'd come across in aeons. Or because of the feel of her hair. Or even the feel of the excitement rising within him. He wanted to have her there, sure, but he also wanted to stand between her and anything that might harm her in any way.

Obsessive?

Oh, yeah, it would be easy to get obsessive over her.

Her eyes remained on his for a long time. It seemed that she was barely breathing. She moistened her lips, and they glistened. Her teeth were tiny and perfect.

"Wow," she murmured, trying to sound light. "That was one hell of a nice statement. Or a very good line."

"Want me to back away?"

"I don't know." He thought her words were honest. Then she seemed to give herself a shake. "I, uh, yes. I guess you should take me home now."

He stood. "No."

She frowned. "I'm sorry?"

"I don't think you should go home."

"Where do you think I *should* go?" she asked.

"I think you should stay here."

She smiled, then laughed out loud. "Now that really *would* be fraternizing."

He shook his head. "No. Not the way I mean it. I'm going to back away. You know, emotionally, socially—even physically. But you should still stay here. If you go home, you'll be afraid. The drinks won't help. I've got a great guest bedroom. There's even a separate head. So you should just stay."

"But…it…I mean…"

"Does anyone check up on you at night?" he asked.

"No."

"Then just stay. Get some sleep. An honest-to-God good night's sleep."

"I slept well last night," she reminded him.

"But was it enough? After this week?"

She still hesitated.

"I bet I even have an extra toothbrush," he offered.

"Maybe you're right," she murmured.

"I have a T-shirt you can sleep in, and I promise I'll stay at my end of the boat. First thing, I'll wake you up. Your car is here, so you can drive yourself home. And just think about this," he added lightly. "No one would ever think anything, should they even recognize your car, because we told Bobby and Doug that I'd be driving you home and your car would be staying here."

"You have a point there."

"Well, that's good."

She looked at him, slightly suspicious again, and bit the bullet. "You were a cop once, weren't you?"

"Yes."

"You weren't fired for anything criminal, were you?"

He laughed. "Hell no." Then he couldn't help himself. "I took part in all my criminal activities before I became a cop."

"Oh yeah?"

"I'm trustworthy. I swear it."

"I know I just thought about that. I've only known you a few days, but I'm choosing to sleep at your place rather than returning to my own—where I'm afraid of what is probably just a cat in the yard."

"Hey, I've already slept at your house."

She laughed. "There you go. True again. Well, then…"

"Well…?"

"Could I have that T-shirt now, please?"

"Absolutely."

Midnight.

He took a cruise by her house again.

The car was gone.

He stared at the front, frowning; then his cell phone rang. Absently he picked it up. "Yes?"

"We've got another problem. No, this one is yours. *You've* got a problem. And you owe me for finding out about this one."

"What do you mean, *I've* got a problem?"

He listened intently.

"So you see what I mean? *You've* got a problem."

Yeah, he had a problem, but still… Half the trouble lately hadn't been caused by him, and he'd coped anyway.

"Don't forget, don't ever forget, that you're in this up to your neck, my friend," he said softly. Very softly.

And then he hung up.

He stared at the house again and felt a rise of fury.

Where the hell was she?

CHAPTER 10

He hadn't been lying down for more than a few seconds when he heard the tap on his cabin door.

Quinn leaped up. As the captain's quarters on a pleasure craft, the cabin was relatively spacious. Still, reaching the door didn't involve much more than getting off the end of the bed.

She was standing just outside. He'd given her one of his T-shirts, and it looked massive on her. It fell almost to mid-thigh. The shoulders and sleeves hung. Even so, the over-size garment somehow managed to cling to her frame. Her face was scrubbed clean, and that ever-present lock of golden hair was falling softly against her cheek.

"Did I wake you?"

He wondered how just the sound of her voice could be so arousing, something that seemed to reach out and tease his flesh. *Did I wake you?* The words woke everything in him. He was sleeping in an old pair of cutoff corduroys. He was grateful he hadn't opted for a light pair of cotton boxers.

He wanted to answer her, but he didn't trust his voice.

He managed a "no" that sounded more like a growl.

She simply stood there for a moment, her scent sweeping around him, seeming to touch raw, bare flesh, like the sound of her voice.

"Is there something wrong with me?" she asked at last.

"What?" Was she looking for a psychoanalyst, someone to assure her it was natural to have fears about things going bump in the night?

She smiled, lifting her chin, hair falling back in a cascade his fingers itched to touch. "I was curious, thinking there must be something wrong with me."

He leaned against the doorjamb, braced against himself, doing everything humanly possible to keep from reaching out for her.

"I don't know what you mean."

Her smile deepened. "Why aren't you trying to come on to me?"

Her words stunned him. He stared at her for a long moment, muscles taut and frozen, on fire inside.

"There's nothing wrong with you. You're incredible. You must know that."

"Then…?"

"You've been drinking."

"I'm not drunk."

"You're not your usual reserved self, either."

"I may not be the wildest party-goer in the world, but even for me… It was just three beers. I don't think I should be driving, but well, you know, they may suggest that you don't manipulate heavy machinery while under the influence, but I've never seen 'Warning! Avoid sex at all costs!' on a beer bottle."

He wasn't sure whether to laugh, send her right back to the other cabin or drag her into his own as swiftly as humanly possible. He chose none of those options and instead folded his arms over his chest as he smiled at her.

Hell.

Who would ever have imagined that he would be standing in his own boat, trying to talk a beautiful woman out of wanting to have sex with him.

"You don't know me very well," he told her, then gave into temptation. He reached out, fingers sliding along the velvet tendril of hair as it caressed the delicate line of her cheek. His thumb stroked the softness there as he looked into her eyes.

You don't know me very well.

When had that stopped him before? How many times had he been out in the last year when it seemed like anyone gave a damn how well they knew each other?

Tonight, it mattered. But why?

Hell, she was twenty-eight. Not a kid, not naive.

But that wasn't what was stopping him. Naive didn't always have to do with knowledge. Her eyes held something deeper. Large, expressive, green and deep as a jungle, usually so careful, so reserved, searching. They held fields of right and wrong, dreams unspent, belief in humanity, art and beauty, truth and honesty. There was something about her that he longed to touch, ached to touch, feared to touch. As if she were fragile. She had never done anything like this before in her life, he knew. Once she had danced, touching the clouds. Then she had broken a bone and never reached into the air the same way again. Ben Trudeau had crushed her, years ago, and she hadn't trusted anyone since. He wasn't sure how he knew all this so well, with such certainty, but he did.

He could step away. He should. He had to, no matter how painful it would be, because it was the right thing to do. But then she spoke again.

"I know you well enough," she told him, the words soft and her eyes openly on his, emerald, sparkling with the strangest glimmer, a hint of tears.

She was still standing at least an inch away. Maybe not even an inch, but they weren't actually touching. And yet he had never felt so sensually caressed before in his life. Her eyes stroked him. That scent of woman and subtle perfume swirled in the air as if it were tangible, and the warmth she emitted seemed to supplely wrap his flesh, then reach down with a grip of steel to sweep boldly right around his sex.

She wasn't even touching him, he reminded himself.

He should make one last stand. Remind her that she had been drinking.

"Quinn?" she asked tentatively.

Ah, hell. He wasn't that noble.

"Come here," he said softly.

She'd aroused him to the point of pain. He felt almost like a teenage kid in the back of a Chevy. He fought the fury wrestling within, pulled her tight against him. Now they were touching, her breasts crushed to him. He felt her ribs against the muscles of his chest, the flatness of her belly, the flare of her hips, the length of her legs. Her body was wicked, her scent pure sin, and, God help him, he was a sinner.

But he just held her for a moment, his breath hot over the top of her head, his chin brushing the softness of her hair. For a moment, he felt her heart beat. Felt the ragged rise and fall of her breath. Then he pulled away, lifted her chin and touched her lips with his own.

Her lips were wicked, too. Full, sensual. Seducing rather than giving, drawing him into a hot wet duel of tongues that took flight in an instant explosion of teased hunger. Her very kiss evoked visions beyond, hinted of deeper pleasure. How could a mouth that was so taut at times melt into the pure exotic?

They were touching.

The clothing between them was suddenly unbearable.

He drew away, long enough to try the buttons on the shirt, then rip half of them off with total impatience.

Hell. It was his shirt.

Shirt gone.

He couldn't shed his cutoffs fast enough.

Their clothing lay on the floor. Her eyes touched his as she slipped back into his arms.

Immense as a field of emeralds, green fire, alive, not hiding, and yet...

That vulnerability. The look that told him, despite her words, the feel of her flesh, that those things were there. *Something deeper.* A need for honesty, a giving that demanded some kind of honor in the midst of excess and desperation and pure instinctive drive and need.

Then they were really touching. Flesh on flesh. Fire and softness, supple vibrancy and heat. Tongues locked again in some desperate dance. His hands all over her. Breasts full and rounded, waist narrow, hips nicely flaring into a roundness of inspiration. He moved back, not breathing, he was so eager for her mouth. He thanked God that the cabin was small; one step, and he could simply fall against the bed, bringing her down.

Good Lord, but she was erotic, and he was drowning in her. Waves lapped against the boat, rocking them into each other in what began a carnal rhythm. He felt her fingers raking his shoulders, back, chest.

Now he was being touched. Really, really touched.

The length of her rubbed against him, evoking a groan that ground roughly from his lips. She was beneath him, and he was seeking to know everything about her. He was burning in all the fires of both heaven and hell, and glorying in the pain. He tasted the curve of her throat, devoured the fullness of her breasts, reveled in the womanliness of her midriff and abdomen, let passion flow as he brought his attentions ever lower, turned them ever more intimate. Her movements were somehow beyond erotic and passionate. He was half-dying in pure sensuality, and still there seemed to be grace and beauty in every twist and cry. Her fingers dug into his flesh, evoking greater arousal. The taste of her seemed to cause novas to explode in his head. He rose over her, straddled her, met her eyes again, emerald burning in the night. Lips parted, damp, breath coming so quickly, a look of astonished pleasure, almost awe, something that touched manhood, then went beyond ego, the body, and touched his soul. Her arms wrapped around him. Her eyes closed.

"Please," she whispered.

His lips found hers again. Locked in a taste of lava and honey, all that had come before along with all that would come next. His tongue teased, entered, thrust, drove and swept.

His body locked with hers, as well, his sex teasing, entering, thrusting, driving in, deep, deeper. Her legs wound around his hips. The waves lapped at the sides of the boat. The master bunk rocked and within her, he felt as if a tidal wave were sweeping over them, as if the ragged violence of a storm at sea were surging through him, into her, allowing them to touch as no one else ever had.

No one moved quite like a dancer, he discovered.

No one else had such flexibility.

No one could create such a raw sense of instinctive desire and need, nor fulfill it with such shattering finesse.

Their bodies were both sheened in a fine, sweet film of sweat. Muscles flexed, tautened, twisted. Breathing came in a rasp of sound as high as the wind, and sounds, ancient, carnal, came keening from them both. He was aware of her face, her beautiful face, eyes half-closed, lashes sweeping her cheeks. He was aware of the length of her, of himself, and then, of that intimate part of himself, as if everything around him was a wrap of hot, liquid silk, while his true self existed in only one spot, rigid as steel, the only true part of his being.

And then that exploding wave of pleasure, as if the ocean itself had erupted, as if the boat were rocking in a perfect storm, pitching, catapulting, shaking over and over again, and finally, after aeons, drifting into calmer waters, edging into the sand, catching there.

He lay draped over her, pulling her into his arms. His words caressed her forehead as he said, "Miss Mackay, I can assure you, there is absolutely nothing wrong with you. In fact, I don't think I've ever known anyone quite so right in my life."

She twisted slightly, eyes rising to his with that slight glint of vulnerability in them again, a hesitancy now, along with something so soft, trusting and awed that it awoke a new wave of sensation in him. Strange, but that simple look made him want to believe in his own invulnerability and strength.

She didn't speak, only touched his cheek, as if she were seeking words. "You really are quite awesome yourself," she whispered. "And honestly, I'm not drunk."

He smiled. "I know."

She nuzzled against him. "It's been so long…. I didn't even remember."

"It hasn't been that long for me, and there's nothing like you in my memory," he assured her.

She rolled slightly, looking at him a bit skeptically. "Really? Or is that something you say to everyone? I'm usually pretty good at spotting lines. I get to hear quite a lot of them, hanging around at Suede."

He shook his head. "It's not a line. But…there is a bit of a problem."

She drew the sheet up around her, as if his simple statement had brought out something defensive in her once again.

"What?" she murmured.

"I would definitely call this fraternization."

She smiled. "I'm afraid so."

"Can you lose your job?"

"Technically? Yes."

"That's serious."

"Indeed," she said gravely. She touched his face. Ran her fingers down his chest, then lower. She had the most elegant fingers.

Elegant…and talented.

"It's so serious that, well, just in case there are repercussions…I wouldn't mind fraternizing again. So I can really enjoy what I might get in trouble for."

"My dear Miss Mackay," he said very somberly. "We can fraternize all night, if that's what you want."

Her lips curved, her lashes fell, then rose. "That's what I want," she said very softly.

"The way you say it, there's absolutely nothing else I can do but my very best to fulfill your every desire," he assured her.

And when he kissed her again, he felt the rise of the ocean once more, the lapping of the waves, and the sheer, erotic beauty of the power and passion of a storm at sea.

When she first heard the knock on the cabin door, Shannon felt panic set in. She felt almost like a little kid. Caught.

Like Quinn had said, this was definitely fraternization.

At her side, he bounded out of the bunk, found his shorts and slipped them on. He looked back to note the panic in her eyes.

"Hey, it's all right. I do know people who have nothing to do with the studio, and they seldom search the boat when they visit." With a smile, he left her.

Shannon listened intently, but the closed door buffered a

lot of sound. After finding the shirt she'd been wearing, she slipped into it, did up the remaining buttons, and went to the door, cracking it just a hair.

"No, I was up most of the night, but knowing what was going on with you, I thought you'd like to hear about it." There was another man in the cabin. Tall, nice looking, well built. He was wearing dockers, a cotton shirt open at the neck and a casual jacket.

Definitely not a uniform, but…

Something about him, his manner, maybe his air of confidence, of intensity, seemed to scream *cop*.

"Of course, and thanks," Quinn said. "Can I meet you on the patio in a few minutes?"

"Yeah."

The visitor left. Quinn turned back toward the cabin, and she opened the door.

"Just a friend of mine. I need to meet with him. You all right?" He smiled, pulling her into his arms. "You looked like the cat who ate the canary. Not all that sorry about eating the canary, either, but scared as hell about getting caught."

She smiled, but she felt uneasy. For some reason, his unknown visitor bothered her more than if it had been Gordon knocking at the door.

"I'm fine. Bright light, daytime."

"And you're glad you stayed?" he queried.

"I told you, I wasn't drunk."

He was tender, cupping her chin, brushing her lips. He was also anxious and in a hurry; she could feel it. Odd. She'd expected him to tell her that since it was Sunday and they'd already been fraternizing…well, she didn't work on Sundays, so…

But he didn't say any such thing.

"I'm not sure how long I'll be. Can I call you later?"

"Sure."

"I have to hop in the shower." He turned toward the tiny head.

"Your friend is a cop, isn't he?" she asked.

He turned slowly, frowning as he looked at her.

"Yes, he is. How did you know?"

"You can just tell."

"He won't be happy to hear he's that obvious."

"Tell him to slump some. His posture is too good."

"You think that will help?"

"Um, no. He just looks like a cop."

Quinn grinned. "Maybe that *is* good."

He slipped into the head and closed the door. She heard the water running and walked back to the other head, wondering if what she was doing was, boatwise, correct. Would she run out of hot water?

Apparently not. She was able to shower. When she stepped out, wrapped in a towel, he was already dressed in jeans and a deep blue polo shirt. He was sliding his wallet into his back pocket.

"I'll talk to you later, right?" he said. He sounded anxious. Either to get going, or he honestly wanted to see her later.

He paused before leaving, hands on her shoulders, eyes doing a sweep of her in the towel.

"You really are beautiful," he said, and his tone was husky. Deep. A grating that touched a lot of newly aroused instincts inside her.

He lingered, as if he honestly would have liked to stay. But then he broke away. "You're all right here alone, right?"

"Of course. I'll be heading home in a few minutes."

He nodded. "I'll talk to you later." He started up the steps, then turned back. "Make yourself at home in the galley, if you want to have coffee before you leave. And hit the lower lock on the cabin door."

"Right." She waved to him, and he went out.

To find out about something important.

Without him there, she felt uncomfortable, standing in his cabin in a towel. She dressed quickly and was about to head out when she hesitated.

It actually felt strangely pleasant to be trusted alone in his personal space. She had been wondering if she should berate herself, feel some strange sense of having given in to something she shouldn't have. But she couldn't begin to remember a night that had felt so good. She'd probably never had one before.

And as for Quinn...

The more she was with him, the more she wanted to be with him. She liked his grin, his laugh, and he wasn't at all bad on the eyes. She liked the feel of his hands, and, most of all, she liked his quick sense of humor and the dimple when he smiled, the way that he talked.

She also rather liked the feel of being in his personal space, trusted to be alone. She hesitated, then decided that since it was Sunday, and she didn't have to be anywhere, maybe she *would* make some coffee before she left.

The pot and coffee were visible on the counter in the galley. Shannon measured some out and reminded herself that there was something going on with him. All he ever did was ask questions, and yet he denied being a cop. It was illegal, of course, to lie and say that you *were* a cop when you *weren't,* but undercover cops had to lie all the time about their jobs.

But him being an undercover cop didn't make any sense. Surely, she wasn't the only one who thought the circumstances of Lara's death had been suspicious. The police had openly questioned everyone. There had been an autopsy, a case file.

A case file that was now closed. Why not close it? One

of the county's best forensic physicians had done the autopsy, they had been told. Human remains didn't lie. Lara's blood had been saturated with prescription drugs and alcohol. There was no denying it.

So…he couldn't be a cop, because the cops had no further interest in the case.

The coffee perked, and she found herself a cup. It was easy to find a small container of milk in the refrigerator, but a search through the cabinets didn't produce any sugar or its substitute, blue or pink, or even off-brand yellow.

"Have some balls, drink it black," she said aloud, as Gordon often did, especially when he had forgotten to buy sugar or cream for the studio.

She made a face. She liked what Rhianna called "evil chemical substitution" in her coffee. Maybe in one of the drawers?

She opened a drawer and found silverware, while another had some kitchen towels. A third drawer held knives and serving pieces. She moved on to the last kitchen drawer.

She didn't find sugar substitute.

She found papers.

Manila files lay atop a stack of receipts and other bits of paper. She hesitated, brows knit, as she stared into the drawer.

She should have closed the drawer, not having found what she wanted.

Except that she just might have found some answers to the mystery of Quinn O'Casey.

And it would have taken a better man—or woman—than she to turn away from what she saw.

Reaching into the drawer, she pulled out the folders. One was labeled Lara Trudeau. The other held the name Nell Durken.

Stunned, she stared at the names for several seconds.

Then she set the second folder down to go through Lara's. There was a police report in the front of the folder. Behind it, numerous statements. An autopsy report. Everything.

She set the folder down and picked up the other. It was organized in the same fashion, but the faces and names were different. Police report, autopsy, pages of statements…the arrest record of Nell's husband.

She heard someone whistling, then footsteps on the pier nearby. She started to shove the folders back into the drawer. They wouldn't go. There was something else in there. She pulled the drawer all the way out and discovered that a videotape was keeping her from stuffing the folders back in and closing the drawer. The tape was labelled with the name of the competition, Lara's name—and "Property of Miami-Dade, Homicide Department."

She adjusted the tape, then the papers, hurriedly putting everything back. She froze and waited, torn between guilt at prying and fury that the man was such a liar.

Fury took precedence.

Along with the fall of her ego, and a geyser of hurt.

Right. She was beautiful. And fascinating.

Humiliation held her at a dead standstill. Yes, she'd come here. Yes, she'd come straight to him. But a man who was pretending an interest in her because he was a lying son of a bitch who was *investigating* her had no right whatsoever to fall so willingly into that kind of intimacy with the person under investigation!

She hoped he was a cop.

She wished fervently that she could get his ass fired!

The sound of the footsteps, and the whistling, went right on by the boat. Whoever was walking by wasn't Quinn O'Casey.

He might come back any minute.

He might not come back for hours.

She gritted her teeth, longing to go through every single thing on the boat—to trash it, as a matter of fact.

A ringing sound stopped her. She paused, listening, then realized with a groan that it was her own cell phone, ringing from her purse.

She quickly dragged it out and surveyed the caller ID.

Justin.

She punched in, feeling absurdly guilty over the night before—yes, this had certainly been fraternizing. And now, on top of having done something she should never, ever have done, she had been used. Pathetically.

Because she basically had no life, other than dance.

"Yes?"

She was breathless as she answered the phone.

"Shannon?" Justin said.

"Yes, of course."

"You sound funny."

"Do I? Sorry. I couldn't find the phone at first. Lost it down in the jungle of my purse, you know."

She heard his laughter on the other end. "That's a jungle, all right."

"Mmm. Right. Funny. So, what's up?"

"We were going to go to the beach. Right down the street from your place. We wanted to know if you wanted to come."

"We—who?"

"Just me, Sam, Jane and Rhianna. We've called Ella and Ben but haven't gotten a hold of them yet. Gordon answered the phone half-asleep and said something really nasty to me, like 'eat shit and die,' because I woke him on a Sunday. But you're usually up…so…hey, how about it? Come join your staff for a day of cleansing sun and sand, huh?"

"Oh, wow, Justin, I don't know…it's been a long week."

"So you don't want to see us, uh? I understand."

"No, I'm happy to see you. But—"

"Come on, please? We'll come by and hound your house until you do."

"No!"

"We will. You'll have to call the cops, and then the studio will suffer. There will be more horrible publicity, and your teachers will be in jail."

"Don't come to the house! Give me an hour and I'll join you."

"Really?"

"Yes."

"You swear? This isn't just to blow me off or anything? 'Cause we will come to the house. We're feeling like a lonely group of kids, you know? In need of our fearless leader so we can have some fun with our lives."

"Oh, yeah, sure," she said dryly. "Fun. I'll come—I promise. Just don't come and haunt my house. We can come back...here, if you want, just give me some time right now."

"Sure, cool. We'll be on the public side of the hotel, straight down the street from your place."

"I'll be there."

Shannon clicked off and slowly put the phone back into her purse.

She should go. Because she was far too mature and sane to trash his residence.

Besides, she had discovered what she needed to know.

She had been right all along.

He wasn't what he purported to be.

So just what exactly was he? He'd taken his wallet, so she couldn't check his ID. She could, of course, search his desk, even see if she could get on the computer.

She shook her head, wanting to get out of Nick's parking lot before her car was discovered there. But then she hesitated and turned around, going back to check the desk drawer beneath the computer.

Pens, pencils, erasers, disks, paper…

She opened another drawer, a file drawer. All she needed to see was the header on the first piece of paper.

"Whitelaw and O'Casey, Private Investigations"

There followed an address in Key Largo, phone number, e-mail, and a state of Florida licensing number.

"That son of a bitch!" she said out loud.

She slammed the drawer, burning.

Oh, yeah, the man sure as hell knew how to investigate.

She started to turn away, wondering if she could actually drive with the rage she was feeling.

Then she hesitated, curious, and turned back to the desk. Picking up the phone behind the computer, she dialed the number for the agency. It rang and rang.

What? Did both Quinn and Whitelaw, whoever he was, suck so bad at what they did that they couldn't even afford an answering machine?

It was Sunday. What the hell had she been expecting?

She was startled when the phone was suddenly answered. By a human being.

"Whitelaw and O'Casey."

Her mind went blank.

"Hello? Whitelaw and O'Casey."

"Sorry, sorry—is Mr. O'Casey in?"

"I'm sorry. He's on vacation. Perhaps you'd like to leave a message for Mr. Whitelaw?"

"Ah, no, thanks. I'll call back. It's Mr. O'Casey I need to speak with."

"Are you from the Quantico office? I can reach him if need be."

"No, no, it's a personal matter. Thank you."

She hung up quickly.

Quantico?

He wasn't just a private investigator. He was FBI. Or had been. Maybe not. Lots of people lived in Quantico, Virginia.

That was bull, and she knew it. He either was, or had been, FBI.

Pleasant, laid-back fisherman, diver, charter manager?

Like hell.

All she knew for certain at that moment was that he had used her.

Tears suddenly stung her eyes, and she brushed them away in self-fury. At the steps, she turned back and looked into the cabin.

"I don't know exactly what you are, Mr. O'Casey, except an absolute asshole!"

She left the boat, forgetting to hit the lock, and she didn't look back.

CHAPTER 11

"There's probably no association at all," Jake told Quinn, looking bleary as he sipped from a mug of coffee.

They weren't outside on the patio that morning. They were in Nick's kitchen. Nick and his wife were still sleeping.

Jake kept a boat moored at the pier, as well, but in the past months, the rocking of the boat at night had kept his wife, fellow officer Ashley Montague Dilessio, awake, so they'd been sleeping in Ashley's old place at Nick's, an apartment off the side of the restaurant/dwelling.

Quinn was certain that the fact Ashley was away in Jacksonville was wearing on Jake's nerves as much as his schedule was. But despite the fact that he was obviously longing to jump into bed, he was taking the time to bring Quinn up-to-date on the latest.

Another corpse.

"Duarte says it's fresh. He knows his stuff, and I've seen them when they've been in the water a while. This one hasn't," Jake said. "He probably won't get to the autopsy until tomorrow sometime, but you know him. He's a worker—he was out there when the call came."

"Did he say anything based on the preliminary?" Quinn asked.

"Rich, at a guess. I'll give you my notes with the exact details, but for the moment…Rolex. Necklace with enough gold to sink a ship and a diamond heart with enough carats to make many a woman green with envy."

"Hispanic, Anglo, black, Asian?"

"Or mark here for 'other'—whatever other may be?" Jake asked dryly. "I don't know yet. Dark. Possibly Hispanic. Hell, down here she could have been blond and still Hispanic. Half the South Americans I know look as if they came from Germany. She was dark. Dark hair, dark eyes, deep tan."

"Any sign of a struggle?"

"She was naked, but if she was raped, there aren't any bruises or signs of violence. Just tracks on her arms."

"So she was a junkie?"

"I don't know about a junkie. But she'd done some drugs in her day."

"Did she match up with any recent missing persons reports?" Quinn asked.

"Not so far. All I can say for certain right now is that a young woman's body washed up on the beach. According to Duarte, she probably died last night. She'd been in the water, so she might have been dumped in from a boat. She showed signs of drug abuse, and it's likely she died from an overdose. As soon as I find out more, I'll keep you informed. I still can't figure how the deaths of two women from prescription drugs can tie in with the illegal narcotics scene, but…hell, like you, I think it's odd."

"Odd enough to reopen Lara Trudeau's case?"

Jake winced. "She wasn't my case and it isn't my call.

I'll have to bring it to my superiors, and to do that, I'm going to have to give them more than another drug death in the same vicinity. As a county employee, I have a lot of rules and regs to follow. You can get away with a lot that I can't."

"Yeah, but you can call a hell of a lot of shots *I* can't," Quinn reminded him.

Jake shrugged. "The whole damn thing is crazy. It's sad, but true—there's a whole high-flying scene, a lifestyle, on the beach. Drugs flow, no matter what the cops do. Every year, people die of abuse and overdoses, or violence escalated by uppers and downers. It happens. Most cases aren't related. Hell, most of them are random. But anyway, I know your interest. If you want, I'll call you for the autopsy. Duarte won't mind having you there."

"Yeah, I want, thanks."

"You all right? You look as ragged as I feel. Who's down at the boat? Someone I know? Hell, someone you know, at least? I hope."

Quinn angled his head as he stared at his friend sharply. "Someone I know. Let's leave it at that for now, huh?"

"Yep." Jake rose. "I don't know what the hell I'm doing, drinking coffee, when all I want is a shower and bed."

Quinn stood, as well. "You're right—coffee probably isn't the best thing for you to be swilling right now. Thanks. I appreciate you letting me in."

"It may mean nothing."

"It probably does. Thanks anyway."

"You bet. I'll see you tomorrow."

"Hope Ashley gets home."

"She's due in late this afternoon."

"Good. I'll see you later."

Quinn let himself out from the side door, facing the parking lot. He could see Shannon's car was gone.

He'd expected her to leave, hadn't he? After all, he'd had

no idea how long he was going to be gone. And the way Shannon felt about being seen with a student…

Fraternizing.

He'd been anxious to talk to Jake, and just as anxious to get him away from the boat, since he hadn't wanted to make her uncomfortable.

And still…

A sense of unease plagued him as he headed back to his boat.

"Now that's bad," Justin said.

They were lying on the sand, the group of them, slicked with lotion, feeling the sun, facing the water.

Justin—who had brought his own beach chair—was doing a lot more people watching than loafing.

"What?" Jane demanded.

Justin pointed. "That is just way too much flesh to be seen."

"Justin, that isn't nice," Rhianna told him.

"You're right. Not nice at all—it's major-league *nasty.*"

"Hey, who told you that you look so great in a bathing suit, anyway?" Jane teased him.

"I may not look great, but I don't look like a beached whale."

Shannon took a look at the woman walking along the shoreline. She was definitely a little large for her suit, but the idea that everyone on the beach looked like a swimsuit model was an invention of the movies and nothing to do with reality.

"Justin, you're being cruel," she told him. "The beach belongs to everyone."

"Yeah, you're picking on women," Jane drawled.

"No, I'm not. There, over there. Look at that old geezer, thinking he's sexy 'cause he's got a package in those skimpy shorts. He's got more skin flapping around than a basset hound."

"Would you stop!" Shannon said.

"I can't. The woman's back. Oh no! She's bending over. I'm blinded by the pure white reflection of her ass."

"Justin…" Rhianna moaned right along with Shannon.

Cruel, Shannon thought, and yet, Justin was funny. He was trying to make them laugh. He wanted the world to get back to normal.

Jane decided to take care of him. She moved her sunglasses down her nose, staring at him. "Since it's so easy to see over your head, Justin, I just got a good view myself."

"Fine, make fun of the poor vertically challenged man," Justin said in mock affront.

"Thank God," Rhianna said, "that at least the cops aren't still crawling all over the place. Those poor guys trudging through the sand in their uniforms and dress shoes."

"The cops?" Shannon said.

"Rhianna," Sam groaned. "We weren't going to say anything, remember?"

Shannon sat up straight, slipping her sunglasses from her nose, staring at them all. "Why were the cops crawling all over the beach?"

"A body washed up," Sam told her. "Someone must have found the corpse at like two or three in the morning. A whole stretch of the beach was closed off until ten or eleven, when they took her away. They were still talking to people until about five or ten minutes before you got here."

"A body?" Shannon said.

"Not a dancer," Justin said quickly.

"How on earth can you know that?" Jane demanded.

Justin sighed. "I heard them talking. She was some kind of ritzy socialite. People who saw her were talking about all the jewelry she had on. Not a stitch of clothing, but tons of jewelry. She had track marks, though. Probably some hot little Latin mama, too into the scene."

"Found with two tons of jewelry," Rhianna mused. "Well, she wasn't killed and then robbed, anyway."

"Who said she was killed?" Jane demanded.

Rhianna sat up, staring at Jane. "What? She accidentally took off all her own clothes and lay down on the beach and died? That's ridiculous."

Yes, ridiculous, Shannon thought, but no more so than the thought that Lara Trudeau would take that many pills when she was dancing. *Knowingly* take them, at any rate.

"Oh, God," Justin groaned. "Read the newspapers. Someone dies every day. We can't take each and every one of them to heart. We're getting over Lara. Let's not start obsessing over a stranger, okay?"

"Do we know that she's a stranger?" Jane asked softly.

Justin sighed. "I don't really know anything," he said. "But come on, think about it. We can't take the woes of the whole world on our shoulders. We're all punch-drunk right now, over Lara and all. We're trying to have a beautiful day."

"Right," Shannon said dryly. "It was rude of that woman to be murdered where we were planning on having fun."

"Definitely murdered, huh?" Jane said.

"Hey, none of us is a cop," Justin said. "We can talk to Doug O'Casey next time he comes in. He should know."

"He's a patrolman—not in homicide," Jane said.

"So? He's got friends. He'll find out the scoop for us," Justin assured her.

Yes, and if he doesn't, his brother can, Shannon thought. His brother, the private eye. Who was apparently there to watch them. All of them.

Why?

And who had hired him?

What did someone else know that they didn't?

Rhianna rose, dusting the sand from her butt. "I think I've had enough of the sun. I'm going to call it quits, guys. See you in the morning."

Jane stood, too. "Justin, thanks for getting us all together. It was a good idea, but I think I'm a little baked, too."

Justin rose with a sigh. "Same here, so…so long."

"I'm going to hang around a while longer," Sam told them. He had laced his hands behind his head to lie back and now looked as if he was caught in the middle of an abdominal exercise. "You should stay, Justin."

"No, he can't—he picked us both up. He has to take us home," Jane told him. "See you tomorrow, Shannon."

She shrugged and waved tiredly. Jane and Sam were the studio's rising stars, willing to work hard. She was just feeling absurdly tired.

Disheartened. Hurt. Crushed, actually. She'd thought she might be acquiring a life with a dynamite guy…and she was just being investigated.

Thoroughly, she thought, with a sense of pained amusement.

"Shannon?" Jane repeated.

"Sure. See you in the morning. Ten-ish."

Jane smiled and waved. Sam lay back in the sand. Shannon remained seated, hugging her knees to her chest, staring out at the waves. She did love the sound of the waves crashing on the sand. She loved the water, the sky, even the salty scent that clung to the air. It seemed bizarre that so much beauty could evoke so much violence.

Suddenly, at her side, Sam gave a deep sigh. "Come on. Let's walk down there."

She started, feeling guilty. She hadn't allowed herself to even form the thought in her head, but she wanted to see where the woman had been found.

"That's morbid, isn't it?" she asked Sam.

"Just natural. Think about it. This isn't far from the studio—not to mention your house." He jumped to his feet and offered her a hand. She stood, and he slipped an arm around her shoulders as they walked down the beach. "We'd all agreed we weren't going to say anything to you, and of course we hoped the cops wouldn't come back."

"Sam, it's sweet of you guys to try to protect me from bad news, but hey, I've got a TV and I do read the paper," she told him.

"No, but Justin was right. You've been so upset about Lara. We wanted you to have a nice, death-free day at the beach. It didn't quite turn out that way, huh?"

She gave him a quick squeeze. "Like I said, it was nice of you guys to try. I'm pretty tough, though, you know."

"Yeah?" He looked at her, a grin curving his lips. "Most of the time, sure. You run a tight ship, you've earned everyone's respect. But a really tough cookie…? I don't know."

"Why do you say that?"

His smile deepened. "I shouldn't encourage you. Because you'd just be new competition for Jane and me. But, if you were really tough, you'd go out there and compete again."

She groaned. "Sam, my ankle will never be what it was."

"Bull. An orthopedist might say that, but it's been years. Your ankle is plenty good."

She was going to ask him to drop it all and leave it dropped, but she didn't have a chance. Sam stopped, causing her to halt along with him. "There."

Actually, there was nothing left "there." The body had been taken away. It had been found on the sand, and there was still an area roped off with crime tape, and some Miami Beach officers hanging around. Two crime-scene specialists were combing the sand inch by inch, and the crime tape was surrounded by the curious. People stared, questioned the cops guarding the area and moved on.

"What are we doing?" Shannon murmured. "It's like slowing down to stare at the scene of an accident."

"But we all do it," he murmured. "People were talking when we first showed up. The kids who stumbled on her first weren't frightened or horrified. They were excited—they kept talking to everyone and anyone. They were celebrities for a day. Weird, huh?"

"Well, thankfully, the poor woman has been taken away," Shannon said.

"Oh, yeah. Can you imagine a corpse lying out on the sand in this heat all day? The kids were talking…. She couldn't have been dead that long, but crabs were already munching on her toes."

"Ugh. Let's go," Shannon said.

She turned, and Sam followed. But as they walked away, she looked back.

Two men were coming through the crowd. Shannon recognized them both. One was Quinn's early-morning visitor.

The other was Quinn.

The first man showed a local cop his ID, then introduced Quinn, who shook hands with the officer. Then both men began to ask questions.

"What's the matter?" Sam asked, stopping.

"Nothing," she said quickly, and kept walking. She didn't know why, but she didn't want Sam seeing their new student at the scene.

"You sure?"

"Yeah, yeah, just a case of the shivers. Let's go."

She quickened her pace. When she had a chance, she glanced back again.

Apparently the men hadn't come alone. They were with a very attractive, very pregnant woman who was carrying a

sketch pad. Quinn had an arm around her. He was talking
to her softly, and he seemed deeply concerned. She looked
up, flashing him a smile. Then she slipped under the crime-
scene tape, hunkered down and started to draw.

"What the hell is it?" Sam asked, looking at her with concern.

"Race you to the blankets!" Shannon said, then started
to tear down the beach. She was fast, and she knew it. Sam
took the bait, flying after her.

When they reached their spot, she sat down first. He followed her, gasping and panting.

"I won," she told him.

Still panting, he stared at her and smiled.

"What?" she demanded.

"Oh, yeah. That ankle is bad. Like hell."

She groaned. "Where's your car?"

"A block from your place."

"Walk me home, then. We can cool off for a while, and
then I'll make us something to eat."

There were times when Quinn was definitely glad he
was no longer a cop or with the Bureau.

There really were no such things as regular hours, no matter what some schedule said. Of course, for him, life was
still that way, but at least he could step back and take time
when he wanted.

He'd intended to be doing just that now, he remembered.
He should have been on a beach, all right, but a beach in the
Bahamas. Cool breezes blowing. An icy brew in his hands.
Kids playing in the sand. Calypso music coming from
somewhere. Salt eroding the tangle of cobwebs that held all
the disillusioned nightmares of his mind.

Then again, had he been in the Bahamas, there wouldn't
have been last night on his boat.

And he wouldn't be with Jane and Ashley, wondering what the hell Shannon Mackay had done on his boat after he'd left and staring at a strip of sand where a corpse had washed up from Biscayne Bay.

A fresh one, thank God, as the assistants down at the M.E.'s office had been saying. Duarte had spent the week so swamped, he wasn't cutting into his newest arrival until the following day. Jake was the head homicide detective on the case, and he'd decided to take another look at the scene in daylight. Quinn had come along, but not until he'd returned to the boat and made a thorough inspection of it, ascertaining that nothing was missing, despite the fact that Shannon had taken the time to make coffee, then left in such haste that she hadn't bothered locking the door. Meanwhile, Ashley had managed to get out on an earlier flight, so Jake had picked her up, and after this quick look at the crime scene, they were going to head over to the morgue. Ashley was going to do a sketch of the woman's face for the paper, hoping to find someone who could identify her.

The cops didn't want a photo of her; they wanted her looking as she would have looked when she was alive.

Ashley had been a rare find for Jake Dilessio—a woman with two loves in her life: art and police work. She never tired. Despite the fact that she was expecting their first child within the month—and looked like she was walking around with a bowling ball under her shirt—she was still intent on work. They were both going to take some time when the baby was born, but until then, as Ashley said with a shrug, what did she have to do except sit around and feel huge? Later, as they drove to the morgue, Quinn couldn't help but ask her if sketching corpses didn't ever give her a queasy stomach, at the least.

"You don't ever get over an unnatural death being horrible," she told Quinn, leaning over the seat to look at him as they drove. "But I've had a great pregnancy. I don't feel ill at all—never had a second of morning sickness. And my work is important. Both Jake and I are creating a better world for the child we're bringing into it." She smiled, glancing at Jake, who was driving. "We can't solve all the ills in the universe, but every little bit helps, right?"

"Ashley, you should be cloned," Quinn told her.

She flashed him a smile. Beautiful and delicate, she could also be tough as nails.

"Thanks." She fell silent, then said, "Whatever the circumstances…you know we're glad to have you back down here, right?" She sounded awkward, but she wasn't the type to pry. "Hey, if Nell Durken hadn't come to you, and you hadn't kept such meticulous records when you tailed her husband, he might have gotten away with it."

"He hasn't gone to trial yet," Quinn reminded her. He frowned. She might not feel queasy, but now, when he thought about the Durken case, *he* did.

They reached the morgue. Jake and Ashley flashed their badges, and an assistant came out to escort them into one of the rooms, where the victim from the beach was brought out.

According to Duarte's initial estimation, she hadn't been dead twenty-four hours yet.

Amazing what the sea and the life within it could do in that time.

And still, certain facts were obvious.

She had been young, beautiful and, apparently, rich. Her nails—on the untouched fingers—were elegantly manicured. What remained of her makeup was expertly applied and apparently long lasting. Her hair was rich, thick, dark, well tendered. High cheekbones graced her face, and, when her mouth was opened, it appeared that her teeth were perfect. Bone structure, muscle tone…everything indicated that she'd had every opportunity in life.

Ashley was already sketching.

The assistant provided gloves, but their cursory inspection provided little additional information, except that they noted the needle tracks in her arms.

"A user…but she hadn't moved beyond her arms," Jake said.

Quinn shook his head. "Her physical condition appears to have been good otherwise."

"She couldn't have been into it long," Jake agreed.

A little while later, Ashley told them that she was finished.

Her sketch wasn't of a smiling, cheerful face but rather one at rest. It was excellent, and far better for a loved one to discover in the newspaper than a photo of what that once-beautiful face had become.

After leaving the morgue, they headed back to the spot where the body had been found. Since the crime-scene detectives were still busy searching the sand, they kept their distance, talking to the patrol officers who had canvassed the area, asking questions.

A delicate matter. The body had actually been found on hotel property, though no one at the hotel recognized Ashley's sketch. Or if they did, they didn't let on.

Jake noted the proximity of the spot where the body had been found to the studio—and to Shannon's house.

He said goodbye to Jake and Ashley, assuring them he would get back to the marina fine, and started walking.

He rang the bell at Shannon's house. He heard movement near the door, apparently someone looking through the peephole, but it wasn't opened.

Then he heard people speaking. Whispering. He leaned his ear against the door.

"What's the matter with you? Why don't you open it?" A man's voice. Quinn recognized it as Sam Railey's.

"It's Sunday—I'm off." Shannon's reply was terse.

He shouldn't have come here, Quinn realized. There was that fraternization thing.

"Well, open the door and tell him that," Sam said.

"No. Just let him go away."

"That guy has a thing for you, I think." Sam sounded teasing.

"He's a student."

"Screw that! He's hardly a student. He won't last. The guy gives new meaning to the term 'two left feet.'"

True but painful, Quinn thought wryly.

"Let's get away from the door," Shannon said.

Great. Thanks for defending me, Quinn thought.

He rang the bell again.

"Oh, for God's sake," Sam muttered.

"All right, all right."

Quinn stepped back just in time. The door flew open.

Shannon stared at him. She didn't simply look angry that he had shown up at her house when a fellow teacher was there.

She looked lethal.

Her emerald-green eyes were harder and icier than he had ever seen them. Her body language was downright hostile. She was stiffer than a concrete pillar.

And she didn't ask him in but left him standing on the porch.

Sam, on the other hand, looked highly amused. "Hey, Quinn," he said cheerfully.

"What do you want, Mr. O'Casey?" Her tone could freeze fire.

"I came by to see how you were." He glanced at Sam. "I knew where Miss Mackay's house was because I dropped her off the other night." He turned to Shannon. "After everything…I was in the neighborhood. I just thought I'd see how you were doing."

"You were just in the neighborhood, were you?" There was saccharine in the query.

Then he knew. Something hit the pit of his stomach like a rock. She'd gone through his place. Well, he'd been a real idiot, leaving her there, with what was in his drawers.

"Are you talking about what happened on the beach? Some kids found a body there," Sam said.

Apparently she hadn't said anything to anyone else yet. That was a relief. Not that his real line of work was a national secret.

"I heard," he said evenly, staring at Shannon.

"Sam and I were on our way out," Shannon said.

"Oh?" She had on a terry cover-up. Sam was in cutoffs. They were both dusted with sand.

"We were?" Sam said. "I thought you were going to cook?"

Shannon glared at him. He stared back, as if really confused. "Well, hell, don't leave our new student out here while we figure this out." He backed away, smiling. "Come in, Quinn. Or Mr. O'Casey. You know, according to the rules, we're supposed to call our students Mr. or Mrs. or Miss all the time. I think those rules must have been written a while ago, because they don't even refer to a possible Ms. We've always gone by first names, though. What do you think?"

"Quinn is just fine," he said, taking advantage of the opportunity Sam afforded him and stepping inside.

He and Shannon needed to talk. Somehow.

"Sam," Shannon said warningly beneath her breath.

"Come on, Shannon, aren't you even curious? Quinn can tell us all about the case."

"You two feel free to chat," she said. By her tone, she didn't mean it at all. "I'm taking a shower. Sam, we *are* going out. Mr. O'Casey, we'd love to invite you, but I'm sure you've heard that we have a studio policy? We don't want anyone feeling we're giving one student more attention than another."

She'd left him little choice. He managed to grin awkwardly.

"Actually, my ride disappeared. I thought I could get a return favor, and you could give me a lift home."

Let her handle that one politically.

"Shannon, let's not be idiotic," Sam pleaded. "Don't you need to talk to Quinn about a charter boat for the Gator Gala, anyway?"

"I don't think Mr. O'Casey has what we're going to need."

"Oh, but I do. Really. And I can get you the best deal in the area," he told her.

She stared back at him. Her eyes were so hard that he could almost hear the word *Liar!* screamed on the air.

"I've been thinking, and I'm not sure we should do business with a student," she said.

"I swear to you, I can give you a charter you won't believe," he said. He leaned a hand against the door frame, and she seemed to understand that, short of having a few honest words right there and then, with Sam present, he wasn't leaving.

"Gordon would want you to hear him out," Sam said pleasantly.

Quinn realized that Sam was actually savoring the situation. He had the look of the devil in his eyes.

"I still need to shower. Sam, if you want, you can rinse off in the guest bath. And, Mr. O'Casey, you can…" Her voice trailed off. He knew exactly what she thought he should be doing with himself. "Have a seat. Wait, if you must."

She spun around, heading for her room.

"Hang tight," Sam said, casting Quinn a sympathetic look. "We'll be ready in a minute."

He, too, disappeared.

Quinn wandered out to the Florida room. It was a day when autumn was becoming more and more obvious—even in Florida. The temperatures were still high, but darkness was coming earlier and earlier.

He leaned against the wall, looking out into the backyard, with its rich growth of palms, key limes, shrugs, crotons and more. A stone trail had once cut a swath through the foliage, but it was largely overgrown now. A gentle breeze lifted leaves and bent branches.

And yet, as he stared out, he thought that far more than the breeze was moving in one area of the yard.

He tensed, watching. He had the eerie feeling he was being watched back.

Lights were on in the house. The shadows of coming darkness were protecting the yard. And…yes, someone was there.

He swore, and reached for the knob of the back door. Nothing happened when he twisted it, and he realized the door was double bolted.

He twisted the locks with a jerk and threw the door open with a bang.

Branches snapped, as someone began to run.

Quinn burst out of the house in pursuit.

CHAPTER 12

Gordon Henson appreciated his Sunday afternoons.

Not that he worked all that hard at his studio anymore. He'd banked on grooming Shannon for the job of managing the place, and he'd chosen well. He could actually have retired already, but he had discovered that he didn't want to. In the past few years, he'd actually begun to make money—real money.

But he couldn't do it without his involvement in the studio.

Not to mention the fact that he would never fall out of love with dance. He didn't teach anymore, but he attended the parties and certainly spent time down at the club. A nice lifestyle. He'd been married once, discovered it wasn't for him, and despite the fact that time was passing, he didn't feel the need for a permanent relationship. Rather, he liked the lifestyle on the beach and in the nearby clubs, where just about everything went. There were so many people out there. So many colors, nationalities, heights, weights, creeds, whatever. Even sexual mores. Gordon was open to anything in life.

He loved the studio, the club, his work week.

But he loved his Sundays, too.

Sometimes Sundays meant spending some off time with his employees. He would have Ella Rodriguez plan a picnic at a park, maybe up in Broward, where there was a small pretense of a water park. He also liked to get his teachers up on skates—roller, in-line, or ice—because they helped with movement and balance. Sometimes he used his Sundays very privately, having found an intriguing person to date.

And sometimes, after an eventful week like this one, he liked to sit in his condo and catch up on movies he hadn't seen, or watch an old classic.

Years ago, he'd fallen in love with dance by watching Fred and Ginger, Cyd Charisse, Donald O'Connor, Buddy Ebsen, Gene Kelly, or any one of the men or women who embodied the grace and spirit of dance. Today he'd chosen to watch "Singin' in the Rain." He would never tire of it.

Gene Kelly was moving across the screen with his own particular brand of sheer genius when the phone rang.

He ignored it, letting the machine pick up. When it did, the caller hung up, then rang again. Persistently.

Gordon swore, clicked the hold button on the remote and answered the phone.

"Hello?"

"You got a good thing going there, at that studio."

"Yes?"

"That's it. You got a good thing going at that studio. A really good thing. Remember that. Remember that at all times."

Then the phone went dead in Gordon's hand, and he stared at it, feeling a bead of perspiration break out on his flesh, along with an eerie sense of chill.

"What the hell is going on?" Shannon demanded, bursting out of her room and flying to the back porch.

The door to the yard was open.

It was like inviting the shadows in.

Sam came running up behind her.

"See, look at that. You were so rude, the poor fellow freaked out and ran away."

She shot a furious glare at him. "Sam, something obviously happened out there. Or there was someone out there."

"Then, let's go see, shall we?" He looked at her raised brows and reached out a hand. "What's the matter with you? What are you afraid of?"

"Um, maybe somebody out there with a gun or a knife."

He laughed. "Why on earth would anyone be running around your yard with a gun or a knife?"

"I think there was a body on the beach this morning, and that we all need to be careful," she said sternly.

"Good thing you've got a muscle-bound student to go after things in the dark, huh?" he said slowly.

"Check the front door—let's make sure it's locked before we head out the back," she said.

Through the yard, out to the street, down the street, through another yard.

His elusive prey remained just in front of him.

Finally they hit the beach.

Darkness had crept its fingers over the daylight, so as close as he got, Quinn couldn't quite ascertain the physical makeup of the person he was chasing.

Then, at last, he was almost upon them.

A woman. A small one.

He collided with her body in a tackle, bringing her down into the sand. She didn't scream; her breath escaped her body with a "whooshing" sound. Then he was on top of her, staring down into her face.

* * *

Along with making Sam check that the front door was locked, Shannon grabbed her tennis racket. They went out the back. She'd always loved her yard so much. Now, it seemed that every tree, every bush and branch, was hiding something.

"I guess we should look through the foliage?" Sam said.

She shook her head. "If Quinn saw something, someone, out here—which I assume he did—he's chased them out."

"Great. We've checked the front door, we have that lethal tennis racket for protection, and we're just going to stand here?"

She scowled at him.

A rustling sound came from behind them. They both swung around.

It was Mr. Mulligan, who lived next door, with Harry, his retriever.

"Evening, Shannon!" he called out. "Hello there, Sam," he added, since the two men had met before, when Shannon had invited the group over for dinner.

"Hi, Mr. Mulligan," Sam said.

The neighbor smiled at them, then stared at the tennis racket Shannon was holding as if it were a baseball bat.

"You've taken up tennis again? Good for you."

"We think there was someone in the backyard, Mr. Mulligan," Sam said. "A friend is chasing them."

"Here? In this neighborhood?" Mr. Mulligan seemed to think that was unlikely. "Must have been Harry, here." The dog, who loved people far too much ever to be an effective guard dog, trotted over to Shannon.

"Hi, fellow," she said, scratching his ears.

"You know, young lady, I'm right next door, if you ever need help," the older man admonished her.

"I know that, thank you," she said, looking at the man,

who—with his wrinkles and bald pate—might have been a hundred and five, in age *and* in weight.

"You just call me any time. Harry, come on in."

The dog trotted obediently back to his master, and they walked back to their own house.

"This is kind of silly," Sam said to Shannon when Mr. Mulligan was out of sight. "Wherever Quinn went, whoever he went after, he's gone, and we don't know where."

"Maybe we should call the police," Shannon murmured.

"Maybe you really did scare the guy off. You *were* awfully rude to him."

"I'm the studio manager, remember? Don't correct me or argue with me in front of students."

"Sorry," Sam said. "Hey! Here he comes. And he's not alone."

Quinn was returning, entering the yard from the sidewalk. He was accompanied by a skinny waif with a cascade of brown hair flowing down her back. She was in jeans and a tank top. Young. Very young. And pretty. With brown eyes that eclipsed her face.

Shannon and Sam just stood, watching.

The girl seemed to be uncomfortable, accompanying Quinn. She was very young, yet it was obvious that she knew him.

Shannon couldn't help staring at him with calculating eyes.

"Shannon, Sam, this is Marnie. Shannon, she's been living in your backyard."

"What?" She focused accusingly on the girl.

"I didn't hurt anything!" the girl said quickly. "I wasn't going to break in or take anything. It's just that it's so overgrown back there…. Some of the trees actually make a little shelter. Honestly, I wasn't going to steal anything."

Shannon thought the girl was telling the truth. "But don't you have a home? Shouldn't you be in school?" she asked.

"Runaway," Sam murmured.

"No, I'm not. Look, my dad died when I was a kid," the girl explained, as if she were now well on her way to old age. "My mother remarried. And he…"

Shannon breathed out a soft expletive, staring at Quinn. "She needs to go to the police. He should be prosecuted!"

"He didn't do anything. Yet," the girl explained. And she did sound as if she were almost one hundred. "You don't understand. My mom was alone a long time. And, like, desperate. And he made her think that…that I was coming on to him. He's not all that old—younger than my mom. And she wants him more than me, and it was just…I had to get out. I graduated from high school last June. I'm over eighteen. It's my right to be out. It's the truth. You can check it all out."

"But you can't…you can't just live in people's yards," Shannon said. She still felt somewhat confused, but sorry, too. There was something about the girl that was defiant; and also truthful. She was like a puppy, thrown out into the cold, determined to adopt the attitude of a Doberman. "Let's go inside," Shannon said. "You can tell us more."

"No," Quinn said firmly.

Shannon stared at him, startled.

"We're going to go see a friend of mine. A cop."

"I don't want you to arrest her," Shannon protested.

"I'm not a cop," Quinn reminded her wearily.

"He's not arresting me," the girl explained, as if she felt obliged to come to Quinn's defense. "He's taking me to some shelter. My, uh, stuff is still in your yard, though."

"Oh." Shannon stared at Quinn again.

"We're going to check out Marnie's story," he said firmly. "Sam, follow what's left of that little trail, and you'll find a book bag. Her things are in it."

"Okay," Sam said, though it was evident he was wondering why he was the one who should look for the book bag, when Marnie was standing right there.

"I'm not going to bolt on you," Marnie said wearily.

"Sam would love to get the book bag for you," Quinn said to her.

"Yeah, sure, I'm going right now," Sam said.

"Quinn…" Shannon murmured. Strange. She'd actually had a few jealous thoughts when she'd first seen him with the girl, but now she felt a protective surge sweep through her. She'd been lucky. She had loving parents who would die before hurting her, and they'd never doubted her word when she'd been growing up. This little waif…

"We're going to the police station," Quinn said firmly. "I have a very good friend who is a victim's advocate. She's wonderful. She'll help Marnie get settled safely."

The girl suddenly smiled, staring at Shannon. "I've seen you dance!" she told her. She flushed. "In fact, that's how I found your yard. I watched you through the windows at the studio. I would trade half my life to move like that."

"You want to dance?"

"More than anything."

"All of our first lessons are free," Shannon said.

The girl stared at Quinn.

He let out a deep sigh. "Tonight, you come and meet my friend, Annie. I'll see to it that you can get to the studio for a lesson. In fact, I'll buy you a guest pass with a bunch of lessons, all right?"

"Really?"

The tiny face lit up. She was more than just pretty. She looked so young, like a child just given the best birthday present in the world.

"Yeah, really." He sounded gruff.

"I don't have a car," Marnie said softly.

"That's the kind of thing Annie can help you with," he explained.

"Actually, I can't even drive."

"Annie will see that you get where you need to go," Quinn told her. "Hell, don't worry about it. We'll get you back down here."

Sam returned with the bag. "Here you go," he said, smiling at the girl.

"Thanks." Marnie turned to Shannon. "I know you didn't exactly have me at your place on purpose, but thanks," she said.

"Let's go," Quinn told her.

"Hey, Quinn, how are you going to get her anywhere? I thought you needed a ride," Sam said.

"I'll call a cab." He stared at Shannon. "Well, now, the two of you can have that dinner on your own. Good night. Marnie, let's move. Night, Sam."

He set a hand on Marnie's shoulder, steering her toward the road.

"Why don't we invite both of them to dinner?" Sam whispered to Shannon.

She'd felt the urge herself. But then she'd remembered that Quinn O'Casey was a lying son of a bitch who had used her.

"He needs to get the girl settled," she said firmly.

"She could get settled after dinner."

"No." She sounded sharper than she had intended.

Sam sighed. "Let's see, you have no life. A terrific guy is apparently interested in you. You shove him out like refuse. Don't come to me when you're old and lonely."

She didn't respond.

"Shannon, that guy may not come back."

She turned around. "Oh, he'll be back."

"How can you be so sure?"

Because he's investigating us. Some of us more than others, she thought.

"He'll be back, trust me. Let's just stay in and order a pizza, all right?"

"Shannon…"

She spun on him hard. "I do not want to talk about it. Bring it up one more time, and I will fire your ass!"

He didn't believe it, but the threat fulfilled its purpose.

"No pizza, please. I'm gaining weight. We can order from the sushi place, okay?"

"Fine. But not one more word about Quinn O'Casey, got it?"

"Yes'm, boss, I got it."

They went into the house. Sam was true to his word. They watched a movie and wound up comparing opinions on the leading man. Sam was gay, and they often spent time dissing or admiring various actors.

He left her house at about ten, and she locked the door, glad to be feeling both safe and ridiculous. She *had* been hearing things—because a kid had been living in her backyard. She wondered who Annie was and where she could be found. Because whether Quinn had meant it or not, Shannon intended to make sure Marnie got her dance lessons.

By midnight, she was asleep.

And she slept well, waking in the morning to feel as if it really was over.

Lara was buried.

And that was that.

Quinn's phone rang at six-fifteen in the morning.

It was Jake Dilessio.

"Sonya Marquez Miller, twenty-nine. El Salvadoran by birth, married an older American eight years ago, became an American citizen. She must have cared for him. Even

Miller's kids like her. His daughter saw the sketch and called in to identify her. The girl hadn't seen her in almost a year, but Sonya would call and chat now and then. When Gerald Miller died, Sonya went a little crazy, realizing that she was still young. She'd gotten big time into the club scene, partying at a place toward the north end of South Beach most of the time. She lived alone and acquired a lot of acquaintances, but, according to Eva Miller, the stepdaughter, no one close. Or not that she knows anything about, anyway."

"Did she ever take dance lessons?" Quinn asked.

"Not that we've discovered so far. The cops have scoured the local hotels and restaurants, and we've found a few places where she liked to eat, shop and party. But not one person ever saw her come in or go out with anyone else. She lived in an apartment on Collins, and the doorman saw her leave her house at about eight o'clock Saturday night. That's the last time we can find anyone who admits to seeing her. Duarte is doing the autopsy in an hour. Show up, if you want. He told me he actually likes having you around."

Quinn thanked him and hung up. Before he could rise and head for the coffeepot and a shower, the phone rang again. It was his brother.

"Hey, bro. You heard about the new body on the beach, right?" Doug asked.

"Yes, Jake Dilessio has the case. I went down with him yesterday, and I'm going to the autopsy this morning."

"Well, that kind of sucks, doesn't it?"

"What? A woman being dead sucks? Hell, yes, it always does."

"No, I'm a cop—you're not. You're invited to the autopsy. I'm not."

"I can get you in if you want."

"Exactly. There's irony for you. No, I'm working, but thanks."

"You *will* make detective."

"Thanks for the vote of confidence. It's just strange some-times, you know? I wanted you on this, and I'm glad you are, but... Anyway, I don't think this woman has anything to do with Lara, but what do you think?"

"Sure, I have a couple of feelings about things. I feel, like you, that something's not right. Do I have any real leads? Not one."

"It's the studio, I'm telling you. Something is wrong there. We can't see it, because the place looks so benign, but something's going on. Hey, do you have a class scheduled for today?"

"No."

"You should. No, maybe you shouldn't. You need to look a little casual, but make sure you show up tonight."

"For...?"

"Group. Beginners' group class. Seven forty-five. Make sure you're there."

"Do you come to beginners' group? They all talk about you as if you're the next John Travolta—what would you be doing in a beginners' class?"

"Advanced tech is at eight-thirty. I'll be in early for that. I'll see you there."

"I'll be there."

Richard Long was Shannon's first student. He ran in be-tween a face-lift at ten and a tummy tuck in the afternoon. After that, she had Brad and Cindy Gray, a married couple she'd worked with since she had started at Moonlight Sonata. Gunter showed up alone for a coaching session, anxious for help in perfecting his bolero.

She had just finished with Gunter when Gordon stuck his head into her office.

"Hey."

"Hey," she returned.

"How was your Sunday?"

"Great. A couple of us went to the beach." She didn't know why she felt so slimy. That was the truth. "How about you?"

"Great. I spent it alone."

"Didn't want to join us at the beach, huh? You've had it with your 'kids,' is that it?"

"I love you kids, but enough is enough. I wanted to check something with you. Didn't you say you were going to charter a dinner cruise for the local students and teachers taking part in the Gator Gala?"

"Yeah."

"I heard you were going to arrange it through Quinn O'Casey."

She hesitated slightly. "I was."

"Have you talked to him about it yet?"

"Um, not really. I started to think that maybe we shouldn't go through him. He *is* a student."

"Find out what he can do for us. I was just looking over some costs. We don't have to make money doing this our first year, but we can't go into the hole too deeply, either."

"I don't know, Gordon."

"Talk to him. Get some costs. I want to go on the cruise well ahead of the gala. Let the students bond, gear up, you know? Talk to Quinn. Is he scheduled for today?"

"No."

"Maybe I'll give him a call."

"He'll show up."

"I'll call him."

"Gordon, he'll show up."

Gordon hesitated, looking at her. "Confident, aren't you?"

Right. Confident. Why didn't she just tell him that the guy was a private eye?

"I'll call him anyway. Want me to handle this?"

Usually, she would have said no. She liked to handle everything. But this time she hesitated, then said, "Sure. That would be great, Gordon. I hadn't expected to be asked to do so much coaching."

"You got it. I'm on it."

He left. Shannon stared after him, chewing on the nub of a pen. She wondered if she should call Quinn herself anyway. She wanted to find out what had happened with Marnie.

No…she wanted an excuse to see him alone. No Sam, no one else.

Among other things, she wanted to tell him just what she thought about his methods of investigation.

Quinn stood with Jake about three feet back from the table, giving Anthony Duarte room to work. A microphone hung over the corpse, and after the preliminary photographs were taken, Duarte, in slow, clear, well-enunciated words, recorded his observations.

Scrapings were taken from beneath the nails. Duarte noted that there wasn't a single bruise on the woman's body. Her excellent, well-toned physical condition was duly noted, as well. Though it didn't appear that she had been in the water long, there were indications that she had been nibbled on by sea life. Her eyes, he informed the microphone and silent room, were dilated. And there were track marks in her arms, though none were found at other locations on the body.

Vaginal swabs were taken, and Duarte voiced for the microphone that there was no sign of rape or recent intercourse. Her last meal had been a good one: lobster, asparagus, rice, largely undigested.

Duarte's voice seemed to drone after a while as he went

through many of the rote, technical aspects of observation as the Y incision was made and organs were removed, weighed, observed, and tissue samples taken. His suspicion that they would discover cardiac arrest due to substance overdose was stated, along with the fact that he would await lab results before final analysis. Duarte was a thorough man.

The brain saw made an eerie sound in the room. The brain was duly weighed, and additional tissue samples were taken.

They had stood silently on the hard floor for hours when Duarte at last stepped back, removing his gloves.

He stepped around the gurney, approaching Jake and Quinn. "Whatever happened to her, it doesn't look like she put up any fight." He shrugged.

"Any chance that she was out with a wild group on a party cruise, got into a state of euphoria and just fell overboard, unnoticed until it was too late?"

"Not unless she managed to die before she plummeted into the water. It's clear she didn't drown. I suspect we'll find she died of cardiac arrest. No, gentlemen, she overdosed, either on her own or with help, and someone with her panicked and tossed her body overboard."

"And then she washed up on the beach," Jake said.

"So she was either helped to her death or died by her own hand, and then she was dumped off a boat," Quinn commented. "But it looks like a case of illegal substances, not overdose by prescription drugs?"

"You saw the tracks," Duarte reminded him.

"But until those lab tests come back, you won't actually know just what was in her," Quinn persisted.

"I'll call Dilessio the minute I get anything. There could be some surprises in the lab work," Duarte said. "I'll have the reports to you by the end of the day, or first thing to-morrow, maybe. We're a bit backed up here. Hell, we're always a bit backed up here. There was a major accident on I-95 this morning. Five people killed, an infant among them. Hell, when will people learn that there's nowhere you have to be in that big a hurry?"

"Thanks. And thanks for letting me hang around," Quinn added.

Duarte managed a grin. "You know, oddly enough, there are plenty of people out there who would like to witness an autopsy. Not like the line for a pop band, but still… Hell, Quinn, believe it or not, I can remember way back to when you were in the Miami-Dade academy. They were dropping like flies around you. You just turned green. I knew you'd make it big."

"I'm a small-time P.I.," Quinn corrected him.

Duarte arched a brow. It wasn't the time or place to get into the things Quinn had done between then and now.

"I have an infant waiting, gentlemen," Duarte said. "I'll get back to you as soon as possible."

They started out, and Jake's phone rang.

He answered tersely, then a smile split his face.

"I'm having a baby," he said.

"Great, get going."

"No, come with me."

"Ashley doesn't want me in the delivery room!"

"No, and I don't want you in there, either. But apparently she's been there for a while already. You know my wife—she wouldn't take me off duty until the moment it was necessary. The baby should be here within the next two hours, at the most. Come on. Spend some time with the living."

Since Jake sounded cool but looked a little nervous, Quinn decided that he could afford the time. All he had planned for the immediate afternoon was some Internet investigation and a call to Annie about Marnie, a call he could make from the hospital.

When they arrived, he was able to see Ashley for a few minutes. She was having contractions every few minutes, and they were obviously painful, but she managed to grin, and assure her husband that she would never have let it go so far that he wouldn't be able to get there in plenty of time. When the doctor arrived for an examination, Quinn wandered out to the waiting room. A few minutes later, Jake poked his head out to tell him that it was time, and Quinn wished his friend good luck. Then he found a quiet spot and called Annie down in South Miami.

"That girl is precious," Annie told him. "And a smart cookie."

"What about the stepfather?" Quinn asked. "Can anything be done?"

"Not as it stands," Annie told him.

"It's got to mess the kid up—knowing the husband is getting ready to really hit on her, only her own mother thinks she's the guilty one, after the guy."

"She's tough. She'll be all right. I've got some time this afternoon, so I'm going to take her for driving lessons."

"Great. She's situated okay?"

"Sure. I've got her in a home. She misses the beach, though."

"Do you think she'll bolt on you?"

Annie thought for a moment on the other end of the line. "No. She wants to make something out of her life. She knows we're giving her real help."

"Good, then. I'll check in later."

When he hung up, Jake burst out into the waiting room. "It's a girl! I have a daughter." He looked dazed.

Quinn rose, embraced him briefly and told him, "Congratulations."

"They need a few minutes. Then you can come in and see her. She's amazing. Nick is on his way down. In a few hours, this place will be like Grand Central Station."

Jake disappeared, and Quinn waited, as asked.

Fifteen minutes later, he got to hold his friend's daughter.

And she was amazing. A big baby, they told him—a few ounces over nine pounds. But she seemed incredibly tiny. She had been born with curling dark hair, her eyes were immense and blue, and she had a grip like steel. He was startled to feel a powerful surge of warmth and protectiveness, and as the baby stared up at him, he found himself thinking about Marnie. Jake's daughter would grow up in a wealth of comfort and love. The innocence in her eyes would remain.

When he returned the baby to her parents, he departed thoughtfully. It was amazing to hold an infant in her first few moments of life.

It made it all the harder to think of the fact that far too many lives were wasted.

Maybe including his own.

Sam came into Shannon's office at about five.

"Hey, did you see the paper this morning?" he asked.

"No, I didn't even put the news on this morning."

"They ran a picture of the woman they found on the beach. I heard on the news that she's already been identified."

"Oh? Did we know her?" Shannon asked, feeling a sudden chill.

"I don't think so. She was a Latin American, got into the U.S. by marrying some rich guy. She got along with his grown kids, though. One of them identified her this morning. Sonya Something. The rich old guy died, and she went wild. Sad, huh?"

"Very sad."

"The old guy finally keels over, she's in the States with money—and whap!"

"Sam, that's terrible. Sonya what?" she persisted.

"I don't remember. It will be on the news again later. I didn't recognize her from the sketch in the paper, though."

"How did they know she was murdered? Maybe she drowned."

"She was found naked on the beach. But she'd been in the water long enough to get chewed by a few crabs. Plus she had track marks in her arms."

"How do you know that?"

"I read the paper, and though cause of death isn't certain, the preliminary suspicion is an overdose."

"Maybe she overdosed herself."

"You think she overdosed, took herself to the beach, stripped and managed to make her clothing disappear, and then died?"

Shannon sighed. "Maybe she was out on a boat with a party crowd, did too many drugs, fell into the water and drowned."

He frowned. "How the hell would I know? I was just mentioning it to you because we were there yesterday, and they ran a sketch of her in the paper with what the reporter had been able to find out. Interesting, huh?"

"Sad."

He shrugged. "They found the body of that prostitute not far from there a while back."

She sat back. "This woman wasn't a prostitute, was she?"

"No, unless she was really high-class. She didn't have on any clothing, but she was wearing thousands in jewelry."

"It's horrible. I'm really sorry. And," she added ruefully, "glad she wasn't a student here."

"No, rest assured, I've never seen her. Hey, aren't you going to go eat? Want to go down to the Italian place with me?"

Shannon hesitated, then shook her head. "I'm taking dinner, but I've got a few errands to run. Sorry. I may be a little late, too. I don't have anything scheduled tonight except for going over the books and making sure the papers are in order for the Gator Gala. Do me a favor and let Ella know I may be late getting back."

She rose, grabbed her handbag and started out.

One inner voice was telling her just to let things alone.

But another voice was telling her that she had to take care of a few matters or else explode.

She opted to listen to the second voice.

There were simply far too many dead people shadowing her life these days.

CHAPTER 13

Shannon Mackay walked out on the deck with true purpose, strides long, every inch of her body speaking volumes.

She was really angry.

Quinn wasn't surprised to see she was still furious with him. He *was* surprised that she was there.

He was sitting at Nick's, where all the regulars had just been treated to drinks in honor of the new baby. He'd opted for a soda himself, since he intended to get to group class, and he was poring over the files on the table in front of him. Somewhere, in either the various police reports or the dossiers on the teachers and clientele of Moonlight Sonata, there had to be a clue.

Shannon searched the crowd, saw him and walked to his table. She didn't wait for an invitation but pulled out the chair opposite from him and sat.

He felt his muscles tighten, and he waited.

"You son of a bitch," she said quietly, evenly. In fact, it was amazing that she could get so much venom into a tone that was so soft.

"You're wrong," he told her.

"Oh, no. I'm not wrong. You are an absolute bastard. In fact, I could go on and on. But I've just come to tell you that, despite your methods, I don't intend to stand in your way, nor have I told anyone at the studio just what you are."

"A bastard?"

"A private eye."

A waitress, Ellen, walked cheerfully up to the table. "What can I get you?" she asked Shannon. "First drink is on the house."

"I'm not drinking, thank you," Shannon said distractedly, staring at Quinn.

"Oh, it doesn't have to be alcohol," Ellen said.

"It's all right. I don't need anything."

Quinn leaned forward. "Have an iced tea, a soda, a coffee. They're celebrating here today."

"Iced tea," Shannon said, then looked at the waitress. "Thank you."

Ellen left. Shannon was too angry to ask what they were celebrating.

"Just keep your distance from me. I'll have Jane or Rhianna take over your lessons. Don't call me, don't come to my house, and stay away from me at the studio."

Quinn leaned back, fighting hard to keep a casual pose. "You're wrong."

"About what? You're not a P.I.? You weren't hired to investigate the people at Moonlight Sonata?"

He stayed silent, staring at her.

"Nice job. You're paid to fraternize."

He shook his head, leaning closer. "No, I'm not making anything on this. It's costing me. I'm looking into it because Doug asked me to."

"That's fine. You keep looking into it. Just stay the hell away from me."

"You're wrong that the one thing has anything to do with the other."

"You were investigating me," she snapped.

"You should be investigated. You might be top of the line in a list of suspects—after Ben Trudeau, the ex-husband. Hey, who would have motive? She stole the man you were living with, your partner. She hit you when you were down." He moved closer and closer, trying to keep his tone low. "You were the best, and you went down completely when Ben left you to dance with Lara, then married her to boot. You even gave up what you loved, competition."

"I never loved competition—I love dance," she grated. "And you are so full of—"

"Iced tea!" Ellen said, arriving back at the table. "They named her Kyra. Kyra Elizabeth," Ellen informed Quinn. "It's a beautiful name."

"She's a beautiful baby," Quinn told Ellen.

"You've seen her already?" Ellen said.

"Yes." He smiled at Ellen. He felt taut, his stomach clenched, and he couldn't think of a thing to say in his defense that Shannon would believe, so he took a certain enjoyment in seeing her try to maintain her temper and refrain from exploding while the waitress remained at their table.

"I'll bet she *is* beautiful, and it's cool that you said that," Ellen informed him. "Most men say all babies look alike—like wrinkly little bald things." She laughed.

"Well, Kyra Elizabeth isn't bald. She came with a head full of curly hair," he said.

"Well, her mother's a beauty, and her dad…he's pretty darned cute, too," Ellen said with a laugh. "Wave if you need me." Then she hurried off to another table.

"Bull!" Shannon enunciated, hard and sharp.

"The baby *is* beautiful."

"*You* are full of bull. The thing with Ben and me ended so

long ago, it's ridiculous. And it's so flattering to know that the only reason you were determined to find out whatever you could about me is because I'm so high on your suspect list."

He felt something snap inside him, and he leaned closer. "Whoa, back up here. I drove you home, I checked out your house. *You* came to my boat. I gave you your own cabin. *You* knocked on *my* door. I made a point of suggesting that it might not be a good time."

"I wasn't drunk," she said icily.

"And I wasn't using you," he snapped back. "What, did that whole thing—over so long ago it's ridiculous—warp you so badly that you can't get on with life at all? Take a look at yourself. Is it so impossible that someone could want you? Enjoy your company? Think you're beautiful?"

She stared at him as if she wanted to scream, or simply throw something at him.

"And is what I do so damned bad?" he asked. "I make a legal living. I'm pretty good at what I do, too. Most of the time."

"Oh, I'll give you that. You're good."

"That sounds hostile. However, I'm going to take it as a compliment."

"Being such an ass, you would," she said. "Listen, like I said, I don't intend to give you away."

"Because you think Lara was murdered."

She hesitated. "Yes."

"So quit hating me. Help me."

"I can't help you. I don't have any idea who might have done it. And now I have to leave. Just stay away from me."

"Great. We've discovered that the danger in your yard was a homeless kid, so now I should stay away."

"I was always honest."

"No. You lie to yourself so often you don't know the truth anymore."

She exhaled a long, exasperated sigh. "I have no feelings for Ben Trudeau! No, that's not true. I feel sorry for him. His life isn't working out so well. I can cope with mine, because I love what I do. Ben needs to compete. He needs applause, to win. I hired Ben for the studio because he's good. And I hired Lara whenever I could, too."

He shook his head slowly, looking at her. "You say you don't want to compete, but you're a liar and a coward. And you say that I used you. I didn't. I found out you aren't just some of the greatest eye candy in the world. You're intelligent, thoughtful, fun and a million other wonderful things. But you won't let yourself accept that. Ben Trudeau hurt you a long time ago. And so, for a *ridiculous* amount of time, you've been a coward, afraid of any man who shows an interest."

She issued a sharp expletive and rose, walking away from the table.

Then she turned back, footsteps brisk as she returned. "How is the girl?"

"What?"

"The homeless girl."

"Marnie is fine."

"You'll really get her to the studio?"

"Yes, I'll really get her there. And for your information, I only met her once before, when she was panhandling on the beach. I'm not a child molester."

She flushed. "I didn't suggest that you were."

"You should have seen the way you looked at me that night. And by the way, I'll handle your charter boat for you, as well. I do own two boats—well, I own half of two boats. Dane Whitelaw and I run the investigations, and we also own boats that we rent out. I do fish, and I do dive. And I can give you the best deal you're going to get."

"Gordon will be talking to you about that."

He folded his arms across his chest. "I won't deal with Gordon."

"It's his studio."

"And I won't dance with Jane or Rhianna. You took me on. You keep me."

"So don't take classes. What do I care?"

"Because I suck?"

"Because you're a jerk!"

She started to walk away, then swung back again.

"Who had the baby?"

"A friend."

"The woman at the beach?"

His eyes narrowed. She had seen him when he had gone to the site where they had found the last body.

"Who else saw me there?" he asked.

She shook her head. "I was with Sam, but he didn't see you."

"Sit down," he told her.

"No!"

"Please."

She inhaled, then sat, perched on the edge of the chair.

"The guy who came on the boat the other day is Jake Dilessio, a homicide cop. His wife is a forensic artist. Cops can get a lot of things P.I.s can't. And Jake is one damned decent guy—he's not threatened when an outsider looks into something. Anyway, I'm happy as hell for Jake and Ashley because they had their first child today. I'm kind of sorry, as well, because they're both going to take time off, and he's been a big help."

She shook her head. "What did the woman on the beach have to do with Lara? She wasn't a student. She was never a student."

He shook his head. "I don't know."

"Then what were you doing there?"

"Trying to figure out why so many women are dying." He hesitated. "You had a student once, a woman named Nell Durken."

She frowned, and at last the tension in her seemed to dissipate. For this moment, at least, she wasn't ready to rip into him. "Nell was very good. She stopped coming, though. She wanted to put time into making things work with her husband. And then the bastard killed her anyway." She shook her head. "But they got him. The police arrested him. He's facing trial."

He nodded. "Nell hired me. A simple case of following him—she was convinced he was cheating. He was. When she turned up dead, his prints were all over the bottle of pills, and since he was seeing someone, he had definite motive."

"Nell was a lovely woman. She had a lot to offer the world," Shannon murmured.

"Yes, she did."

"If her husband killed her, then…well, then these deaths can't be related," Shannon said. "But it just seems a little too strange that both women might have died the same way and it's a total coincidence."

"Well, that's the point, isn't it? Things *are* a little too strange."

Shannon stood abruptly, as if remembering how angry she was. "I'm working. I have to get back. And as for you, I'll certainly cooperate in any way I can to help you find the truth. But other than that…"

"I know. Keep my distance. Because I know just a little too much about you, right?" His voice had an edge, a sound of bitterness he was surprised to hear himself betray.

"Yes, you've got it," she informed him.

As she started to turn away, he caught her wrist. "There's something you're not telling me. There has to be a reason you were so edgy in your own house."

There *was* something. He could tell. But either she was afraid it was just something minimal or silly, or she was afraid she might give someone else away.

She shook her head. "I don't know anything. I wish I did."

"Maybe that's not a very good wish."

"Why?"

"Maybe people die because they *do* know something," he said.

She pulled her wrist free. "I'm sure I'll be seeing you, Mr. O'Casey."

"Very soon. In a matter of hours."

She frowned.

"Group class," he reminded her pleasantly.

She turned on her heels. Her footsteps clicked in a no-nonsense manner as she walked along the path to the parking lot.

Rhianna was leading the beginners' class. From her office, Shannon could hear her directions.

"Slow, quick, quick, slow. Slow, quick, quick, slow… there you go, Mr. Suarez, look at that, Cuban motion already taking flight. Mr. O'Casey…think box. Just a box. Slow… quick, quick, slow. Think of the way we've been working, fox-trot, rumba. Two very different dances, one smooth, one rhythm, and yet we're still talking box right now. There will always be two aspects involved. The step itself, and then the technique of the step. Belinda, good motion! Just because it's slow, that doesn't mean that it's a stop. Eventually, each step flows into the other. A count doesn't necessarily mean a foot movement but rather a body movement, and though each is distinct, it flows. Feel the music, Mr. O'Casey. Slow, quick, quick, slow…slow, quick, quick, slow."

Shannon stepped outside to watch. All the men—Ben,

Justin and Sam—were engaged in private lessons at the moment. Jane didn't have a private, so she was the one assisting Rhianna, who was trying to show the men the proper dance hold so they would one day, be able to lead properly.

Tonight the newcomers group was small. Just the pretty little dressmaker who had started about two weeks ago, Quinn O'Casey and a construction worker, Tito Suarez, who was about to attend his daughter's wedding.

As she stepped out, she heard Mr. Suarez speaking in confusion. "I'm sorry, which of you is being the man?"

"I'm the man right now," Rhianna told him. "Just call me Reggie—that's my name when I play the guy. Jane's guy name is Jason. You'll get used to it. Hey, you should see it when Justin Garcia does his Judy thing when Ben is leading. They're great."

For a moment Shannon leaned against the wall, feeling a brief sense of strange relief. She didn't think she'd heard real laughter in the studio since Lara had died. Tonight it seemed that they might be getting back to normal at last.

Or maybe nothing would ever be normal again.

She caught Quinn's eyes across the room.

You're next.

Why hadn't she told him what the waiter had said to her? Because…it wasn't proof of anything? It might be as silly and paranoid as jumping when a bush moved in her backyard.

But maybe not.

"Small class, huh?"

She nearly jumped a mile. It was just Gordon, standing behind her, speaking softly and glumly.

"Business will pick back up," she said.

"I hope so."

"There's a large group waiting for the advanced class already," she told him.

"I guess you're right. Have we had any cancellations for the Gator Gala?"

"No, not one," she told him.

"Hey, Quinn got us the boat."

She spun around.

Gordon nodded, pleased. "Casual buffet, trip out into Biscayne Bay—he even knew a great band to play for us, and the price is right. Be sure you make the announcement tonight, after advanced. We're going out of Coconut Grove at eight. Everyone should meet at the dock around seven. Tell them that dress is Miami-casual-chic."

"And what the hell is that?" Shannon asked him.

He shrugged. "It means they can wear whatever the hell they want."

He turned to head back for his office. Rhianna announced the end of the group class, and told her students to applaud their partners and themselves. Then Belinda started to chat with Tito. Quinn smiled casually and sauntered over to Jane and Rhianna.

Shannon was amazed to hear her teeth grate as she wondered what investigative techniques he would be using with her staff.

Quinn walked into Gordon's office. "I hear there's some kind of a meeting tonight for the Gator Gala people."

Gordon Henson leaned back in his chair, smiling. "Not a real meeting. Shannon has an advanced class tonight, so a lot of the participants will be here. She's just going to give them a little advice, get them hyped, talk about outfits, shoes, hair—makeup. Your brother will probably stay, though he's heard most of it before."

"Can beginners enter the Gator Gala?"

"Of course." Gordon brightened up, as if his eyes were on the prize. "You interested?"

Hell, no! Quinn thought. But aloud he said, "Maybe. Would it be all right if I hung around for the meeting?"

"Naturally. Hey, I know you feel you don't have much of an aptitude for this, but believe me, most people are clumsy when they start out."

"Right."

"Your brother looked like a real clod," Gordon said, maybe a little too honestly. "And look at him now."

"Well, I'll hang around. And think about it."

"You'd have a lot of work to do." A lot of work—a lot of classes. More income for the studio. It was the American way, it was what they did.

"I'll give it some thought," Quinn assured him. "Do a little watching."

"Go right ahead. Do that."

Quinn walked back out to where the advanced class was being taught. It was Shannon's class, and they were working on rumba technique. He was amazed to see the individual motions that actually took place in one little step. He was amazed to watch her do it, as well. The twist of the hips, the bend of the knee, how everything combined to become so incredibly fluid that no one watching would realize how complex the motions really were.

She was a good teacher. And she used Doug to demonstrate a lot of what she was saying.

He'd never seen his brother look so damned good.

A twinge of jealousy swept through him and he firmly stomped it down. They were dancing, just dancing. But when dancing looked like that…

Motive…

Jealousy was a major motive for murder. Jealousy, unrequited love, hatred spawned by envy.

She worked with each member of the class. He knew a few of them. The doctors Richard and Mina Long. Gabriel Lopez, owner of the club. His own brother. There was also a much older man, who performed the moves with applaudable finesse. Two other couples, a beautiful younger woman, and a middle-aged woman.

Bobby and Giselle showed up during the class. They stood near Quinn, watching.

"Those are the crème de la crème of the students," Bobby told him. "Katarina and her husband...she's really good. I don't think she's as much in love with dance as she is with showing off her outfits, but hey, whatever works. Richard Long is really good, better than his wife, but they get along amazingly well, anyway. You should see some of the fights between husbands and wives around here—wife accusing husband of not leading right, husband accusing wife of not being able to follow."

"Not us, of course," Giselle said, grinning.

Bobby grimaced. "We don't fight that bad, do we?"

"Let's hope not, we're still newlyweds."

"It looks as if the two of you get along all right," Quinn told them.

"Better than the professionals," Giselle said. "We were here one day when Lara Trudeau and Jim Burke were working. Shannon was coaching. Lara was going on and on about Jim missing the beat, and Shannon told her that Jim was right, she had to actually let him lead."

"And Lara Trudeau just took that?" Quinn said, surprised. From what he had heard about the woman, she wouldn't accept anyone else giving her instruction.

"Oh, no. She said something to Shannon, and Shannon told her that she didn't waste her time with people who didn't think they needed any improvement. She walked off and Lara and Jim got into a big fight. Then they realized that some of the students had arrived and were watching, so Lara went to get Shannon, and everyone started over as if nothing had happened at all."

"Jim must have had some major patience," Quinn said.

"He wanted to compete—she was the best, I guess," Bobby said with a shrug. "I haven't seen him around much, not since she died."

"Was he here a lot?"

"Sure. He knew Shannon could teach. He would come for coaching sessions without Lara."

"The woman was a bitch," Giselle whispered.

The advanced class was over, and Gordon had come out to talk to them about the Gator Gala. Shannon, seeing him in the back of the group, arched her brows.

"I told Gordon I was thinking about entering," he said, not caring that everyone in the room could hear, in response to her unspoken question.

"Oh," she murmured.

"As a beginner. He said there's a beginner category," Quinn told her. He almost laughed aloud at himself. He had sounded defensive. Yes, he thought. *There's a category for people who can't dance. It's the two-left-feet award.*

"Hey, that's great," Sam Railey said. "Our newest student is entering."

The room applauded for him. To his amazement, he felt the dark heat of a flush creeping over his face.

"Maybe," he said.

"Some of you have competed before, some of you haven't," Shannon said, perching on one of the small tables against the wall. "Some things may sound silly, and some may sound fun. I've actually acquired students through the years just because they like the dance outfits, so... Okay, beginners—something dressy is all you really want. And students entering other categories are still free to opt for something simple. Whatever makes you comfortable and works with the dances you've chosen. We have all kinds of catalogues for shoes and clothing, and, of course, we have Katarina right next door, and I can vouch for the beauty of her designs. We'll also have someone to help with hair and makeup. Long hair's best swept up out of the way. There's nothing like throwing your partner off by smacking him in the face with your hair. Makeup should generally be very dark and dramatic—best for pictures and videos. This next is very important. Competitions move fast—always make sure you know where you're supposed to be and when. Be in line or you're disqualified. Your teachers are responsible for you, as well, but try not to torture them too much. Everyone will have an opportunity to see the floor and try it out before the competition begins, and, of course, there will be a professional show at our awards dinner."

Mina Long piped up. "What about shoes?" She hesitated. "Last competition, Lara Trudeau was appalled because I was wearing black shoes. I mean, it was like Joan Crawford in that movie, telling her children there would be no wire coat hangers in the house."

There was laughter after that statement. Uneasy laughter.

Shannon answered casually. "Flesh-colored shoes are best, unless you're doing a cabaret act and need a specific shoe for a specific outfit."

"Black shoes don't go better with a black outfit?" Giselle, seated on the floor with Bobby, asked.

Rhianna, hovering near Shannon, answered. "This may be in opposition to all the fashion advice you've ever heard, but think flesh, think beige. The right shoes are important, because the judges will be looking at your feet. When you're heading out on the town, black heels may look good with your black dress, but in dance, go for the flesh-colored shoes, beige, tan."

"Why?" Mina asked.

"You create a line," Shannon said. "The leg looks longer, movement looks smoother. Check out some of the tapes we have and you'll see. Compare the dancers with 'blending' shoes with those who have color, and you'll see."

"You mean we're going to be judged on our shoes?" Giselle asked.

Shannon shook her head. "No, and of course, there's nothing in the rule books that says you can't buy any dance shoes you want. But take a look at the tapes, and you'll see what Rhianna is saying for yourself. If you don't agree, then you don't agree. There are no laws."

Quinn looked around the room, noting that all the teachers, even Ben, were present. It made sense. They all had students entering the competition. Ben, who had been married to Lara and might have hated her. Jane and Sam, learning to compete together, always losing out. Rhianna, also a competitor. Justin Lopez. Shannon, who had good reason to hate the woman. Then there was Gordon Henson, who had given Lara her start. Jim, who Lara abused, but who needed her for what he craved in life.

Then the students. Gabriel Lopez, who managed the club, and Katarina, who created the clothing. Lots of reasons for hatred, but lots of reasons for need. None of it gelled. Because why would any of them have hated Nell Durken? And what could they have to do with women found dead on the beach with drugs in their systems?

None of it made sense. What *would* make sense would be that none of the deaths were related. Still…

"So thank you all for coming. We'll meet once a week until the competition, just for questions. Don't forget to schedule your private lessons with your teachers, and thanks for coming," Shannon said, rising.

The meeting was over. Students were saying goodbye. Kissing goodbye—everyone here seemed to kiss everyone else goodbye on the cheek. It was like leaving after an Italian wedding.

There was no reason to linger. The teachers were anxious to lock up and go home. In fact, Justin Garcia was out the door along with the students. It was nearly eleven, Quinn realized.

But he had to linger. He stayed behind, avoiding his brother and Bobby as they left. He approached Shannon.

"I can hang around, walk you to your car."

"No, thank you," she said firmly. Coldly. He itched to take hold of her, shake her, tell her she was the best thing that happened to him in ages. In forever. He watched her dance, watched her move, and was afraid for no reason. Still, he felt a rising desperation to be near her.

"Gordon and I will leave together," she lied. Again, that ice in her voice. *You do your thing. And leave me the hell alone.*

"All right, good night, then." He turned to leave, then turned back. "Make sure you let Gordon walk you out."

"Absolutely."

He left. He had no choice.

The last student left. Sam and Jane departed together, discussing the Gator Gala. Rhianna muttered something about having to stop for milk and flew out as if she were being chased by a banshee.

Ella Rodriguez had gone out with her mother for her birthday that night, so Shannon went to the schedule board to make sure that any last-minute appointments had been filled in properly. She looked up to see that Ben, moody and grim, was hovering near the reception area.

"Anything wrong?" she asked him.

He shook his head. "Except that…"

"What?"

"There's a rumor going around that you're going to start working with Jim Burke."

Her brows flew up. "I don't compete anymore. You know that. Who told you that?"

"Gabe. Gabriel Lopez. He said it's the talk down in the club."

"It may be talk, but it's not true." She sighed. "Ben, I don't compete. I don't want to compete. I really like what I do."

He looked away for a minute, then looked back at her. She was surprised by his expression. Ben was very good-looking—suave, dark, with deep, expressive eyes. They were on her intently right now.

"What I was going to say was this—if the rumor was true, I was happy for you. You may think you don't want to compete, but you do. I see your eyes sometimes when other people are on the floor. I see your mind working, and I know that you're calculating steps. I screwed you over once. Big time. I wanted to get ahead too badly myself. You should compete. Not with me—I understand how you feel about me—but with someone. Someone good. And Jim is good. I just wanted to say that you didn't need to try to hide anything like this from me. I would be happy to see you compete with anyone, especially Jim."

She almost fell into the chair behind her, but instead simply stared at him for several long seconds. "Thanks, Ben. Thanks very much. But what you heard is a rumor."

He nodded. "Think about making it not be a rumor," he said, then turned and walked away. "Good night—hey, go ahead and lock up when you leave. Gordon left a few minutes ago."

"Sure, thanks. Good night."

She heard the door close as Ben left.

The music was off. There suddenly seemed to be an eerie silence in the studio.

And she didn't want to be there alone.

She hadn't finished with the schedule, but she didn't care. She wished she hadn't been so surprised by Ben's words that she had let him leave; he would have stayed to walk out with her.

She wished she'd kept Quinn O'Casey around. Why the hell hadn't she?

Because she'd been hurt.

Maybe it was like her dancing. She'd been hurt, so...

Stop, she told herself. Get your purse, get your keys, lock up and leave, rationally.

She left the reception area and started to walk to her office for her purse. It was when she bent down to get it that she heard the noise.

A cranking. A shifting. Something being opened then closed.

She stood very still, trying to tell herself the noise was natural. There was a club on the floor below, after all.

But the noise hadn't come from below. It had come from the second floor.

"Hello," she called.

She forced herself to throw her purse over her shoulder and walk calmly out to the studio area. There was no one there. Nothing had moved, nothing had changed. She felt a ripple along her spine.

Maybe Katarina was working late.

No, she and her husband had gone home directly from the meeting, they'd said good-night to her.

Get out, get out, just get out, a little voice said to her.

She fought the unreasoning sense of fear. Even if someone was around, they probably had a valid reason.

No attempt at logic seemed to help her any. She just wanted to get out, and get out fast. Instinct screamed at her as if she were being chased by a menace she could actually see and touch.

She hurried to the back door, flying out of it, then reminding herself that the noise might not have come from within the studio but from without. She could see no one in the area that led toward the back. The stairs that led to Gabriel Lopez's apartment above seemed swamped in shadow. The door to the storage room was locked.

Even if someone was out here, it could be for a very valid reason.

"Katarina? Hey, Kat, David…are you two here?"

No answer.

She looked at the shadowy stairs leading up to Gabe's place.

"Gabriel?"

Not a whisper sounded from the shadows.

She fled toward the stairs that led down to the rear parking area. As she stepped on the first, the grating sounded again.

From behind her.

She didn't look back but started quickly down.

Footsteps followed.

She started to run.

Her car was only forty feet away, and she had her keys and clicker out as she moved toward it, absolutely certain she was being followed.

She hit the button. Her car clicked a friendly little beeping sound, and the lights went on.

Shannon flew to the driver's door and nearly wrenched it open, then slid into the seat, slamming the door shut instantly.

She hit the locks.

Then she screamed as a tap sounded against the window.

CHAPTER 14

Seated at the table of the galley, legs stretched out on the boothlike seat, Quinn chewed the nub of his pen and stared at his notes. Nell Durken, Lara Trudeau. Dancers with the studio in common. Art Durken in jail, more than a hundred witnesses when Lara died. Two more women found dead from drugs in the area of the studio, neither of them dancers. What could be the connection—or was there one?

He glanced over his list of students and teachers, and realized with a growing headache that motive was not a problem with most of them.

Eliminate. Get rid of the impossible, and whatever was left, however improbable, had to be the truth.

Shit. Who the hell to eliminate?

He started writing another list. Least likely, most likely. Least likely—Justin Garcia. A small burst of pure speed, didn't work with Lara, loved salsa. And probably not her type. Being tall herself, she had apparently liked tall men, though what Quinn knew of her lovers other than Ben

Trudeau and his own brother, he didn't know. He wrote down Ben's name and, beneath it, ex-husband still bitter.

Gordon? Which side did he go on?

There was a tap at the cabin door. "Yeah?"

"It's me. I'm here."

He rose, leaning up the steps to open the cabin door and allow his brother to walk down. Doug looked eager. "You've got something?" he asked.

Quinn grimaced. "No."

Doug frowned. "I thought maybe you asked me here because you had something."

"Sit."

"Yes, sir," Doug said, sounding a little irritated.

"Did I interrupt something?" Quinn responded in kind. "You're the one who got me into this."

"Right. I'm sorry," Doug said quickly.

"Who else was Lara seeing? How hot and heavy was your affair? You've got to give me more. I can't get to know all these people overnight."

Doug drummed his fingers on the table, lowered his head for a minute and looked up. "I think she was seeing someone else."

"Was it Ben again?"

"Maybe, I'm not sure. But she was ready to call it off."

"How do you know that?"

"She told me there was something in her life that had to change."

"Why would that be a man?"

"Because she was Lara."

Quinn shook his head and muttered ruefully, "Bring that into a court of law."

Doug sat up straight, giving Quinn his full attention. "You had to know her. She could be the most exquisite person in the world, and she could be cutting and cruel."

"How did you get involved with her, exactly, and when did your involvement with her start?"

"About three months ago."

"Where?"

"Down at the club. We were dancing one night. She'd had a little too much to drink. I suggested I should give her a ride home and maybe stay awhile. I was just playing around, really. I never thought she'd say yes."

"Then?"

"She said no—there was no way she'd take a chance on anyone knowing she was inviting me in. Then, in the same breath, she suggested that she come to my place. And she did. And after that, we saw each other at least once a week. Always at my place. She didn't want anyone to know. I was trying to keep it casual, as if I knew she was a free spirit. But I honestly think she was beginning to care about me. Because, once, I pressed it. I said she didn't work for the studio—we could be a couple if we wanted to be. And she said it wasn't just the studio, that she had a few other problems she needed to solve. And the way she said it, I knew there was someone else. At least one other person."

"Ben?"

Doug shook his head. "Maybe. Someone who was always at the studio, anyway. And I doubt it was Sam, 'cause he's gay, and I doubt it was Justin, because she didn't go for guys who weren't over six feet."

His assumption had been right, Quinn thought.

"Gordon?" he queried.

"Gordon...he's a lot older, but he's still a nice-looking man. Known to go both ways, but I don't know. If they were suddenly a hot ticket, there was no chemistry on the floor."

"What about her partner, Jim Burke?"

"I don't think so."

"Why not?"

Doug stared at him and shrugged. "Lara liked her own strength, but she wasn't attracted to a pushover. Jim did everything she said. I don't see him as a lover for her."

Quinn leaned toward his brother. "There were hundreds of people there the night she died. Do you remember her having any confrontations?"

Doug hesitated. "Can I get a beer?"

"Help yourself. Just answer me."

Doug walked to the refrigerator and pulled out a bottle of beer. He arched a brow to Quinn, who reached up and caught the Miller his brother tossed his way.

"She had a bit of a confrontation with me."

"Oh?"

"Well, not exactly *with* me. *About* me. She told Jane that she needed to follow, that I knew my stuff and Jane was being too strong, that she needed to let me lead. Under her breath, Jane muttered 'Fuck you, bitch.' Lara heard her and told her that they'd talk about it later. She could be really vicious when she wanted. In a cool, deadly way."

"Yeah, well, she's the dead one. She and Jane were major competition, huh?"

"Rhianna is more the current belle of the studio." As Doug spoke, his cell phone rang. He reached into his pocket with a quick, "'Scuse me."

Quinn looked off. He saw that his brother was glancing furtively at him.

"Yeah, I'm a little busy," Doug said quietly, then listened for a moment.

"I'm not sure," he said next, then glanced at Quinn, looking oddly guilty.

"Who is it?" Quinn mouthed.

For a moment he thought Doug was either going to lie to

him or tell him it was none of his business. But Doug covered the mouthpiece of the phone and whispered, "It's Jane."

"Ulrich?" Quinn said.

Doug nodded. "I...uh, I can tell her I can't see her tonight."

"You're not supposed to be seeing her at all, are you?"

"No." No wonder he'd looked so guilty. "You can't say anything," Doug told him quickly. "I mean, she could get fired. Look, I'll just tell her that I can't go over."

"No. Don't. Go over. And don't forget that you're a cop, and don't forget that you dragged me into this."

"Don't forget I'm a cop? You mean, question her."

"Hell yes."

"Doesn't that seem a little...slimy?"

"No. Murder seems a little slimy."

Doug nodded. "You're right."

Quinn shook his head. "You were having an affair with Lara, and she's only been in the ground a few days."

Doug nodded. "I know. But like I said, she was seeing other people, too. She meant something to me, yes. And solving this means a lot to me. I work with Jane. I've worked with her a long time. We're good friends. And she's shaken up right now. It's not so much that we've begun something. She just doesn't want to be alone. You think my spending time with her now is so bad?"

Quinn drummed his fingers on the table. "No, I guess not. But, Doug, if you were so close to Lara, shouldn't you have some idea of who she might have been alone with—if only for a few minutes—at the competition?"

Doug waved a hand in the air. "People move quickly. Before the dinner and competition that night, there was a cocktail hour. People were all milling together. Plus the women instructors had a dressing room, and the men had another, but they were connected by a little outside balcony. So someone having trouble with a tie or a hook or whatever might have slipped out on the balcony and gotten whoever was there to help. And even the pros had some champagne or a cocktail of some kind."

"The glasses from the dressing rooms should have been analyzed," Quinn said, wondering how such a simple procedure had been omitted.

"You have to remember, it looked like a natural death," his brother reminded him. "You don't really think it could have been one of the women, do you?"

"Why not? History has proved that women are certainly capable of murder. And when they do commit murder, they often opt for poison."

"This wasn't poison."

"Drugs act the same way. But what I mean is, no knives, no gunshots, no shows of strength. Silent killers."

"But…Jane? If it were a woman, it would more likely be Shannon. She's the one with the grudge."

"That's true. And if it were just Lara's death, I'd be more inclined to think we should be looking at the fairer sex. But Nell had a connection to the studio, and the circumstances were just too close. And I still don't know if the illegal narcotic deaths were associated or not. My gut reaction says yes, but there's nothing concrete to connect them yet. So I'm suspicious of everyone."

"Even Jane."

"Even Jane. Find out what she takes. If she does drugs. And if she has prescriptions. And if so, find out where she gets them."

"I still feel slimy. But…you're right. I got you into this, and I'm the one who wants to make detective. But you *were* a detective. And when you were with the FBI, you analyzed the ways people acted, their psyches. You've got to have more of a feel for what's going on than I do."

"Nothing but hunches," Quinn told him. "But, hell," he added dryly, "they seem to be just about as good as any other method I learned."

"Should I go now?" Doug asked.

Quinn nodded, then frowned. "She's still on the phone?"

Doug indicated his hand, still tightly clamped over the mouthpiece. Then he moved his hand and spoke into the phone again. "I'm on my way."

On the other end, Jane said something. Something suggestive, Quinn imagined from Doug's reaction.

After Doug left, Quinn stared at his notes.

Coincidence.

Art Durken in jail.

Lara Trudeau dead from the same drug that had killed Nell, combined with alcohol. The prescriptions from different doctors, both with reputations above reproach.

How did the other dead women fit in? Maybe they didn't.

Nell and Lara, both dead by the same drug. Different doctors.

That didn't mean they hadn't gotten more of the drug from different sources.

He glanced at his watch. It was late. Didn't matter. He picked up the phone, intending to call in a few favors.

"Ben!" Shannon exclaimed in relief, reflexibly hitting the button to lower the window, then wondering if she should have.

"Shannon, are you all right?" He sounded anxious as he stared in at her.

"I'm fine. Why did you bang on the window like that?"

"Because you came running out of the studio like a bat out of hell."

"Just nerves," she said. But had it just been nerves? Had she imagined the sound of footsteps coming after her?

"Then you're all right?"

"Yes—other than the near heart attack you gave me."

"I'm sorry, really sorry. I thought something was wrong."

She shook her head, then frowned. "Where the hell did you come from, anyway?"

"I'd walked around from the front. I needed a few things from the convenience store down the street. But my car is back here."

"Oh. You—you didn't go back upstairs, did you?"

"No, I came from the street. Why?"

"I don't know. I thought I heard something."

"Buildings creak. Especially old ones, like ours."

"I suppose," she agreed.

"Want me to follow you home?"

"It's all right."

"I won't get out of my car. I'll just see that you get in your house."

"Sure, fine."

Ben went to his car, and Shannon revved hers into gear. Her house was so close she wondered why she drove.

Because she didn't feel like walking along any shadowy streets right now.

The trip went quickly. As she turned into her own driveway, she saw Ben watching her from his car. She hurried up her walk, opened the door and went in, turning to wave to him before she closed the door.

He waved back, then drove off.

Alone, she leaned against the door and stared around the house. She had left on several lights, but despite that, shadows greeted her.

Silence and shadows.

You're next!

Those two words, spoken to her by a waiter at a competition, where they could have meant anything at all, could have been—must have been—spoken to her by mistake. And yet, they continued to haunt her.

"So just break down already and check yourself into a hospital for the insane," she murmured to herself.

She felt the unbelievable urge to leave home and head for a boat on the marina called the *Twisted Time*.

No.

"Screw this!" she exclaimed aloud with irritation. But once again she found herself going through her house room by room, looking in closets and under the bed, checking out everything, assuring herself that the back door had remained locked and bolted in her absence.

At last she drank a cup of tea and swallowed an Excedrin PM.

After she did, she swore, thinking she would stay up all night long next time, rather than take anything, anything at all, even so much as an aspirin.

It was late when she went to bed, lights blazing in the other rooms, only her own darkened. She would be in shadow and look out to the light. That thought eventually allowed her to close her eyes.

Maybe Christie had been right. Maybe she did need a dog.

She suddenly sat bolt upright, cloaked and chilled by the darkness in her room. Ben had said he'd gone to the convenience store.

For what?

He hadn't been carrying anything, anything at all, when he'd come to her window.

Home again, home again.

She was home again.

Alone. Surely, by now, stretched out in bed, glorious eyes closed, lashes sweetly sweeping her cheeks.

No dog, no alarm, and it wasn't difficult at all to don a pair of gloves and use the key he had to slip inside.

She had no idea how vulnerable she was.

At any time...

Just what the hell did she know?

Nothing, he assured himself.

Except that...

She was listening. Hearing what she shouldn't even be noticing. Maybe, in time, she would start looking for the source of the noise.

There was more.

He'd overheard her one time too many. He'd seen the way she acted. And now, when he could, he watched her around the studio.

But she'd known something tonight. She'd heard something.

Vague, that was all. She had a vague sense of danger.

He hesitated, thinking how easy it would be to slip in.

But why?

He could take her any time he wanted. If he needed to.

He would really hate to see her dead.

Right now, he would watch. Just watch.

She shouldn't die in her own house. Unless...

No.

There were far better ways. Should it become necessary.

He had been standing on the sidewalk, in the shadows of an elm. But his car wasn't parked far away.

Actually, he tried never to be very far away. Ever. She never even noticed.

Morning was coming.

He would see to it that they were close during the day.

He would watch and wait.

Tonight, he could have touched her.

So close, he could have reached right out and touched her.

He had to remember that. He was always close. Always watching.

And she never knew.

He would always be watching.

Always be close.

Close enough just to reach out...

And touch.

CHAPTER 15

Art Durken entered the jail conference room accompanied by a thirty-something, bulky guard and an older man in a rumpled suit. The older man introduced himself.

"Theodore Smith, Mr. O'Casey. I'm Mr. Durken's attorney, and my client has agreed to see you only in my presence, so if I don't like your questions or attitude, I intend to remind him that he doesn't have to see you at all. Mr. Durken insists on his innocence and is convinced that you may now have a few reasons to believe him—since you requested this meeting."

"I realize Mr. Durken is under no obligation to speak with me," Quinn said. "I appreciate both of you agreeing to the interview."

Smith nodded, looking for all the world like a king granting a subject a special favor, despite his harried appearance. He took a chair on the opposite side of the table, indicating that Art should sit next to him. As Durken did so, Quinn took his own chair.

The burly guard remained in a corner of the room.

Durken was in his early thirties, with sandy hair and light

gray eyes. Slender but wiry, he had a certain charm about him. Apparently that was how he had kept Nell.

And acquired a college senior as a mistress.

"I didn't do it," Durken told him, staring right at him. "I know you were tailing me for Nell, and I know you know exactly what I did with my time in those weeks before she died. But I didn't kill my wife. I swear it."

He looked ill, not at all the same man Quinn had tailed. His hair, so neatly combed in those days, looked ragged, as if he spent his hours running his fingers through it. He had always worn the look of a man who had the world captured between both hands, but now his face was lean, haggard, and there was a sheen of sweat on his upper lip. He might just have looked nervous, like a killer who'd been caught and was ready to deny everything.

But there was something about the way his eyes held Quinn's that seemed to speak of honesty. He didn't start in by scowling, or by accusing Quinn of being the reason he had been arraigned for murder.

"Your fingerprints were all over your wife's pill bottle," Quinn reminded him quietly.

"I handed her the damned thing often enough. And I told her she shouldn't be taking the things. Hell, I even told her that I wasn't worth her having to be on the things. But she had me convinced she knew what she was doing, that she knew when to take them, and that she didn't overdo it. They kept her from mood swings and depression, and fear."

"Let's say you didn't do it, Art," Quinn told him. "Who could have forced her to overdose like that?"

A look of desolation swept over the other man, and he shook his head. "I don't know. You see, the thing of it is…I think Nell was having an affair months ago. She knew…well, she suspected, until she hired you, that I fooled around." He lifted his hands. "I…I did before. And I think her way of getting even with me might have been to have her own affair. I accused her once, and she told me that she *should* be fooling around, maybe we could stay married that way. It would be messed up as hell, but…she said she loved me and wanted to stay married. Anyway, I went into a big guilt thing, and I wasn't even angry that she was running around, too. I just…you see, I wanted to stay married, too."

"So what happened?"

He shook his head. "It's not in my nature, I guess, to be monogamous. I met Cecily, told her I wasn't married, and you know the rest. Actually," he said, wincing, "I told her that I worked for the CIA, and that's why I was away so much, unable to see her, be with her…and she believed me. I guess you know all that, but…look, I might have been an asshole, a liar and a cheat, but I didn't kill Nell."

"You weren't at all angry, thinking she might have had an affair? You haven't mentioned any of this before. It's not in any of the reports," Quinn pointed out.

"Art, be careful of what you're saying," Smith warned him.

Durken shook his head impatiently. "I didn't mention it before because no one asked me, and…shit, why volunteer that kind of information when I already had a motive and no one wanted to look any further? And while I'm at it, yes, it was always her trust fund that we used for our lifestyle."

"Art, this man can use what you're saying against you in court," Smith warned firmly.

"Was it during the time that your wife was dancing that you thought she was having an affair?" Quinn asked.

Durken looked surprised. "Yes."

"Do you think she was having an affair with a teacher? A fellow student?"

He shrugged. "I never went around the place. Bullshit

dance like that just doesn't appeal to me. She'd asked me to go when she started. I probably should have. Who knows? But, yeah, I suppose she could have had her affair with someone there. We made up big time back then, though. She stopped dancing—and I think she stopped her affair. I didn't press the point, because I didn't want her pressing any points with me. I was guilty as hell, so if she was guilty, too...well, you know."

Durken brightened up suddenly. "I heard about that dancer dying. She died of an overdose, too, huh? Or drugs and booze, something like that." His face fell. "But she died in front of a pack of people, didn't she?"

"Yes, she died before hundreds of people."

Durken looked ill again.

Quinn rose, nodding to Durken's attorney and the guard. "That doesn't mean she wasn't alone with someone before the performance," he said. He pulled out his card, handing it to Durken's attorney. "If there's anything you can think of that might help, could you give me a call?"

He started from the room. Smith called him back. "Mr. Durken is in here because of you, Mr. O'Casey."

"Mr. Durken is in here because his fingerprints were all over the bottle of pills his wife had taken. I merely provided the police with a chronology of his activities prior to his wife's death."

Durken was shaking his head, ignoring his attorney. "I don't care if you got me in here or not—if you can get me out. I'll be thinking. Of anything that can help. Anything at all."

"Thanks," Quinn said.

A guard on the outside opened the door, and Quinn found himself anxious to leave the jail as quickly as possible.

Once outside, he hesitated only a minute, then put through a call to Annie. Though he wasn't scheduled for an appointment himself until the following day, he wanted to get back into the studio.

Marnie was excited.

Dressed in jeans and a polo shirt, she was worried that she didn't really have clothing in which she could move.

"And my shoes," she told Quinn. "My shoes are horrible."

He glanced at her as they drove across the causeway. "I don't think it matters too much—not at first, anyway."

"You sure?"

"We'll find out, won't we?"

She nodded, and he knew she was watching him. "Thanks, by the way," she told him quietly.

"The studio offers a free first class to everyone," he reminded her.

She shook her head, and her long dark hair floated on her shoulders. "I mean, thanks for setting me up with Annie and all. Annie is great. I've been working, you know. At a boutique, right by the shelter. And I can stay at the shelter until I get on my feet. The boutique is great, really cool clothes, and I'll get a fifty percent discount after six months. But you know what? There's an older woman who is a friend of Annie's, and she doesn't have any local family. So Annie's trying to set the two of us up. You know, she'll give me a room, rent free, if I take her to some doctor appointments, buy groceries, take her to church, you know. And if it works out, I can buy the lady's car. Okay, so it's a fifteen-year-old Chevy, but it was never driven anywhere."

"Sounds great," Quinn told her.

"No, it's incredible!" Marnie exclaimed. Then she shook her head again, as if she didn't want to get too sappy. "So, you know, thanks. It's working out well. Better than living in a yard, anyway. Even if it's a pretty decent yard. Besides, the yard was getting a little creepy."

"Creepy? You mean bugs and things?"

She shook her head and said dryly, "No, you live on the street, you learn to live with bugs. No, it was weird sometimes. There was a car that used to cruise by really slowly…then take off. Probably just someone looking for an address."

Tension knotted Quinn's fingers, causing his grip on the steering wheel to tighten. "What car?" he snapped.

"Hey, sorry! I don't know. I didn't get a license number or anything. It was night, dark, you know? It was a car. Maybe beige, maybe gray. Lightish."

"What kind of lightish car?"

"What do you mean? A car—like the kind people drive."

"Big one, little one?"

"Medium."

"Chevy, Ford, Olds, Toyota, Mercedes—what kind of a car?"

"I don't know. I don't have a car, remember? I've never even been shopping for a car. I only know that old Mrs. Marlin's car is a Chevy because Annie told me. It was a medium-sized sedan, I guess."

"If you saw it again, would you recognize it?"

She must have felt his tension because she went very stiff herself. She was staring at him, looking a little scared, as if she'd trusted in a mentor who'd turned out to be slightly insane. And yet she still looked as if she wanted to help him.

She shook her head. "I'm sorry. Really."

"How many nights did you see this car?"

"It was only twice—if it was the same car."

"So why did it make things…creepy?"

"I don't know. It just did. Hey, pay attention—you're going to miss the turnoff. I do know how to get to the beach."

They reached the studio. Quinn parked at a meter but told Marnie they would walk around the back, where the teachers, seasoned students and other employees at the building parked.

"Recognize any of them?" he asked, but before she could reply, he knew her answer.

Every flipping car there was gray or beige.

And every single one of them was a sedan.

"Quinn, I'm sorry. They all look alike," she told him, turning her large brown eyes to meet his. "It might have been any one of them."

"Or none," he said.

"Or none," she agreed.

He nodded. "Well, thanks for looking. Let's go on up."

She smiled again. "My first lesson," she breathed happily.

Shannon returned from a meeting to see Marnie out on the floor with Sam Railey. The girl looked like a child getting a Christmas present for the first time. And when she moved, following Sam's instructions on a rumba step, it was with a natural grace.

The girl had caught her eye, but then Shannon looked quickly around, certain Quinn would be there, as well.

He was. By the reception area, with Gordon and Ella, all of them watching the girl.

"You're back," Ella called out to her. "Meeting go well?"

"Yes, everything went perfectly," she said, walking over to join the group. As courtesy required, she forced a note of welcome into her voice as she greeted Quinn.

"Great. You've got a class in fifteen minutes," Ella told her.

"Oh?" Who? she wondered. Quinn wasn't scheduled until the next day.

"Me," he told her, smiling.

"Oh?" she responded, trying not to sound too icy.

"Well, I've decided to enter that Gator thing," he said. "And that means I have a lot to learn in very little time."

"You're really going to enter the Gator Gala?" she asked.

"Why not?" Gordon boomed. "There's a beginners category."

"Gordon, he's had one private lesson!" she said.

"Well, that's the point. I'm going to need a few more," Quinn said.

She nodded. "Fine. Let me get my shoes on."

Trying very hard not to give away her irritation, Shannon went to her office and changed her shoes. Gordon might be delighted that a brand-new student wanted to enter, but she wasn't.

Still it was good for the studio. It would mean lots and lots of classes. Lots and lots of money. Of course, she knew now that he wasn't any poor fishing captain or struggling charter service. Then again, did P.I.s make the big bucks?

Of course, Doug O'Casey felt free to book as many classes as he wanted. On a cop's salary.

There was a light tap on her door. "Hey, Shannon," Ella said softly. "He signed up for this hour."

"Well, he shouldn't have. I just got back," she muttered.

"Gordon was really excited."

"Then Gordon should teach him."

"Shannon, what on earth is the matter?" Ella demanded.

"Nothing. I'll be out in a sec."

Katarina was in the studio, minus her husband David. She was dancing with Ben. They were working on an advanced waltz, with Ben showing her how to create a beautiful arc with her body. "It's easy to forget the body when you're learning the steps," Ben was saying seriously. "But now that you have the routine down, it's time to work the body. Think elegance. We dance together, but you've got to remember your position—your universe."

"And get the hell out of your universe, right?" Katarina

said, laughing. "I know what you mean, Ben. I just keep forgetting."

"That's why we'll keep going over it," he said. They waltzed away. Quinn two-left-feet O'Casey was waiting.

She walked over to him and took his hand, leading him to the other side of the floor. Justin Garcia was there, teaching salsa to a pretty young Oriental girl taking her first class. Sam Railey was still with Marnie. Her class was over, but they were talking by the kitchen, where Sam was fixing her a cup of coffee.

There was really nowhere private in the studio, but most of the time the music drowned out any conversation.

"Why are you taking classes at all?" she asked Quinn, leading him to her stash of CDs.

"Because I'm dying to be the Irish salsa sensation of the city," he said dryly.

"Really?"

"Sibling rivalry? Doug has gotten so good, I can't stand it."

"Really."

"It's the best way to be here."

"It's an expensive way to be here."

"True," he agreed. "But if I hang around enough, I can find out all the deep, dark secrets going on around the place."

"Yeah, like our lives are deep, dark secrets," she said dryly. "We don't have lives. That's the sad truth."

"Lara had a life. An active one."

Shannon waited for Justin's salsa to end, then slipped a basic waltz into the player. "Come on," she told him. "Get the count. It's very basic. One, two, three…one, two, three…"

She was amazed to discover that he actually had it.

"Not bad," she told him.

"My mom made me do this one when I was growing up,"

he admitted. "But you seem really unhappy teaching me. So let's talk."

"Can you talk and keep count?" she asked.

"Yes!"

"Don't bark at me. Lots of times, in the beginning, people need to count. Then they learn to move and converse at the same time."

"Let's see, you know what I am, what I do. So let's start with you. On the day Lara died, did you spend any private time with her?"

Shannon stared at him, realizing that he was far better at dancing than he had let on. Or maybe it was just the waltz. He seemed extremely capable of moving around the floor and grilling her at the same time.

She stared at him hard in return and answered. "No. I got along with her fine. When she came to the studio, I wrote her checks, chatted pleasantly and applauded her triumphs. But we weren't friends, and we didn't go looking for each other's company. So no, I was never alone with her."

"Did you see anyone alone with her?"

She shook her head. "I wouldn't have been watching her."

"So what shook you up so badly that day?"

"Nothing," she said, then stopped, inhaling sharply.

"So you've been lying?"

She shook her head. "No, not lying," she said, and hesitated. "I...I've been pretty angry at you."

"Gee, you're kidding." His eyes were sharp as crystal, cool, distant. He was working now. And he was good at it. She felt as if she should be ready to spill everything. She reminded herself that he was a P.I., not a cop.

But he had been a cop once. Maybe he'd left in hopes of making more money as a private citizen. She felt as if she was dancing with Eliot Ness.

"Tell me," he persisted. "And tell me, too, why you haven't told me yet."

"Because it isn't really anything," she insisted.

"I'll decide that."

"When Lara was dancing, a waiter came up to me and said, 'You're next.'"

"'You're next'?" Quinn repeated.

"Yes. That's why…well, I'm assuming he just mixed me up with someone else. I wasn't competing, so I couldn't have been next. But that's also why it freaked me out a little. You know…*you're next*. As if I were next…to die. I assumed it's just part of the paranoia I picked up after Lara died."

"You should never assume. You're sure the man was a waiter?"

"He was dressed as a waiter."

"I'll check into it," he told her.

"How are you even going to know what waiters were working that day? Never mind—it's what you do."

The music stopped. Justin slipped a salsa CD back into the machine. Shannon determined to tone her temper down. After all, he wasn't the enemy. He was trying to find the truth.

And that was what she wanted.

"Thank you," she managed to tell him. "If I can find out that the man really was just mixed-up, then I will feel better."

"I'll find out," he said flatly. "And here's the deal—when you think of anything, no matter how silly, you tell me."

"Yes," she said.

"And…" he said firmly.

"And what?"

"My time isn't nearly up. I think I've proved I've got the count on this. What I don't know is any more steps. And why are you arching away like that, trying not to look at me?"

"Because I'm not supposed to look at you in a waltz. There's a way to hold your partner in close contact, but you're not really ready for that yet."

He arched a brow. "Try me," he said softly.

"You're a beginner—two left feet. You said so yourself."

"Not in everything."

She wasn't sure exactly what he meant, if there was an innuendo there, or if he was referring completely to dance.

"Excuse me. I'll get your book and put on a waltz as soon as Justin's disk ends."

She walked away from him, grabbed his new student folder from the bookshelf and headed back over to the stereo system. The salsa ended. She got ready to slip in another waltz.

There was a second between the disks. A split second.

And in that fraction of time, she heard it.

That sound, a scraping, like nails against a blackboard, like metal against metal, like…something moving, opening, closing….

Then the music started again, and Quinn came up behind her.

She turned, frowning. "Did you hear that?"

"What? Something in the music I should have heard?" he asked.

"No…no…like…"

"A car backfired down on the road somewhere," he told her.

She shook her head again.

"What did you hear?" he demanded.

"I don't know. Nothing, really. I guess it was the car." It was broad daylight. The studio was filled with people. The streets below were busy. It could have been anything.

Except she had heard that noise before.

When his lesson ended, she was very surprised to realize that it hadn't been mercilessly painful, and he seemed ruefully pleased himself. Maybe the classes were just a byproduct of his work, but he was getting somewhere with them, at least.

He left right after his lesson, taking Marnie with him.

And after he was gone, the day seemed to drag on. She made a point of wandering into every room, studying it. Trying to figure out what might make the noise she kept hearing.

Nothing. She had to make a lame excuse about checking the toilet paper when she ran into Sam as he walked into the men's room while she was on her way out.

"Slow day for you, huh?" he teased.

Then Justin came in. "We never had a lineup like this in here before," he said.

"I was just checking supplies," she said.

Then Gordon entered. "What the hell is this? Grand Central Station?" he demanded. Hands on his hips, eyes narrowed, he looked at her suspiciously.

"I was making sure there was enough toilet paper."

A bushy white brow hiked. "In the men's room? The cleaning lady does that once a week."

"Someone said we were out," she mumbled. Then, both exasperated and embarrassed, she pushed her way out.

Despite her search, she continually found herself listening. And watching Ben. Finally, when she was in the reception area and Ben came to check his schedule, she asked him about the night before.

"Ben?"

"Hmm?"

"Last night...?"

"Yes?"

"You said you'd been at the convenience store."

He looked from the book to her. "Right."

She shook her head. "But you didn't have a bag or any-thing with you. What did you buy?"

He frowned, staring at her. "Something personal," he said. "And really none of your business."

"Sorry."

"Are you accusing me of having run up here to follow you?"

"No, I was just asking."

He set his hand on her chair and leaned toward her. "Condoms."

"What?"

"If you must know, I was buying condoms. And if you don't believe me, go ask Julio. The little Honduran guy. He was the one working there last night."

She felt a flush cover her cheeks, but it didn't matter. Ben had stepped away from her chair.

"Thanks for the info," she said, rising and pushing past him.

After that, the day became even more tedious, with the tension rising between her and Ben.

That night, a number of the others were going down to the club. Shannon was glad she wasn't going to be leaving the studio alone.

But as she started to close down, she realized Ella was already gone, and the group going clubbing was already on the way down.

She was going to wind up in the studio alone after all.

She ran into her office, grabbed her purse, then froze. There were footsteps coming toward her office.

She swung around, ready to wage battle with her purse.

But it was Gordon. He arched a brow slowly. "What is going on with you, Shannon?"

She lowered her purse but kept it clenched tightly in her hand.

"Shannon?"

His voice seemed low and quiet, and yet his features were tense. He was holding a pen at his side. He seemed to be clutching it very tightly.

Gordon Henson had been her mentor from the beginning. He had given her this job, had given her his trust. He had brought her through the ranks.

He had also been the first to teach and encourage Lara Trudeau.

"Nothing. Nothing is going on." She looked at his pen. He was clicking it open, then clicking it closed. Continuously.

"Hey."

She looked past Gordon. There was someone else in the studio.

Quinn.

"I just wanted to see if Shannon was going down to the club. Or you, Gordon," he said casually. Both of them stared at him. He offered them a slight grin. "Hey, guys, I'm not a ghost. I've been here for a while. I came back to watch the group class."

"I'm going home tonight," Gordon said. "Since you're here, you can walk Shannon out. Ben told me she's been getting a little freaked out at night lately. Good night."

Gordon lifted a hand, waved and left.

"Are you going clubbing tonight?" Quinn asked Shannon.

She shook her head. "I'm really tired. I just want to go home."

"Did you drive?"

"Yes."

"I'll follow you, then."

"Thanks, but you don't have to, not if you want to go to the club."

"Not tonight."

She almost asked him to wait, to let her walk around the studio and try again to find what it was that made that sound.

But she didn't hear it then. And she didn't know how to describe it. And for some reason, she was still disturbed because of what seemed like a strange encounter with Gordon.

She walked out of the studio, locking the door behind her, then paused, listening.

"What's the matter?" he asked.

"Nothing." And there was nothing. Just the sound of the music from down below.

"So…?" he said.

"Let's go," she said with a shrug.

He didn't say a word, just followed her to her car, and when she was in it, slid into the driver's seat of his own Navigator. He followed her to the house, parked and walked up the front door behind her.

"Thanks, thanks a lot," she told him.

"I think I'll sleep on the couch in back," he told her.

"I didn't ask you to."

"I know. I'm telling you that I'm going to."

"What if I don't want you to?"

"Trust me—you want me to," he told her.

He stepped inside, closing and locking the door behind him. And she had to admit, he was right. She *was* glad to have him there.

CH**A**PTER 16

He cruised by. Easy enough…just cruising. People did it on the beach all the time. Drove around, saw what action was going on.

Except his cruising was a little off the beaten path.

What was it? Had he always had a bit of a thing for her? She moved like liquid. The tilt of her head, the arc of her back, just the reach of her hand, slowly moving to the music…yeah, she was liquid. Elegance in motion.

Had it been that, or…

Or had she always made him a little bit nervous?

Whatever had caused his obsession, she had never known of it.

He suddenly damned his partner, who was causing the trouble now. Strange, but once it started, murder came easy. And he had to admit, his partner had an ungodly finesse….

But his partner could also cause them all to get caught.

Wrong choice of people.

Because, here on the beach, with the garish, shrieking beat of the night, anything could happen. Rich and poor, they came. Ecstasy flourished—the drug and the feeling it enhanced. New designer drugs hit the streets every night.

People died. They couldn't handle it. Everyone in the world knew it: drugs killed.

But now…

She made him nervous. And she made him angry. Because…

He was obsessed. So if she pushed him too far…

He could solve both his obsession and his problem in one little night.

He was smart. And dangerous.

But she was always watching. And listening.

Hide in plain sight. It was good advice. She could watch and listen, but what could she see?

Lara had known. But Lara had wanted money. She'd actually found the whole thing amusing. Sins weren't sins to Lara Trudeau, not unless they were against her. She had probably dropped dead having no idea of what had happened, or why. Pity. He'd wanted her to know. She shouldn't have pushed the wrong people too far.

He slowed the car as he neared her house.

The Navigator was there.

He swore, feeling his anger—and his obsession—grow.

Jealousy shot through him, like the piercing blade of a knife. He stared at the house, imagining what might be going on inside.

The fury grew.

At last he drove on by, anger now a fierce flame.

It took root, wrapping around his gut like a fist of burning steel. His fingers were so tense around the steering wheel that he jerked the car to the side of the road.

He gave himself a mental shake.

His time would come.

Her time would come.

* * *

There he was, Quinn O'Casey, in her house and heading for the kitchen.

She followed him. "You can't stay here," she informed him.

"What have you got in here?" he asked her, opening a cabinet. "Coffee? No good, I don't want to stay up." He opened the refrigerator.

"You can't stay," she repeated.

"What, not afraid tonight?" he asked her. "Tea," he said. "Hot tea, I guess it's got caffeine, too, but they say it can make you sleep."

She reached for the box of tea bags. "You can't stay."

There was a strange look in his eyes. A bright glimmer of dry amusement. "What? Afraid of me being on your couch? Afraid you won't be able to keep your distance?"

She snatched the box out of his hands. "I guarantee you that I can keep my distance. What you don't understand is this—I can't have your car out in front of my house all night."

"Why? Do your friends—employees—check up on you? Does Gordon make a habit of driving by at night?"

"Of course they don't check up on me. But they drive by occasionally. They stop by in the morning sometimes."

"You're the mother hen, huh?"

"The point is, they may come by."

"I'll move the car," he said.

"Move it where?"

"Out to Alton. People hang out on the beach until the wee hours of the morning. I can leave it there and no one will ever notice."

She couldn't argue with that. But she shook her head. "There's no need for you to stay. I was uneasy, but it turned out that Marnie was living in the yard. Now that she has a home, I'm not afraid anymore."

She was lying. She remained nervous, with no tangible reason, and it was driving her nuts. She wasn't usually such a chicken.

But then, she didn't have a defensive talent to her name. She wasn't a weakling, but she had never shot a gun in her life nor taken a single course in self-defense. She should probably rectify that situation, but everything she had ever said about having no life was true. She spent far too much time at the studio.

She reflected briefly that even Lara Trudeau had allowed herself to have a life.

That didn't matter tonight. He shouldn't be in her house.

Tomorrow, she decided, she was going to go through every room in the studio again. Yes, even the men's room. She was going to find out what that noise was. She was going to find out why she heard not just noises, but footsteps that followed her when she fled the building.

Quinn was watching her. It was almost as if he could read the thoughts running amok in her mind. "I think I should stay," he said firmly.

"But I'm not inviting you!" she said. Then she felt uneasy, wondering just why he was so sure he should stay. "Do you think that I may be in danger?" she demanded.

"Well, let's see, we both know I'm a P.I. working a case. Maybe I think—"

"You *are* a P.I." She cocked her head suddenly.

"Yes, that's been established."

"Couldn't you rig me with a surveillance system?"

"Sure. But they cost. And they take time."

"Tomorrow, maybe?"

"I can do it on Thursday," he told her. "For tonight, I'll move my car." He indicated the box of tea bags in her hands. "I like sugar and milk in mine," he told her, heading for the door. "And lock up while I'm out."

He left the house, and she just stared after him for several seconds. Then she flew to the front door and locked it. Irritably, she threw the box of tea bags on the counter. Then she waited impatiently for him to return.

When he did, she didn't open the door until she saw his face through the peephole.

"Honey, I'm home," he teased. "Where's the tea?"

"I'm exhausted, and I'm going to bed. I'm sure you know how to boil water."

"I do," he told her. "I make a pretty good cup of tea, too. Want one?"

"Thank you, no."

"You don't have to sleep with me just because I make you tea."

"Cute. I don't want tea."

"Still afraid you'll get too tempted with me sleeping out in the Florida room?"

"Not a chance."

"Pity."

"I told you, I don't like liars."

"I never actually lied. But it doesn't matter, not if you're going to be that bitter."

"I still say there's no reason for you to be here."

"Just protecting your interests—in the pursuit of my own. And if there's no chance of you forgiving me, there's no reason for you to be so irritable about me being here."

She shook her head. At least he wasn't coming anywhere near her. He'd done some teasing, but he certainly seemed to have no difficulty keeping his distance.

"You want to sleep on the couch, sleep on the couch," she said at last.

"Good night, then."

"Good night."

She made a good exit, turning, heading straight for her

bedroom, then closing and locking the door. She leaned against it for a minute, listening.

She heard him filling the kettle with water and shook her head. Last night, she'd lain awake listening for noises and wondering about Ben.

Tonight she would feel safe.

But she would still lie awake, knowing this man was in her house.

Shannon moved away from the door and went into the bathroom, where she brushed her teeth, she showered, then found a ripped-up flannel nightgown. She put it on, then went back to the door, leaned against it and listened again.

She heard the sound of the television and the drone of his voice. He was on the phone, she thought.

Screw it.

She crawled into bed, reminding herself how angry she was at the way he had used her.

Ah, but he knew how to use a woman well.

She could get up, invite him in and sleep in the real comfort of feeling those arms around her. Feeling...

More. A lot more. Excitement that was raw and seductive and exhilarating. Carnal and lusty and sensual, hot, slick, vibrant...

She turned, slamming a fist into her pillow.

Absolutely not.

Why? It was so much better to lie here, in a cool dry blanket of dignity.

Yes.

No.

She stood up and walked to the door, listening again.

She could still hear him on the phone, thanking someone for taking care of something that would happen tomorrow. She slipped the door open, trying to hear more clearly.

He said goodbye to the person on the other end of the phone as she did so.

"There's still tea in the pot!" he called to her.

She stiffened. "I was just going to ask you to turn the television down a bit."

He turned, seeing her down the length of the hallway. "Really? I thought maybe you were going to come on out and seduce me again." His eyes slid up and down her, taking in the ragged flannel nightgown. "Guess not, huh?"

"Not a chance," she told him solemnly.

She closed the door and went back to bed, swearing.

Later, even as she burned with discomfort, wanting what she refused to allow herself, she began to drift, until finally she fell into a deep refreshing sleep.

Tedium.

Half the work was pure tedium.

There had been dozens of waiters on duty the night of the competition. But thanks to Jake, he had a list of names and phone numbers.

And when he called people, they seemed to think he was a cop, even though he identified himself immediately. At any rate, it worked.

A few of the men he talked to were hesitant at first. He had a feeling that a number of them weren't quite legal. Once they ascertained that he wasn't with INS, they tried to be helpful.

On some of the calls he made, the numbers just rang and rang. On some, he hit answering machines. On some, he hit really sleepy people. Seemed most of the guys worked nights.

He kept dialing, marking off those he had spoken with. The next guy to pick up sounded uneasy. Quinn assured him that he wasn't with INS.

"The waiters didn't help line up the dancers," Miguel

Avenaro told him. "The judges do that. They had their clipboards, and their lists of names and schedules, and handled all that themselves."

"Thank you for your time," Quinn told him and hung up.

How many calls had he made? Twenty-something already.

He tried the next name on his list. Manuel Taylor. A true Miami name.

The man who answered spoke English perfectly, no hint of an accent. He listened to Quinn's question.

"Who are you?" he said.

"I'm a private investigator. My name is Quinn O'Casey."

"You're not a cop?"

"No."

"I don't have to speak with you, then, do I?"

"No, you don't. I can have a cop call you," Quinn said.

"They don't think any of the waiters had anything to do with that woman's death, do they?"

"No."

"Then…"

"I'm just trying to find the man who spoke to Miss Mackay and find out who instructed him to do so."

There was silence on the other end.

Then, "It was me," the man said.

In the morning, Quinn was gone. The bottom lock on her front door was in place, though the bolt, which had to be latched from the inside or with a key, had necessarily been left unlocked.

There was coffee waiting in the pot, along with a little note.

Since it seems you're not fond of tea, I made you coffee. See you later. I have a lesson today. Can't wait. Know you can't, either.

* * *

"Funny, funny," she muttered.

She poured herself coffee. She leaned against the counter, feeling a little chill. She hadn't experienced any of the wild, carnal excitement that had teased her memory and stirred her senses. She had gotten a good night's sleep, instead.

She wondered which she might really have needed more.

An edge of hurt came creeping back. He had just been using her, getting to know her, getting close, investigating...

At the same time, he definitely seemed like a decent guy. And decent guys didn't come by all that frequently in life.

Would it be so bad to have another memory of an incredible encounter?

Stop, she warned himself.

She had to teach him today. She didn't want to feel any little electric jolts zapping through her while she danced. And she had a busy day ahead of her. Gunter and Helga, practicing for Asheville. A double appointment with Richard Long, coaching for Jane and Sam, the studio "party" that night, when the students danced with the teachers, practicing the steps they'd learned.

There was a tapping at the door. Still in the ragged flannel nightshirt, she walked to the door and looked through the peephole.

It was Gordon.

Unease filtered through her. She remembered the way he had clicked the pen last night, open, then closed, open, then closed. With such agitation.

Asking her what was wrong with her.

After he'd discovered her prying in the men's room.

She hesitated.

He stood on the step, hands shoved into his pockets, glancing around. He looked at his watch, then pounded on the door again.

"Shannon, what the hell are you doing in there?" he demanded.

It was broad daylight. And it was just Gordon, being impatient. It wasn't the strangest thing in the world that he was there—he had stopped by in the morning many times before over the years. She hesitated a moment longer, then opened the door.

He arched a brow, scanning her attire. "Not out to seduce anyone this morning, huh?" he asked.

She grimaced. "I just woke up."

"Well, take a quick shower and come with me."

"Come where with you?"

"To get something to eat."

"I have a really full schedule today," she said.

"You still have to eat. Don't make your old boss go out alone. I don't want to be alone right now."

"Grab some coffee then—you have to give me a few minutes."

She started back to her bedroom, but as she did, the phone rang.

"Want me to get it?" Gordon asked.

"No, I'm right here." She picked it up, glancing at her watch. Ten o'clock. She really had slept late.

"Hello?"

"It's me, Quinn. Meet me at Nick's in thirty minutes. Can you do it?"

"I have company right now, and a killer schedule today." She winced at her casual use of the word *killer.*

"This is important."

"I was just heading out to eat."

"I've found the waiter."

"Who?"

"The waiter who told you that you'd be next."

"My boss is here," she said. "I'm going out with him."

"Gordon Henson is there? Now?"

"Yes, we're going to lunch. Breakfast. Brunch. Whatever." She glanced at Gordon. He had wandered out to the Florida room as if he were totally uninterested in her conversation. Even so, he could probably hear her.

"Tell him I'm coming to get you both," Quinn said.

"Wait a minute!"

"Just do that. Tell him I'm coming to get you both. That we're going to talk about the trip out on the bay. Tell him that. Make sure he knows I'm on my way over."

"All right. But tell me—"

"Get into your room and lock the door. And make sure he knows I'll be on the doorstep any second."

She felt a chill and lowered her voice, staring out at Gordon, a sinking feeling already seizing her. "It was Gordon, right?" she whispered.

She clutched the phone more tightly.

"Yes, it was Gordon. And he didn't just ask him to say it to you—he tipped him fifty bucks to do it. Hang up, and lock yourself in your room until I get there."

"Right."

She nearly dropped the phone, trying to return it to the base. "That was Quinn," she called out. "He'll be on the doorstep any second. He's going to take us to lunch, discuss the trip this Saturday. I'll be right out!"

She fled into her bedroom, wrenching the door closed, instantly hitting the lock.

For long moments she remained there, her fingers curled around the handle, afraid to let go, even though the lock was in place.

Then she heard Gordon. Walking back from the Florida room.

"Shannon?"

His hand was on the doorknob. She felt it twist beneath her fingers.

CHAPTER 17

Quinn was in his car in a matter of seconds.

Gordon Henson had paid the waiter to say those words to Shannon. *You're next.* Seconds before Lara fell down dead.

That didn't make him a murderer.

And if he was a murderer, he was of the more devious variety. He would not head to Shannon's house in broad daylight to commit an act of violence.

He wasn't going to hurt her. Especially not now that he knew Quinn was on the way.

Quinn felt as if he was rocketing down US1.

He was amazed he wasn't stopped by a policeman.

I-95 took him to the causeway. He watched the clock on the dashboard. Just a matter of minutes. He must be making record time.

It didn't make sense. What could Gordon Henson possibly gain from the death of Lara Trudeau?

He swore softly. He didn't need to be in such a panic. He hit the digit on his phone that called Shannon's house. Gordon picked up.

"Gordon, hey, it's Quinn."

"Hey there. Thought you'd be here by now. The way Shannon spoke, I though you were just about in the front yard."

"I *am* just about in the front yard."

"Take your time. Shannon isn't ready yet. She must be in the shower."

"I thought we could talk about the cruise."

"So she told me. Looking forward to it. You got us a hell of a deal."

"Right."

He was turning the corner onto her street.

"I'm there," he said, and hung up.

In seconds he was out of the car and running up the path to her house.

Shannon heard the thundering on the door. Heard Gordon walk across the living room to answer it.

Gordon. She couldn't believe it. She'd known him for years; he'd done everything in the world for her. And yet...

She was still standing there by the door, frozen, as time elapsed. Maybe not that much time. Maybe it only felt like it.

Quinn was there. She could let go.

She did. Then she flew to get dressed.

When she came out, both men were seated in the living room. They'd been talking casually, it seemed. Quinn looked as if he didn't have a care in the world.

Gordon only looked hungry.

"I've seen her change outfits five times at a show faster than that," Gordon said, half joking, half aggravated.

"But she's ready now," Quinn said.

"Yes," Shannon said. "I'm ready."

"Well, then, do you mind going to Nick's? There's someone who should be there that I'd kind of like to run into," Quinn said.

"The cop hangout? Sure, I've never been. I'd love to see the place," Gordon agreed, heading for the door. "Maybe we should take two cars. That way Shannon and I can head over to the studio if you have other business during the day," he continued.

"I don't have any business. I'm coming into the studio," Quinn said.

Shannon stared at him, trying to maintain a neutral expression. Had he actually figured out that Gordon had somehow killed Lara? Was he having him arrested? And if not…

"Suit yourself," Gordon said cheerfully.

Quinn seated Shannon in the front seat of the Navigator. She looked at him questioningly, but he didn't say anything as Gordon got in the back, complimenting the car. In fact, as they drove, he seemed laid-back and content, commenting on how nice it was not to be driving but just enjoying the scenery. "It's easy to forget how beautiful it is out here, isn't it?" he said, leaning forward.

"Water, water everywhere," Quinn murmured.

"I hear that Nick's is a nice place. He a friend of yours?"

"I hung around there for years. And a friend of mine, a homicide cop, married Nick's niece. Who is also a cop."

"Cool," Gordon said. "So your brother hangs out there, too?"

"Yes, Doug has always liked the place."

"Maybe we'll run into him," Gordon suggested. He didn't seem worried about fraternization. "Then there's his buddy—the wedding student, Bobby, and his bride, Giselle."

"We won't run into either of them. They're both on duty right now, toeing the line, sticking to their assigned districts," Quinn said. He glanced at Gordon in the mirror. "Doug wants to be homicide eventually."

"Too bad. He could be a pro," Gordon said.

"Maybe he can be both," Quinn said.

Gordon laughed. "You haven't really realized what the world of true pros is like yet, huh? They dance. They dance, and then they dance some more."

"Is Doug really that good?" Quinn asked. He glanced at Shannon.

"I think he could be. He's got a lot going for him," she said.

They had left the causeway and I-95 and were shooting down US1. They would be at Nick's any minute. Gordon didn't seem in the least alarmed.

But why would he have paid a waiter to say such a thing? Shannon wondered.

They parked and got out of the car. Shannon followed Quinn, who immediately headed for the outside patio. Gordon was behind her.

The girl who had waited on them the last time she had been there saw them arrive. Apparently Quinn often wound up in her section, judging by the friendly way she greeted him.

"Welcome back!" she said cheerfully to Shannon, who winced slightly.

"You've been here before, huh?" Gordon said. There was a curious, teasing light in his eyes.

She smiled weakly.

"That friend of yours is in at the bar," the girl told Quinn. "Did you want coffee?"

"All the way round?" Quinn asked, looking at the other two.

"You bet. And orange juice, at least for Shannon and me. You, too, Quinn?" Gordon asked.

"Yeah, great," he said.

They slid into their seats. Before Gordon could ask about

Quinn's friend, the man himself came walking out to the patio. Gordon stared at the tall, attractive, Hispanic man coming their way. He squinted slightly, as if trying to remember where he knew him from. Then he said, "Hey! That guy was one of the waiters at the competition. I recognize him."

Shannon inhaled sharply, holding her breath.

Quinn looked intently at Gordon. "That's right. And you *should* recognize him."

Gordon stared at Quinn. The man reached the table.

"Manuel, have a seat," Quinn said.

The man nodded and took a chair, looking a little awkward.

"Manuel, hello. How are you doing? Leaving the hotel business and working here now?" Gordon asked pleasantly. "Or are you two friends?" he asked, looking from Manuel to Quinn.

"Mr. O'Casey asked me to come out," Manuel said.

Coffee and orange juice arrived. "Sir, I brought you fresh coffee, too," she told Manuel cheerfully.

"Thank you," Manuel said.

Gordon waited for her to leave. Then he sat back, crossing his arms over his chest and staring at them all one by one. The biggest accusation in his eyes was for Shannon. "All right. What the hell is going on here?"

"Gordon, right before Lara died," Shannon said, "this man came up to me and said, 'You're next.' You paid him to do that? Why?"

"How the hell did I know Lara was about to drop dead?" Gordon said irritably. "And if you dragged me—and this poor man—out here just to have him as an eyewitness, we can let him go home now. I paid him to go up and talk to you, yes."

"Is it all right if I leave? I'm working a luncheon this afternoon," Manuel said to Quinn.

"Sure. Thanks for coming."

Manuel grinned. "No problem. I'm making pretty big bucks off your group. I wouldn't mind working a cruise, sometime, though. Call me if you need help."

"Sure thing," Quinn replied.

As soon as Manuel left, Shannon turned to Gordon. "Gordon, why? Why pay someone to say something like that to me?"

"I thought it might slip into your subconscious somewhere," Gordon said. "Remind you that you should be next to dance. Awaken the spark of competition in your soul. Hell, it's no secret that all the rest of us think you should be out there. Wait a minute." He stared at Quinn then. "Hell, I was pretty damned slow there, huh? I think I'm finally getting this. Shannon, you think that someone killed Lara. And since I paid Manuel here to say 'You're next' to you, I must be that person. Great. You think I killed her."

Shannon wanted to crawl beneath a chair. Gordon had never in his life looked so much like a beaten bloodhound.

"Gordon, you don't understand the way those words have haunted me!" she said.

"Lara was my pride and joy. My creation," Gordon said.

"She bit the hand that fed her many a time, too, so I understand," Quinn said.

Gordon shook his head in disgust. "You don't understand. If I were an architect, Lara would have been one of my greatest buildings. We can tease and nit-pick and argue among ourselves, and I'll grant you, she was as impressed with herself as anyone could be, but she was still…family, I guess you'd say. There was a relationship. Good sometimes, aggravating at others. But in a thousand years, I'd never have hurt her. And you?" he told Shannon. "Fine. You want to throw away years of work and an ocean of natural talent, do it. You not competing saves me from any work I might have needed to do in these last few years before re-tirement." He shook his head in hurt and disgust. "What, you don't believe me?" he said to Quinn. "Is that why we're here? Have you got the cops lined up to arrest me?"

Quinn shook his head. "No. But when Shannon told me about those words, we had to find out why the waiter came up to her and who told him to."

Gordon sighed, closing his eyes, opening them on Shan-non. "So you've been spilling your guts out to this guy, huh?"

"I mentioned a few fears, yes."

"Makes sense," Gordon said.

"Oh?" Shannon murmured.

"Sure. He's a private investigator."

"You knew that?" Shannon said.

"Go through a few channels and you can pull him up on the Internet." Gordon was staring at Quinn. "I shouldn't have been surprised this morning. Finding the waiter was a piece of cake for him." He kept looking at Quinn, but Shannon knew that he was speaking for her benefit. "He had to have his record expunged—he was thrown out his first year of college for drugs and disorderly conduct—but then he made a nice turnaround. A psychology major who became a cop, made it to homicide in record time, then applied to the FBI, where he joined the behavioral science unit—you know, the profilers' division—and then he up and quit and came back here, join-ing up with a friend who was already in the business."

Shannon stared from Gordon to Quinn. "Everything is available on the damned Net, huh?" Quinn said.

"Hey, you were a civil servant. What do you want?" Gor-don said. "Do they serve food around here? I mean, I know you don't trust me, I don't know what to make of you, and Shannon would probably just as soon we both jumped in the bay, but I'm still starving."

"Yes, they serve food," Quinn said, looking around to catch their waitress's eye.

Gordon was hungry. He ordered a breakfast special that included eggs, pancakes, steak, hash browns and toast. Shannon opted for just the last. Quinn stuck with coffee. Which was fine, because Gordon kept trying to get them to help him with the huge platter the waitress set down before him.

Quinn and Shannon were both quiet throughout the meal. Shannon couldn't help feeling a slow boil of anger again when she thought of just how much she hadn't known about Quinn's life. Things he apparently hadn't thought to share, even when insisting on being a protector rather than an investigator.

"Shall we get to the boat?" Gordon said.

"What?" Quinn said.

"The boat. Saturday is almost here. Let me ask this—do you really have a boat?"

Quinn nodded. "She's down in the Keys right now, but I'll have her up here with a crew, the whole bit, by Friday night."

"I need you to speak to the catering company, just to make sure everyone has what they need. And I'm hiring a trio to play—we'll need space for them."

"She'll be just what you need," Quinn assured him. "You can do a walk-through Friday night."

"Great." Gordon threw his napkin down at last. "We need to open up the studio. Are you two ready?"

"I'll get the check," Quinn said.

"Hell, no. I'll get the check. You can put your money toward your entry into the Gator Gala," Gordon told him.

"He's not really entering," Shannon said.

Quinn stared at her, his look suddenly hard and stubborn. "Yes, he really is entering. And I brought you here so I can get the check."

"No, I've got it," Gordon insisted.

Shannon stood. "I'll get the check. Let's just go."

It was a very busy day. Wednesdays always were. The studio's weekly "party" didn't start until late, but students came all day to brush up and be ready.

Katarina, the designer from next door, was busy, too, making adjustments to costumes for the gala. Gabriel Lopez took a lesson first with Shannon, then one with Jane, and later, he told Quinn, he would be taking a lesson with Rhianna, as well.

"I think it's important," he said. "I run a club, and I ask lots of women to dance to keep the floor moving, keep the wallflowers happy. So I learn from all of them. And the lessons," he said with a grin, "are tax-deductible. It's a deal."

The doctors Long were in, taking a lesson with Justin Garcia as a couple, to work on their salsa, then separating to take individual lessons.

Quinn lounged around, drinking coffee, speaking with the others as they either waited for or finished their sessions. At last it was his turn.

And Shannon was more aloof than ever.

"Gordon is really angry with me," she said, green eyes flashing as she led him through a fox-trot by rote. "He hasn't actually said anything, but I know. I've hurt him really badly."

"I think I'm supposed to be leading," Quinn said.

"You don't know how to lead."

"Right. But you're supposed to be teaching me how."

"Why?" she demanded. "This whole thing is just a joke to you. You think that we're all a bunch of silly prima donnas."

"That's not true," he said, forcefully taking the lead. "I admit, I thought I would hate it. But I don't. And if Gordon is mad, that's the way it goes. What happened to you needed to be checked out. And besides," he added firmly, "who knows? Maybe Gordon is the best actor on earth."

"You think he was lying? That's ridiculous," Shannon protested.

"No, I don't actually think he was lying. I'm just saying it's still a possibility. I wish it wasn't. I wish *someone* could be eliminated."

"I suppose you haven't even eliminated me yet?" she said coolly.

He shrugged. "I don't think you're guilty of anything. Either that, or you really are deserving of an Academy Award."

"Right. And you should have a stack of them," she said. "*Left* foot. Left."

"Why?"

"Because it's the foot you're supposed to be on."

"No, dammit." He stopped dancing. "Why do I deserve that stack of awards?"

"FBI? You might have mentioned that."

"Does it matter? I left the Bureau. I work down here now."

"You should have told me."

"We've never really had an opportunity to talk about our lives, you know. Either one of us."

"What on earth don't you know about me?" she demanded.

"Why you won't compete," he said.

"Oh, God!" she groaned. "That again. I told you. I like to teach. I had an injury."

"You had an injury once."

He stopped speaking, turning to see that Gunter and Helga were doing a fantastic lift. "I don't want to fox-trot. I want to do that."

"You can't even dance."

"I can do that."

She was about to tell him about his left foot again. He didn't give her the chance. Before she could protest, he lifted her, repeating the motion he had just seen, swinging her around his back before he set her on the floor again.

She was flushed, startled, angry—and maybe a little awed.

"Okay, what did I mess up?"

"You didn't give your partner a clue as to what was happening," she snapped.

"But I'm leading. You're supposed to follow. Men lead, women follow. That's the way it is in ballroom dance. No bra burning here."

"That's a cabaret move. People practice it," she muttered.

"Well, there you go. I'm trying to practice my…what? Does it have a name?"

She sighed. "Here in the studio, we call it the pooper-scooper."

"Pooper-scooper?" he said, his brows shooting up. "How…elegant."

"Pooper-scooper just came to mind when we did it the first time. I don't even remember who named it," she said impatiently.

"When we did it the first time?"

"I did it in a piece with Sam for a dinner we had once," she explained impatiently.

"I want to do it for Gator Gala," he insisted.

"You're a beginner. You need to do beginner steps in a long roster of dances. Later—"

"I'll do that. But there are individual routines, right? I want to do a waltz, with a pooper-scooper in it. Look, you know I can do it."

"I know you have the strength. What you need are the skill, balance and coordination."

"Then start teaching me, because I'm going to do it."

"This is really going to cost you."

"Yes." He looked at his watch. "And you're wasting my class time right now."

She stared at him indignantly. "You...asshole!"

"What a way with words. Pooper-scooper. Asshole. Can we work, please?"

For a moment she looked as if she would explode. Then she started in on a waltz, which he thought he knew.

But there was so much he didn't know, he discovered.

And yet, by the end of his forty-five minutes, he actually looked good. Because his partner looked good. And when they choreographed the pooper-scooper into the end of the short routine she planned as they went, there was a spurt of applause.

Quinn looked around to see that the others in the room had stopped to watch them. His brother had arrived, having picked up Marnie, as he had asked him earlier in the day to do. Bobby and Giselle were there, as well, along with a number of the others Quinn was coming to know as regulars.

Gordon walked over to them, laughing. "Hell, you really can teach anyone to dance," he said to Shannon, his tone teasing. He shook Quinn's hand. "Not bad."

"Tell him that he still needs to learn a lot of basics," Shannon said.

"I can tell him anything you want. Doesn't mean it will work with this guy." Gordon seemed to have forgotten the morning. "I see you had Doug bring that girl in again. I understand she's a street kid but over eighteen, an adult. A broke adult."

"Right. I bought her a guest pass that gives her a few lessons," Quinn said.

Gordon nodded. "I'm going to give her a few more. The kid is good—better than you."

"What a surprise," Quinn said dryly.

"I'd thought of that," Shannon said, as she looked at Gordon. "But I was afraid, with the cost of things, that the other students would get mad."

"I can explain it as a community service award," he said. "Not bad, O'Casey. Shannon, Richard Long has signed up for another lesson. He's looking a little irritated over there. Nice guy, but he does like to be a star."

Gordon walked away, and Shannon turned to join Richard. Quinn started off the floor to feel a hand land hard on his back. He turned. Doug was grinning at him. "That was great. You slimy liar. You're good."

"At least I can waltz, thanks to Mom. Listen, let's get out of here. We need to talk."

Ella called to them as they started out of the studio. "Hey, you guys going to be back for the party?"

"Wouldn't miss it," Doug assured her.

Quinn took his brother to the café across the street and chose the front table he'd opted for before. From there, they could see everyone coming and going. Once they had ordered, Quinn filled Doug in on what Shannon had told him, how he'd found Manuel Taylor and had him confront Gordon.

"And Gordon said it was just to get Shannon competing again?" Doug said.

Quinn nodded. "And he was convincing. Thing is, he'd been looking me up, as well. Knew everything about me. My work, at any rate."

"Interesting, but not startling," Doug said. "He's one of those people who really knows his way around the Net. He checks out all the students."

"I wonder why."

"Curiosity, I think. He never tells one student about another, though."

"So how do you know he's into checking up on people?"

"I was in his office talking to him one day. He doesn't hide anything. I happened to see his computer screen, and he'd pulled up the info on Richard Long's practice. He saw me looking and said you could find out practically anything about anybody on the Net."

Quinn sat back. He'd quit smoking a long time ago, but at that moment he really wanted a cigarette. He saw their waitress and ordered another espresso.

"Marnie thinks that a gray or beige car has been cruising by Shannon's house at night," he said.

"Who has a beige or gray car?"

"Everyone in the place, I think."

"I'll get tags tonight, and pull up the owners, makes and models," Doug said.

"Good idea. How's Jane doing?"

"Shaky. She's as convinced as Shannon is that someone killed Lara. Have you heard anything more about the woman they found on the beach?"

"No, but I'll check with Jake later."

"I thought he was taking some time off?" Doug said.

"He is, but I guarantee you, he's still on the phone a few times a day, and if he can't give me anything, he'll direct me to someone who can."

"Like Dixon?" Doug almost spat out the name.

Quinn lifted his hands. "When you hit a guy like Dixon, you just work around him." He leaned forward. "Did you see Gordon hanging around Lara that day? Buying her a drink? Anything?"

"No, the one person I didn't personally see anywhere near her was Gordon. Why?"

"I don't know. Something is still bothering me. It's something Manuel Taylor said, but I can't put my finger on it right now. I'm hoping it will come to me later."

"You done?" Doug said. "I've got my class in about fifteen minutes. Have to put my Latin shoes on."

"You bought special shoes?"

"Of course. You better buy some shoes yourself, bro."

"Right."

"Your pooper-scooper will be even better."

Doug was laughing at him. Quinn shook his head. "Murder, Doug. Come on, we're here to solve a murder."

By party time, Shannon was exhausted, even though she had to admit she'd had a decent night's sleep because of Quinn.

But it had been one hell of a long day.

They started by playing music that ran the gamut of everything they taught. The teachers all danced with the students at first; even Gordon came out on the floor. Then students danced with students, which was usually a time she really enjoyed, watching the more advanced students help out the beginners. Men asked women to dance, and women asked men. Old studio friends chatted, and the more advanced students quizzed the newcomers, making them feel welcome.

In the past, Shannon was aware, many people had considered studios like theirs to be something of a lonely hearts club. She had spent her years as manager trying to make sure that the place wasn't that but that it was instead a warm and hospitable environment where people came to have fun, and where, even if they already had busy and active lives, they met new friends. She thought she had done well. She was, in fact, incredibly proud of the studio. And heartsick that it now seemed to be a place encased in fear and shadow.

After the first set of dances, they had the students sit. Then either she, Gordon or Ben would give a speech about dance. Tonight, she spoke about the awkwardness of first learning to dance. Sam and Jane played a couple coming to their first lesson, with Jane pulling Sam in by the ear. They stepped on one another's feet, argued with each other. Then they improved a little, a little more, and then a little more, until they were whirling around and the room was applauding.

Gordon came and took over the microphone. "Now's the part where a newcomer asks to see a dance."

"Bolero!" Mina Long called out.

"I said a newcomer," Gordon said, laughing.

Shannon was startled when Quinn O'Casey called out, "A waltz. I'd like to see Shannon do a waltz."

"Yeah, Shannon, go, Shannon!" his brother said.

Then an echo went up, as if they were at a football game.

The next thing she knew, Ben was in front of her, reaching out a hand to her, a slight smile on his face.

She accepted his hand, having little other choice.

After all these years, she knew him so well. Knew his lead, every tick of his body. She forgot the audience and was only aware of the music, of how it made her feel, and move.

She was almost startled when it came to an end and she was posed as they had finished their last competition, arched over his knee, her head just above the floor, one leg extended parallel with the length of his body.

The room was alive with applause. She nodded to Ben, rose and went to steal the microphone back from Gordon.

"Let's change pace. Anyone?"

Marnie shouted out, "Samba!"

"Hey, can I be guest teacher?" Gunter called.

"Sure," Shannon told him.

He went to Jane, whirling her out to the floor. Gordon had found the music, and when it started up, Gunter stepped forward, Jane in his arms.

Shannon started clapping, inviting audience participation. The samba was fast, and the pair were well matched, spinning across the floor with perfect motion and speed. Then the music ended and Gunter spun Jane out so she could take an elegant bow.

Then she straightened, and for a minute, pain tensed her features.

Then she doubled over.

"What...?" someone said.

Jane screamed, clutching her abdomen, doubling over, then literally falling to the floor.

"Oh, God! Oh, God, the pain!" she shrieked.

She wasn't acting.

The entire room went still, frozen.

"Ella, call nine-one-one!" Shannon ordered, springing to life, flying over to land on her knees by Jane's side. "What is it? What hurts?"

Gunter was down on his knees, too. Gordon was there, while Ben made sure that the others didn't rush in too close around her.

Jane let out another screech, tightening her hold around her belly. Her dark blond hair spilling on the floor, she turned her huge dark eyes to Shannon.

"Oh, God, help me. Help me. I don't want to die. I don't want to die! Oh, God, I don't want to die like Lara!"

CHAPTER 18

Once he'd ascertained that something was seriously wrong, Quinn was on his feet. Ben Trudeau was doing a good job of holding the others back, but he knew that both Doug and Bobby were behind him, and they were both trained in CPR.

"Let me get to her," Quinn told Shannon, who looked up at him, eyes dazed, features frozen into a mask of concern.

A hand fell on his shoulder. He turned to see that Mina Long was behind him, and her husband was behind her.

"We're actually physicians," she reminded him quietly.

He stepped back. Richard was already down on his knees. He might have been a plastic surgeon, but he obviously remembered the medical basics, as well. His voice was firm but reassuring as he spoke to Jane, and his hands moved with amazing expertise over her abdomen. "It's your stomach, right? And the pain just started?"

Jane seemed to choke on her answer at first, but then she managed to speak past the pain. "There were a few twinges…before. Then…it's like a knife. I'm in agony. It's like I've been…poisoned."

"Poisoned?" The whisper echoed through the crowd like the chorus in an ancient Greek tragedy.

"No, no," Richard told her, his lips twitching in a smile. He looked at his wife, across Jane's body. "Do you think we agree on the possibility of an acute attack of appendicitis?"

Mina smiled at Jane and touched her gently.

Jane moaned. "Appendicitis?" she said.

"I'd say it looks like surgery for you tonight, but we're just minutes from the hospital. You'll be all right," Mina said. She looked up, searching the sea of faces around them. "Ella, you called emergency, right?"

"Yes, the second Shannon told me to," Ella said.

Jane was reaching out, groping. She wanted Shannon. Shannon curled her fingers around Jane's hand.

"You'll come with me? To the hospital, right?" Jane asked breathily.

"Absolutely."

They could already hear the sirens. Within a minute or two, emergency med techs were coming up the front stairs. Questions were asked; vital statistics were taken. Gabe Lopez opened the doors and led the way so that a stretcher could be brought up, and Jane, still moaning, was lifted and brought down the stairs.

Shannon crawled into the back of the ambulance with Jane.

"I'll follow in the car," Quinn told her.

The door was shut, and the sirens blared again.

Quinn realized that not only had everyone in the dance party come down, but people had spilled out from the club. The line waiting for admittance to Suede was also out on the sidewalk. People were talking.

"My God, is she dead?" someone asked.

"A woman was found dead on the beach Sunday," another voice whispered.

Richard Long turned to the crowd. "No, folks, it's all right. Just a case of appendicitis."

Doug pulled out his badge. "There's no danger, just go about your business. Folks, come on, please, break it up."

People began to mill away until only the dance crowd was left.

"I guess the party is over for tonight," Gordon said dryly.

"Ella, you make sure you call us all and tell us how she's doing in the morning," Mr. Clinton said. "Hell, I'll just stop by and see her. Bring her some flowers. Richard, you're sure it's appendicitis?"

"It certainly appears to be, Mr. Clinton."

"You're a plastic surgeon," Clinton reminded him.

"They still made me go to medical school," Richard replied, rolling his eyes with a wink toward his wife. "Mina gets little ones with appendicitis now and then—not frequently, but enough to spot it when she sees it." He slipped an arm around his wife's shoulders. "Shall we go up, change our shoes and get on home? Gordon is right—I'd say the party is over."

"Can someone take me back?" Marnie asked softly.

"Sure, I'll take you," Doug said. He looked at Quinn. "You are going to the hospital, right?"

"Yes."

Quinn realized his brother was looking at him with anxiety.

He had been spending time with Jane, because Jane had been so unnerved.

"Hey, Doug, would you follow them to the hospital? I'll get Marnie back, and then I'll join you there."

Doug gave him a nod of appreciation.

"Come on, Marnie, let's go."

She followed him around back. Quinn paused, staring at all the cars again. There were more colors in back now. The club attendees who could had snagged spaces in back.

As they drove, Marnie said, "You think it's really appendicitis?"

"That's what the doctors said," Quinn replied.

"Why did she scream about being poisoned?"

"Probably because she's in pain."

"Can appendicitis really come on that quickly?"

"I think so, yes. It can be very sudden."

Marnie was quiet for a minute, staring out the window. "You can die from it, can't you?" She sighed softly, then turned to him. "I love it. I love the studio so much. I love dancing so much...but it's a little scary, isn't it? Strange, it's scarier than sleeping on the street."

"Scary, how?"

She shook her head. "People around it...things happen to them."

They reached the shelter where she was staying until Annie could get her squared up with the older woman she was going to assist. Marnie jumped out of the car. "Hey, please don't think I'm a chicken. And please don't stop bringing me to the studio. I want to dance more than anything in the world. And I'm good, honestly, they said so."

"I won't stop bringing you," he promised, thinking that he would keep his word, though he wasn't so sure he wanted her there when he wasn't.

She smiled. "Will you call me, and let me know how Jane is doing?"

"Sure. It's late, though."

"It doesn't matter. The shelter is pretty cool."

"I'll call," he promised.

He watched her enter the shelter, then drove away.

Even Marnie knew it. Something was not right at the studio. In fact, something was very, very wrong.

When he arrived at the hospital, he found that Jane had already been seen in emergency and rushed upstairs for surgery.

The Longs had made the right diagnosis. She had been on the verge of a ruptured appendix. Shannon wasn't alone in the waiting room.

Gordon, Ben, Sam, Justin, Rhianna and Ella were all there. Gordon sat in a chair, his hands folded before him. Sam paced, passing Shannon as they walked the length of the room, turned and walked back again. Ben was fighting with a coin-operated coffee machine, Justin was stretched out on one of the sofas, and Rhianna was half-asleep, draped over Justin and using him as a pillow. Gabriel Lopez was there, and Katarina, but not her husband. They were on one of the waiting room sofas, apparently half-asleep but determined to wait on Jane with the others.

Quinn took a seat by Gordon.

"That was fast," he said.

"She was in a bad way," Gordon said. "And thankfully, there was only one guy with a broken toe in there when we arrived. Hey, they know when they need to move. The guys from fire rescue were great. Shannon said the hospital was ready to take Jane the minute the ambulance pulled in. They had a surgeon all ready to go. They say we caught it in time. She'll only be out of commission for a little while. A matter of weeks, probably. Not too bad."

"Where's my brother?" Quinn asked.

"Down the hall, just outside surgery," Gordon said, staring at him as if he could read something he wanted to know from Quinn's face. Gordon shrugged. Maybe he didn't really want to know. "He seemed really anxious."

"Yeah, anxious," Ben muttered, slamming a fist against the coffee machine. "Why the hell don't these things ever work?" He turned, facing the others. "Just her appendix. That's pretty serious, actually. But around here, it's a relief."

There was a silence in the room then that went beyond exhaustion and worry. Shannon and Sam both went still.

"I think we should cancel the Gator Gala," Shannon said.

"What?" Rhianna said, bolting to an upright position.

"There's been too much trauma," Shannon continued. "Lara…gone. And so close to the studio, that poor woman found on the beach."

"Sadly," Justin said, "there have always been bodies in Miami. You know how many people have been dumped in the water that we'll probably never even know about? And hell—none of us knew that woman. Shannon, we can't take on grief and concern for the whole world."

"We knew Lara. And before that, there was Nell," Shannon said.

"Her husband killed her," Sam said sharply.

"We can't cancel the Gator Gala. We've sunk too much money in it already," Gordon said.

Shannon stared at all of them. "I'm afraid. Afraid that something else is going to happen to someone. Let's be honest, for once. We're all afraid."

Quinn was silent, watching the reactions of the others. Before anyone could speak, the door to the waiting room opened. Richard and Mina Long had arrived.

"Thought you two went home," Ben said.

"We started for home," Mina said.

"But then we decided that we wouldn't sleep until we found out how Jane was doing," Richard explained.

"She's in surgery now," Gordon said.

"We heard."

"You both gave an accurate diagnosis."

"There you go," Richard said lightly. "See, I really did go to medical school." He paused, expecting laughter. None came. "Well, she's going to be fine," he said. "It was actually the best thing in the world that it happened when it did—she was with a crowd, and she got medical attention immediately. If she had been alone, if she had failed to reach a phone and call for help…well, then, it could have been really serious."

"So what's going on?" Mina asked.

"Shannon wants to cancel the Gator Gala," Justin said.

"No!" Richard said, sitting down, but staring at Shannon with a frown. "It's still almost three months away. Jane will be up and kicking by then."

Gabriel Lopez walked over to Shannon, slipping an arm around her shoulders. "*Chiquita,* it will be fine. The way the hospitals do things these days, Jane will be out by tomorrow afternoon."

"I certainly hope not," Mina said.

"Okay, so I'm exaggerating," Gabriel said, winking at Mina.

"Look, Jane carries a lot of the student burden, and she's going to have to be out for a while," Shannon said. "And wasn't she planning something with you, too, Ben? She had a heavy load. It's going to be too much for her."

Ben walked over to Shannon. "*You* can dance with me. You know I'm good."

"Ben, of course you're good. That's not it."

"Jane is going to be all right, but there's nothing suspicious about what happened. And we can cover for her."

"Ben, even if I dance with you, we'll be down one instructor."

"I have an idea," Sam said suddenly. "Marnie. That girl is the most natural dancer I've ever seen in my life. Shannon, seriously, in a few weeks' time, I could turn her into an instructor."

"Sam, think about how hard it is to learn all the steps as one sex. To be certified, she has to learn all the steps for both sexes. There's no way she can do that in time," Shannon said.

Justin shrugged. "When she was a little kid, she said, she

took years of ballet, modern and hip-hop. She knows a hell of a lot already."

"She has the natural talent," Rhianna said.

"We'll work with her, right, Justin? Please, don't think about canceling the Gator Gala," Sam said.

Shannon sighed. She stared across the room at Quinn. "What do you think?"

"About the Gator Gala?" he asked, surprised. "I'm the least capable dancer in the room. How would I know what could happen in a few months' time?"

She actually smiled, shaking her head. "Would Marnie want to do it?"

"Are you kidding? That girl would die to come on as a teacher," Rhianna said.

The room fell silent. The word *die* was not a good one at the moment.

"I promised to call her about Jane's condition," Quinn said. "I can ask her."

"Do it," Gordon said. He was staring at Shannon again. "We can't cancel the Gator Gala. We can't. We're in too deep."

Doug came into the waiting room looking haggard but relieved. "They won't let me anywhere near her, but she's going into recovery, and they say she's going to be fine."

There was a collective sigh of relief.

"Sweetheart, we've got to go home," Mina Long said to her husband.

"Right. Well, good night all," Richard said.

Gabriel stood, as well. "There's no need for all of us to be hanging around here, that's for sure."

"Are you going back to the club, Gabe?" Gordon asked.

"Yeah." He shrugged. "I'm not tired. We never close until five."

"I don't remember if I locked up. Check the studio for me?"

"Sure thing."

"You can give me a ride back," Katarina said. "My car is there."

"All right."

"I'm heading home," Gordon said, rising.

"I guess we could all go," Rhianna commented with a yawn.

"I'm staying here a while. I want to see her when they take her out of recovery," Shannon said.

Ben said, "Then what? Your car is at the studio, too."

"I'll wait around," Quinn said.

"Yeah, well, I was going to hang around, too," Doug told them.

"Were you?" Gordon queried him, looking at Shannon.

"Good night," she said simply.

Gordon nodded. They all began to file on out.

Then they were left alone in the waiting room, Doug, Shannon and Quinn.

"It really was just appendicitis?" Shannon said, sinking into a chair.

Doug sat next to her, taking her hand. "Really. Just appendicitis."

She let out a long sigh and leaned back. Then her head jerked back up, and she stared at Quinn. "What about that woman they found on the beach?"

"There's nothing new," he told her. "I'm expecting to hear anytime."

Quinn pulled his cell phone out and put a call through to Marnie. When he explained that the teachers had suggested she come in and train for a job, her scream of delight was so loud that Quinn had to hold the phone away from his ear.

"I mean, oh, Lord, I'm so sorry about Jane, but...I don't think she'll mind about me, do you? Oh, God, it's like a dream come true. I was on the streets, and now...I'm a dancer." She giggled over the line. "And I don't even have to go to some raunchy dive and dance with a pole. I'm going to be a ballroom instructor. Oh, I could kiss you, all of you, even old Mr. Clinton." Another giggle. "I guess I will be kissing him. You know, the kiss on both cheeks every time someone comes in. Thank you, tell them all thank you, and I'll work so hard they won't believe it. Tell Gordon and Shannon thank you so much!"

"I think Shannon heard you," Quinn said dryly.

"There's a problem," Marnie said suddenly.

"What's that?"

"How am I going to get to and from the studio from here?" She was still talking loudly enough for Shannon and Doug to hear.

"Tell her she can stay at my house. *In* my house, this time," Shannon said.

Quinn stared at her for a moment, then repeated her words to Marnie, who went into another fit of gratitude.

"She won't be sorry. I'll clean the house. I'll cook. I'll do anything!" Marnie said.

Shannon took the phone from Quinn. "Hey, just work at becoming a teacher—that's going to be quite a load. And, work for yourself, too. The world of competition is out there, you know."

Quinn heard Marnie exclaim that she could never be that good. Shannon just shook her head. "Get some sleep, Marnie. You'll need it."

"Thank you, thank you."

"You're welcome. And you're doing us a favor, too." Shannon was smiling as she handed the phone back to Quinn, who managed to calm Marnie down and hang up quickly.

"It's a shame we didn't think of offering her a job to begin with," she murmured, looking at Quinn. "Lots of teachers start out knowing nothing at all and don't have half the natural ability of that girl."

"Fate," Doug said from across the room.

"What?" Both Shannon and Quinn looked at him.

"Sometimes fate is good," he said. "Marnie needed a life, now she's got one. Jane will be all right soon enough, and Marnie will have a job, not just selling clothes, but a real vocation."

A nurse came in then, telling them that they could see Jane briefly.

Quinn decided to remain in the waiting room while Shannon and Doug went in. A while later, his brother came back out.

"There's a chair that becomes a bed," Doug told his brother. "Shannon is going to stay the night."

Quinn nodded, looking at Doug. "You all right?"

Doug nodded. "I'm on first thing in the morning." He shook his head. "Hell, tonight…at first I was terrified. I thought that… It was just too much like déjà vu."

"It was appendicitis," Quinn said.

Doug looked at him. "But there *is* something wrong. You know it now, right? Quinn, I know I dragged you into this, but I was right, wasn't I?"

"Yeah, you were right."

"But I still don't get it. That woman who washed up on the beach…what can she have to do with this?"

"I don't know," Quinn said. "But there's something, and I intend to find out what."

The next morning, Jane awoke moaning. Shannon rushed to her side.

Jane's eyes widened. "You stayed all night?"

"Sure."

"You must be exhausted."

"Actually, the chair was quite comfortable."

Jane tried to smile. She looked at Shannon anxiously. "I'm really all right?"

"You're really all right. You had honest-to-God appendicitis."

Jane tried for a smile.

"Jane, after you fell down, you said you'd been poisoned. Is there some reason why someone would want to poison you?" Shannon asked.

"No, we'd just gotten to talking around the coffeepot, and Mina Long was saying that she can't figure out how Lara could have been dumb enough to take so many pills. The alcohol didn't surprise her—she said she'd seen Lara belt down a few, then go out on stage like it was nothing. I'm trying to remember who was back there at the time...not that it matters now. But Mina said maybe someone had put the pills in her drink or something like that. Then I had coffee, and then I was in agony."

"I see," Shannon told her, suddenly certain she didn't want to drink coffee in the studio ever again.

"Silly, huh?"

"Well, you're all right, and that's what matters."

A look of dismay swept over Jane's face. "They said I just made it. That if my appendix had actually ruptured, I could have died."

"But you're going to be fine."

Jane shook her head. "What about all my students?"

"It will all work out."

"It can't. We don't have enough teachers to go around."

"We're going to bring Marnie in, give her a crash course, and she can take over some of the beginners."

"Marnie?" Jane said, surprised. Then she mulled over the idea. "If someone really works with her... Actually, I didn't know anything at all when I started. There's only one problem."

"What is that?"

"What if the students like her better than me?"

Shannon laughed, squeezing Jane's hand. "We always have enough students to go around. And anyway, your students love you. It will be fine."

"Maybe," Jane said after a moment.

"Hey, I'll be back later, okay? Your nurse will be coming in any minute, and I've got to take a shower and head to the studio."

"Of course. Thanks for staying."

Shannon hesitated. She had always thought it best not to know things, but at the moment, she couldn't resist. "If I hadn't stayed, someone else would have."

"Who?" Jane said, but she was blushing.

"Doug O'Casey."

"Really?" Jane didn't seem able to prevent her smile.

"Yep."

"Hmm. You know…never mind."

"Do I know what?" Shannon asked a little sharply.

Jane shook her head. "I can't say I'm really going to miss Lara."

"What does that mean?"

"Nothing."

"Jane!"

"Hey, don't harass me. I just had emergency surgery last night."

"Jane?"

"Okay, well, I think I've had one of those 'things' I'm not allowed to have on Doug for a long time. But when he saw Lara…well, he just had a look about him. Now Lara is gone. And he doesn't just think I'm the most wonderful teacher in the world, he…well, like I said, never mind."

Shannon hesitated. "I think you should watch out for everyone right now," she said quietly.

"Doug is a cop."

"I know."

"Then…?"

"I just think we should watch out for everyone."

"Lara was murdered," Jane said firmly. "You know, there are all kinds of top professionals who might have wanted her dead."

Shannon grimaced. "Maybe. But something lately…something about the studio… I keep hearing something, a strange noise. I'm going to do a little prying, find out just what it is."

"Don't be there alone, Shannon. Don't pry when you're alone."

"Hey, the club is right downstairs, Katarina is right next door. But anyway, you just lie low and keep quiet, okay?"

"Yes, ma'am," Jane said. "I don't have any choice, do I?"

"Nope."

Shannon gave her a kiss on the forehead and departed, figuring she could take a cab to her house, then walk to work.

Early.

She would lock herself in, then figure out what in hell was making the noise that was driving her so crazy.

As she left the hospital, she suddenly felt very determined. She was tired of being frightened.

A little prying…

He'd been just about to enter the hospital room when he had heard Shannon's voice.

Flowers in hand, he stepped back, listening.

No, Shannon, you little fool. Don't pry. Don't be an idiot.

As he stood there, listening, he realized that there was no help for it.

Shannon Mackay would look just as beautiful as Lara Trudeau…in a coffin.

She was coming out!

He started to back away, then dropped the flowers and threaded his way between two nurses and an old lady in a wheelchair. He hurried down the hall. Turning, he could see Shannon.

He didn't wait for the elevator but took the stairs.

Once on the ground, he was furious with himself. What an idiot he'd been. He should have walked right on in and put his flowers down.

He waited until Shannon Mackay was on the street. He watched as she hailed a taxi.

Then he ran back into the hospital, took the elevator and hurried along the hall.

His flowers were still on the floor.

He picked them up, looked in on Jane. She was sleeping again. He walked down the hall and entered a room, dropping the flowers on the table beside an older woman.

"Your lucky day, honey," he told her, then exited the hospital once again.

As he came out into the sun, he remained irritated with himself. Cops always said that killers were bound to mess up somewhere.

He'd been an idiot, running away like that. What the hell had been the matter with him? Like the cops said, he'd fucked up.

No. He could walk in anywhere, any time, and act normally. Shannon had just given him a moment's pause.

He wouldn't mess up again. He was far too good for that.

He would be even more careful, more clever.

When he finally went for her she would never know.

Richard Long's offices were magnificent.

He practiced with another man, Dr. Bertrand Diaz, and between them, they did quite a business. The waiting room was crowded with women when Quinn arrived, and all of them attractive, even if a few did look a little…plastic.

At least Long did plastic well.

He spoke to the receptionist, and with the amount of people in the office, he was surprised to be shown into the doctor's office rather quickly.

Richard Long seemed pleasantly surprised to see him. "I'm sure you're not thinking about surgery, are you, Quinn?" he demanded, half-sitting on the edge of his mahogany desk and folding his arms over his chest with a look of amusement. "So…to what do I owe the pleasure of this visit?"

"I thought you could give me some help."

"Oh?" Long said.

"Well, it occurred to me that you and your wife are physicians."

"Yes?"

"Well, how do you think those drugs got into Lara Trudeau?"

Long stared at him for several seconds, and as he did so, his face began to mottle. "Are you suggesting that *I* would dispense drugs illegally? Never. Lara was not my patient. Nor would I have accepted her as a patient—ever. She would have been far too demanding."

"So how do you think she got all that Xanax into her, then?"

Long's eyes narrowed angrily. "Who the hell are you to be asking? I thought your brother was the cop and that you were a…a fisherman, or something."

"Licensed private investigator, Dr. Long," Quinn told him. What the hell, hiding it hadn't gotten him anywhere. Maybe the truth would serve him better.

"And who hired you?"

"I'm not at liberty to disclose the name of my client."

"Well, I'm sorry, I'm not at liberty to waste any more time with you. I never gave Lara Trudeau a prescription for narcotics. She had her own doctor. Question him."

"I did. I was just curious, thinking you might be able to give me a little help. Now your wife is also—"

"Don't even go there. My wife's reputation is spotless. I can promise you, she wouldn't have given Lara a prescription or supplied her with free samples or anything of the kind!"

"I'm sorry, but let me just ask you this—the day of the competition, did you see Lara alone with anyone at any time?"

"Well, if I'd been there, too, she wouldn't have been alone, right?" Long said sarcastically.

"I think you know what I mean."

"I was busy the day of the competition," Long said. "This is my profession, but dance is my love. I had my own amateur ranking to worry about."

Quinn rose. "I'm sorry I took up your time."

"You could have talked to me at the studio," Long said.

"Well, you know—everyone is at the studio."

"Lara did herself in. That's my professional opinion. Sorry, Quinn. I have patients out there."

"Of course. Sure."

Quinn put his hand on the door handle.

"If anyone spent time with Lara Trudeau, Mr. O'Casey, you might want to look closer to home."

Quinn turned back.

"Most of the students think he was having an affair with her," Long said. "Talk to him. In fact, come to think of it, I think he managed to be alone with her, out on the balcony that joined the dressing rooms, right before she went on stage. And I think they were arguing. Yeah, if you need some help, go to your brother. Ask Doug your questions."

"Thanks, Dr. Long," Quinn managed to say easily.

He exited the office, nodding at the blonde with the fantastic boobs to the left of the waiting room door and the older woman with the tightly stretched face on the right.

Doug!

Dammit. Why did it keep coming back to his brother?

And why the hell wasn't Doug telling him the truth—all of it?

CHAPTER 19

Shannon was irritated to reach the studio early—after a very quick shower at her own house—and find out that Gordon was already in. So were Ella and Ben.

Ella was going through the books; Ben was practicing steps by himself, and Gordon was on the phone. When he saw her, he waved her into the office.

"Right, Richard," Gordon said. He grimaced as Shannon took the seat next to his desk. "Richard, I was aware of Mr. O'Casey's profession, yes." A moment's silence as Richard spoke on the other end. "Richard, I'm sure he came to see you for help, not to make an accusation, and of course everyone knows that Mina is beyond reproach." Again silence. "Oh, come now, Richard, you and Mina have to join us on the cruise... As you wish," Gordon said with a sigh. "We'll miss you."

Gordon hung up the phone.

"Richard Long?" Shannon said.

"Totally indignant. O'Casey was over at his office, questioning him."

"Really?"

"Well, you know, the man is a doctor. Doctors can get prescription pills."

"But Lara had a prescription from her own physician," Shannon said.

Gordon shrugged. "At any rate, Dr. Long is pissed off. Says he's not coming on the cruise, and he may just quit taking lessons."

"You didn't try very hard to cajole him," Shannon said. "Want me to call him?"

Gordon shook his head, grinning. "He'll call back any minute. By noon, at the latest. Richard thinks he's Fred Astaire reincarnated. He won't stop coming."

"I hope you're right," Shannon said, rising. "And by the way, Jane seems to be doing all right. I left early, but she was awake."

Gordon nodded. "I stopped in briefly to see her. She said you had just left. I met her doctor. They're going to keep her two or three more days, then she has to lie low at home for a while."

"Maybe I was too panicky last night. I guess she'll be back to teaching in less time than I thought."

Gordon mulled that over. "Whether you were panicky or not, it's kind of a good thing. I think that young lady we're bringing in is going to be quite an asset." He leaned back in his chair, reflecting. "I hope she never changes, though. Her enthusiasm is so wide-eyed, and her energy is so unlimited. She just loves dancing and being here. Lara was like that when I met her. She let it all go to her head, though. She was a champion, but not really a winner."

"I hope it works out well, and I definitely hope she stays sweet—since I said she could live with me," Shannon told him.

"Speak of the devil," Gordon said.

Shannon turned. Marnie was standing hesitantly just outside the door. "Sorry, I didn't mean to interrupt. Quinn dropped me off. With my things. They won't take up much room. I got the impression I needed to get started right away."

"Good call," Shannon said, rising. She smiled, slipping an arm around Marnie's shoulder. "Come on. You'll work with me first. I'm early." She winked. "I'm also the best—and most qualified—instructor."

"Really?" Marnie said.

"Well, in my own mind, anyway," Shannon told her. "Let's get started."

When she moved back into the studio dance floor area, she saw that Quinn had not only brought Marnie, he had stayed. He was in the back by the coffeepot, and Ben had joined him. They seemed to be deep in conversation but broke it off the moment she appeared.

"Coffee, Shannon?" Ben asked.

She hesitated, remembering Jane's words and her earlier decision. But they both appeared to be drinking coffee from the pot.

"Sure, thanks."

"I saw Jane," Ben said.

"You, too? So did Gordon."

Ben laughed. "The hospital is going to be thrilled when they get rid of her—Gordon was just leaving when I arrived. Mr. Clinton showed up with chocolates and flowers. Doug was up to see her, and Gabe and Katarina came together, right when I was leaving. I'm willing to bet that the rest of our group—the teachers, at least—will all show up to check on her."

She smiled. Once that had been the good thing about the studio. They might squabble with one another once in a while, but they were always there for one another, too.

But now...

Now it seemed that a shadow lay over them, that there was some kind of malady among them that could never quite be cured.

Ben handed her a cup of coffee and said to Marnie, "Hey, kid, do you drink coffee?"

"Of course. I am eighteen," she said.

"Let's hope she keeps it to coffee," Quinn murmured. Marnie made a face at him, but she also looked at him with a certain amount of adoration.

"Quick cup of coffee. We're going to start working," Shannon said.

"Are you? I was hoping to catch you early and get a class in," Quinn said.

"We're not even officially open, Quinn," she said. "Sorry, I—"

"I can start with Marnie," Ben said. "I'm in because I'm restless."

"Yes, but—"

"Don't worry. I'll leave the finer points to you. Marnie has so much to learn, she might as well start some basics with me."

"I really need the help," Quinn said.

"Fine," Shannon told him, unable to come up with another excuse. "Let's go, then."

She usually linked arms with a student to walk across to the stereo and choose a working disk, but she let Quinn O'Casey follow in her wake.

She slid in a fox-trot.

"No, let's work on that waltz."

"You know the waltz—you suck at the fox-trot."

"But we're doing a waltz routine. I'd rather get that right than anything else."

"You can get it right, but if you're going to compete, you need to do the fox-trot."

"You just want to do the fox-trot because you know I hate it." He was grinning.

She sighed. "You need to learn it."

"Why? Do you make everyone learn the fox-trot?"

"We don't *make* people learn anything."

He grinned. "I promise I'll learn the fox-trot. Let's do the waltz today, though. I really want to excel at the pooper-scooper."

"Great."

She put in a waltz and slid into his arms. He really did have this one down.

"You caused some trouble," she told him.

"Only some?"

"Richard Long is refusing to come on the cruise."

"Oh, I bet he'll be there."

"That's what Gordon said. But you went into his office and started accusing him of dispensing drugs illegally."

"Nope."

"You didn't go into his office?"

"Sure. But I just asked him a few questions."

"Great."

"That's what investigators do. Ask questions."

He arched a brow at her. "Yeah, you know, like I did with you. Such an ugly thing."

She shook her head. "You're killing time now, aren't you?"

"Still investigating."

"Me?" she said. "I would have thought you had me down pat by now."

He shook his head. "Not really."

"Oh? And what don't you know?"

"How did you break your ankle?"

She inhaled, shaking her head. "What are you after?"

"The truth."

"I broke my ankle because I wasn't good enough. How's that?"

"Not true."

She let out a sigh. "We were at a competition. I was dancing with Ben at the time, and Lara was dancing with a man named Ronald Yeats. We were all out on the floor during a Viennese waltz and…she crashed, and I went down, too. My ankle was broken."

"So basically, Lara caused all your woes."

"So I murdered her?"

"You didn't, did you?" he said, and his tone was both serious and mocking.

"No," she snapped.

"I didn't think so. But…"

"But what?"

"You're still a coward, you know."

"What are you getting at now?"

He didn't answer her. They'd moved across the floor, following the steps in the routine, and he flipped her up and around in a perfect rendition of the pooper-scooper. Then he spun her into perfect position to take a bow.

She turned to him. "Your mother must be one good dancer."

"She is," he said.

"Are you really planning on dancing at the Gator Gala?" she demanded. She lowered her voice. "Because if all this isn't solved by then…"

"What?"

"Nothing."

"What?"

"I'll be insane, that's what," she admitted.

"The amazing thing is this—okay, I suck at the other dances. But I do want to learn them. It actually feels…great, I guess. To be able to do this. That's the truth."

"Ah," she said.

"And that means?"

"That's the truth, but it's not the whole truth. Why didn't you mention the FBI? And why did you leave the Bureau? And for that matter, you and Doug seem to have a lot of money. You're not drug smugglers in your spare time, are you?"

He shook his head. "Cops don't make big money, FBI agents don't make big money, and P.I.s just do all right. My father died years ago and left us all trust funds."

"Was he a drug smuggler?" Shannon said, only partially teasing.

"Real estate. He came here when land cost nothing, bought tons of it and made some pretty good money. I try pretty hard not to touch mine. Don't know why, except that I like to make my living on my own. Planning to check out my bank accounts?"

"Maybe. But that would be illegal, wouldn't it?"

He shrugged, and she had the feeling he had the ability to check out just about anything he wanted.

"I'll put the music back on," she murmured, dropping the subject of his finances.

In all, they went through the routine several times. Then they went into the fox-trot, which was just as bad as it had been. Still, as they worked, she realized that she loved teaching him. Loved his rueful smile when he didn't get what she was saying, and the flash in his eyes when something made sense. The scent of him seemed very rich to her, seductive. The feel of his hands on her was magic. She was startled when he suddenly said, "I think I'm way over time. I've got to move on."

They *had* gone over.

She stared at him. "You managed not to answer me before. Why did you leave the FBI?"

He hesitated for a minute. A shield went over his eyes. Then he said, "I made a mistake. A big one."

She stared at him, then shook her head. "You're really something."

"Why?"

"You call me a coward, but you're worse. You made one mistake, so you copped out. You're worse than me."

He stared at her and didn't reply. He walked by, saying something to Marnie and Ben, then departed by the back door.

She followed him, but the door had already closed. Then, as she stood there, hesitant, she heard it.

The grating sound.

She couldn't place it. Was it coming from inside—or outside? Ben turned up the music, and she rushed over, turning down the stereo.

"What are you doing?" he demanded.

"Didn't you hear that?"

"Hear what?" he asked, trying not to sound annoyed.

"That…noise."

"There's noise from all over, Shannon. What noise are you talking about?"

"Never mind," she told him. "When you two are done, let Marnie take a little break, then I'll see what she's learned," Shannon said.

She left them and walked into the ladies' room.

Nothing. And yet…

The noise, she decided, was coming from the rear of the studio. But from where, exactly, and what the hell was it?

Quinn found his brother at Nick's.

Luckily he was alone. He was also looking very worn.

Quinn took the chair opposite him. "You look like death warmed over."

"Yeah, I'm tired," Doug admitted.

"Should you be taking lunch?" Quinn asked.

"Why?"

"Well, you took time off this morning to go by to see Jane."

Doug flushed. "I had to."

"Patrolmen aren't supposed to mess around like that. Your beat is Kendall."

"I only took a few minutes. What's the matter with you? You're coming on like a ball-buster sergeant."

"What were you and Lara fighting about at the competition?" he demanded.

Doug avoided his eyes, looking off in the distance. "Fighting?"

"Yes, fighting. Balcony area, outside the changing rooms."

"I was…angry."

"About what?"

"Her behavior."

"How so?"

"She was…she was drinking more than usual, and really flirting. I thought Katarina was going to deck her once when she made a real play for David."

"You knew she slept around."

"That didn't mean I liked it. She was in rare form that day. Talking about a million places she was going to go." He hesitated. "I'd let her know once that…well, I had told her I might be a cop, but I could take as many lessons, pay for a coach as often as I wanted, because I had a trust fund. That was probably why she got interested in me. But that day, she told me that if I didn't like something, I could just piss off. She'd fool around with anyone she wanted, and she didn't need money—she'd acquired a source for all she needed. I thought she was just talking through the alcohol. I said something to her about that, too, about how much she was drinking. And she told me she could dance no matter what, she was that good, and that I should just piss off."

"And then?" Quinn prompted.

Doug shrugged. "I did. I left her."

"And you didn't see anyone else with her?"

He shook his head. "I went to cool down, to remind myself that I was just in it for the fun, that I'd always known she would never get serious. Then, not too much later, I watched her dance, and I realized she would never really love any guy, because she was too much in love with being Lara Trudeau. Not just dancing. But in being herself, out on the floor, making everyone want her. Or envy her." He took a swallow of iced tea. "Have you found out anything, anything at all?"

Quinn nodded. "Yeah. I found out that if any two people look the most suspicious, it's you and Shannon MacKay." He rose. "Make sure you're back on your beat on time."

Quinn went back to his boat and sat on the deck, going through the files again, looking at his own notes.

Find waiter.

Well, he'd found the waiter. Dead end.

But something was still bothering him. Something Manuel Taylor had said.

He pulled out the sheets with the listing of names Jake had acquired for him, wondering what it was. It eluded him.

He hesitated, then called the man. He got his answering machine, but left a message. "Hey, this is Quinn O'Casey. You said you'd like to work a cruise sometime. How about Saturday night."

He hung up and called down to the Keys, making sure that Dane could still bring up the party boat they owned for Saturday night.

Then he swore to himself.

He'd forgotten all about getting an alarm installed at Shannon's house. Now Marnie would be living there, too, and he didn't want the two women alone without protection.

He swore to himself and pulled out his phone book, then put through a call, hoping his friends in the area remembered who he was.

Carlos did, and agreed to go out to Shannon's house himself, saying that he could arrive around five-thirty. "An after-hours job," Carlos told him cheerfully.

"Thanks. Really."

"Hey, it's my business," Carlos said. "No problem."

Quinn hung up and pulled out the picture of the woman who had been found dead on Sunday, the drawing that Ashley had done for the paper. Pocketing it, he headed back for the beach.

Late in the afternoon, Shannon finally stopped, smiling at Marnie. "Let's take a real break. Get your things. We'll go to my house and settle you in, grab something to eat."

Marnie nodded, then said, "Hey, are you sure? I mean, I feel like Cinderella, some kind of a fairy-tale princess."

"I'm used to living alone," Shannon admitted. "But we'll manage."

Shannon told Ella to make sure that Gordon—who was in his office with the door closed—knew where she was going. She led Marnie to her car and then drove the short distance to her house. The girl's possessions were truly meager. So far, though, they'd fitted her with some of the used shoes in the studio, and though Shannon and Jane were taller than Marnie, Rhianna was just about her size and had generously seen to it that Marnie took a few of the jeans and shirts she kept in her locker. They would plan a little party for her, Shannon thought, a welcome-to-the-staff party, and everyone could buy her some little thing and she would begin to have real belongings.

"There isn't really an extra bedroom, because I had it made into a studio," Shannon told her. "But we'll fix up some space for you in that closet, and the couch is comfortable. You won't have an actual bedroom, but you'll have a television set, and tons of DVDs and tapes to choose from."

Marnie grinned at her. "Hey, I thought I was lucky when I was living in your yard." She walked in, turned around and said, "Remember, I'm Cinderella. And I mean it. This is like a castle."

"Things were really that bad at home?" Shannon asked her.

Marnie nodded, looking away. She squared her shoulders. "The thing of it is, I'm an adult. I should be able to make it on my own. But once I was out…God, it was harder than I thought it was going to be. I had nothing to start with, I guess."

"Well, now you've got a room, for what it's worth," Shannon told her.

"A lot." Marnie hugged her arms around her thin frame. "If it weren't for you…and Quinn… God, he's really something, isn't he?"

"Oh, yes. He's something," Shannon agreed. What could she say to such hero worship? Especially when he was the best "something" she'd come across herself. Ever.

"I think he's in love with you," Marnie said.

"He's a student," she replied sharply. Too sharply.

Marnie grinned. "Sorry. It's just…don't you ever notice the way he looks at you? Boy, if anyone like that ever looked at me that way, well, I wouldn't be a silly fool and let him get away. Fraternization rule or not."

"I'm going to make tea," Shannon said. "Do you want some?"

"You mean like hot tea?"

"Yes. We've got about forty-five minutes. That's the meal-time. All the teachers make sure to schedule meals around their appointments."

"I know, I know. I got the speech."

Shannon put the water on. Marnie walked down the hall, looking in at the extra bedroom-slash-studio. "Wow."

"I like it," Shannon said when she got back to the kitchen.

"The only thing you're missing is an alarm," Marnie said matter-of-factly.

"There's a dog next door."

"Quinn said something about getting one installed for you. I think he meant to do it today, but after last night, what with Jane and all, I think maybe he forgot." She grinned. "So I bet that means he'll be around tonight."

"Why should he be?"

Shannon crawled up on one of the bar stools that sat at the counter between the kitchen and the family room.

"Because of the car, of course. The car that kind of cruises by your house. I guess maybe he didn't say anything to you. He probably didn't want to freak you out, because, you know, it's probably nothing."

The water boiled. The steam hit Shannon's face. Despite it, she felt a sudden deep, debilitating chill.

Suede hadn't opened for business when Quinn arrived, but the handsome black doorman recognized him and let him in, telling him that he would go find Gabe.

Quinn sat at the bar, sipping a soda water, waiting.

"Hey! It's the new student. I hear you may rival your brother one day," Lopez said pleasantly, taking the chair beside him. "Can I get you something besides the drink? We don't really have a menu, but we've got snacks."

"No, no, thanks. I was hoping you could help me."

"Sure, if I can."

He pulled out the picture of Sonya Marquez Miller. "I was trying to find out if this woman had ever been in the club."

Gabriel Lopez shook his head sadly. "The cops were in here after she washed up on the beach. I had all my help come out and take a look. I've never seen her. They haven't found out what happened to her, huh?"

"One big overdose," Quinn said.

"I wish I could help." He hesitated. "You know, of course, that weekends down here get wild. And Miami has a little bit of every kind of Mafia known to man—Russian, Italian, Cuban…then there are the Colombians. Hell, someone even told me that we have Haitian drug lords here. And you name a country from Central or South America, and we get their criminal element on the beach. I get every nationality known to man in here on a Friday or Saturday night, and most of them are fine people, just out for fun. And trust me, there are lots of executive types—clean and pure Monday through Friday, nine to five—who do recreational drugs on weekends. But we've kept the club clean. The bartenders and wait staff all know to watch for anyone getting too drunk. We cut them off. And we're known as the toughest club in the district, as far as checking IDs goes."

"Yeah, I've heard. I was just hoping you might have seen her."

"I would have told the cops if I had. Hey, are you going to group class tonight?"

"Not tonight, I'm afraid."

"Well, keep up the dancing. And come back here any time."

"Thanks." He got off the stool.

"You doing some work for your brother?" Lopez asked him.

Quinn turned back.

"I didn't know you were a cop yourself," Lopez explained.

"I'm not," Quinn said. "Private investigator."

"Ah. Well, that's good. Did the woman's family hire you?"

"Can't say," Quinn told him.

"Big secret, huh?"

"Client privilege," Quinn told him. "See you later. Are you going to be on the boat Saturday night?"

"You bet."

"See you then."

He left Suede and went upstairs, where he found that Shannon was at her house. He called and Marnie answered. He told her to tell Shannon not to freak out when the man from the alarm company arrived. "He'll be there any minute."

Marnie went off to talk to Shannon.

"She says we have to go back to work."

"Fine. I'll be there any minute, too, then."

He hung up before there could be any protest.

When he arrived at Shannon's, Carlos Rodriguez was already there, and Shannon was standing at the door, ready to leave.

"Do you know," she told him, "you really need to discuss it with someone when you're ordering something for their house."

"We talked about this. You need an alarm," he told her, and added impatiently, "And I'll pay for it, if that's the problem."

"Trust fund, right?" she said coolly. "Don't be ridiculous. I make a decent income."

She was rigid and entirely aloof. It made him want to grab her and...

He wanted to touch her face. Run his thumb along her

cheek, thread his fingers into her hair. Hell. Crush her against him. Every body part he had suddenly came up with a physiological memory of what it was like to be with her.

"I've got to get back. Since you wanted this, you stay here until it's done," she said.

"I intend to stay here," he informed her, noting the grating tone of his own voice.

Marnie gave him a shrug as Shannon started down the walk for her car, then ran to catch up with her.

"Told you," the girl said, and Quinn could hear her. "He's really got a thing for you. Like he's in love with you or something."

"This is what you want, right?"

Quinn jumped. Carlos was in front of him. "What?"

"The system—you want a standard system. Windows and doors, a keypad, and an automatic alarm if they're breeched?"

He nodded, looking after Shannon's car as it drove away down the street.

CHAPTER 20

By the time she drove back home that night, Shannon was exhausted.

She'd intended to get back by the hospital to see Jane, but she never had, because the studio had been so busy.

It amazed her, because she had thought that the death and burial of a major ballroom dance star like Lara Trudeau might have given people pause.

It hadn't.

It seemed that everyone wanted to be at the studio.

One of the important factors in planning the Gator Gala had been encouraging the students to compete, and therefore, to take more classes.

It was working.

On top of that, Jane's attack of appendicitis seemed to have drawn people out of the woodwork. The regulars were all there, and then some.

Gunter and Helga came by, saying they had stopped to see Jane on the way. Christie—who only made an appearance when she was coaching—arrived, as well. Doug showed up and stayed a little while, saying that he was going by the hospital. Bobby Yarborough and Giselle came, saying they had already stopped by the hospital. Both Katarina and David were there. Gabriel was up, bringing a few friends from the club, trying to introduce them to the magical world of dance.

Despite having sworn that he wasn't showing up, Richard Long came, and Mina was with him.

He barely mentioned Quinn, except to note with a certain pleasure that the man wasn't in attendance. Their younger crowd, a number of the high school girls and boys, showed up, as well as some of the newer students. People stayed, chatting after the last class.

Shannon was ready to scream.

She didn't think about noises, or leaving the studio. She wished that she didn't have a new housemate, because Marnie was excited; she had never tired during the day, despite working with each of the teachers in succession. Christie had watched her and given her a number of pointers, then commented to Shannon that they had found someone who could excel.

"She reminds me of Lara, actually," Christie said.

"Her talent, yes," Shannon agreed.

Christie gave a rueful smile. "Certainly not character-wise. Lara always had...well, never mind, it isn't nice to speak ill of the dead. Oh, what the hell. From the time she started, there was something cutthroat about Lara. With Marnie, it's pure love and enthusiasm. Maybe she reminds me more of you. Once."

At that point, Ben had joined in. "Shannon is going to do some dancing with me."

Christie's face lit up. "Really? If you do go back into competition, I'd love to work with the two of you again."

"Maybe," Shannon murmured. She *had* told Ben she

would dance with him. And for the first time that night, she felt a spur of excitement. *Yes. Maybe…yes.*

Grudgingly she admitted to herself that if she did indeed go back into professional competition, Quinn O'Casey would have been the one to stir her into it.

That made her even more tired.

Since Marnie was bubbling all over with enthusiasm, she forced herself not to ask the girl to please just shut up as they drove.

Yet when they reached house and she saw that Quinn's car was still in front, she felt a strange ripple of emotion—one she didn't want to analyze. Could he possibly really care about her? And could she possibly care about him?

"Quinn is still here," Marnie said.

"Yes, well, that's a good thing," she said, realizing that if he hadn't been there, she would have been in trouble—she had left with the alarm man working and her house keys on the counter. "I didn't bring my house key," she reminded Marnie.

"Oh," Marnie said. "And there's an alarm." She grinned. "There's an alarm system on Cinderella's castle now."

When she knocked on her own door, it took him several minutes to answer it. His hair was tousled, and she realized he'd fallen asleep on the soft couch in back. Even the way his hair looked caused electricity to take flight down a path in her spine.

"You ran late," he murmured. But he seemed to have the ability to shake himself to full wakefulness easily enough. "Let me explain the alarm to you." He showed her the keypad, and told her what to punch when she was home and they were both in for the night, and what to punch when she left the house, and what to punch when she wanted the alarm off if she happened to be coming in and out for any reason.

He stood near her, arm over her shoulder as he demonstrated, and she was more tempted than she had ever been in her life just to lean back and rest. She didn't, though. No matter what Marnie had said about the way he looked at her, she wasn't sure she was willing to give her trust so easily.

"Have you got it?" he asked her.

"Yes, I think so."

"Well, the instructions are on the counter, if you have any difficulties."

"Quinn!" Marnie said, throwing herself at him with a childish abandon, hugging him, then letting him free. "It was great, it was so wonderful. Even the coach…what's her name, Shannon?"

"Christie," Shannon said patiently.

"Even Christie said I've real potential."

"That's wonderful." His eyes met Shannon's.

"Can we have some tea?" Marnie asked.

There had been nothing Shannon wanted more than to crawl straight into her bed, but now Quinn's and Marnie's eyes were on her.

"Sure," she said, resigned.

"You'll stay, right, Quinn?" Marnie asked.

"I really need to go."

"Just stay for a cup of tea," Marnie prodded.

"One quick cup of tea," he said, looking at Shannon.

"Have you eaten anything?" Shannon asked. She added, "You did get this alarm in for me. I mean, I owe you."

"No, you don't owe me," he said firmly.

"I'm sorry, I didn't mean it that way," she murmured, wishing she weren't flushing. "Anyway, please go sit down…I'll brew the tea." She smiled. "Marnie can tell you about her day for a while."

He arched a brow, a slow smile curving his lips. He was well aware that Marnie had been talking nonstop.

"All right. Make tea in peace," he said.

He walked toward the back of the house. Marnie stood still for a minute. "Hey, sorry, I should help, huh?"

"No. Go entertain Quinn."

Shannon boiled the water, fixed a pot of English breakfast tea and found some oatmeal bars to set around it. Then she dug around in the refrigerator and found some cheese squares, and decided to add toast points. When she had fixed the tray and was ready to bring it out to the coffee table in front of the couch, she realized that the room was strangely silent.

Marnie was curled into the chair, sound asleep. Quinn was leaning back on the sofa, legs extended on the coffee table.

Sound asleep as well.

As Shannon stood there, Marnie's eyes opened.

"Oh," she murmured. She uncurled herself. "I was talking to him and then I realized he wasn't answering me anymore," she whispered. "I guess we should wake him."

Shannon turned back, putting the tray on the pass-through counter.

"No," she said softly.

"But what do we do?"

"Let him sleep. Come on in the kitchen and drink your tea. We'll sleep in my room."

Marnie leaped up and came around beside Shannon. "You think he'll be all right?"

"He'll be fine." Shannon turned and went into her room for a blanket, then brought it out and swept it over his outstretched legs. "Come on," she said, bringing her fingers to her lips to indicate that they should be quiet.

Marnie nodded and followed Shannon back into the kitchen. They drank their tea, and Marnie went through half the food on the tray. She looked famished.

Well, she'd worked really hard, Shannon thought. And she certainly didn't have any fat stores to draw on.

When she had finished, she seemed to realize that she had inhaled everything. But she didn't apologize, just looked at Shannon a little morosely. "I'll clean up."

"Leave it. We'll get it in the morning. Come on, we'll take turns in the bathroom, then get some sleep."

She was afraid Marnie would want to whisper all night. She didn't. She accepted the new toothbrush and nightgown Shannon gave her with a simple thank-you, then insisted Shannon go first.

At last, way after midnight, they were in bed. Marnie kept carefully to her own side, as if she were afraid to offend her benefactor in any way.

After a minute, she said, "Thank you so much for everything."

There was something in the way she spoke that made Shannon smile, glad in a way she had never imagined.

"It's okay, really."

"Good night. I swear I won't make another sound."

Shannon laughed softly, tousled her guest's long hair and turned her back on her.

Strange. This was not at all the night she would have been having in her dream of dreams.

But at least she felt safe and secure with her house full. In minutes, she was sound asleep herself.

Jake was still taking time off.

He offered to come into the station, but Quinn flatly refused to let him do so. Jake had a new partner though, a woman named Anna Marino, and she was a blessing—pleased to meet Quinn and happy to help. She was tall for a woman, probably a good five-ten or five-eleven, but she was slim and as wiry as a polecat. She was very pretty, with naturally light hair, vivid blue eyes and classic features. She might well have graced a runway had she not decided to become one of Miami-Dade's finest.

"I'll give you anything I can," she assured Quinn, digging through Jake's files for him. "I wish we had more. That's one of the sad facts of this work. When we have a suspect, modern forensics do wonders for us. But when we haven't got a prayer of a suspect… Here. Here's the old one. Sally Grant." She skimmed the file before handing it to Quinn. "Twenty-two, working the streets, her address is a boardinghouse known to be a little less than reputable but not a drug house, just one of those places that doesn't ask for a lot of background information and doesn't much care what you do in your room as long as the door is closed. Transient, out of Oklahoma, folks dead, one brother found, and he didn't come for the body, he just asked if there was life insurance on her. I found her case one of the saddest. So did Jake. We combed the streets, and narcotics came in on it, too, doing a real rundown on the clubs. No matter how hard we tried, we came up with zilch." She hesitated. "We took up a collection in the department just to get her a decent burial. One of the funeral homes helped out."

Quinn nodded, taking the file and sitting across from Anna. She folded her hands on the desk, watching him. "I'll get the Sonya Miller file. Jake is convinced that these two are associated, though we don't know how. Sonya Miller had money and a family that claimed her. The two women were from totally different social arenas."

"I can see that."

The case of Sally Grant was truly sad. She'd been so young. The photos taken at the scene were truly pathetic. Her eyes were wide-open. She was staring. Long brown hair spilled over the sidewalk, reminding Quinn of Marnie.

He looked up at Anna. "No sign of sexual assault in either case?"

Anna shook her head. "Sally was a hooker—there were enough street people around to assure us on that point. But she hadn't even had any business the night she was killed."

Quinn gave a grim smile as he looked at Anna. "Could have been an accidental death."

She shook her head. "She was found on the sidewalk, with the needle still in her arm. Staged, but staged badly. Where the hell was her stash? Her source for getting the heroin into the needle? It's been called possible homicide, probable homicide and death by misadventure. Call it what you will. She was murdered."

"The two deaths were months apart," Quinn mused.

"Right. Like I said, though, Jake and I are convinced that they're related. I understand that you're investigating the 'accidental' death of the dancer?"

"That's right."

"I wish it had been assigned to Jake and me. But it wasn't. And Dixon closed the case. Though, quite frankly, I'm not sure what correlation Jake or I could have made, either. Your dancer died of prescription drugs and alcohol. There were definitely no street drugs."

"Another woman died recently of a massive overdose of prescription medication," Jake said.

She nodded. "Nell Durken. Husband arrested. Joel Kylie has that case. He said the arrest was easy, you had such great records on the husband."

Quinn winced. "I'm not so sure anymore that the guy is guilty."

Anna looked surprised. "His prints were all over the pill bottle," she reminded him. "What makes you think he's innocent?"

"Well, he says so, for one thing," Quinn told her.

She smiled. "Most murderers claim to be innocent. You know that. You can see a guy pull the trigger, and he'll still look you right in the eye and deny it."

"Like you, I think the two deaths are associated. And I also think they're associated with your drug overdoses."

"There have been other deaths by drug overdose, you know. Even though we've actually cut down on murder cases per capita recently, we're still talking hundreds a year in the general area. You worked here—you know that many go unsolved."

"Sadly, I do know that."

"So what makes *you* think the deaths are all related?"

"Nell was a dance student at Moonlight Sonata. Lara Trudeau was a coach there and got her start there. The beach where Sonya Miller was found is right there, and, according to this report, Sally Grant was found just down the street."

"I don't think our hooker, Sally Grant, took dance lessons. And she would have been thrown out of a club like Suede before her little toe passed the door. Sonya might have been in the place, but we grilled everyone in there as hard as we could, within the limits of the law," Anna assured him. "The other business in the building belongs to a designer, and our hooker couldn't begin to afford her clothing. Patrolmen canvassed the area after both bodies were discovered. Officers spoke with the designer and her husband, and they talked to people at the dance studio, as well."

Quinn stared at her, then paged through the file on Sonya Miller again. An Officer George Banner had spoken with Gordon Henson on Monday and been assured that the woman had not taken classes there at any time, nor did he recognize her as anyone who had ever been around.

Strange, Gordon had never mentioned the fact that the police had been in on Monday.

Gordon had a way of keeping quiet about things, he had realized that the other day at Nick's, when Gordon had revealed all he knew about Quinn.

"Anything else?" Anna asked him.

"After these deaths, narcotics did a sweep of the area clubs," Quinn said. "What happened there?"

"After the first girl was found, we acquired search warrants for Suede and a few other clubs. Ted Healey, in narcotics, told me that when they arrived at Suede, they almost had to force the folks there to look at it. Management said they were welcome to tear the place apart if they wanted to. Suede prides itself on—"

"I know, I know. Controlling alcohol consumption by drivers and putting heavy pressure on their people to make sure that IDs are good," Quinn said.

"Right," Anna agreed, looking at him strangely.

"I know the guy who owns the place," Quinn said. "Hey, you have extra pictures in here, sketches, of your first victim. Can I take one?"

"Absolutely."

"Thanks. For this, and for all your help."

"Hey, if you can find something we didn't, it'll be great." Her eyes darkened for a minute. "Every unnatural death is sad, but you know, you come to live with it. When we found Sally Grant…I don't know. She got to me. Such a kid. And with no one. No one who cared at all. I'd give a lot to see that justice is done for her, even though she's dead and can never know."

"I understand."

"Since you think these deaths are related, as far as your dancer goes, do you have any suspects?" she asked.

He grimaced ruefully. "Too many," he said. *And too few. The two people with the best motive seem to be my brother and the woman I'm falling in love with.*

When he left the station, he returned to the *Twisted Time.* After checking his messages, he discovered that Manuel Taylor hadn't returned his call, so he made another and left another message.

Then, at his desk, he drew a map of the studio and the surrounding blocks.

He looked over his lists, making comparisons, looking for similarities. The only thing in common between the four deaths was proximity to or association with the building that housed Moonlight Sonata.

Someone had to know something.

The same someone, he was certain, who drove by Shannon's house in a gray or beige sedan.

He checked his e-mail.

His brother had come through on one thing. There was a list of plates and cars belonging to everyone who worked at the studio or at the building, or went there on a regular basis.

Elimination time. Shannon—it was unlikely she was casing her own house. Jane—she drove a red Chevy minivan. Rhianna Markham drove a blue Mazda.

Gordon had a beige Lexus. Ben had recently purchased a "pre-owned" gray Mercedes. Old Mr. Clinton owned a "taupe" Audi. Figured. He eliminated Clinton anyway. He went down the list. Gray or beige sedans were owned by Jim Burke, Mina Long, Justin Garcia, Christie Castle, Sam Railey, Gabriel Lopez and four more employees of Suede.

At least his own brother, the one who had definitely argued with Lara Trudeau the day of her death, drove a dark green aging Jaguar.

As he sat there mulling the cars, he finally realized just what Manuel Taylor had said that had bothered him, that he wanted to pursue.

He put through another call, but the man still didn't answer. He left another message, then headed out.

Quinn was gone when Shannon awoke, but he'd left coffee on again. "Schedule me for late afternoon," was the message he left behind that day.

Determined to spend some time at the studio alone in nice bright daylight, Shannon slipped out before Marnie awoke, leaving her a note that she would be back later to pick her up. She hurried to the studio, letting herself in and locking the doors once more before determinedly looking around. She didn't know what she was looking for, but she went so far as to knock on walls, search the area around the toilet stalls, and then, at the end, let herself out the back door into the little hallway-balcony area off the stairs that led down to the back lot, up to Gabe's apartment, and over to Katarina's design shop.

She paused, then opened the door to the storage area. The costume on the dressmaker's dummy still seemed eerie, even in the glare of the light. She noted that the back shelves weren't actually very full and made a mental note that she could move more of the boxes of old paperwork back here, and also that she had lots of her old outfits back here, and some of them were in excellent shape. If she was considering competing again, she should start going through them. As she stood in there, surveying the shelves, she thought she heard someone out in the hallway. Glancing at her watch, she realized that the others would be arriving soon.

Suddenly the light went out.

"Hey!" She turned, not really afraid; it was daytime, after all.

But then the door closed, and the room was plunged into darkness.

"Hey!" she called again, and rushed forward, toward the door, just in time to hear retreating footsteps.

The pitch blackness caused her a moment's disorientation. She plunged into the dressmaker's dummy and struggled with it, trying to keep it upright at first, then trying to maintain her own balance. As she teetered backward, she would have frozen if she could have, because she was suddenly certain she heard the sound of breathing...right next to her ear.

It was right there.

While the footsteps had been outside, even when the light had gone out and the door had closed.

Suddenly the dummy seemed to collide with her. She fought wildly for her balance, then went crashing down to the floor. Her head struck a shelf, or, she thought rather bizarrely, the shelf struck her.

And as the blackness became complete, she thought that she heard a strange groaning sound, although it might have been issuing from her own lips.

Things were getting out of control, and it was all because of her. What the hell was she doing now, suddenly digging around in the storage room? Should he just have waited? She might have turned around, walked on out.

They all came in.

And they all walked out.

The cops had been through the building. Not because of the studio, but because of the club. They had gone over it with a fine toothed comb and found nothing. Because the club was clean. There was nothing to worry about.

So why had he moved so quickly?

Killers always made a mistake eventually, or so they said. Not true. People definitely got away with murder. So...

Slow down. Calm down.

What did she know?

Too much. Somehow.

She knew too much. Suspected too much. Those beautiful eyes were not as innocent as they looked. But he had known. He had watched. And he had wanted.

And now...

Some things were simply necessary.

All he really had to do was get a grip and remember to act naturally.

Quinn walked in with a handful of flowers, looked around the room and thought that his own bouquet was a bit shabby. But Jane, who was sitting up a little in the hospital bed, smiled radiantly at him.

She might have been in absolute agony on the floor the other night, but she was already glorious again. Her hair was brushed; she was wearing makeup.

"Quinn, hi. This is really nice of you. Thanks for coming by. And thanks for the flowers—they're beautiful," she told him. She reached out, something like a queen awaiting a subject. He realized she was just used to greeting everyone with those double cheek kisses.

He obliged, then sat on the bedside chair.

"You're looking great."

"I'm feeling awfully sore," she said. "But, with the new keyhole surgery," she added, brightening, "at least I'm not going to have one of those really long scars."

"What a relief," he murmured, only slightly amused. She lived off her body—and not in an evil way. He'd started to see more and more of what went on in her world. She was young, and very pretty, and the costumes she wore were often skimpy, exposing the length of her perfect back and toned midriff.

"That sounds petty, doesn't it?" she said with a sigh.

"I'm sorry. I understand."

"Your brother just left," she said.

"Did he? He's supposed to be on the job. He was lucky to get a regular nine-to-five patrol beat."

"He only comes for a minute, just to say good-morning."

He nodded. "So you two are seeing each other?"

"You can't tell anyone," she said, plucking at the sheet nervously.

He smiled. "It might become evident."

"If it reaches that point, I may have to quit." She stared at the sheet, then looked up. "Gordon and Shannon are both willing to look the other way as long as they can, but...then again, maybe Shannon will be more understanding now."

"Oh?"

Jane laughed out loud. "Hey, she hasn't taken on a new student in a long time."

"I thought you were stuck with someone if they fell your way when they came in for their first lesson."

"Not if you're Shannon. She's the manager. She chose to keep you."

"Only because she was investigating me."

Jane smiled again. "Because you're an investigator."

"Everyone knows now, right?"

"Well, to be honest, Doug told me. But Katarina was in yesterday and told me you caused a real flurry, going to Dr. Long's office."

"I see."

"Actually, I can tell you a secret."

"And what is that?"

"I don't think Shannon held on to you to try to find out what you were about," she said with a conspiratorial smile.

"Well, she's not very fond of me at the moment."

"You're wrong, you know."

"Am I?"

"She's very proud. I wasn't around at the time, but Christie told me once that she never let anyone see how it hurt her when Ben decided to dance with Lara, then marry her. Christie said Shannon behaved as if it was the most normal and natural thing in the world, and she held her head high any time she saw them. As if he had meant nothing to her and it was a relief to teach and not have to mess with all the games involved in competition. Well, she does love to teach, of course. But…" Her smile deepened. "Wouldn't it be cool if Doug and I got married, and you married Shannon?"

He had to laugh out loud. "Wow, you two are moving fast."

She wrinkled her nose. "You mean because of his thing with Lara?"

"Uh, frankly, yes."

"Lara knew I liked him. Really liked him. And that I was proud of him as a student. That's why she went after him. I didn't blame Doug. I just kept telling him that I was his teacher, and that…well, we couldn't go out. But after Lara died, I don't know, maybe I realized that life could be short. And who knows? We're an independent studio. No corporate brass can come down on us or anything like that."

"All right, maybe you and Doug have a longer relationship than I realized," he told her. "But I can't say Shannon and I have aeons of experience together. And as I said, I'm not so sure she likes me very much right now."

"That's because she's falling head over heels for you, and she's afraid of herself," Jane said. She grinned deeply. "I know Shannon pretty well. She's different, since you've been around. I have a feeling you two know certain things about each other really well—if you get my drift."

"We'll see. At the moment, Jane, I have two questions for you. You said you were afraid you'd been poisoned when you fell."

She flushed. "Silly, huh? I was just convinced that someone had put something in the coffee because of the chat we'd been having. About Lara. Like how maybe someone might have slipped her some extra pills in a drink or something."

"And who was in on this conversation?"

She grimaced. "Lots of people. The Longs, Mr. Clinton, even one of the new girls—I don't remember her name. Gabe, Katarina…I think David was there. Ben…Doug, and Gordon was nearby, watching the floor. And Sam was near Gordon. Lots of people."

"Did any of them say anything suspicious?"

"Um…David Mercutio, Katarina's husband, he was the one who said you could probably slip pills into a drink."

"Okay, second question. Do you have any idea who might have been alone with Lara at the competition and argued with her? Or even been really friendly?"

Her face darkened.

"I know about my brother," he told her.

She sighed. "Besides Doug…she fought with Jim Burke, her partner. They always fought. There would have been something suspicious if they *hadn't* fought!"

"Anyone else?"

"In the little bar area in front of the actual showroom floor, I saw her talking with Gordon, Ben, Justin…Gabe, both of the Longs, I think. And Shannon."

"Shannon?"

"I told you, there was never a time when you would have known that Shannon had anything against her. I think she bought her a drink. Or maybe not. Maybe she just went up to her to tell her good luck. You can't imagine how busy it is then, how fast everything moves. And remember, Sam and I were in that competition, too."

"Right. You two are really good together, right?"

"Sad to say, maybe we'll have a chance now. We won several times when Lara wasn't there."

He nodded. "One last thing. Do you mind taking a look at a picture?"

She shook her head.

He showed her the sketch of Sally Grant he had gotten from the police file. Jane looked at him right away, shaking her head. "No. I remember when they found her body, though. I mean, actually, I do recognize that picture, because they ran it in the paper. But I never saw her around the studio."

He thanked her and rose.

"Are you going to the studio?"

"Yes, why? Do you need something?"

She shook her head. "You're a good student."

"I have a lot to learn before the Gator Gala."

"Yeah, right."

"I have to keep an eye on people."

"Including Shannon, huh?"

"She is pretty suspicious," he said.

She just grinned, settling into her pillow.

"What the hell are you doing in here? And on the floor?"

Shannon blinked, looking up. Gordon was standing over her.

She sat up, then clutched her wobbling head. "Someone tripped me, bumped me, something."

He arched a brow, looking around. The storeroom was empty.

"What did you do? Walk into a shelf? Oh, I see. You had a major fight with a dressmaker's dummy."

"I came in here, and then there were footsteps in the hall."

"Me," he told her.

"And you turned out the light and closed the door?"

"I thought some idiot had left the light on and the door open. I turned off the light, and closed and locked the door."

"When?"

"Just a few minutes ago. When I went into the studio and

found your purse in the office and no you, I came running back out here." He looked concerned. "Are you all right? Hell, we'd better get you to the hospital, if you knocked yourself out."

She looked around the room, noting that, indeed, nothing, no one was there—except for the dressmaker's dummy, down on the floor beside her.

"No one came out?"

"I locked the door from the outside," he told her. "I guess I should have looked in. It just didn't occur to me that you were in here."

She had to be imagining things. It had gone black, and she had panicked. Because, if anyone had been in the room with her, Gordon would have seen him. Or her.

He sighed. "Can you get up?"

"Of course." She rose, only a little unsteadily, to her feet.

"Come on," Gordon said. "Let's go start canceling your lessons for the day."

"No," she protested.

He gave her a stern look. "You probably have one hell of a lump on your head somewhere."

She probed her own skull. She had a lump, but it was a little one.

"I'm okay, Gordon."

"You should—"

"Gordon, I swear to you, I'm okay. And if, during the day, at any time, I feel funny in the least, I swear, I'll let you know. I don't want to go to a hospital, or home, and I sure as hell don't want to cancel my classes."

"But—"

"Really. And, Gordon, don't say a word about this, please?"

"But…?"

"Please? Look, if I'm out of it for any reason, there will

just be more talk. And we could wind up having to cancel the Gator Gala."

That gave him pause. He sighed.

"Gordon, not a word. And in turn, I swear I will tell you if I have so much as a headache."

"Deal," he said after a minute.

They walked out into the hall together. Ben was there, just outside the studio's rear door. "What the hell is going on?"

"What?" Shannon asked guiltily.

"Doors open, music blaring…and no one around."

"I was just…" She paused, looking at Gordon. "I was checking on some of my old costumes."

Ben's dark brows arched slowly. "You're really—seriously—considering competing again?"

"Yes."

"With me?"

"Yes, Ben."

"Thank you," he said. She had never heard him sound more humble.

He walked back into the studio, and she and Gordon followed him. Shannon had a feeling it was going to be another long day.

CHAPTER 21

Something was off all day.

Or maybe she was feeling a sense of heightened awareness after being hit on the head, however it had happened. Friday was usually slow, but today it was busy.

She spent time training Marnie, as well as her students, after getting Ben to run back to her house to pick up the girl. Richard was peevish, saying that he wanted to learn more lifts, and she wasn't sure he had the ability to do them.

She had a student named Billy that afternoon, one of her regulars, who suffered from cerebral palsy. He tried so hard but continually got frustrated with himself. Still, she respected him for trying, where others might just have given up. She worked with him especially hard, knowing how good the basic movements were for him.

Then there was Quinn.

Unbelievably determined and adept at the waltz, lifting, turning, moving as he should. She wondered how it was possible for him to be so good at the waltz and so horrible at the fox-trot. Students tended to do better at smooth dances and have trouble with rhythm, or do well with rhythm and have a hard time with smooth. She'd never come across anyone who could waltz with the best, then trip over his own feet in a fox-trot. Even tango steps came more naturally to him.

They worked for a while with Rhianna and a student on one side, Justin and Mina Long on the other. It wasn't until the others had gone over to the other side of the room to work rhythm and she moved to the stereo that he said to her, "Any trouble with the alarm system?"

"None whatsoever," she told him. After hesitating, she said stiffly, "Thank you."

"Sure. And thanks for letting me sleep."

"No problem."

She was tempted to tell him about her wild panic in the storeroom that morning. But the more time that passed, the more convinced she was that her imagination had really begun to run wild.

"What?" he demanded. She looked up. He was against the wall, trying to catch her eyes, which were lowered as she stared sightlessly at the floor. She shook her head. "Nothing."

"There's something."

He wasn't going to let up. She turned the tables. "Exactly what mistake did you make with the FBI? What did you do?"

He looked aggravated, as if he was going to tell her to mind her own business.

"I was with profiling."

"Profiling?" She didn't know why she was surprised that that was the root of his issues. Maybe because she'd had a sense that he had shot the wrong person, or someone had died, that something really terrible had happened.

"Yeah, profiling. There was a case in Indiana. I should

have been on top of it, but gave an entirely wrong assessment. I was certain the killer had to be late twenties, early thirties, with some kind of a menial day job, maybe even a wife. They arrested a guy who fit our description."

"And?"

"The community let down its guard. The next day, there were two more dead women. The killer left evidence that time—he dropped his wallet. He was fifty, and an executive at a local bank."

"But profiling isn't an exact science. You could only work with what you had."

"Maybe that was the point. I felt that my work was useless. So I came back home, and started working with Dane, an old friend. I figured I couldn't do too much harm on surveillance, that type of thing. I was wrong. I followed a guy named Art Durken, and he wound up killing his wife."

"Nell," Shannon said softly.

"Nell," he agreed. "Kind, pleasant, the type of person who should fill the world. But she wound up dead, and Durken wound up arrested, and now, well, now I'm not at all sure Art is guilty, but I'll be damned if I can figure out who is. Except…"

"Except?"

He stared at her with a shrug. "Well, that's obvious, isn't it? It's someone associated with this studio."

She swallowed hard. "It might not be," she said.

"You don't want it to be," he corrected.

She looked at him again. "Some murders are never solved."

"This one had better be. When Doug talked me into coming here, he told me he was afraid someone else would die. I think he was right."

"Is that what it takes to learn those lifts—lots of long conversation?" Rhianna teased, coming over to them. "Shannon," she asked, "are you going to play anything or can I have a cha-cha?"

"Sure, a cha-cha. Whatever."

Rhianna put in a CD, and moved out to the floor.

"I'll follow you and Marnie back to your house later," Quinn said.

"It will be around ten by then," she told him. As happy as she was to improve someone's life as it seemed they had Marnie's, she suddenly desperately wished she didn't have a roommate.

"It's all right. I'll see you two home."

"I have an alarm now, you know," she reminded him.

"And it's great—once you're inside to be protected by it."

His lesson was over. He gave her the perfunctory and studio-necessary kiss on the cheek, then left.

After that, the day seemed to drag endlessly, even though students kept coming.

At the end of the night, she remembered to announce to the group class that everyone involved with the Gator Gala and who wanted to attend the cruise get-together should be at the marina by seven.

She thought Quinn had forgotten her, but just as they were locking up, he arrived. Since Gordon evidently knew exactly what he did for a living and what he was doing at the studio, it didn't seem to matter that Quinn had come for the precise reason of following her home.

He didn't even get out of his car when they got there. He watched her enter the house with Marnie, waved, and was gone.

So much for his being in love with her.

There was still no word from Manuel Taylor when Quinn reached the *Twisted Time*, though, frankly, he had expected that if the man was going to call him back, he would have called his cell phone.

"No problem. I'm making pretty big bucks off your group," the man had said.

Sure. He'd made money off Gordon, and off Quinn, for showing up to confront Gordon, who had seemed to have such a glib answer.

But the sentence, Quinn was certain, implied more. Someone else in the group had paid the waiter, as well.

But for what?

Did they all tip that well, just for drinks?

He doubted it. He had a feeling someone had tipped Manuel to give Lara Trudeau a drink. A special drink. A drugged drink.

It was late. Still, he tried the hotel and got through to a beverage manager.

The man was no help. He was irritated. Manuel Taylor was supposed to have worked a dinner the night before, but he hadn't shown up.

"Is he usually fairly dependable?"

"Yeah, sure, usually," the beverage manager told Quinn over the phone. "But he was a no-show once before. Went off to Orlando with friends. I told him if he pulled one like that on me again, he'd be fired. He's a good waiter, though. I'm going to be sorry to fire him."

Quinn hung up, aggravated himself.

There was little else he could do that night. He was restless, feeling that he should be at Shannon's house, even though there was an alarm there now, and she wasn't alone.

Nothing to do. He lay in the cabin, awake for hours— events and ideas floating around in his mind like pieces of a puzzle.

Shannon, here, on the *Twisted Time,* not so long ago, a lifetime ago. Wearing his old shirt and framed in the doorway, a silhouette, a shadow of seduction. One night and his world had turned. The boat still seemed to carry the elusive scent of her perfume, permeating his sheets, the cabin, his memory. The sound of her voice echoed in his ears, the dance she practiced between the sheets more hypnotic than the sway of the rumba, as passionate as the steamy encounter of a *pasa doble.*

He was losing it, he told himself.

But he couldn't erase the memory of her coming to his cabin door, and he was chagrined to realize that an eighteen-year-old street waif had seen with clarity the depth of what he had thought was just attraction and arousal. She had touched him once, and now the world revolved around her, both his waking moments and his dreams. He wasn't just after the truth to vindicate himself, but because he had to fix her world and create one in which he could touch her once again. He'd known what it was to care, but never before had he felt that someone had slipped into his skin and was haunting him, flesh and blood. She teased and taunted his dreams. He saw her in the realm of memory, breathed the scent of her, heard her whisper, even above the lapping of the surf against the hull.

Nick's stayed open late on Friday nights. He could hear laughter and conversation from the patio. Men and women, some together, some looking to be together, seeking what could be real, what could be permanent, and others hoping just to get lucky, to get laid. Not that Nick's was really much of a pickup joint. It was usually too full of regulars, married and co-habiting couples, and friends. Sometimes the old jukebox played, and sometimes, on weekends, Nick brought in a band.

Tonight he would be keeping it down. Ashley was home with her new baby. She and Jake had always intended on moving on and buying their own home, but Jake had his boat here, and Ashley's place was a separate apartment, anyway. Plus they had both been too involved with each other and their work to do any house hunting. Nick's reflected that kind of commitment. Not like the places on the beach. Not like Suede....

Searched up and down by the narcotics squads, who had found nothing. So it was hot, a hot club, a hot pickup place. It was also an establishment that followed the law, crossing the T's and dotting the I's.

But two women had been found nearby, dead. A socialite and a hooker. Illegal substances...not like prescription drugs.

He gave up, dressed and went over to the patio at Nick's. Lots of cops tonight. The old jukebox was playing softly. Dixon was there, eating a cheeseburger.

Inside at the bar, the television was on, though the music from the jukebox drowned out the sound. Quinn ordered a beer, staring at the screen. He froze, his drink halfway to his lips.

There, on the screen, was a picture of Manuel Taylor, and beneath it ran the words, "Caught in the crossfire?"

He rose, walked to the television, turned up the sound.

"Hey!" someone complained.

He ignored the man, turning to stare icily at the protester, and the guy turned away.

The newscaster came back on. "Manuel Taylor was pronounced dead on arrival at Jackson Memorial from a single bullet wound to the head. It's believed that he was an accidental casualty of a gang war currently under way. In other breaking news..."

On Saturdays the studio itself opened for business earlier than on weekdays mornings. Despite the charter that night, plans were no different this Saturday.

Shannon dropped Marnie off, told Ella that she was just hopping over to the hospital, then went to visit Jane, who was both delighted and angry—she was being released the following day with a slew of instructions about what she could and couldn't do until she was healed, which was great, of course, but not in time for her to go out on the boat. "It's not fair," she complained.

"It's not, and I'm sorry. I'd change things if I could," Shannon told her. Jane was restless; she'd been in bed too long. She'd heard all about Marnie's progress, and she was both excited and worried, afraid that the younger girl might end up stealing some of her students.

"We have too many students. None of us can handle so many," Shannon said soothingly. "Besides, pretty soon, you'll be too busy winning competitions everywhere to do much teaching."

"I can't even dance again for weeks," Jane moaned.

Unable to make her friend feel any better, Shannon told her that she would pick her up the following day and get her settled back at home. When Jane told her that she already had a ride arranged, Shannon didn't push the point. She assumed it was going to be Doug O'Casey.

"Watch out for my students tonight, huh?" Jane asked her.

"You bet. I'll keep old Mr. Clinton from flirting."

Jane shot her a dry glance, and Shannon laughed. "Jane, just get better. It's all going to be fine. Just get back on your feet."

Shannon had more paperwork than classwork during the day, since it was time to arrange the group schedule for the following month, and she wanted to read all the notes in the suggestion box and find out what dances the students wanted on the roster.

Gordon wasn't in—he was heading straight down in the afternoon to check out their charter boat and make sure the caterers were ready, that the trio was going to have enough room to set up, and that the dance floor was all it should be.

By three o'clock, the studio had emptied of students, with everyone anxious to get out and get ready, so they could make it to the marina by seven.

Ben was strangely helpful, though, anxious to hang around and help Shannon close up. Marnie was there, as well, and was the most helpful when it came to clearing up the bits of Saturday doughnuts and croissants left around the room, making sure they wouldn't get bugs over the weekend.

As she locked up, Shannon realized that she was listening for the grating sound, but she didn't hear it.

There wasn't that much for her to do at home, since she had decided to adhere to the casual side of the dress code, wearing a pair of studded jeans and a halter top. Despite Marnie's slimness, Shannon found a cocktail gown that fitted the girl perfectly. She also finally got Marnie to quit thanking her, reminding her that the studio needed her.

"But don't you know how neat that is?" Marnie asked. "I've never actually been needed by anyone before."

They made it to the marina by six. Gordon was already on board and as happy as a clam. He explained the arrangement of tables in the salon area, and introduced Shannon to the caterer and crew. Buffet tables lined the sides of the main salon, surrounding the dance floor. The trio would play in the rear, so they could also be heard on the open deck in back.

Shannon was somewhat surprised that Quinn wasn't around, but Gordon told her that he'd had a few things to do but would be there by seven.

The cruise seemed to have been perfectly planned, and Quinn had definitely come through. The boat was great. Perfect for the fifty or so they would have aboard.

Long before seven, their group started arriving.

The staff of Moonlight Sonata lined the boarding plank from the dock to the boat, greeting their friends and students.

"Leave it to old Mr. Clinton to arrive first," Sam said.

"You know," Shannon teased, "his first name is actually John—not *Old Mister.*"

"Well, I don't call him old Mr. Clinton to his face," Sam protested.

"Oh, my God! He's brought old Mrs. Clinton," Rhianna whispered, watching the older gentleman escort a spry little white-haired lady toward them.

"His wife died years ago," Gordon commented.

"He's found a lady friend, apparently," Ben said.

"I know all about it," Ella whispered. "He lives at a retirement home, you know. And he says that it's great—women outnumber men by two to one, and when you're a man who can dance, you have the pick of the litter at every occasion."

Mr. Clinton introduced his date, a retiree named Lena Mangetti. She seemed charming, and was delighted to be out on the cruise. They headed aboard, and others followed, including the group from their sister studio in Broward. The Longs came with the Beckhams, another couple that attended classes together, and Katarina and David arrived with Gabe, saying that they'd all shared a cab from the beach, since they intended to have more than a few drinks. Christie, who was both a student and a judge, also arrived—with her dog, as usual. She went nowhere without it. And whether the students were canine lovers or not, they all made a fuss over the animal.

It wasn't until the boat was almost ready to go out that Quinn arrived, his brother in tow.

"You almost didn't make it," Shannon said lightly. "Late for what is actually your own party."

He didn't so much as crack a smile, but said, "Well, I'm here now."

Doug gave Quinn a dry gaze and turned to Shannon, shaking his head. "We're both here now. Guess he didn't notice me with him." He was trying to be polite, when Quinn was acting liking a jerk.

Quinn ignored Doug and walked by. Shannon thought, Oh, yeah, he's madly in love. Can't live without me.

She glanced at Doug.

"Don't say anything yet," Doug told her, "but…that waiter was killed. He was caught in some kind of gang war, but Quinn is seeing something else."

"What?" she said incredulously. "Waiter—you mean Manuel Taylor?"

"Don't look so panicky," Doug told her quickly. "He was shot—no overdose of anything. It's got nothing to do with us. It's all right."

It had to be. She had too much to do.

She was shocked, but she couldn't afford to worry about Quinn's state of mind. There was too much going on. As they set sail, there were questions from all quarters. Cocktails were already being served as the boat moved out, but the caterers wanted to know how she wanted the food brought out. Cheese puffs and shrimp balls first? And the trio wanted to know when to play, when to give it a break. She noticed that the Broward and Miami-Dade groups seemed to have chosen opposite sides of the boat, and she wanted to tell the trio that they needed to sing the number from the musical *Oklahoma*, about how "the cowboys and the farmers must be friends," or whatever it was they said exactly. She accepted a glass of champagne herself and went over to sit with Mary and Judd Bentley, who owned the Broward studio.

"Hi, Shannon," Trudy Summers, one of their longtime

students said. "Glad you're here. Mary was just talking about how hard it was to dance with her husband."

"Well, it shouldn't be," Judd said, perching atop a table and setting an arm around his wife's shoulders. "It's just that she's a teacher, and she wants to lead all the time, even when we're dancing together."

"Especially when we're dancing together," Mary said, laughing. "Seriously, I do not try to lead."

"You two *will* be dancing together tonight—it's a fun evening," Trudy said.

"Yeah," Judd teased. "It will be a lot of fun. We'll dance out on the deck. We'll do one of those lifts she likes so much."

"Right," Mary said. "He plans on lifting me right overboard, I'm pretty sure."

"Heck, you can swim," Judd said.

"Not a good idea, there's a propeller or something back there," Shannon said lightly. "Trudy, don't forget to mix and mingle. We're all South Florida, you know."

"No problem. Introduce me to some of your guys. Our studio is heavily weighted on the female side. Hey, that guy is really cute—and that one, too." She pointed to Doug and Quinn. "Jane's student. I've seen the younger guy before, but not the other one. Hey, they kind of look alike."

"Brothers," she told Trudy, then couldn't help teasing, "I'll introduce you to Mr. Clinton, if you haven't met him yet. He says that women always outnumber men, two to one," she said with a laugh, and moved on.

She didn't actually sit to eat with anyone, moving from table to table as others helped themselves to the buffet. Dancing went on along with the dinner, but picked up in earnest once the tables were cleared and it began to grow late. They were due to return by midnight.

Gordon and Judd introduced some of their people, who

then did one-and-a-half-minute bits of the routines they were going to do at the Gala.

She was startled when Gordon announced that she and Quinn were going to do their waltz, and she was sure Quinn was equally startled, but he rose to the occasion.

She was glad to slip into his arms, feeling that electricity he could so quickly create. But she was troubled by his eyes.

"Are you all right with this?" she asked him.

"With this? Yes," he said simply, and when the music came on, he proved it. The waltz was definitely the man's dance. Dancers, especially beginners, were supportive of one another, but she was surprised by the applause that followed his movements, and the oohs and aahs when they went into their final turn, and he spun and lifted her into the "pooper-scooper."

He smiled; he was charming. When people rushed up, saying they couldn't believe he was a beginner, he said that they should see his fox-trot. He accepted Doug's warm hug and sincere congratulations, but he wasn't really paying attention, not even to his brother. He was watching Gordon, she thought.

She didn't get a chance to stay with him, though, because Judd announced that she and Ben were going to do a bolero. Another surprise.

Ben asked her, "Do you mind?"

"No, let's do it," she told him.

They did, and she had to admit that, as partners, they were good together. Better than good. They excelled.

"Will you really enter as a pro with me at the Gator Gala?" he asked her, hugging her in a brotherly fashion as their number ended and applause sounded.

She squeezed his hand. Something about Ben had changed since Lara's death. She took the microphone herself to announce, "Thank you. Thanks so very much. And here's some news. Ben and I will be entering the professional division at our first ever Gator Gala!"

Ben gave her a look of pure gratitude, but she sidestepped him, anxious to find Quinn. Gordon announced that Judd and Mary would be dancing, followed by more dancing.

Shannon moved toward the aft deck. A few of the students had milled outside, but having heard the announcement, they were now returning to the main salon. She wandered out as they moved in, wondering where Quinn could have gotten to.

She paused, feeling the breeze. The night was beautiful.

The last dance was starting. She hugged her arms around herself and stared at the wake, the foam spewing out from the propeller at the back of the boat. Standing still and silent, she heard the rush of the water and the hum of the engine.

Then, slowly, she became aware of the voices.

Whispers, hushed.

She turned, not sure where the sound was coming from and unable to make out the words.

"...has to stop."

"There is no visible connection!"

"She was too close. They'll see the connection eventually."

"Shannon!" someone called.

She turned back to the door to the salon. Judd was calling to her. Silently she damned him.

Gritting her teeth, she turned to stare out to the rear again, noting the way the water flowed violently from beneath the boat.

She felt a rush of wind and started to turn just as the boat did, starting to head back to the marina.

There was something...someone...

But what, she didn't know.

Suddenly she was flying off the boat, falling toward the water, where it churned violently beneath the giant propeller.

CH**A**PTER 22

"**S**he fell! She was there a second ago, and then…!" Mr. Clinton called out in horror.

Quinn had been looking for Shannon. He'd wanted to tell her, before they got off the boat, that, to the best of his knowledge, no one but Gordon had known about the lunch meeting he had staged with Manuel Taylor. Maybe the man really had been caught in the crossfire of some gang war, but just in case, Quinn didn't want Shannon alone with Gordon.

Threading his way through a friendly group of Broward students, he had searched the crowd for her but he hadn't been able to find her. Then Clinton had yelled.

The *she* in "She fell!" had to be Shannon.

Panic gripped his heart with fingers of sharp ice.

He pushed past people, heedless of who they were. He practically knocked old Mr. Clinton right out of the way. At first it seemed no one was near the area from which Shannon had disappeared, but by the time he got there, a crowd had already formed.

Tearing across the deck, he plunged into the water.

Someone turned on floodlights; the motor was killed. As he hit the water, chilled by night and depth, he feared to open his eyes not just to the sting of salt but because he was afraid to see a blur of red, if she'd been caught in the propeller.

He scissored himself to the surface, shouting her name.

"Shannon!"

"Here!" she called.

Though the motor had been cut, the boat was now a good distance from them, due to sheer momentum. He could hear the crew lowering lifeboats, so that people could come after them.

"Where?"

"Here!" The word ended with a gurgle. He shot toward the sound of her voice.

"What the hell are you doing?" He swam toward her strongly, then realized that she was treading water with no difficulty, actually pushing away from him when he came close.

His heart was still pounding. Her hair was slicked back from her face, and in the expanse of the night sea, she looked frail and delicate—and defensive.

But all in one piece. She had missed the blades of the propeller.

He fought the frantic urge to reach out for her despite her apparent competence.

"What am I doing?" she repeated incredulously. "I'm just out for a midnight swim."

He reached her in the water. "You fell overboard?"

"I think I was pushed."

"By who?"

"I don't know."

"You didn't see anyone?"

"No."

"How do you know you were pushed? Could you have been leaning over? We took a bit of a sharp turn—is that when you fell?"

"No. That's when I was pushed."

The seas that night were two to four feet, causing small swells around them. Since she seemed to be doing fine on her own, Quinn made no attempt to reach out for her.

"Mr. Clinton saw you go over, but there was no one else there."

She glared at him but didn't respond, instead swimming toward the lifeboat that was now coming their way.

Gordon was aboard with two of the crew members, Javier Gonzalez and Randy Flores. Quinn knew them both, since Randy was a permanent employee and Javier often worked the cruises. They were ready to help them both aboard. It wasn't cold, but definitely cool, and Shannon shivered as she was helped up. There were blankets on board, and one was quickly wrapped around her. "Are you all right?" Gordon asked Shannon, seeming genuinely anxious about her.

"Either of you hurt?" Javier asked.

"No," Shannon said quickly.

"Fine," Quinn said briefly.

"What the hell were you doing?" Gordon asked Shannon.

To Quinn's amazement, she said, "I don't know. I must have been leaning over too far when the boat veered to head back toward the marina."

"Thank God, you didn't hit the propeller," Gordon said vehemently.

"He's right," Suarez said.

Quinn stayed silent. A minute later, they reached the boat, and the anxious captain was there to greet them. Doug helped Shannon from the boat, then assisted his brother, looking at them both in silence.

Shannon quickly assured everyone that she was fine, as her friends, associates and students swept around them.

"I'm so sorry, everyone," she said. "I guess my balance isn't what I thought. You all can remember that when I'm giving you grief when you're dancing."

A little ripple of laughter rose, but despite her words, Quinn knew she was still convinced she had been pushed.

Someone pushed through the crowd. It was Richard Long, and he was carrying take-out cups. "Coffee and brandy, one for our lovely-even-when-wet instructor, and another for the man willing to risk his life to save her. Whoops, wait a minute. He owns the boat we're out on, right? Maybe he's trying to make sure he doesn't get sued." Long spoke teasingly, and laughter rose again.

"Sued? Are you kidding me? I couldn't take the chance that my instructor might drown. I'm just beginning to catch on to the whole dance thing," Quinn said lightly.

"All's well that ends well," Sam said, stepping forward to give Shannon a warm hug.

"Drink the coffee," Ella said. "You're just standing there shivering."

"Coffee sounds great. Thanks, Richard," Shannon said, reaching for a cup.

Once they were docked, Quinn had a few words with the captain, who swore that he hadn't taken any turns too sharply, something Quinn assured him he was already certain of.

When he was ready to debark himself, Quinn saw that Shannon, a bit damp, her clothing still hugging her frame, had taken her place with the rest of the Moonlight Sonata group, saying good-night to everyone. Her trip overboard had become part of a good time, something they would all talk about for years to come.

Quinn had made up his mind. Screw policy.

As the instructors began to say good-night to one another, he came up to her. "We need to talk."

She arched a brow, looking around her, silently reminding him that they were surrounded by her entire staff.

"I need to take Marnie home," she said.

"No, you don't," he said. "Someone else can take her. I can have Doug do it."

A strange expression filtered into her eyes. He thought that she was going to refuse him again, and belligerently. Instead she turned around and called softly to Sam, asking him, "Can you take Marnie home, and—" she hesitated briefly, looking at Quinn "—stay with her tonight?"

Sam looked surprised at first, stared at her, then glanced at Quinn and smiled broadly.

"Sure."

"And stop grinning."

"Absolutely. No grin."

Everyone continued the process of kissing each other good-night, but finally almost everyone had straggled off the dock toward the parking lot.

Gordon lingered, asking Shannon, "You're sure you're okay?"

"Absolutely. Honest, Gordon, I'm sorry I caused such a stir."

"I wouldn't be sorry for that. After it turned out you were okay, the students enjoyed it. Hey, how often have any of them gotten to see you uncoordinated?"

She smiled. "There you go. I was the entertainment."

Sam was still hovering nearby with Marnie, and Doug remained, as well.

"Doug, looks like everything is all right. Go home or...wherever." She smiled knowingly, and he waved, then walked off toward his car. "Sam, quit looking like a two-year-old in training pants. Go ahead and drive Marnie out to the beach."

"Well," Sam murmured.

Marnie gave them each a kiss on the cheek, casting them a look that was too wise for her years. "Have a good night," she said, preceding Sam along the dock. He shrugged, a smile still hovering on his face, and followed her. With a last, curious look, Gordon left, as well.

Quinn and Shannon turned to each other, both feeling the worse for wear.

Boats knocked against rubber guards at their docks; a bell clanged from somewhere; waves lapped against boats and pilings. From a distance, they could hear the drone of conversation, the sound of a mellow reggae band playing at Nick's.

Quinn stared at Shannon, ready to argue the point as to whether or not she had been pushed, but she shook her head before he could speak. "Stop," she said. "Don't…. Just don't."

He frowned, slowing arching a questioning brow.

God knows who might be around, but she took a step toward him.

Then she slipped her arms around his neck and pressed against him, rising on her toes, the length of her body like a caress, and pressed her lips against his. She tasted like salt, like the sea breeze, like a promise of sweet and decadent sin. He returned her kiss, parting her lips with a ragged and swift hunger, sweeping her mouth with his tongue, deep, returning her initiative with passionate insinuation of what could come. She was trembling in his arms, whether shivering from the touch of the breeze or trembling with anticipation, he wasn't at all certain. Nor did he care. The *Twisted Time* was just yards away. And when her lips parted from his, the words she whispered against his ear were liquid fire. "Don't you ever want to forget it all…just for a few hours, forget it all and…"

His response was so guttural and startling that it evoked an eroticism beyond memory. He drew back, staring at her, cupping her cheek in his hand, a smile slowly taking hold of his lips as tension streaked through him, muscle, sinew, blood and bone.

"Hell, yes," he told her. And he lowered his head, whispering back, "You mean like feeling so desperate that nothing else matters except crawling right into someone? Not time, place, words, anything?"

She nodded, drawing a line down his damp chest. Low. Down to his soggy belt line. Below.

"You're wasting time now," she informed him.

He swept her up into his arms because it seemed the simplest, easiest and fastest move to make at that moment.

His own balance and agility were put to the test when he jumped the distance from the dock to the deck of his boat, but necessity seemed to be the mother of coordination as well as invention.

Balancing her weight, he fumbled in his pocket for his key, then burst into the cabin, banging his elbow and her head as he made his way down the steps into the salon. They were both laughing then.

And then they weren't laughing, they were gasping for breath, heedless of everything else as they struggled to peel away wet clothing and crawl into each other's skin.

Draped over Quinn's bare length, Shannon smiled and then winced. In the heat of the moment, they had wound up on the floor, in the narrow space between the table and the sofa, and she had apparently banged more body parts than she had realized in the process. Now it was awkward trying to rise. She made the attempt to avoid him, but wound up with her knee right in his abdomen.

"Ow!" he groaned.

"Sorry."

He eased to his side, laughing. "Could have been worse. How about I get up first? But what's the urgency?"

"Shower. I'm pure salt."

"I'll come with you."

"We won't fit," she told him.

"We'll make do."

The shower was ridiculously tiny, but the water was steamy and hot, and despite the fact that they barely fit, the rush of warmth brought on by the spray that covered them was delicious. Purely sweet at first. Then purely sensual. Quinn's hand was braced on the Fiberglas wall behind Shannon, and his mouth seemed as hot as the water, moving over her flesh. His wet hair teased against her skin, and she was both breathless and laughing again at the erotic maneuvers he managed in the tiny, tense space. His hands laced around her midriff, and she found herself lifted to stand on the seat of the commode as the sensual movement of his tongue continued down the length of her body. When her knees gave, she was pressed against the Fiberglas herself, aware then of the pounding of water, the rush in her ears, and the force and thrust of his body, bringing her crashing over a brink of sweet forgetfulness and raw abandon once again. Climax shuddered through her with the strength of the rushing water, and she shivered and was held upright only by the power of his body and the smooth shower wall. They stayed there as moments slipped one into another, crushed together, still one, caught in an intimacy that seemed to go beyond any act of love.

At last they stirred, found soap, found shampoo, and, since there really was little choice, washed and soaped various body parts for each other until that too became so intimate and arousing that there was nowhere to go except back where they had been, but this time, when the level of arousal escalated to insanity, Quinn slammed off the showerhead, opened the door and dragged them both back into the cabin, oblivious to the fact that they drenched the floor and sheets.

But there was space…space and limitless comfort, and here she had the freedom of his body, room to slide and creep and crawl all over him, taste and savor and caress the length of his body, hear the thunder of his heart, the gale wind of his breath, the feel of his arms and hands, know his eyes when he rose over her, drowning in the first slow, excruciating moments as he sank into her with the full force of his body, hunger and being. Then, finally, when it seemed to Shannon that her whole world had rocked and exploded to the highest peaks, she drifted down in comfort and warmth and lay at his side, totally relaxed for what seemed like the first time in forever. Then her mind began working, because it was impossible to turn off her brain, and she felt the first sense of self-defense, because it was frightening to feel so desperately for someone, to want him so badly, not only in such a sexually passionate manner, but in moments of laughter, fear, purpose and just plain existing.

His fingers moved through her hair as he pulled her close, and she was stunned by the first words that left his lips.

"She's right, you know."

"Who?"

"Marnie. I *am* falling in love with you."

She was afraid to reply.

He gripped her harder, pulling her taut to the curve of his body, into something that had surely been a male hold since the beginning of time. She was wrapped in him, and it was good, very good. She wanted to whisper something back, but fear kept her silent.

"Okay," he murmured softly. "Don't reply. Though that is one of those things that kind of demands an answer."

She wasn't facing him, instead lying flush against him, her back to his chest, her rump curved into his hip.

"I think you were pretty incredible."

He laughed. "Always the judge. We're not talking performance level here."

"Cocky, too," she murmured.

He rolled her to face him, and the laughter was gone. His eyes were the deepest, most piercing blue she had ever seen, and his features were striking, strong and taut.

"I don't want to play games anymore. I quit being a student. Screw the friggin' Gator Gala. I want to be with you."

"I'm…I'm…"

"A coward. A chicken."

Anger flickered through her.

"I am not!"

"Then at the least admit you want to take a chance."

She hesitated, uncomfortably aware that he was right. "I want to stay with you until morning. I want to sleep with you over and over again," she said.

"Why?" He smiled. "Other than the fact that we really are great together. Better than the most erotic dance known to man."

She smiled, and then his smile faded, and his words were a promise of everything to come. "Because you are the best waltz I've ever known. The most erotic rumba, the greatest exhilaration, the wildest, most beautiful music."

He kept staring down at her. Then, after a moment, he said, "Okay…so I think you *are* falling in love with me. At least a little bit."

"I *am* falling in love with you," she managed to say. "More than a little bit."

He kissed her again.

She thought later that there was so much they needed to say. So much was happening that she needed to convince him, needed him to see, to understand….

Nothing could be real, nothing could be right…until the trail of corpses shadowing them came to a halt.

But that would have to wait until morning. Because now, more than anything, they needed the night.

CHAPTER 23

"I swear someone pushed me over," Shannon said.

She was more appealing to Quinn than ever, hair fresh washed, dressed in a pair of jeans and a denim shirt borrowed from Ashley Dilessio, sitting at his table on the boat and sipping one last cup of coffee.

He was going with Jake down to the main station.

She was going to go home, check on Marnie, and let Sam have the rest of his Sunday for whatever he wanted to do. Strange, Marnie had been a street kid, but now Shannon didn't even want her left alone during the day.

They'd spent a nice morning taking time for themselves, then having breakfast at Nick's and spending an hour playing with the new baby, Shannon getting to know Ashley, Ashley getting to know Shannon, finding out they were fascinated by each other's professions, quickly becoming friends. They had talked about the case, too. Shannon had expressed her sadness over Manuel Taylor but had been quick to point out that she had overheard Gordon mention him in a group, so his "role" was common knowledge at the studio.

Quinn couldn't help it. He wasn't satisfied with the possibility that the man's death wasn't connected, so Jake had offered to go down to the station with him, look at the report, then take a ride down to the area of the Grove, where it had happened. But first, he and Shannon had gone back to the boat so Quinn could get ready to go.

"The really strange thing is that right before I went overboard, I heard people whispering."

"Saying what?" he demanded.

She frowned, thinking. "Something about having to stop, about there being no visible connection."

"Connection to what?"

"I have no idea. I was eavesdropping. Well, not really. I was just there and heard pieces of the conversation."

"I'm telling you, everything's connected. I want you to watch out for Gordon, especially. Don't ever be alone around him."

"Gordon has been like a second father to me, you know," she told him.

"I don't care. Watch out for him."

There was a call from topside. "Quinn, you ready?"

"Yeah!" he called back. He gave Shannon a kiss on the top of the head, suddenly loath to leave her, even for a few hours.

"See you later?" he asked.

She nodded. "If Sam doesn't have plans, the three of us will probably head to the beach and get some sun."

"Great." With a wave to her, he headed topside.

"You know," Jake told him, "I'm a big one for hunches myself, but we're beginning to move a little strangely here. Two overdoses by prescription drugs. Two deaths by heroin overdose, both victims found near the studio. But this…

okay, so Manuel Taylor was a waiter the day of the competition. But he was in Coconut Grove, not on the beach, when he was killed. And he was shot."

"I know," Quinn said.

"So?"

"I still say everything's related."

Jake shrugged. "All right. Am I driving?"

"Let's take both cars." Jake stared at him, and he shrugged. "I'm heading back out to the beach after we hit the Grove."

At the station, Quinn pored over the report, which had been prepared by Jake's partner, Anna. The woman was thorough. Everything pointed to an innocent man being caught in gang war crossfire.

"I'll make you a copy, then we can head out to the site."

Jake disappeared. The station was staffed on Sunday, but it was still slow. When Quinn's phone rang, it sounded like an alarm going off.

It was Marnie.

"Hey, is Shannon with you?" she asked.

"No, she was heading home."

"She isn't here yet." Marnie sounded a little plaintive. She went into a whisper. "Sam is like a little kid. He wants to go the beach."

"Try her cell. I left before she did. She might still be on the way."

"I just tried her cell. She didn't answer."

"Try her again and leave a message, but I'll drive on out there, okay?"

"Great. Thanks."

He hung up. When Jake returned, Quinn told him he was going to head straight out to the beach. "Shannon's not answering her cell," he explained.

"She could just be out of satellite reach," Jake told him.

"I still feel kind of antsy about this," Quinn said. "Too much happening too fast. This may have nothing in common with the rest—or far too much."

"Want me to follow you?"

Quinn shook his head. "No, I'm probably acting a little panicky. I'm just concerned, I guess."

Jake made no comment on why he might be overly worried. "Call me if you need me."

"Great. Thanks."

As he walked out to his car, Quinn tried dialing Shannon himself.

Her phone rang and rang, and then he heard her voice.

"Shannon! It's Quinn."

"If you'd like to leave a message, I'll get back to you as soon as possible."

He swore. "Dammit, yes, get back to me as soon as possible!"

He pocketed his phone with a growing sense of danger.

Shannon hadn't meant to do anything other than drive straight to her house. She knew that Quinn was worried about her, and that he'd probably come close to insisting that she hang around on the boat until he returned. And he seemed so down on Gordon. She couldn't believe that Gordon could be responsible for the things that had happened, even though she'd had her own brief flights of fear regarding the man. No. Not Gordon.

She hadn't even mentioned the incident in the storeroom to Quinn. In retrospect, the whole thing seemed ridiculous, an instance when panic had caused her problems, so she'd kept quiet.

It took her only minutes to reach the beach. It was getting a little chilly these days for the locals, and they weren't into tourist season yet. But when she reached the turnoff for her house, she found herself driving to the studio.

Sunday. The place would be empty. Katarina wouldn't be working, and there wouldn't be a soul around the studio. No music, no noise. She would only stay a second.

And maybe figure out what the strange sound she kept hearing was.

She parked in back and hurried up the stairs to the outer hall and balcony. She slipped her key into the lock and entered, carefully locking the door behind her, then walked around the space.

Nothing had changed since they had left yesterday.

Feeling a little foolish, she stood in the center of the dance floor.

Then she heard it again.

The grating sound.

It was coming from the direction of the men's room.

She turned and went into the men's room, checking it out stall by stall. Nothing. And yet, clearer than ever before, she could hear the noise.

She paused, hurried back to her purse and found her key chain with the little container of pepper spray she kept there. So armed, she went out back and stared at the door to the storage room. She should wait. Call someone and tell them about the noise.

But hell, every time she wanted someone to hear it, the noise didn't come. It was undoubtedly nothing.

Maybe they just had a resident rat, or an army of cockroaches.

She slipped the key into the lock and entered, wedging the door open. If there was something in there, she wanted to be ready to run.

Turning the light on, Shannon went in.

Shelves held their multitude of boxes. Katarina's dressmaker's dummy was back up, standing sentinel again. Shannon slowly walked to the back, tiptoeing, listening.

And then she heard it. It was coming from the back wall.

She walked back determinedly, stood and listened. She looked back to the door and then again to the rear of the room.

The room wasn't as deep as it should have been, she realized suddenly.

She went to the shelves and started moving boxes.

Quinn made it to the house but didn't see Shannon's car.

When she heard him drive up, Marnie came running out, followed by Sam.

"She's not here, I take it?" he said.

Marnie shook her head, leaning in his window, frowning. "What?"

"Why is that woman's picture on your front seat?" she asked.

"What?" he asked, distracted. She pointed. A sketch of Sonya Miller was on top of the file folders stacked on the passenger seat.

"You know her?" he demanded.

"No, I don't know her. But I've seen her go up the back stairs at the studio."

Quinn glared at Sam.

Sam put his hands up. "I've never seen her before. She wasn't a student, Quinn. I swear it! Maybe she went to Suede."

"You're certain you've seen this woman?" Quinn asked Marnie.

"Yes. And she didn't go to the club, she went up the back stairs," Marnie said stubbornly.

He jerked the car into reverse with Marnie still leaning in the window. "I'm going over there. Call the cops."

Marnie moved back just in time.

He shot back out onto the street. He didn't know what the hell it meant, exactly, that Marnie had seen Sonya Miller.

He only knew he felt a sense of urgency unlike any he had ever known before.

Finally she had all the boxes removed from the area of the back wall.

She stepped closer, noticing what looked like either a crack in the wall or a structural juncture. She pressed it and felt nothing.

She tapped it, and the sound was hollow.

She pressed again, putting weight behind the effort. The wall began to give. She realized she hadn't needed to move the boxes—the shelving was part of a false door.

The door opened. That had been the creaking sound. But opened to what? Maybe she didn't need to know—not now, anyway. It was time to get the hell out. She started to back away, ready to reclose the false door and put the boxes back.

"Ah, Shannon. I knew it was just a matter of time before you got here. Actually, I've been waiting for you."

She opened her mouth to scream and prepared to flee. But before she could do either one, fingers of steel wound around her wrist, jerking her forward.

Quinn raced up the back steps and saw the door to the storage room standing open. He raced to it and looked in just in time to see Shannon heading through the false wall.

For a moment he was stunned into stillness.

Shannon was hiding something at the studio. A sense of illness pervaded him. No, it couldn't be.

But there she was, at the studio, when she had said she was heading straight for the house. No other cars in the lot. No one around, no sound…

Just Shannon, disappearing as he stood.

He hardened himself and flew into action. Behind the false door was a long hallway.

He followed.

She was being jerked along so fast she could barely breathe, much less scream. The pepper spray was in her pocket, but she couldn't get to it because her wrists were being held in such a vise. The hall was narrow. The only light came weakly from the secret doorway back into the storage room.

The hallway ended. She thought she was going to be slammed through a wall, but, like the other, it gave when pressed.

She burst into a room. A narrow room, four feet at best in width, eight feet in length. It was tight and only dimly lit, but when her eyes adjusted, she was able to make out details. At one end were shelves filled with plastic bags that held a white powder. At the other end was a narrow circular stairway that led up.

To Gabriel Lopez's apartment.

Gabriel thrust her away from him, and she saw that he had pulled a gun.

She was terrified into speechlessness at first. Then something kicked in. She stared at the gun, self-preservation telling her to talk, to do anything, say anything, to keep him from shooting her.

"You son of a bitch! Why?"

He shook his head. "Money, *chica,* money. And the life, of course." He gave her a disdainful look. "Dancers! You were the best cover in the world. All your silly little people, awed by the club, always waiting to catch sight of a celebrity. And this building…perfect. Everyone was so pleased with the renovations. When the cops would come by, they met a dressmaker and dancers, and they could check me out and check me out and search the place…and find nothing. Nothing but boxes of costumes and student records."

She had to get out, and she knew it. Taking a chance, she pulled out her key chain.

He lifted the gun, playing with his thumb and finger, showing her how quickly he could cock the weapon. "Drop it."

She didn't dare. She hit the plunger. He ducked, swearing, coughing, choking, wheezing.

But she'd missed his eyes. The gagging fumes of the spray filled the area, and she was trapped, too. Then he was flying toward her. They struggled, but in the end, he had her.

"Let her go. Now."

The voice stunned both of them. Shannon found herself thrust in front of Lopez, coughing from the spray herself, his gun against her temple. Her eyes watered. She blinked and saw that Quinn had come, that he had followed the hallway and found the two of them.

"Let her go, Lopez. Now. I don't want to shoot you. The cops are on the way, and I want you to go to trial. I don't know why you killed Nell Durken, but her husband doesn't deserve a death sentence for what you did."

"You don't know the half of it, buddy. You don't know the half. But the cops aren't here yet. And you're not a cop, just a fuck-up P.I. Get out of the way. I get out of here, and I throw her back to you. That's the way it goes."

Quinn stood his ground, his gun level on Lopez. "Nice little place you've got here, but you'll never get her up the stairs, so it's kind of a trap, isn't it?"

"Not when you get out of the way."

"You'll hear the sirens any minute."

"That's why you'd better move. I'll kill her. And she's

such a pretty little thing, huh? I could have taken her for a nice ride. You know, she turned me down all the time. Since she was such a good cover, I had to just smile and take it. But then she went off and slept with a prick like you. Now move!"

Quinn shifted a little.

"Funny thing is, Lopez, I almost thought she was in on it. You know, I came here, saw that false door…you should have thought to close it. Might have taken me and the cops ages to find it. Too bad you didn't think of that."

"Put the gun down and let me out of here."

Shannon was afraid she was going to drop, whether he let her go or not. Her knees were rubber and the pepper spray was burning her eyes. On top of that, she couldn't breathe.

And still, Quinn was standing there.

"I'll shoot her right now!"

"All right, all right, I'm going to put it down."

He started to lower his weapon. Shannon felt the slightest easing of Lopez's hold, but the barrel of the gun was still against her skull.

"Asshole!" Lopez said. "You *both* have to die."

He was going to pull the trigger. This was it. Not even time for her life to flash before her eyes.

The sound of the gunshot was deafening in the small space.

She felt nothing….

Behind her, Lopez crumpled, dragging her to the ground. Only then did she begin to scream when she saw the gaping bullet hole in his head.

She vaguely heard the sirens. Then she felt Quinn's arms around her, heard his voice as if from far, far away.

"Come on, it's over. The cops are here. They'll take it from here."

She couldn't rise on her own; her knees were too wobbly.

But his arms were around her.

And he was going to lead her from the shadows into the light.

CHAPTER 24

"**B**ut why did he kill Lara?" Ben demanded.

They were down in Key Largo, guests at Quinn's place, a beautiful home with a pool, right on the water, where he could dock the *Twisted Time*.

There was nothing ostentatious about it, and Shannon loved it. There were three bedrooms; one converted into an office, but it still had a futon that could sleep two. Since the police had requested that the entire studio building be closed for a few days, Gordon had decided that Ella could leave all messages for their students—in case they didn't quite get the concept of crime tape—and since they weren't working, and the entire situation was so traumatic, they should bond together. Thus, these days in the Keys.

Sunday had become something of a blur, with police pouring through the building, Shannon answering the same questions over and over again, Marnie and Sam appearing, first distraught, then relieved, Doug showing up with a pale Jane, freshly out of the hospital, in tow. Shannon had accepted drops for her eyes from the emergency personnel who had arrived but refused the suggestion she be looked at in a hospital. She had insisted she was fine.

Quinn was actually in worse shape. He'd said something about being sorry he'd had to kill Lopez, because there would be so many questions to be answered. She had remembered that he had followed her, *suspected her,* and even though he had saved her life, something had come over her when he bemoaned the death of the man who had been about to kill her, and she had hit him. She had rued the instinctive reaction immediately, but she had done it, and apparently she had a fairly decent hook, because even on Monday, he was still rubbing his jaw. That hadn't, however, interfered with Sunday night, when she had once again slept on the *Twisted Time,* while Sam stayed with Marnie at Shannon's house. That night, more than ever, she had needed to feel alive, and he had been pleased to help her explore every sensation. And, of course, they had talked and talked, before being awakened early the next morning, when Gordon had called with his idea of a studio-group getaway. Quinn had politely suggested his place in the Keys, not the least bit worried about fraternization, and now there they all were.

They headed south and all went out on the boat together. Doug, Ben and Quinn went diving, while Gordon, Sam, Marnie and Rhianna did some fishing, and Shannon mainly lounged around, with Justin, Ella and Jane joining her. Justin worked on his tan and Jane just tried to relax and follow doctor's orders.

On Monday night, they sat around in Quinn's living room, eating dinner. Drapes in the back opened to the pool area, the dock and the bay, a breeze drifted in, along with the smell of the barbecue, and it really did feel like a vacation. Until they started talking and Ben voiced his confusion.

Quinn glanced at Shannon. "Maybe she got too close to him, or maybe she knew too much."

"But…somehow he managed to drug her at the competition. I mean, he got a hold of prescription drugs to do in two of his victims, and he shot the other two women up with heroin. And," he added, gazing at Doug, "if I've got this right, he also shot Manuel Taylor. Why Taylor?"

"He definitely killed Taylor," Doug said, looking at Quinn.

"Ballistics came back with a positive match. They found the gun that killed Manuel Taylor when they searched Lopez's apartment, and his prints were all over it," he told them. "I imagine Gabriel was afraid Manuel would remember that Gabe had tipped him to make sure Lara got the drink he'd prepared especially for her." He shook his head. "I'm sorry as hell I didn't examine the whole night more thoroughly with Manuel when I talked to him. I was so into the concept that he had told Shannon she was next that it didn't occur to me that he might know more. Anyway, I think Gabe panicked when it came to Manuel, so he shot him."

"And he killed Nell Durken, too?" Ben said, and shook his head, giving Quinn a questioning stare.

"So it seems. At least, Art Durken's attorney is counting on the evidence to get him out of jail," Doug told them.

"But what if Art Durken *did* kill her? What if the murders weren't related? It all seems kind of…I don't know. Weird," Ben persisted.

"Ben," Sam said. "It's over. Let it be."

"I'll bet Lara was having an affair with Gabe Lopez," Gordon said, looking around the room."

"She hadn't been around in months," Ella protested.

"Okay, then maybe…he wanted to start something with her, so he talked to her about it, but she turned him down. He didn't like being turned down. He played the charmer, but he hated Shannon for turning him down, right?" Jane said.

"So he said," Quinn agreed.

"We're supposed to be bonding, not rehashing this whole thing," Gordon moaned.

"I'm not rehashing," Ben said. "I'm making sure I've got it all straight in my mind. Okay, so maybe that poor little hooker, Sally Grant, scored drugs off Lopez and somehow saw the secret room, so she had to die. Sonya, he probably met in another club, or on the beach, or somewhere, but she, too, was into getting high, found out too much and had to die. Lara wasn't a likely candidate for an overdose of heroin, but…he already knew what he was doing because of Nell Durken. He was probably having an affair with her, then got tired of her or something and decided to kill her. He'd gotten away with killing her by prescription and seeing it nailed on the husband, so he figured he'd do the same thing with Lara. And since she was wearing gloves…it was logical that there were no prints on the bottle. She'd die in front of hundreds of people. No murder, no crime."

"As much as we can figure," Quinn said, "that's about the picture."

"And Manuel," Gordon added dryly. "Manuel was executed purely for purposes of insurance."

"So it appears," Doug said.

Gordon groaned. "My business is going to be in the toilet."

"Gordon, he owned the club, not the studio," Shannon protested.

"Yes, but the club will go right to hell now," Gordon argued.

"Maybe not. Someone else will want to own it—it will have a real reputation now," Sam said. "You know how people love a little bit of the illicit in life."

"It all remains to be seen," Shannon said.

Ben stared across the room at her moodily. "He almost killed you, Shannon." He shook his head. "In retrospect…he was always watching you. I think he was worried for a while that you thought something was going on."

She shook her head. "I didn't think anything at all—until Lara died, and then…there was the noise. When he was coming and going through the secret door. Too bad for him that he didn't come and go more often from his apartment. I'd never have known."

"The point," Doug said, "was that his apartment and the club itself were free of drugs, just as clean as most of his employees believed with their whole hearts."

"Most? You think other people were in on it?" Rhianna said worriedly.

"Maybe," Doug said. "But both homicide and narcotics are on it. They'll find whatever contacts he had."

"Okay, okay, we're bonding here," Gordon said. "Please, let's watch a movie or something. Quinn, you got any good movies?"

Dinner was cleaned up, popcorn was made, and they settled on *The Lord of the Rings* on the wide-screen TV in the living room.

Shannon was glad when Quinn tapped her on the shoulder and they slipped away to his room. She had thought it would be the hardest thing in the world to accept a relationship again, to really live in one. But it wasn't. It was easy.

The easiest thing in the world just to be with him, and the most exciting thing in the world just to know that they could slip away and make love.

But late that night Shannon awoke to find Quinn staring up at the ceiling. He started when she stroked his cheek.

"What is it?"

"I don't know. Don't you dare hit me again, but I really wish I hadn't had to kill Lopez. There's too much that's still going to be up to a jury. Did Lopez kill Nell—or did Art do it?"

"There will be the shadow of a doubt now," Shannon

said. There was no lie to tell Quinn, and she knew that his work on behalf of Nell Durken still haunted him.

"Remember how he said, 'You don't know the half of it'?"

She nodded. "I remember everything he said."

"Well, that still bugs me. I don't know the half of it. And I hate like hell to guess."

She was quiet for a minute. "I guess there are some things that will never be solved. There *is* one thing, though."

"And what's that?"

"You saved my life and I'm eternally grateful."

"I'm not so sure. You might have saved mine."

"Because maybe one day you'll be able to cha-cha?"

"Because I've learned that I can't solve everything, but that I can be the best possible person for someone I really love."

She smiled and rolled into his arms, and, for a while, at least, she was certain she made him forget the questions that still plagued him.

"Dear, dear, dear!"

Christie was in the studio a week later, donating an hour of her time to help Marnie. "You're trying to step and turn all in one. They're individual movements. You need to learn to focus if you do want to do all these high-speed turns. Break it down. Step, turn. Heel lead. Step, turn."

Marnie caught Shannon's eye and grimaced. "Dear, dear, dear!" she mouthed.

"Keep working," Shannon ordered. She wondered suddenly how anyone could have allowed a kid like Marnie to live out on the streets, failing to take care of her when she was so young and sweet. But it took all kinds. She was learning that lesson well.

She was awfully grateful to Marnie, too. Quinn, not finding her at home that Sunday, was coming to the studio any-way. But thanks to Marnie recognizing the picture of Sonya Miller, he had come prepared, gun loaded. She had also been able to connect Sonya to both the building, and Gabriel Lopez, since she had witnessed Sonya coming up the back steps.

Shannon watched the pair for a minute, grinned, and headed for her office. Ella had just told her that Quinn was on the phone for her.

She grinned. He was taking his mom out to dinner. He had been feeling really guilty because lately he'd been lax about seeing her or even calling her. Tonight he was going to atone. Doug had explained the family situation to Shannon. Their father was dead, but they had a terrific mother, one who didn't nag but *did* worry. And Quinn had a habit of closing off when he was disturbed or busy, which only worried her more.

"What kind of a son are you? I haven't even met your mom yet—and you've competed!" she had told Doug.

"I had to be a little more confident first," he'd said. "But now…she's going to love it. You'll be surprised. She can dance. Wait until you see her," he had told her with pride.

Shannon picked up the phone in her office. "Hi. So where are you taking her?"

"A new place in North Miami. I probably won't make it back until late. Hey, this restaurant is supposed to be gour-met Scottish cuisine. Have you ever heard of such a thing?"

"No, but it sounds interesting. Steal a menu if you can."

"I'm an ex-cop. I can't steal anything."

She laughed. "Hey, um, do I get to meet Mom soon?"

"Oh, yeah. She's already been hearing all about you."

Shannon smiled. "Hey, listen, have a great dinner."

"Thanks. See you later."

She hung up. When she walked back out, the crowd was beginning to thin. It was close to time for her advanced group, but there were few private lessons on a Monday night. It seemed that Monday was kind of a blah day, no matter what business you were in.

Blah…

Actually, she thought, she enjoyed feeling that there could be blah days again. Or could there? Quinn, she knew, was still uncomfortable about the death of Gabriel Lopez. There was something unfinished, something that didn't quite fit altogether.

You don't know the half of it.

She walked back to the kitchen and poked through the refrigerator. Ben walked back to join her. "What're you up to?"

Sam, with no more classes, had driven Marnie home. Jane had left early, as well. She wasn't working with her students again yet, but she couldn't quite stay away from the studio. Tonight, however, Doug had remained behind. Though he loyally claimed that he wasn't going to dance with anyone but Jane at the Gator Gala, he was taking lessons with Shannon and Rhianna, and not missing any of the group classes. Katarina and David were in, and Richard Long was there, though Mina had gone home, tired from the onslaught of childhood injuries, which always seemed to multiply after a weekend. Gordon had told her earlier that he was leaving by eight because he was the owner and he had good management, so he, too, was gone.

"Hey," Ben repeated. "What are you up to?"

"Champagne. Thought I'd wake up our advanced group a bit."

"Richard just made coffee for that same reason."

Richard came up behind Ben. "Whatever. Champagne sounds good to me."

Mona O'Casey had never remarried, but neither had she fallen into any kind of lifelong depression. Left with an ample income, she had given up her job as a nurse and instead spent her time on a number of charities. She was five-five, slim, with short-cropped silver hair and bright, powder-blue eyes, a little dynamo of energy.

"I was bad, huh?" Quinn said.

Mona smiled. "I guess I know you when you're in your moods. When I can talk to you, naturally, I feel better. But I know you'll always call when you're ready." She sighed softly. "And since you and your brother both insist on dangerous professions, I've learned not to stay awake nights worrying. Besides," she added, "Doug assured me that you were all right, just moody. And," she added, taking a sip of merlot and grinning, "I hear that I'm going to get to see both of you dance very soon."

"Hey, the waltz. I owe it all to you."

She laughed. "Well, thank goodness I taught you something of value."

He took his mother's hand, running his fingers over it. "You taught us both all kind of things of tremendous value. Took me a while to catch on, but Doug was a pretty good kid straight from the start."

Mona grew serious suddenly. "Strange, isn't it, what does and doesn't bother people? Your brother went through everything at the academy, crime scenes, the morgue visits, the tests, and was as stalwart as a tree. But when it comes to his dancing…I would have loved to see him compete, but he didn't want me to watch him. Dancing makes him nervous."

"Heck, I'm afraid for you to see me waltz," he told her.

She looked unhappy for a minute. "Maybe. But nervouness just isn't a good reason to take drugs. I told Doug that."

"Doug?"

"Yes, can you believe it? Your brother got a prescription

for that drug himself, just to take the edge off before he dances."

A gut-deep, miserable sensation speared through Quinn. No. Not his brother. Lopez had been the killer.

Lopez had also looked right at him and said, "You don't know the half of it."

His brother had been sleeping with Lara Trudeau.

He'd known something was still wrong with their picture of the crime.

But not Doug. Not his brother.

"What's the matter, dear?"

"Excuse me, Mom, okay?"

He dialed the studio. The machine picked up.

He dialed Shannon's cell phone and was asked to leave a message there, too.

There was no reason to feel that anything was wrong. All sorts of people had been at the studio all week long. Shannon wasn't alone now. Her advanced class would be in progress any minute.

"Quinn, you're scaring me," Mona said.

"I'm sorry. Forgive me just one more minute. I'm going to give Doug a call."

When he got his brother's answering machine, as well, his muscles tightened.

"Mom," he said, standing, "I'll make this up to you, but I've got to go."

She met his eyes. "If you don't call me by midnight, I'll send the cops out after you."

"If I don't call you by midnight, make sure you do."

He threw down some cash and hurried out of the restaurant.

Shannon set down her glass of champagne, hearing the distant beeping of her phone. "Excuse me, everyone, will you? Advanced class in two minutes, and no champagne, ever again, if anyone blames their lack of balance on it."

She found her cell phone and checked her messages. There was one from Quinn. She called him back and was frustrated when she got the message service. Strange, she should have gotten him at the restaurant. But maybe he had left and was going in and out of coverage areas on the highway.

"Hope all went well with your mom," she said cheerfully. "Call me. We're quiet here, but everything's fine."

She hung up thoughtfully and waited a minute, drumming her fingers on her desk. She started up, but then sat again, grabbing the phone as it rang. "Quinn?"

"Sorry, it's me. Marnie. Just wanted to make sure you were okay."

"I'm fine, why?"

"Quinn called here, said he couldn't get through to you."

"Well, I just left him a message. All is well."

"I'll try to get him back for you again."

"Thanks, Marnie."

She hung up, then frowned. The studio was very quiet except for a waltz playing very softly.

She stood up and left her office. When she reached the dance floor, she came to a dead halt, staring around her.

They were on the floor. All of them. Katarina and David were on top of each other. Richard Long was a few yards in front of her office, facedown. Ben and Rhianna just steps away from him. Doug O'Casey was almost beneath her feet. It looked as if Justin had fallen on his way out of the men's room.

Ella was slumped over the reception desk.

She exhaled in confusion and shock, fear seeping into her. She dropped to her knees, set her fingers against Rhianna's throat and gasped out a sigh of relief.

She could feel Rhianna's pulse.

She rose and spun, anxious to rush to the phone and dial for help.

But she couldn't.

Because one of the fallen had risen.

And for the second time in a little over a week, she was staring down the barrel of a gun.

Quinn got Shannon's message, and while he was listening to it, swearing at the poor reception he got despite the ads the phone company ran all the time, another call beeped through. It was Marnie, telling him that things were fine.

He thanked her and hung up.

But despite her words, and Shannon's, he felt the need to reach the studio quickly.

That was it, wasn't it? The *half* of it. Gabriel Lopez hadn't worked alone.

Doug had been taking a prescription drug for his nerves. The same drug that had killed both Nell Durken and Lara.

"Not my brother!" he swore aloud.

He pushed harder on the gas pedal, swearing at himself for letting his guard down.

He had known it wasn't over.

"You didn't drink your champagne," Richard Long told Shannon. "You should have."

She stared at him. "Richard?"

"You really need to drink your champagne."

"Why are you doing this?"

He sighed. "Well, you see, too many people know that something just isn't right in Denmark, or however the saying goes. I was sweating it big time at first. I was sure Lopez would give me away, but he didn't. Then that damn cop had to come here—sleeping with Lara, for God's sake! And then his big brother, the private eye, showed up. The questioning started all over again. The homicide cop and all his friends, the narc guys. Sooner or later, they're going to come knocking. So, you see, I have to fix things now."

"How can you fix things this way? You know Quinn will come here. And then his friends will come after him—the homicide cops, the narc guys."

"Shannon, I really don't want to hurt you. So drink your champagne. I can't tell you how easy it will be. Like falling asleep."

"Right. And how is all this supposed to have happened?" she asked dryly, gesturing around the room.

He grinned. "The last to arrive will be Mr. Quinn O'Casey. I don't think he knows it, but I wrote Doug a few prescriptions. There's one in his pocket right now. Everyone knows already—whether they admit it or not—that he slept with Lara. So his brother shows up, and knows what Doug has done, so he confronts him on it. Of course Doug's already drugged himself—suicide being the only answer for what he's done—but he has a little juice left and gets into a shoot-out with his big bro. He's the better shot, kills Quinn, and then dies of an overdose, just the way he planned. Everyone in the room dies. I was lucky enough to get tired and leave the class early. Otherwise, I'd have died, too. What a terrible tragedy."

"You're insane," she told him, then wished she hadn't spoken that way, because he was twitching. "Richard, I don't get it. How did you and Lopez…?"

"I introduced Gabe to many of my clients. You can't begin to know how many rich people enjoy their recreational therapy. They never knew he was the supplier. They just knew they could come to his club, leave payment and get their drugs delivered. We both made good money. It started with Nell. She was lonely—and Mina, quite frankly, bores me to tears. Then Nell stepped back. She was going to make up with her husband, who, quite frankly, is a creep. I went to talk to her, we argued…she insulted me. Preferred the creep to me. So I took matters into my own hands. As for Lara…you knew her. What a bitch. First, for fun, she decided to seduce me. Then, for fun, she started following me, and she figured out what I was up to with Lopez. Then she decided she was going to blackmail me, and she taunted me, letting me know she was sleeping with the cop, too. He was younger, she said. So…I had to take care of her. Gabriel got careless with the prostitute and the socialite, so they were his to clean up. I simply got mad—and then even—with Nell. And Lara. Come on, the bitch deserved to die."

"Lara could be a bitch," Shannon agreed placatingly. How much had all those on the floor ingested? How long could they survive?

"You have to understand. This will put an end to everyone saying that something just wasn't right, that Lopez couldn't have done it all."

Shannon jerked around, certain she heard someone rushing up the stairs.

Richard heard it, too. He grabbed her, dragging her down to the floor, the barrel of the gun against her heart.

He burst in and felt if he had come across the scene of a strange massacre. They were on the floor, all of them, Justin Garcia's body nearly tripping him as he came in. He fell to his knees, checking for a pulse.

Faint, but there.

He rose, carefully moving across the floor.

There was Doug, down like the others.

He thanked God briefly as he checked his brother's throat and found a pulse.

Gun in one hand, he reached for his cell with the other.

But before he could hit a single key, a shot exploded, searing across his hand.

His gun flew across the room, and his phone fell to his feet as he instinctively reached for his injured hand, damning himself for his stupid vulnerability.

He turned. Richard Long was halfway up, and it was definitely a moment of déjà vu.

Shannon was in front of him, his gun against her temple.

"The doctor, naturally," he said calmly. "You know, you son of a bitch, I almost suspected my own brother."

"It *was* your brother," Long said.

"Like hell."

"Well, everyone else is going to believe it was your brother. Too bad he's going to shoot you."

"You're a fool. Forensics will come here and figure you out to a T. You'll go up for capital murder. You'll die from lethal injection."

"No, I won't. I have it figured out absolutely logically."

"So why isn't Shannon unconscious on the floor, too?"

"She wouldn't drink her champagne. However, you can get her glass and give it to her, so she can die more easily."

"I am not drinking that champagne!" Shannon said. Quinn met her eyes. She didn't look terrified; she looked furious.

"It will be easier for her. Tell her, Quinn."

Quinn rose slowly, his hands in the air. He flexed his fingers, grateful to realize that the shot had only skimmed his flesh.

"I'll tell her to drink the champagne, Richard," he said evenly, his eyes on Shannon. "But I want something from you. You need to set up your little scene properly, and I'll help you. But I want something from you first."

Richard didn't ease his hold on Shannon.

"What the hell are you talking about, Quinn?" Shannon demanded darkly.

He looked at Richard then. "You let Lara die poetically, and she was the biggest bitch in the world. Shannon has treated you like a king, taught you...face it, she's been great. And as for me, well, I came in off the street and learned something of elegance here."

"So?"

"One waltz," Quinn said. "We get one waltz."

"A waltz? Are you crazy?" Shannon whispered.

"I can shoot you right now!" Richard said.

"Yes, but it won't look right. Let me have my waltz. What have you got to lose?"

Richard still hesitated, then shoved Shannon toward Quinn. She was frowning fiercely as she reached him. He smiled, trying to explain with his eyes. Trying, in seconds, to say that he needed her help. That they had one chance.

"Our routine," he said aloud.

"You're crazy," she told him. Tears stung her eyes. "We're about to die, and you want to waltz?"

"Our routine," he repeated.

She arched a brow to him. He went into a competition position, inviting her to him. She moved into his arms, and they began dance.

Chain steps, turns...promenade, one, two, three, rise and fall...

"Get on with it," Richard said.

"It's our routine," he snapped back.

Aloud, he continued to Shannon, "One, two, three, one, two, three, turn...and pooper-scooper coming up."

At last something registered in her eyes. Knowledge of what he wanted.

Fear that she couldn't follow through.

"Hey, I can do the lifts," he told her. "And you're the dancer—you can do them, too."

"What the hell does it matter?" Long exclaimed.

"One, two, three…now."

Shannon moved around him. He dipped to sweep her up into the lift. He spun.

And she performed magnificently, body flying out with the force of his spin…and slamming hard into Richard Long, forcing him backward, forcing him to fall…then falling, and herself landing hard atop him.

Then Quinn was down, as well, pushing Shannon away, going for Long. The other man rolled, desperate to elude Quinn, to reach the gun that had fallen from his hand when Shannon smashed into him.

Quinn dragged him back. Long lashed out. Quinn slugged him hard, in the jaw, just as Shannon flew across the floor, retrieving both the gun and Quinn's phone, which she handed to him.

Straddled over Long, Quinn dialed 911. "Emergency, major emergency. We need several ambulances, stomach pumps…"

Before he finished talking, they could hear the sirens.

EPILOGUE

The beach was always crazy, that night more so than ever.

Highly publicized, written up in every magazine across the country as "The little contest that could," the Gator Gala—the first-ever competition sponsored by the Moonlight Sonata Dance Studio—was creating pure traffic havoc.

The hotel hosting the gala was booked to overflowing, with people spilling into the neighboring facilities and even beyond. Restaurants thrived. The wicked tale of adultery, narcotics, the wild side, and murder among the elite and famous connected to the studio—which had survived all the ills assailing it—had made the competition taking place that night not notorious, but so fascinating that many of the big names in ballroom dancing had felt that they had to be there to get their share of so much publicity. The more big names that were offered, the more tickets that were sold, the more the prestigious the judges who wanted to be associated with the competition, the more the students who poured in.

It was almost out of control.

And there was more, of course.

Shannon Mackay, who had retired nearly eight years ago, after a broken ankle, was back.

Back in a big way.

She was, quite simply, dazzling. Poetry set to music. Her gown shimmered, exquisitely molding her elegant curves, billowing softly beneath the lights with each movement of her body. She seemed to create such splendor effortlessly, blond hair in a shimmering knot at her nape, studded with jeweled stones to match those on the gown.

Just a stretch of her finger spoke volumes. The tilt of her head, the look in her eyes. She was dance at its most complete, every part of her attuned to the music and the steps. She was lost in the rhythm, and those who watched were lost with her.

It was fairy-tale music, and a fairy tale that was created. She was tall, slim, delicately curved, and her smile was infectious. Her partner was tall, dark, handsome, assured and equally talented. Together they went beyond human belief, sometimes moving in such perfect unison that they appeared almost to be one.

"Lord, she's incredible," Gordon breathed.

"She makes Ben look damned good, too," Sam added.

"Ben can dance," Quinn commented, smiling.

"They complement one another," Rhianna approved. "As dancers, of course," she said quickly, causing Quinn to laugh.

"We were almost as good," Jane said, squeezing Sam's hand.

"Almost," he agreed, smiling.

"I'd say that Marnie and I have a good chance of taking the salsa trophy," Justin said.

Quinn felt another smile coming on. He glanced at Marnie, the street kid, the runaway. She had come into her own. She hadn't made enough yet to afford her own clothes, but with Katarina's help, they had reworked one of Shannon's old Latin dresses, and it would be difficult to point to a figure more perfect than Marnie's at this moment. She had turned nineteen, and it looked as if she had matured far more. Like the others, she had her hair neatly coiled, making the fine lines of her profile more evident, along with the size of her eyes. She smiled back at Quinn. "A very good chance," he told her affectionately.

Perhaps just because of the circumstances of her life, she still tended to be nervous. And Sam still tended to be protective. He had taken a larger apartment, and she had moved into one of his bedrooms. Neither one was allowed to go out unless the man was first approved by the other. They were jokingly considered the "Will and Grace" of the dance world.

"Rhianna, you were striking tonight, too," Gordon said. "You and Doug."

Doug had quit the police force. He had really liked being a cop; he had simply decided that he loved dance more. Besides, with the popularity that had descended upon Moonlight Sonata, they'd been in need of another male teacher. He and Marnie still didn't have the certifications to teach at the higher levels, but they were favorites among the beginners.

"While we're all getting sticky and gooey here," Doug said, "may I compliment your waltz tonight, big brother?"

Quinn laughed. "We came in second. With another partner, Shannon would have won."

"You're a beginner, and you were excellent," Doug said.

"Both my boys were terrific," Mona commented, sliding between them to squeeze their hands.

"Hush. The finale," Gordon commanded.

It almost seemed that Shannon paused in flight, above Ben's head, then alit in his arms, sinking slowly into a perfectly timed stillness.

The applause was deafening.

But after her bows, Quinn saw Shannon searching the room. For him. She flew to him, made another fantastic leap and landed in his arms.

She accepted his congratulations on her performance, and he smiled as he brought her slowly down, kissing her. The act of dancing would always mean more to her than a trophy. And the approval of those who loved her would always mean more than any other judgment.

There were others, of course, from whom she accepted accolades. Her new mother-in-law, her co-workers, her old friends, his old friends, total strangers. But eventually the last of the awards was given out. As expected, she and Ben took the crowning prize of the night, leaving Gordon to boast about the studio. It got a bit ridiculous at times, but even so, it was both gratifying and exhilarating.

But in time they were in their room together, a fantastic suite they'd taken at the hotel, since Shannon had so much to do for the gala that she needed to be on site. Moonlight poured in from the heavens beyond their balcony, and she walked up to him, slipped her arms around him. "I'd never have done it without you."

He gave her a smile. "And I'd never have rejoined the Bureau without your encouragement. And I am good at what I do."

"You're good at everything," she assured him, her eyes searching out his. "You would have taken first for that waltz if I hadn't...well, I back led you, and I shouldn't have."

"I forgot the step. Besides, I won when it mattered."

"I took the trophy with Ben, but I should have taken one with you, too."

He could tell she was anxious. He knew that she had wanted to win far more for Ben than for herself. And she had wanted a win for him.

He cupped her face in his hands. "We won together once," he told her. "We won together with that silly pooper-scooper—and the most incredible waltz ever mastered by man. Ben may have his trophy, but I get to go home with you, and that's all that matters."

"That was one hell of a pooper-scooper, wasn't it?" she whispered.

"There will never be another like it."

She smiled, moving against him, touching his ear with her whisper. "It's amazing when you know your life is the best applause you'll ever earn. I can't tell you how I love it. It's like my life is a dance I'll never do better with any other partner but you. It requires all kinds of very special moves."

"Leaps and bounds?"

"The most incredible ones."

"Ah, well, you *are* the instructor. Show me."

"Even teachers can learn."

"A dual session. Sounds fascinating."

He swept her up.

And like everything else that night, it was beautiful beyond belief.

They were alive; they were together. Now the years and the world stretched out before them with assurance hard-won, confidence earned, and the dance of time the one they would practice forever.

HEATHER GRAHAM

Slow Burn

Faced with the brutal murder of her
husband, Spencer Huntingdon demands
answers from the one man who should
have them – David Delgado – ex-cop, her
husband's former partner and best
friend…and her one-time lover.
Their search for the truth takes them from
the glittering world of Miami high society
to the dark and dangerous underbelly of
the city – while around them swirl the
secrets and schemes of a killer driven to
commit his final act of violence.

MIRA®

HEATHER GRAHAM

Hurricane Bay

Nothing and no one is safe...

Dane knows something about
Sheila Warren that no-one else knows.
He knows she is dead. He has seen a
photo of her body, taken on his private
Florida beach...strangled with his own tie.
The crime has all the hallmarks of a
serial killer currently terrorising Miami,
and Dane is being set up to take the
blame. He just doesn't know why.

MIRA®

HEATHER GRAHAM

If looks could kill

Witness to a murder?

Madison Adair didn't witness her famous
mother's brutal murder. But she saw it.
Saw the gloved hand…felt the knife
strike…knew her mother's terror.
That was a lifetime ago, but now the
nightmares have returned; only this time
they're of a faceless serial killer stalking
women in Miami. A killer she can't see
but who knows she is watching…

MIRA®

HEATHER
GRAHAM

Picture me dead

A dangerous rite of passage...

Ashley Montague is nearing the
end of her police training—but
nothing has prepared her for the
rite of passage that will take her
on a deadly ride into the underbelly
of Miami's drug world.

M286

ERICA SPINDLER

After a strange message and then the disappearance of her sister, Liz Ames heads to Key West to investigate. She finds a community terrorised by a mysterious suicide, and another teenage girl's murder. With every step forward in the search for her sister there is another death, uncovering evil at every turn, an evil she cannot escape from, even at a DEAD RUN.

DEAD RUN

ON PARADISE ISLAND, EVIL STILL REMAINS...

MIRA

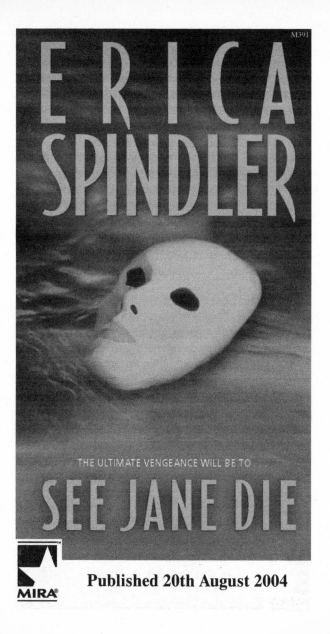

M391

ERICA SPINDLER

THE ULTIMATE VENGEANCE WILL BE TO...

SEE JANE DIE

Published 20th August 2004

GWEN HUNTER

A Dr Rhea Lynch novel

DEADLY REMEDY

A mysterious power to cure – or kill?

Published 20th August 2004